I0576313

# Red Rock Canyon
## Return to Red Rock
*A Tyrell Sloan western adventure*

Written by Brian T. Seifrit

Email: **briantseifrit@gmail.com**

Web site: www.booksbybriant.ca

**Cover art by**: Getty Creations, Burnaby, British Columbia

Published by

Edition 2
ISBN: 978-1-7773280-6-1 Paperback
ISBN: 978-1-990215-07-0 Hardcover
ISBN: 978-1-7773280-7-8 eBook

*"Let me take you to a place you have never been."*

*BTS 2000.*

# Chapter 1

It was six years ago when Tyrell Sloan last stood on the ridge that overlooked his Grandfather's forgotten homestead. He gave it all up to two special people, Grandma Heddy and the woman of his dreams and desires, Marissa McDowell. The year then was 1890. Things had changed since he last laid eyes upon the homestead. Two dozen cows grazed in the open field and a couple of horses trotted around inside a fence. He noted all the changes as well as the wagon near the entrance of the cabin.

Black Dog sat vigilantly at his side. Worn and tired as he was, his cunning, loyalty, and willingness to kill to protect Tyrell at any cost, remained his objective in life. *Nothing would ever change that.* His days were numbered though the years were starting to take their toll. Both Black Dog and Tyrell knew that, but nothing could change it. He was old, that's all there was to it.

"There it is Black Dog, Red Rock Canyon." For a moment, he fell silent. It was then that he noticed the woman removing clothes from a line. A beautiful vision from where he stood. His heart skipped a beat and he swallowed hard, *I wonder if that might be Marissa down there,* he thought.

Tyrell squinted as he averted his eyes once more. The woman now skirted toward the cabin with a basket clutched under her arm. He watched with pride and regret as she entered the cabin, memories of Marissa, Grandma Heddy and a life he could have had flooded his mind.

At 42 years old, he was no less quick with a pistol than he was with his wit and charm. He sat on his horse his hat tilted to block the sun, a red kerchief around his neck. His shoulder length dirty blond hair blowing gently in the fragrant forest air. A .45 Winchester rifle was strapped to his horse and around his waist were two Colt .45 revolvers. Tucked snugly away in his right boot was a two-shot derringer and in his left a skinning knife. His clothes were buckskin.

For the past six years, he had no choice but to live in obscurity. After meeting up unexpectedly and killing the two men responsible for his Grandfather's death. Now accused of murder, the Mounted Police wanted the man who killed Heath Roy. He had kept a low profile ever since. It wasn't his intent six years earlier to disappear or for that matter kill, the men he suspected of killing his Grandfather, but all the pieces certainly fit. It was accidental or perhaps by coincidence that he even met the two. One lonely night in 1890, he bequeathed all he owned to both his one-time-lover Marissa McDowell and a woman who saved his life, Grandma Heddy, the sole proprietor of Heddy's Mercantile.

Near the homestead and less than an hour's ride up stream of the Hudu Creek were three gold claims, the Sloan 1, 2 and 3. At the time of his reprieve, the claims were contracted for a two-year term with the Wake Up Jake, a mining company.

In the letter, he wrote and left behind on that fateful night stashed in the sacks of gold left in Grandma Heddy's care. He bequeathed to Grandma the gold and his share of whatever the Wake Up Jake produced, during the term of the contract.

To Marissa, he left behind the homestead, all 300 acres. With plans to head north and back to his hometown of Hell's Bottom, he was side tracked. A recurring dream of his Grandfather's death and the men, who killed him, as well as the face-to-face encounter with the villainous men of his dream, took over the next six years of his life.

It didn't take that long to kill them, just two shots. They met innocently enough at a Black Jack table in a little town called Willow Gate, two hundred miles north of Red Rock. At first, he thought nothing of the men. They were loud, obnoxious, and no different from most men at the table that night. Then it occurred to him that the man to his right wore an odd-looking glove. Only the man's trigger finger and thumb were evidence that he had a hand at all.

At that moment and as though from Hell, a young woman darted forward, cursing the man to his left. With the man's own knife that she managed to pull from his belt, in one fluid motion she cut him deep and fast. The man rose. Turning to meet his foe, he pulled his pistol and laughed. "I could've blown your head clean off Emma, clean off."

"You should have you filthy pig bastard. I wasn't good enough for you huh, that you had to take my sister too. What is a matter with you? From now on you can get your kicks elsewhere, Heath Roy."

"C'mon Emma, think about what you're sayin'. What went on between that sister of yours and I, ain't for public discussion. Besides it meant nothin' at all." Heath Roy turned toward the man with the odd glove as though he was looking for assurance and he smiled. "Now, hand back my knife b'fore you hurt yourself and get out of my sight." Heath Roy spat as his eyes turned cold and dark.

The young woman shook her head and without skipping a beat, threw the knife dead center between Heath Roy's feet. With a solid thud, it stuck into the wooden floor. "Don't ever come around my sister and I again, Heath Roy. I fear what I might do if I ever see you again." Tears streamed from the corner of her aqua eyes and down her tanned angelic face. Her jet-black hair was long and well kept; she was a vision of beauty.

Looking now at the knife stuck in the floor between his feet, Heath Roy shook his head. Angered at Emma's nerve to defy him, with an opened hand he blatantly slapped her, knocking her to the ground.

As though this treatment was common, Emma stood, blood trickled from the corner of her mouth, embarrassed and full of rage she turned and stormed away.

"That ought to keep her in check for now Heath Roy. Damn woman anyway, now let's get back to playin' cards." The man with the odd glove spoke out.

"Give me a minute, Ollie. I need to use the facilities to wipe the blood from my face. That Emma, she always was good with a knife. Deal me in whilst I'm gone would ya?" Heath Roy knelt and pulled the knife out of the floor. Before putting it back in its sheath, he wiped the blade across his shirtsleeve and then proceeded to the only restroom that the saloon could accommodate.

The entire fiasco may have lasted three minutes and Emma did indeed provoke the incident. Still, Tyrell believed any one of the men in the saloon that night, including himself could have stood between them both and prevented the whole episode. Feeling ashamed he tossed in his last card and folded his hand, then exited the establishment.

At an eatery directly across the way from the saloon, he ordered a hot cooked meal. Noticing Emma was seated at a table alone and obviously upset, their eyes locked momentarily and he nodded, tilting his hat in respect. "Can I buy you a coffee ma'am?" he questioned. "I was present when that man of yours sprawled you out on the saloon floor. Only a coward does such a thing to a woman."

Emma smiled slightly. "He's no man of mine, at one time maybe he was. I know different now. Heath Roy is a scoundrel and a thief. A two-timing womanizer, I dislike him with Godly passion. That piece of work thought it fit to seduce my sister not once, not twice, but five times in the year, he and I have been acquainted. It's as much her fault as it is his I'm sure. For crying out loud though, he's a grown man for Pete sake. Angie is only a nineteen year old kid." Emma stood from her table and joined Tyrell at his. "By the way mister, my name is Emma." She reached out her hand before sitting.

He stood remembering his own manners. Taking her hand into his own, he introduced himself. "It's a pleasure to meet you, Emma. My name is Tyrell." He gestured for her to sit and gently pushed in her chair.

"That was kind of you Tyrell, thank you."

He nodded and returned to his own seat. "Now about that coffee, can I buy you one Emma?"

"No need for you to buy it. I'm working on owning this place," Emma smiled. Turning she looked over to the woman behind the counter. "Gabby, could you please bring both Tyrell and myself a fresh coffee?"

"Yes indeed, Miss Emma. Would you both like sweetener and cream?"

"Thank you Gabby, yes, sweetener and cream in both."

"Right away Miss Emma."

"It'll only be a minute Tyrell. Tell me, what are you doing in such a Godforsaken place as Willow Gate?" She was curious to know.

"I'm only passing through actually. I'm heading further north to Hells Bottom," he answered.

"That's quite a hop, skip and jump."

"Indeed, Emma it is. Another three weeks of travelling easily enough. It's all right though, I'm used to it."

"Sounds as though you've been there before, yes?"

"Yep. Born and raised actually."

"Where are you coming from? Sorry, if I sound a little snoopy, really I'm not. I'm a curious sort though, I've been told that before." Emma smiled sheepishly.

"No worries. I'm coming from Red Rock Canyon. Some family business needed tending. I was the only one of my kin that could deal with it."

"Red Rock Canyon?" she repeated as she pursed her lips. "I've heard Heath Roy mention that place. Is it south of here, towards Fort Mount?"

"As a matter of fact it is," he felt a sudden urge to press her for more information. "When would that have been, Emma?"

"I couldn't tell you. I know it was before he and I were together, perhaps 1886-1887 somewhere in between there."

He felt only rage as he listened to Emma's response. Could it be that Heath Roy and his numbskull friend Ollie were the two men in his dream, the murderers of his Grandfather? They both seemed to be the type. Although Emma continued to speak, Tyrell heard nothing as his mind filled with vengeance. The sound of another voice, that of Gabby, jolted him back to reality and the here and now.

"The coffee is done Miss Emma." Gabby set the two cups down.

"Thank you Gabby," Emma cooed.

"Ah, yes, thank you from me too Gabby." Tyrell responded as Gabby turned and walked away.

"Are you okay?" Emma questioned.

"Sorry about that I'm fine," he chuckled. "I was thinking how odd that Heath Roy once passed through Red Rock and here I was talking with you, his better half."

"Correction, Tyrell, the ex-better half."

"Still seems strange that he too once spent time in Red Rock or thereabouts, and that he and I have had the pleasure of your company."

"A great waste of time, that's what it was. Brought on by convenience and desire, tonight however was the last time Heath Roy will ever lay a hand on me. I'm finished with him for good." Emma brought the cup of coffee to her lips and gently blew the hot beverage, then took a drink.

Spellbound by Emma's cherry lips, he brought his own cup to his mouth and took a deep swallow. His mind raced with visions of Marissa, he thought there would never be another woman who could hold a candle to her. Yet across from him, there sat Emma. In comparison the two women shared more than one trait, both were *desirous, young, confident, and carefree.* More important though, and in his mind they were honest.

Suddenly and without cause there was a loud smashing as someone hurled a wooden bucket from a nearby water trough, through the eatery's front window. It was Heath Roy, he was standing outside on the quiet street cussing at Emma and blatantly threatening Tyrell.

"What ya doin' sittin' all cozy with that riff-raff Emma? Ya say I ain't man enough for ya…what about that pig farmer sittin beside ya. Think he's any better than me?"

Emma stood quickly from the table. "He's a gentleman, Heath Roy, something you haven't got the courage to be. Now, leave me alone go on, get out of here you pig." Emma knelt down, grabbed the wooden bucket, and began picking up the shards of glass.

"You callin' me a pig, Emma? In case ya have forgotten, my ol' man owns your establishment and this shit-hole town. I don't have to listen to your drivel." Heath Roy started toward the front entrance cussing as he approached.

Tyrell by now was standing next to Emma, as Heath Roy opened the door he drew his pistol in a drunken rage and fired, the bullet whizzed above Tyrell's shoulder and smashed into the wall behind him. Missing with the first shot Heath Roy cocked his pistol once more, but before he could squeeze the trigger, Tyrell had pulled his own .45, and in one fatal shot put to rest, the man named Heath Roy. Blood spurted from his chest and he sounded off some obscenities before finally going silent as he fell to the floor. At that instant another shot echoed and Tyrell felt the sting of a bullet as it grazed his brow.

Turning to his left without faltering, his gun returned the echo as the bullet took off the top of Ollie's skull. It seemed like an eternity as Ollie stood there, his eyes wide as his brain bubbled over from the crater left behind. Like a volcano spewing lava, brain matter and blood ran down the side of his face. Wobbling, he finally fell to the blood soaked ground.

"Goddamn it!" Tyrell expressed as he brought his hand to the wound above his eye. "Those stupid bastards!" he said out loud, as he looked over to Emma. "I'm sorry about that Emma. It was self defense I had no choice." He slapped his pistol back into its holster, as a small crowd of people gathered in the street and gawked at the two dead men.

"One of these fellows is Heath Roy," a bystander commented. The crowd was awed.

"Someone go get old man Roy and let him know!" Another shouted.

Somewhat shocked but still able to have a presence of mind, Emma shook her head. "I saw it Tyrell. Heath Roy and that Ollie Johnson had that coming. I only wish now it was sooner than later. Come on, we have to get you out of here. Quickly, into the back room, I'll bandage up that wound of yours. Once Heath Roy's father finds out that he's dead there is going to be a lynch mob and I'm afraid they'll be coming for you.

Even if it was in self-defense, he'll want retribution." Emma began pushing him in the direction of the back room. Closing the door behind them, she cleaned up and taped the wound above his eye as best she could with what she had to work with. "There, that will keep it from bleeding. Now hurry, you must go." She opened the door and led him through the back entrance, and into an ally. "Keep that wound clean as you can Tyrell, and stay safe. I will do my best to stall those who will be looking for Heath Roy's killer for as long as I can. Now go."

"Do me a favor Emma, once the law hears of this let them know I was simply defending myself and that Heath Roy and his sidekick Ollie, drew on me first."

"I will. And Tyrell, rest assured I won't give up your name or much of a description of the man who shot those two. Waste no more time, get as far away from Willow Gate as you can."

Tyrell tilted his hat and walked away as Emma closed the door. For a few minutes he was disoriented from the dizzying pain, but his need to get out of town soon took over, and he made his way as calmly as possible, to where he tied up his horse Pony. Looking back once, he left behind the town of Willow Gate.

For the next few years, he travelled through life as most drifters did when the law was on their tail. He heard through the grapevine that Heath Roy's father paid off the law and that they were going to put a noose around his neck no-matter what. Avoiding the growing cities, Tyrell preferred the loneliness of startup townships that could offer him a piece of mind, and the companionship of the odd can-can girl. Never settling down and always on the go, he worked as a miner, a cowhand, a personal bodyguard for a few rich and arrogant landowners, but eventually settled as a quick drawing bounty hunter. Never revealing his true identity he went by the alias of Travis Sweet, and that alias was near as legendary as Tyrell's real life, but it wasn't. It was a made up life, there was nothing real about it.

He sat on his horse, looking down at what was once his home and reminisced about the events that led him to Red Rock Canyon for the second time. It was late summer and the fields below were golden brown and the grass danced as the breeze picked up. His old horse Pony, from back in the day when he lived in the area was long dead. However, his travelling companion and guardian Black Dog was at his side. His new horse was nothing at all like his old horse Pony. This one listened to his commands. It was a six-year-old Dutch-Warm blood stallion and as black as night.

It was supposedly sired by one of the first of its breed. In all honesty, he cared little about the horse's history. Yet he accepted and carried the papers in his saddlebag that proved its breed. The horse's name was long and one he didn't like. Instead, he simply called it Dutch. He won the horse in a poker game from a European aristocrat two years earlier. He liked the thing but it lacked personality something Pony never lacked.

A movement in the distance caught his cobalt-blue eyes as he brought his hand up to block the yellow rays of the setting mid-day sun. He could see clearly now and looking down toward the ramshackle cabin he saw that the woman was pointing a rifle at him. He knew that the old Henry she held against her shoulder couldn't make the distance if she fired. It would be a different story though, he knew, if the woman was Marissa, she never missed.

He raised his hands. "I'm unarmed lady," he said loud enough for her to hear.

"What is your purpose for being here?" The woman yelled back.

"Just passing through, I don't mean any harm. Can I put my hands down now?"

"Hold on a second, your voice sounds familiar. Do I know you?"

"That depends on who you are." Tyrell responded.

"Mister, in case you are blind it is me who holds a gun on you. What's your name?" It was then a young boy darted out from behind a stack of wood and ran to the woman's side.

Tyrell squinted with his hands still raised. "Name is Tyrell Sloan."

"You're lying." The woman cocked her rifle.

"No ma'am, I'm not. This used to be my Grandfather's homestead. Can I put my hands down now?"

"Tyrell Sloan has been dead for six years. Keep your hands up mister and move along." She motioned with her rifle.

He began to say something but before he could finish he heard the authentic loud bang of the Henry rifle, at the same time he felt burning lead, as the bullet ripped through his shoulder, and knocked him clean off his horse. He fell hard on the moss-covered ground and grabbed his shoulder, as his horse darted out of sight. Before he could sit up to speak the woman came closer, but not close enough, that either of them could recognize the other. Looking around quickly to see where Black Dog was, he was disappointed to learn, that the dog was nowhere in sight.

"I'll tell you again mister, gather up your horse. Move along or the next bullet is going to be right between your eyes."

"Hold on, hold on," he sat up slowly clutching his shoulder. "I can prove I am who I say I am if you'll give me the chance ma'am."

"How is that? You are way up there and I'm way down here. And I don't aim on getting any closer."

He was squinting now in pain, his right shoulder spewing blood. "The boy..." he began to say as waves of agony and what seemed like the fires of hell continued to burn his ragged shoulder. "The boy, have him go over to that lilac bush...buried below it is a big old cast iron pot...it holds the deed to this place," he was pointing weakly toward the lilac bush.

The woman looked over to the boy and nodded for him to go ahead and dig, keeping the barrel of the rifle pointing at Tyrell. "You better not be lying," she held the rifle steady. "If you are the boy and I will be burying you out back."

Tyrell was laying on the ground, his eyes staring up to the heavens above as his world seem to spin. *Out of all the times, I have been shot at, and wounded it is a damn woman that knocks me off my horse...* That was his last thought before darkness overcame him.

# Chapter 2

Tyrell cautiously opened his eyes he had been out cold for two days. He had no idea on where he was, that is until the cobwebs cleared from his mind. It only took a minute to realise that he was lying on a bed in his Grandfather's old cabin. He remembered the room. Things had changed though since he had been there. It was decorated with frilly this and frilly that. The smell in the room was that of rose water and lilac. The furthest wall he noticed had been knocked out and a new room built.

Hearing the shuffling of feet coming his way, he closed his eyes. It was then he felt the dampness of a woolen cloth press against his wounded shoulder. Taking a chance, he peeked and for the first time looked at who was swabbing his wound. His heart sped up when he recognized Marissa McDowell, a woman he once loved but at the time could never have. She was as beautiful as ever. As she turned to dampen the cloth, he once more closed his eyes and let the soothing hands of Marissa caress his fleshy wound.

He was too weak to speak, and couldn't even muster the strength to mutter. Then he felt her moist cherry lips on his cheek as she kissed him.

"I am so sorry Tyrell, for the harm I have caused you. Please get well." Marissa whispered as she patted his brow with the damp cloth. "There is someone you need to meet..." Rising from the side of the bed, she exited the room. Her mind was full of memories of the Tyrell she knew. The man who wandered from Hells Bottom, the man who bed her and slipped into the void to never be heard from again, that is until now.

Marissa often thought about him, but how couldn't she? Every-time she looked into her son Caleb's eyes she saw his father. With the rumors spreading about Tyrell's death for all those years she never spoke of Caleb's father. Born Caleb Mackenzie McDowell on February 16, 1891, a few weeks pre-mature, Caleb wasn't expected to live, but the Sloan blood that ran through his veins, wouldn't deny him his place on earth. It only took a short while for little Caleb to triumph over his shortcomings, proving to Marissa and the world that he was a Sloan and that he was here to stay.

Marissa sat down at the table next to the woodstove. Caleb was lying on the deer-hide rug that draped over an old rustic Victorian couch that Marissa had shipped in. He was fast asleep. Even when he slept, Caleb looked every bit like Tyrell. It brought a smile to her face and at the same time, she grew angry.

Tyrell was Caleb's father, and where had he been for the past six years? Why hadn't he stuck around long enough to discover the life he left behind? These questions she knew could be answered only by Tyrell, and by God, she was going to ask them once he was able. With her temper cooling to embers, she looked over to the wall where Tyrell's holsters and saddlebags hung.

Curious, she stood and walked the short distance to where they hung. Opening one of the bags, she knew it wasn't the proper thing to do and even felt a bit rattled that she even had the nerve to do it, she proceeded. Slipping her hand inside she pulled out a rolled up piece of paper, undoing the band and rolling it out she was shocked to see a $5,000 wanted poster with the name UNKOWN, and a sketch of a face. It simply read: 'Wanted Dead or Alive for the killing of Heath William Roy'.

For a brief moment, she thought it looked a little like Tyrell, but not enough she decided to be concerned. Or for that matter even question him about. She rolled it up and put it back. Guilt ridden and ashamed that she snooped, she turned and made her way into the kitchen and prepared her and Caleb's lunch, again it would be venison stew and biscuits. It was something Caleb liked. He especially liked the huckleberry jam that he smothered the biscuits with. A little over five-years old, he was an early talker mostly due to

16

Marissa constantly reading him stories. He even began reading words on his own. He loved to sit next to the fire and read the books Marissa read to him.

It was the banging of the pots as Marissa finished cooking that woke Caleb. "Momma, you make too much noise. You waked me up," he said as he trotted into the kitchen.

"Hello, Caleb. It is 'woke', not *waked*," she corrected him. "Did you have a good sleep?" she asked as she scooped him up into her arms.

"Yes," he said as he rubbed his eyes. "When will that man eat supper with us?" he pointed toward the room where Tyrell lay.

"He has to get better first, Caleb. I am doing all I can to help him." She lowered him to the floor. "Now go and wash up. Get ready for some of my famous Venison stew." She watched in admiration as Caleb darted over to the washbasin and scrubbed his hands and face. "You do that so well Caleb. Good for you." She always encouraged him in all that he did.

"Have to go feed the chickens," he said as he burst toward the door.

"Hold on, Caleb. You just washed up. How about you eat first? Then I'll help you with their feed. How does that sound? It will be ready in a few minutes."

"I'll go sit," he darted passed her and sat down at the table. "I'm here and I'm waiting," he teased with a spoon in his hand.

She chuckled as she stirred the stew. Letting it simmer a few more minutes she removed the biscuits from the cooking stove and placed them on the table. "Now, Caleb, these are fresh from the oven and are very hot. Don't touch them yet. I'll spoon you out some stew and be right back." She only made a few paces before she heard the blood-curdling cry of Caleb, who obviously didn't listen and reached for one of the hot biscuits. Marissa turned around quickly. "See Caleb, I told you those are hot. Let me look at your hand."

As she approached, he began to laugh. "I was pretending."

Marissa stood stock-still and glared down at him. "Pretending to be hurt is not a laughing matter. One day you might really be hurt, and if you have joked about it too many times, then no one will believe you. Do you understand?" she cooed.

"Yes. I not pretend I hurt anymore."

"It is, 'I *will* not pretend *that* I am hurt anymore'," she corrected his grammar.

Caleb nodded his head. "Okay."

Smiling, Marissa turned and walked over to the cooking stove and scooped out stew for her and Caleb. For a brief second she thought she saw a shadow pass by and she cautiously turned around but saw nothing. As she made her way back to the table, she was in awe with shock and excitement. Sitting next to Caleb and smothering a warm biscuit with huckleberry jam sat Tyrell. Marissa looked at him for a few seconds, her mind racing. "Tyrell, you are up. I'm so sorry for shooting you…" she was lost for words as their eyes met.

"Hello, Marissa," he said as he handed the biscuit over to Caleb. "Quite a nice boy, ya got here."

"It is *you*, not '*ya*'." Caleb replied as he took the biscuit from him.

"Well, you are right there. What's your name son?"

"Caleb."

Tyrell smiled. "Nice to meet you Caleb, my name is Tyrell Sloan. I used to live in these parts," he averted his eyes once more toward Marissa who was still standing with the two bowls of stew in her hands. "Can I help you with those Marissa?"

"No, no, I'm okay." Making her way to the table, she asked if he would like a bowl.

"That's okay Marissa, you sit down here with Caleb, and I'll get my own." Tyrell stood and let her sit, pushing the chair in for her. "I haven't smelled a meal like that in quite some time," he said as he made his way to the stove.

18

Scooping out a man-sized portion, he returned to the table and pulled up a piece of stove wood to sit on that hadn't yet been split. "This sure looks and smells good Marissa, thank you very much."

Marissa, who was sitting opposite of him couldn't even touch her stew. He caught her a few times looking at him and he smiled to himself. *Boy, she ain't changed. As beautiful as ever,* he thought as he finished his bowl of stew.

"That was some good stew. I imagine by now yours is cold," he was pointing to Marissa's bowl. "Would you like me to get you another?" he offered.

"Umm, yes, yes. Thank you Tyrell," she pushed her bowl over to him. Taking his and Caleb's empty bowls as well as her full one he moved over to the stove and dumped what was left of Marissa's untouched bowl into the pot. He stirred the stew a couple of times, bringing the warmer stew up from the bottom, then scooped a dollop of the hot stew into her bowl and brought it to her. "Hot and fresh," he said as he set the bowl in front of her.

"Thank you."

"No, thank you. I haven't eaten a meal as good as that in a long time. Hit the spot just right," he rubbed his belly. Marissa took her time eating and there were a few minutes of awkward silence. Not even Tyrell had any words to say. But Caleb did.

"Do you like chickens mister?"

He looked toward Caleb and smiled. "I sure do. As a matter of fact I think you have some don't you?"

"Yep, want to come and see them?"

"You bet. Lead the way Caleb." Tyrell said as he stood.

"This way mister," Caleb was already at the door.

"Right behind you," Tyrell said as he donned his hat. Together they walked the distance to the chicken-coop, neither one saying much to the other.

"There is a real bad rooster, he doesn't hurt me though, but sometimes momma and Sebastian."

"Who is Sebastian?" Tyrell asked with curiosity.

"He's my cousin and lives near the old Heddy Mercantile."

It was then he realised who Sebastian was. He met him years ago along with Marissa's brother Len and his wife Liz. He was glad to know that the McDowell family still resided in the area. "Does, Sebastian visit often?"

"Yes. Sometimes they all come to visit."

*Huh, interesting,* Tyrell thought as he and Caleb approached the chicken-coop.

"All right mister I'm going to open the door. Watch out for the rooster." Caleb untied the leather lace used to keep the door closed and stepped in. The chicken-coop came alive as the chickens scattered and took to partial flight, most landing on their roosts. Tyrell stayed outside and waited for the ruckus and chicken feathers to settle down.

Then slowly stuck his head in; he hadn't even taken a step inside when from the corner of his eye a big black rooster flew at him, its talons opened and ready to fight. "Whoa," he managed to step aside and the rooster landed on the floor. Its feathers ruffled trying to make itself look even bigger as though it was something it needed to do. It was big enough that it didn't need to put on the charade. "You weren't kidding. That is one mean rooster. Looks like, he's getting ready to pounce again."

"Nope, you got lucky this time, he's okay now," he said as he picked it up and cuddled it. "His name is Captain Black."

Tyrell stood there and nodded. "Well, ya have certainly given him a good name."

"No, no, mister, it is '*you*' not 'ya'." Caleb said as he set Captain Black down. "Want to help me feed and water them? They like to have three scoops of wheat at feeding time." Caleb reached into a barrel and started scattering the wheat on the floor. "I'll do this, how about you get them their water?"

Tyrell looked around. "Where do I get that?"

"Outside in the rain trough, sometimes I have to gather it from the spring. It's not far from here, but you are lucky today the trough is pretty full."

Tyrell half chuckled as he stepped out and walked around the corner to where the trough was. His horse Dutch was drinking out of it. "Good to see ya, Dutch," he reached over and patted him. "I'm so used to talkin' to ya, that I seem to have forgotten how to speak. Seems Marissa's son Caleb is always going to correct me too," he chuckled. "Anyway, it was good to see ya, got to get some water to the chickens. I'll stop by later." He scooped a pail of water up as he looked around for Black Dog.

"I don't suppose you have seen that dog around have ya, Dutch?" he asked of the horse as though it could answer. "Ah, I'm sure he ain't gone too far." He waved his hand through the air and headed back to the chicken-coop. As he opened the door to step in, again, Captain Black the rooster attempted an assault, and again he managed to avoid the violent barrage of rooster talons, but spilled most of the water that was in the bucket down his leg, and into his boot.

Seeing this, Caleb started to laugh. "Don't worry mister, it's only because you are new."

Tyrell shook his head as he dumped out his boot. "I sure hope so otherwise you'll be doing this chore on your own." Retrieving a second bucket of water, he simply called Caleb and handed the water to him. "Here, you give them their water. I ain't sure that rooster wants to see me again so soon."

Caleb, reached for the bucket and rolled his eyes. "I think you are scared."

"Am not." Tyrell responded as he reached into his shirt pocket and pulled out a cheroot. Bringing a flame to it, he inhaled deeply. "It ain't because I'm scared. I plain don't like animals, which, want to cause me harm or those that have a bad sense of humor. You could say I'm not too fond of animals that don't have a personality. Take my horse for instance, it don't have a personality a personality at all. It's some big named breed, but that don't mean a thing if it ain't got a personality. I once owned an old horse named Pony now that was a horse with personality. I'll tell ya about him someday." He took another draw from the cheroot dangling from his lips as he reminisced and waited for Caleb to respond. He knew he hadn't spoken as proper as Caleb would have wanted him to, so he waited for him to correct his bad English. Caleb though never did.

# Chapter 3

As mid-day came to Red Rock and Caleb was having his afternoon nap, Marissa and Tyrell reacquainted themselves with each other. He got a tongue-lashing from Marissa, regarding his sudden disappearance six years earlier and his lack of compassion to stick around and wait for her to return from abroad.

"I did stop by Marissa, I truly did. In fact, I even met your brother Len and his family. Didn't he ever tell ya that?"

"No he didn't, it was Grandma Heddy that told me that you left. I was only a day behind your visit to her. I always waited and waited hoping one-day you'd return."

"Well I did, didn't I?" he responded somewhat sheepishly.

"You certainly did, years later I might admit."

He scratched the top of his head as though in contemplation. "Still, I'm here now, ain't I?"

"Don't you 'ain't I', Tyrell Sloan. I expect you to use proper English around Caleb so start using it now."

"Damn it woman, I ain't been around many folks lately give me a break." It was at that moment that they both broke out in peals of laughter.

"I, I, can't believe I shot you…" she said between breaths as she laughed even harder.

"A damn good shot it was too." He looked at his shoulder then back at her. There were tears streaming down their cheeks they were laughing so hard. "I said to myself before I passed out, that out of all the times I've dodged bullets, it was a bullet fired by a woman that knocked me off my horse."

More laughter ensued when Marissa told him that she wasn't even aiming. When their moment of laughter dissipated, Tyrell spoke up.

"Tell me, whatever came of those I was once acquainted with, like Grandma Heddy, Wilson, Fry, and those that worked the Sloan one, two, and three?" he grew silent as he waited for her response.

"Grandma passed away about two years ago." There was sadness in her eyes as she related the news. "The workers of the Wake Up Jake fulfilled their contract. They did well. Before they left, Jake told me that there was more gold to be discovered but I have never found the time or cared to look. Grandma made a better living with the claims than the mercantile during the last few years before she died. She always said that she tossed what gold she didn't need back into the creek that ran passed the mercantile and Len's cabin.

No one knows if that is true or not," Marissa paused. "As for old Wilson and Fry they are still living. Wilson continues to stop by every now and again. What he tells me about Fry, is that he still works his claim on the other-side of Grizzly Mountain."

Again, she grew silent as she reminisced. "I go to the old mercantile a couple of times a year and take care of Grandma's grave. I decorate it with flowers. Although the mercantile is boarded up now, and the road is more than overgrown, I enjoy the journey. I use Len's cabin when I go up there and of course Len uses it when he takes Sebastian hunting, that's all it is used for these days."

There was more that she wanted to tell him, like the fact that there had been a feral child seen in the wood around Red Rock. The child on more than three occasions had been seen, twice by the crew of the Wake Up Jake and once by her. What she didn't know was that Caleb had befriended the child and he called the child Teeka.

As far as anyone knew, Teeka was Caleb's made up friend. Teeka though, was very much real. No one knew where the child came from or the child's age and sex, but Marissa knew firsthand that the child did exist. A few of the men from the Wake Up Jake tried tracking the child once, but the child outwitted them and disappeared. She wanted to tell him the tale but now wasn't the time. He'd likely think she was off her rocker if she did.

Tyrell felt as though she wasn't telling him something, but he didn't pry. "Did Grandma go peacefully?" he asked as tears pricked his eyelids.

"Yes, in her sleep. She suffered for a few weeks as she battled a fever. But in the end, she simply fell asleep and never woke again. I think it was her will, she was so lonely."

"Where has she been laid to rest? I'd like to pay my respects if I could?"

"I'll take you there sometime if you are planning on sticking around? How about you tell me how things have been in Tyrell's world."

"I guess I do owe you an explanation, I always wanted to have the opportunity to tell ya. Now is as good of a time as any I reckon." Pausing for a moment, he reached into his shirt pocket and pulled out a cheroot. Lighting it he took a long pull and exhaled a bit nervously. *It is going to be a long day,* he thought as he proceeded to tell Marissa about his reasons for leaving and the life he led afterwards. He never told her about the alias he once used or that he was a wanted man.

He would keep that secret to himself for now. He told her half-truths and felt badly that he had, but it was all he wanted to share. Pressing out the cheroot on his boot heel he looked into Marissa's eyes, they were as beautiful and clear as he could remember. "That's my story Marissa. I've been drifting trying to figure out where I belong," he paused for a minute. "I think it is here in Red Rock. That is of course if you'll allow me to stay on."

"What do you mean '*stay on*'? This place is more yours than it is mine. Especially, since you are alive."

Tyrell scratched the side of his face. "I wasn't much of a gentleman to you all those years back. I'd like to prove to you that I had no intentions on hurting you in any way. I wouldn't feel comfortable just moving in and all. I reckon if the placer claims on Hudu Creek could use some work, I'd like to start working them. And if there is any man's work you have, I'd be appreciative if you'd let me do it. Fencing and repairs that sort of thing."

Marissa nodded her head. "All right Tyrell. I'll accept your offer." She knew he was right they couldn't simply pick up where they left off. "I know that the Wake Up Jake left an old shack behind. You are welcome to stay there."

Tyrell nodded. "That'll do. Any chance the old tools and whatnots that I left behind are still around?"

"Wilson put them out back under an old wagon canvas when we made room for the chickens. I believe everything is there."

"Good. I'll be taking them. It's getting late now, I best get a move on." He rose from the table and walked over to his gun-belt and saddlebags hanging from the cabin entrance. Securing his holster and tossing the bags over his shoulder, he looked one more time at Marissa. "I'll come back tomorrow sometime to pick up the tools. Plus I reckon I need to pay old Grandpa Sloan a visit…" Tyrell paused for a minute. "Umm, you did know that he's buried out back, right?" he questioned empathetically.

"Of course I know. It was Caleb who found the spot. It was during the first days that we moved here, Caleb was only a year and a half old. We've kept it up and have planted a honeysuckle nearby. I hope you don't mind?"

"Not at all."

"I love the epitaph you wrote, it is very touching. Would you like to go see it now?" she asked.

"I reckon not. Tomorrow is better. I'm a bit weary and think it is best that I get gone." Opening the door he was about to step out when Marissa spoke up.

"Are you sure you'll be okay with that wound?" she pointed at his shoulder. It was more of an excuse to try to get him to stay the night.

"You did a fine job in fixing it up I reckon. I don't see it causing me much grief."

Marissa rose from the table herself and walked the short distance to where he stood. Leaning toward him, she kissed him on the cheek. "I'll see you tomorrow."

Tyrell nodded and stepped out. Black Dog was back, and was lying near the old lilac bush the same as he did when they first lived there, six years earlier. Tyrell patted him and welcomed him back. "Glad you made it, Black Dog. You ought to consider sticking around a bit more, you're getting old... remember that." The dog licked its chops and wagged its tail as Tyrell turned and walked away.

He gathered his belongings and saddled his horse. Then the three companions headed along the brush line. The pots and pans that dangled from his saddle, clanged together in a din of sound as he went. Hudu Creek was in a westerly direction, and he headed in that direction, until he came across the old worn and dilapidated trail.

It gently turned back south then west again until finally the trickle from the slow moving creek was audible. Black Dog panted at the horse and Tyrell's side. Tugging gently on Dutch's reins, he steered him up the middle of the creek. "We're getting close, I can feel it," he inhaled deeply with his nostrils flared, *sure smells nice up here,* he thought as he got Dutch to stop. "Here we are- here is home."

Slipping off his horse, he led him to the edge of the creek. Black Dog frolicked nearby and Tyrell whistled for him. He could see the old shack it was about 50 or so feet from the creek and tucked beneath a thick forest of cedar, fir and dying ferns. Removing his hat, he wiped his forehead with his kerchief. *It certainly don't look like much. But, I reckon we'll make do.* Tyrell smiled as he tied Dutch to a tree and walked over to the shack, Black Dog trailed behind curious and cautious.

The door opened with an awful creak that made the entire forest fall silent. Stepping in he looked around. There was a well-used potbelly stove in one corner, the stovepipe rusted through in places made it look like someone purposely-poked holes in it. Next to that was a single bunk. A couple of crudely built chairs and table was dead center. There was a set of shelves and a gun rack on one wall, the east wall boasted a window and counter that faced the front of the shack in the direction of Red Rock Canyon, giving one the view of the forest and sunrise.

On the wall at the entrance was a set of Deer antlers. He put his hat on one of the prongs and walked over to the dusty window. Using the side of his hand he rubbed it clean to let in the little bit of daylight that was left. *This is it...this is where I'll make things new. Here is where I'll start fresh,* he thought as he looked out. Turning on his heel he stepped over to the old stove and opened it, *it'll do,* he thought, as he looked it over and closed the door.

# Chapter 4

Pulling up one of the chairs to the table, he sat down and reached into his shirt pocket to retrieve one of the eight cheroots he had left. Bringing a match to it, he inhaled deeply. Earlier he felt some pain coming from his wounded shoulder and took the time to look it over. It was healing up nicely, as far as he was concerned and he saw no reason to worry.

Standing, he exited the shack and gathered his bedroll, oil lantern, saddlebags, rifle, and cooking utensils. He set them down and removed the old saddle from his horse. Dutch seemed to sigh in relief. "There you go. I reckon that feels better." Tyrell pointed toward the creek, "I'll tether you closer to the creek and that patch of grass in a minute, hang tight." Picking up his belongings, he traipsed back to the shack. Black Dog was content as he lay there panting beneath a mountain ash, shaded slightly from the late after-noon sun. Tyrell stepped into his new domicile and tossed his bedroll and saddlebags onto the bunk. He carefully put his rifle on the rack and set the lantern on the table, the pots and pans he set down on the counter beneath the window. "There, feels like home already," he said to himself as he once more exited.

He led Dutch to the edge of the creek and the horse slurped a drink while he filled his canteen. Black Dog still hadn't moved and was catching up on his sleep from the day's excursion. The sun was setting and it painted a picture in the sky. Tyrell smiled as he stood and gazed at it. Taking Dutch by the reins, he tethered him for the night. "There you go Dutch. You got both plenty of water and grass to get you through. We'll find a more appropriate place near the shack to bed you down tomorrow."

He turned and looked at the sky then once more headed indoors. Drawing a match, he lit the lantern. It flickered to life casting his own shadow on the wall behind him. Sitting down he stared out the window, his feet up on the table. The shack was small, but not small enough that he could reach across the room and grab his saddlebag. Standing, he took a few steps and retrieved it. Digging through it, he pulled out a soft leather pouch that contained beef jerky and gnawed a piece. What he really wanted was a hot cup of coffee but the jerky and a cold drink of water from his canteen would have to suffice. He was tired and didn't have the energy to brew coffee.

Marissa however was feeling the exact opposite. She was happy that Tyrell was back in her life, and felt better now, that he apologized for leaving her without so much as a kiss all those years ago. She gathered a few things she thought he would like to have, when he came to retrieve the tools he'd need on the placer claims. She removed the maps from the wall that he left behind in 1890 and that she kept tacked to the wall.

With those items, she added a couple of tin cups, plates, and eating utensils as well as a down-filled pillow one of the four she had. She wrapped up some smoked venison and a few pounds of potatoes, salt, coffee, tea, flour and sugar, things she knew he didn't have a lot of. *There,* she thought to herself as she stepped back and looked at her offerings. *That ought to keep him happy for a few days. Anything else he may need he's going to have to round up himself.* Marissa heard the kettle boil and made herself a cup of mint tea. The mint grew wild and she harvested it and used it. Just like the wild onions, asparagus, and raspberries that grew. She did have her own garden out back near the old fire pit where she grew potatoes, carrots, beans, and corn as well as a few edible flowers that she used for medicines, lotions, and oils. She was very self-efficient, she always had been. Still, she did miss adult companionship, now with Tyrell only being a hop, skip, and jump away, she couldn't be happier.

It would take time for them to overcome their past relationship and how it turned out she knew that as did

Tyrell. It was obvious that each of them wanted the same thing and that they wanted to reinvent their long lost love that they shared for each other. Only time would tell if it would ever be worth it. Marissa sipped the last of her tea as Caleb played on the floor with one of his wooden toys, his eyes sleepy. She smiled as she watched him, "Come on Caleb it's time for a story. You look sleepy."

"Okay Ma, can we take turns reading?" Caleb asked excitedly.

"We sure can. Do you want to go first?"

Caleb rose from the floor and rubbed his eyes. "Maybe I am too tired. Tomorrow night I'll read first." Marissa took him by his hand and walked with him to his bed. "Ma, will that man ever visit us again?"

"Who? Tyrell?"

"That man that you shot with the big gun." Caleb responded as though what his mother had done was nothing at all.

"As a matter of fact he's coming for a visit tomorrow."

"Do you think Captain Black will ever be his friend?"

"I don't know. I've known that old rooster for a long time, so has Sebastian and he still doesn't like us much."

Caleb took a deep breath. "Maybe I should have a talk with Captain Black and tell him to be nice. He's never bothered Teeka."

Marissa ran her fingers through his hair and kissed his forehead. "What story do you want me to read, Caleb?" She was looking at the bookcase and all the titles it held. They had read most of them twice, and some three or four times. Even Caleb was starting to get bored with them. She looked over her shoulder to Caleb but already he was fast asleep. Marissa brought the covers up around his neck and tucked him in. "Sleep well Caleb and God-bless." Standing from his bedside she gently blew out the lantern and exited his room. Night had come to Red Rock. Tired herself Marissa tidied up and made for her own bed, anticipating what the following day would bring.

Back at the placer claim shack, Tyrell was smoothing out his bedroll. He too was getting ready for bed. In the distance lonely howls from a pack of wolves echoed eerily in the darkening forest. Their chorus lasted for a few minutes then once again the sounds of crickets and birds took over. He made his way over to the small table and sat, listening to the sounds of night.

A calming effect of inner-peace and realisation enveloped him. He attributed this to three facts: one being that he was finally on familiar ground. For now it didn't matter who it belonged to, him or Marissa. The land was familiar and he knew most of it. The second reason was that here was his opportunity to put things right between himself and Marissa. The third reason of course was Caleb.

Looking at his pocket watch, he noted the time and he yawned. The shack it seemed started getting musty for one reason or another. He stood from the table and walked over to the window then swung it open. A sudden gust of wind tousled his hair and made the papers he left on the table skid across it and land on the floor. The lantern flickered and the door swung open then slammed shut. It startled him and he jumped.

"Damn," he said as he spun around and walked over to it. He set his saddlebags against the bottom of the door to keep it shut. The problem with the door was simple. Over time it had warped and didn't fit properly, even the littlest gust of wind would have the same effect. *Project one,* he thought as he looked it over. *That's an easy fix.* Making his way to the bunk, he took off his boots and buckskins and lay down. His holster hung on the wall above him, and the two shot derringer that he kept in his boot, was snugly under the rolled up wool blanket that he was using for his head. As long as he could get to either in the blink of an eye, he was content.

The opened window didn't only let in the cool mountain air, but also a couple thousand mosquitoes, or so it seemed. He swatted at a handful of them cussing the whole time, then stood and closed the window. *Well, that wasn't very pleasant,* he thought as he again lay down. It didn't take long before his eyes got heavy. Yawning, he turned on his side with his back to the wall and fell asleep. An hour later, he thought he heard a ruckus outside and before his eyes opened, he held the derringer in his hand. Swinging his feet to the floor, he cautiously took hold of one of the Colts that hung from the wall, and crept over to the door. Kicking the saddlebags out of the way, he slowly opened it and peered out. To his relief all was silent.

Black Dog traipsed over before he closed the door and made his way in. "Did you make that noise? Or was I hearing things?" he asked as Black Dog scurried over to the table and sat precariously still. Tyrell scratched his head, if there was ever any danger around Black Dog would have been the first to let him know. It was then he realised what the dog wanted, and he chuckled. "I get it. You didn't get jerky today. I guess I best get it for you now."

Opening the leather pouch that he carried the jerky in, he picked out a nice-sized chunk and tossed it to Black Dog, who then immediately headed back to the door to be let out. "Not going to stay for a brief visit ol' boy?" Smiling, Tyrell opened the door and the dog darted out. "See ya in the morning Black Dog." Making his way back to the bunk, he noticed the half-smoked cheroot sitting on the table and he picked it up. Bringing it to his lips, he lit it. *Out of all the years I've known that dog, tonight was the first time I forgot to give him his jerky. I must be getting old.* Tyrell inhaled the acrid smoke as he reminisced.

# Chapter 5

When he rose in the morning, his body itched with mosquito bites. They covered his arms, neck, and face. It was a wonder that any blood coursed through his veins at all. He scratched at the ones on his arms until they bled. *I've never been eaten alive like that before. I sure hope I don't get the fever. Damn things anyway,* he thought. He rounded up his coffeepot and gathered some water from the creek, checking up on Dutch as he did so.

Night one had come and gone. Before he was going to spend another night in there, he needed to find a way to keep the damn mosquitoes at bay. They practically ate him alive overnight. He looked Dutch over to see if he too suffered the same wrath. It didn't look like he had and he was glad for that. Patting the horse, he headed back to the shack. Firing up the old potbelly stove, he added some coffee to the pot and set it to boil. It didn't take long before he was coughing from all the smoke that escaped from the holes in the stovepipe.

He opened the door to the shack and stepped out. It was a good thing that he did. Looking up to where the stovepipe poked through, he saw that flames were dancing through the roof. Moving swiftly he ran the distance to the creek a bucket in his hand. Scooping up water, he darted back and tossed the water inside the stove. The flames hissed and puffed and finally the fire went out. He kicked the stovepipe down and using his bedroll swatted at the flames that were burning the rafters. It took some doing but he finally got the upper hand and put the fire out. The rafters now smoldered and there was a huge opening in the roof where the old stovepipe once was, and where the flames had burned through.

Covered in soot and sweating bullets he exited the shack to get a breath of fresh air. Black Dog who watched the entire charade from the sidelines looked at him as though he was strange. Tyrell sat down on an old log and looked toward the shack and the hole in the roof. "Project one," he said as he shook his head. *The door is going to have to wait,* he thought. Rising he walked the short distance to the creek and splashed water on his face. The early morning sun reflected and a light wind rustled the willows that grew along the creek and tousled his hair.

Taking a long cool drink, he wiped his mouth with the back of his hand as he contemplated on whether or not he should simply rebuild. He could use the good lumber and logs from the old shack to make a new one. There were enough trees in the vicinity to accomplish the task. Time was a constraint though, it wouldn't be long before the snows of late fall and winter blanketed the valley. He decided he'd patch up the roof as best he could for the time being and in the spring build anew. He wasn't in a rush. Even if he managed to build another cabin by next fall, he would be ahead. There were plenty of places to build. He needed only to find the right spot.

Black Dog approached and sat next to him. "Quite the thing you saw going on here this morning eh?" Tyrell scratched the dog behind its ear. "Guess I should've taken the time to look the roof and stovepipe over. I almost turned the shack into ashes. Live and learn I suppose. One thing is for certain, I ain't going to be getting any coffee here today. We best saddle up Dutch and head to Marissa's. Got some tools and stuff I need to gather. I reckon she'll be awake by the time we get there. C'mon on Black Dog let's get." Saddling up his horse and with Black Dog in tow he set off downstream.

He paid little attention to the forest as he made his way and was completely unaware of the staring yellow eyes watching him. Crouched behind some bramble was the feral child. She was watching the newcomers motionlessly as horse and rider passed. It was an odd sight for the child to see, this new man, horse, and dog. There was an odd scent in the breeze and Black Dog slowed to a stop and sniffed the air. Looking around not even his keen eyes spotted the child.

Unstirred he continued on catching up with Tyrell as he crossed to the other side of the creek and onto the trail that led them out of the woods.

An hour later, they emerged from the forest and into the opened fields of Red Rock Canyon. Looking at his pocket watch he noted it was almost 7:30 a.m. "A few minutes ride and we'll be knocking on Marissa, and Caleb's door. Hopefully she ain't going to train the sights of her old Henry on me and shoot." Tyrell half chuckled as he said that.

In all honesty, though, from his perspective it wasn't at all that funny. "I'm kind of glad that she did shoot me and even gladder that I'm alive to speak of it. It tells me she ain't afraid to shoot a man, and that tells me she can certainly take care of herself if the need arises. Knowing that makes me feel a whole lot better about her and Caleb being alone," he looked down to Black Dog. "You ain't even listening are you? Here I am conversing with you, and you won't even wag your tail. Thanks for the ears ol' boy."

Pulling up to the horse post outside Marissa's cabin, he dismounted and tethered Dutch. It was Caleb that opened the door when they heard Tyrell knocking. "Good morning, Caleb." Tyrell said in his best English.

"Good morning mister. Last night ma gathered some stuff for you to have and when I woke up I added a few books. I think you should read them." Caleb said as he stepped aside to let Tyrell in.

"Thank you very much Caleb. That is mighty kind of you," he responded as he removed his hat and looked across the room to Marissa, "Morning, Marissa."

"Hello Tyrell. How was your first night up on Hudu Creek?"

"Except for the mosquitoes I slept well. This morning though was another story." Walking across the room, he sat down at the table. "I don't suppose you have any coffee brewing? I missed mine this morning due to a mishap and some carelessness."

"I sure do. Would you like some fresh fried eggs and salt pork to go with it?"

"Thank you very much Marissa. If it isn't a problem I'd be quite obliged."

"No problem, sit tight I'll get them for you. Then you can tell me about the mishap that caused you to miss your morning coffee." She rose from the table leaving him and Caleb sitting together.

"So." Caleb said as he looked at Tyrell.

"So...what?" Tyrell questioned a bit confused.

"You said that you would tell me about your horse Pony one day. What about right now?"

"Ah, that's what you meant."

"Yes, ma told me a few things but I think she was fibbing. Was Pony really as crazy as she says?"

"I don't know Caleb what did she say?"

"She said that he didn't like bears and that was how she met you. That Pony saw a bear one time and bucked you off. She said that Pony brought you to Heddy's all by himself and that you were hurt. Is that true?"

Tyrell chuckled as he reminisced about Pony. He certainly missed that horse. "That is true Caleb. He also saved me once from a mean old grizzly. Bears weren't the only thing Pony didn't like. He didn't like grouse either and chased them down too. Plus, I could swing off his back while he was moving and pee behind a tree if I had to. He wouldn't slow down either, he'd keep right on moving. He was so big and slow that most times I could jump right back onto the saddle." Tyrell was smiling as he said that.

"Wish I had a horse like that. We have an old mare and a gelding but they're just plain old horses." Caleb finished his biscuit and milk as he conjured up visions of a horse that did all the things Pony did. "What happened to him?"

"He got old." Tyrell was hoping that Caleb would leave it at that. He didn't want to relive what really happened. Pony died tragically fighting off a sow grizzly with cubs. Tyrell lived with the heartbreak for some time. He was the one that found Pony torn up and bleeding to death. It was the horses eye's that haunted him whenever he thought about it. Tyrell shook his head as he tried to erase the memory.

Marissa's voice brought him back to the here and now. "Are you ready for some breakfast Tyrell?" She set the plate and tin cup down in front of him.

"Thank you Marissa, I appreciate it." Looking at the plate of food, he smacked his lips and dug in.

Marissa smiled and nodded. "So, what was the mishap this morning that caused you to miss your morning coffee?" she asked as he finished chewing.

"It all started when I threw some sticks into the old stove," he took a slurp from the cup in front of him. "I stepped outside to catch my breath when the thing started smoking because of all the holes in the stovepipe…" he put another mouthful of eggs in his mouth and swallowed before he continued. "It was a good thing I did too, I don't know what it was but something made me look up, onto the roof of the old shack and as sure as I'm sitting here, flames were punching through. It took a bit of a fight but I got it under control soon enough and doused it.

Only thing was, that by then the flames had burned right through. I can look to the heavens every night now when I'm sitting at the table," Tyrell chuckled as he took another drink from his cup. "Could have prevented the whole thing if I took the time to make sure everything was okay."

"What are you going to do about the hole in the roof?"

"Ah, with a bit of work I reckon I can fix it with some poles, sod, and mud." Putting the last of the salt pork in his mouth, he finished up. "I might build myself a new shack in time. In fact, I likely will. Until then I'll make do." He slid his empty plate to the side, and took up the cup again and finished what was left of his coffee. Marissa offered him another as she removed his plate from the table. "Thank you, I'd appreciate another cup."

"What are your plans for today?" she asked as she returned with his fresh cup of coffee.

"I reckon I'll gather up whatever tools I need for the work up there on the creek. It'll likely take a couple of trips and keep me busy for the rest of the day. Is there anything you might need done down here that I can help you with?"

"Nothing that is pressing, I do have a question though."

"What's that?"

"How do you feel about Caleb and me helping you today with all the tools and stuff?"

"I wouldn't complain one bit. I'd love the help."

"We can load up the wagon and do it all in one shot. Caleb has wanted to have an adventure for the past little while. I think he'd enjoy it. I'll build us a lunch and we can all have a picnic up on the creek."

"The problem with that is I'm not so sure a wagon could follow that trail."

"What, the trail that the crew from the Wake Up Jake blazed?" Marissa asked somewhat confused.

"Huh?" Tyrell questioned even more confused than Marissa, "they blazed a trail?"

"Isn't that how you got up there?"

"I got up there all right but there is no way a wagon could travel the trail I took. I didn't see any other trail going up or coming down."

"They must have blazed the trail after you were gone. Sorry about that Tyrell, but I thought you knew about the wagon trail."

"I do now, thank you very much for telling me." They started to chuckle realising where and how all the confusion started. "Where the heck is this trail?"

"Come on, Caleb and I will show you." Marissa stood from the table and Tyrell followed suit. Caleb was already at the door and he opened it for them. It was a beautiful morning made even more beautiful and special with Marissa and Caleb at his side. The sun was egg yolk yellow in the pale blue sky. "It is going to be a warm day," Marissa commented as they walked around the side of the cabin in the direction of the wagon trail.

Tyrell was familiar with the place where the trail began and confused at the same time. It was where he gathered his stove wood and fell poles and posts that he used to build up the place when he lived there. The crew from the Wake Up Jake simply carried on what he inadvertently started.

"There, there's the wagon trail," Marissa said as they walked the short distance to where it started to cut through the forest.

"They couldn't have picked a better spot. What confuses me though it doesn't even go in the right direction, the Sloan claims are north-westerly, and if this leads up to the claims where does it exit?" he removed his hat and fiddled with the brim.

"It cuts straight through to the creek then west and follows the creek bed right on up. That's probably why you never crossed the trail or saw where it came out. The creek is the trail." Marissa was smiling as she said that.

Tyrell was looking at her and smiled back. "It makes perfect sense now. I suppose I could have figured that out. I told them they should use the creek to transport their equipment. I knew it was a direct route to Fort Mount, and that the creek was only a little more than a trickle in the summer, yet wide enough for wagons to travel. I must've been a greenhorn because I never once thought about blazing a trail through to the creek myself. I'm sure glad they did."

"Don't get to excited. I've only travelled it a few times to accompany Grandma when she wanted to check up on the work that Jake and his crew were doing. I haven't been up that way in the three or four years that the Wake Up Jake has been gone. The route is likely pretty much overgrown and there is at least ten miles of forest between here and the creek."

Tyrell nodded his head. "I suppose you're right. There could be obstacles and I'm sure a few years of growth does change things. Nevertheless, as long as we find the creek we should be okay. Besides, it does sound like quite the adventure doesn't it Caleb?" he looked over to the child holding Marissa's hand.

"It sure does, mister. Can we go now?"

Marissa and Tyrell chuckled. "First you have to help load up the wagon with Tyrell's tools and stuff and help him harness the horses. And I have to make us a big picnic lunch." Marissa said as Caleb let go of her hand and ran back toward the cabin, excited to get the work done, so they could go. The two of them followed in his wake. Making the distance back to the cabin themselves, Marissa left Tyrell and Caleb working hand-in-hand loading up the wagon with all the old tools and sluicing equipment, while she went inside and prepared  a picnic.

It took them well over an hour to finish. The sun beat down on them hot, hard, and steady. Finally, with the last piece of equipment loaded and everything secure and safe the two of them rested in the shade and sipped on lemonade. "That was quite the job, wasn't it Caleb?" Tyrell wiped the sweat from his brow and took a long cold drink from his glass of lemonade.

"It sure was," Caleb sighed as he imitated Tyrell and wiped his own brow.

"You're a good worker you know that? I'd work alongside you any day of the week Caleb, yes sir, I truly would."

"You're a pretty good worker too, mister."

"How old are you Caleb?" Tyrell wanted to know.

"Almost six."

"I'll tell you what, when you turn six you can start calling me Tyrell."

"No sir. I couldn't do that, ma would get mad. She says it is rude to call elders by their names."

Tyrell chuckled. "You let me deal with your ma, if I say you can call me Tyrell when you turn six. Then, as far as I'm concerned when you turn six, you can call me Tyrell and it won't be rude at all."

"I don't know mister. I'll have to see I guess. Do you think that maybe we should harness up that old mare and gelding to the wagon?"

"I suppose now is as good of a time as any." The two of them stood up and walked over to the corral. "Do the horses have names?"

"Yes." Caleb pointed to the dun mare. "We call her Tiger Lilly, and that buckskin we call him Buck. Tiger Lilly is his momma. But you know what mister?" Caleb crossed his arms.

"What's that Caleb?"

"They don't come when you call them by their names."

"That isn't surprising. Most animals don't pay much attention to names. It is our voices that they learn to listen to."

Caleb shrugged his shoulders. "Why do we name them then?"

Tyrell, leaned up against the corral, and removed his hat. "I guess it's because we want our animals to have names. Take for instance, that horse of mine he's got a God awful long name that I can't even say. How a horse could even understand it is beyond me. So I call him Dutch, either he's forgotten his real name or couldn't understand it in the first place. It's my voice and the tone of it at any particular time that he has learned to understand and obey. Not his name."

Caleb was looking at him as though that was the silliest thing he ever heard. "Mister, that doesn't make any sense whatsoever," he said as a matter-of-fact. Shaking his head, he turned and opened the corral gate. "I'll get the horses."

Tyrell stood there dumbfounded by Caleb's response and mannerism, but it was quite refreshing and he softly chuckled to himself. "All right, I'll wait for you and then we'll harness them up." He watched in admiration as Caleb gathered the two horses and led them over to where he waited to receive them. "Geez, you sure made that look easy. They're two well-behaved horses I'd say." Tyrell took them by their leads and led them over to the wagon. "Does it matter which side of wagon they go on?"

"Tiger Lilly on the left and Buck on the right." Caleb replied as he closed the corral gate. With the task done, he walked toward the cabin. "I'll go let ma know that we're almost done, okay mister?"

"Sure." Tyrell responded

"Hey Caleb, how is the work going out there with Tyrell?" Marissa asked as Caleb came inside.

"It was fun, all done now. Can we go?"

"You bet we can. I know you've been working real hard but could you please help me with these last things that we need to load up?" she handed him the basket of food. "Get Tyrell to help you get this onto the wagon and then come back and help me with the rest okay?"

"Yes Momma," Caleb turned with the basket in hand and exited the cabin. He set the basket down on the ground next to the wagon. "We need to get this up onto the wagon, mister."

Tyrell picked it up and found a place to put it. "How does that look? Figure it'll stay snug?"

Caleb looked on and studied where Tyrell stowed it. "Yes sir. That won't go anywhere except into my tummy. Ma's got more stuff waiting for me."

A couple of trips back and forth they were finally ready to go. According to Tyrell's pocket watch it was 11:00 a.m., there was one more thing he needed to do. He walked around back of the cabin his hat in his hand. The honeysuckle and few patches of wildflowers certainly added beautification he noticed. "Hello, Grandpa Sloan," Tyrell began softly. "As I told you six years ago, when I fist stepped foot on this vast land, that if I ever came across two men that may have been the cause for you lying there in the cold earth, I'd send them to Hell. I'm here to tell you that's what I've done." He stood in silence for a few brief moments, and bowed his head, then turned and walked away. Marissa and Caleb were waiting for him as he came from around back. They were sitting in the wagon ready to go. He swung up onto his horse and pulled up next to the wagon. "Are we set?"

"We are."

"All right then let's get," he said as he turned his horse and headed toward the wagon trail.

# Chapter 6

The blazed trail grew dark as they travelled deeper into the wood. Tyrell rode alongside the wagon and Black Dog trailed behind. The trees that canopied the old trail blocked out the sun in places. At times it was as welcoming as a cool drink on a hot day, other times it was a nuisance, especially in the marshy areas where handfuls of black flies, mosquitoes, and no-see-ums swarmed them.

As they predicted the trail was overgrown and they spent some time wrestling with fallen logs, overgrown mountain ash, willow, and thorn berry shrubs. But they were indeed making progress. In the distance they could faintly make out the sound of a creek. They were close. Tyrell dismounted and helped Marissa and Caleb step down from the wagon.

"We've been going steady and hard for three hours. I think here is a good place to catch our breaths. Besides, I'm a might hungry, how about you Caleb?"

"Yes, but I'm sleepy too," he rubbed his eyes as he sat down on the blanket that Marissa laid out.

"Have something to eat first Caleb, and then maybe Tyrell and I can make a place for you to lie down in the back of the wagon."

"That is easy enough to do. Right up close too."

"Okay." Caleb said as he yawned. The three of them shared the lunch Marissa packed and drank lemonade as they spoke amongst themselves. Every now and again they would sit in silence to listen to the sounds of the forest and all that lived in it. Tyrell never wanted the moment to end. But, of course it did, and before long they were once more on their way. The old wagon trail granted them a safe and uneventful passage as Hudu Creek came in to view.

"There it is," Tyrell pointed. "Hudu Creek, from here we'll follow it upstream. I don't know for how long, but I speculate you do?"

"From what I recall it was about an hour ride from here. I can't imagine it being much longer than that. There is one spot on the way that might slow us down, but after that we should make it to your shack in an hour or so."

Tyrell looked at his pocket watch, "I guess that'll put us up there around four thirty, a total of a five hour trip from your place to mine."

"That is what I suspect."

"There isn't no way that you and Caleb can make it back before dark. You know that, right?"

"I do. The wagon will sleep Caleb and me easy enough. That is if you don't mind some overnight company."

"I wouldn't allow you to leave regardless."

"What does that mean? Do you mind having the company or not."

"Hell no, I'm surprised you'd think otherwise. I won't let you and the boy sleep in no wagon either. The two of you can sleep in the shack. Least wise the four walls will keep the two of you safe. I'll sleep outdoors."

"Good, than that is settled." Marissa snapped the reins and the wagon continued onward. Tyrell watched for a few brief seconds as she steered the horses into the creek and headed upstream. A smile crossed his face as he heeled Dutch's flank and caught up to her.

"It is sure peaceful ain't it?" He hollered over the sound of the sloshing water as the wagon wheels dug into the creek bed spewing mud and water in an upward direction.

Marissa looked over her shoulder and nodded in agreement. "Yes, beautiful too, you know what makes it even more beautiful?"

"Yeah the fact that you are by my side is what makes it even more beautiful."

Marissa smiled. "Yep," she said as she snapped the reins and the two horses sped up. Water sprayed up from the back wheels with a frothy coolness soaking Tyrell from head to toe. He could hear her laughter as she sped away. Soaked and laughing himself, he heeled Dutch's flank again, and the horse reared up catching him off guard. Dutch slammed his front hooves down digging them in and with a great fury took off in a sprint so fast Tyrell almost fell off. He held on for dear life as the horse dashed passed Marissa and her wagon like it was standing still.

"I didn't know you had that in you Dutch." Tyrell looked back and shrugged his shoulders at Marissa, "I don't know what got into him." Dutch slowed to a comfortable trot and finally stopped. "That was quite the ride Dutch, what was eating at your behind for you to get up and go like that?" Tyrell questioned as he patted Dutch's muscular neck.

Marissa and her wagon caught up a few seconds later. "Man, can that horse ever move," she pulled up next Tyrell.

"That was the craziest thing ever. I don't have a clue on what caused him to do that, nor has he ever got up to speed like that before. I almost took a tumble when he first started off. Not even Pony ever went that fast." They conversed back and forth as the continued onward.

"I was going to ask you about that." Marissa began as they rested.

"About what?"

"Pony. Whatever happened to him?"

"He got old." Tyrell replied as he reached into his pocket and pulled out a cheroot. Sticking it between his lips he drew a match across its striker and brought the flame up. Taking a deep breath he held it in for a minute then exhaled. "I'll tell you about it sometime. Come on, we got a bit further to go I reckon," he said as he sped ahead.

"I suppose. Lead the way." Marissa got her team to start moving. She knew that there was more to the Pony story than him simply getting old, she wouldn't pry though. "Come on Tiger Lilly let's get. You too Buck, giddy-up." Neither Tyrell nor Marissa spoke much after that. Instead, they were content to listen to their surroundings, the horses splashing hooves and the ever squeaking and creaking sound that the wagon made as it traversed through the water, rock, and clay. Taking a final pull on his second cheroot of the day, Tyrell flicked it into the creek. He and Dutch had gotten quite ahead of Marissa and now they waited for her and her team to catch up before carrying on. They were getting close he could recognize the bend up ahead. It would only be a few more minutes. Finally, Marissa and her wagon team caught up.

"I'm starting to feel every bump and burp this old wagon makes when it hits them."

Tyrell chuckled. "Getting a sore behind eh?"

"Sure am," she responded as they continued. Ten minutes later, they pulled up to the old shack.

"Here we are." Tyrell slid off his horse, tethered him and helped Marissa down from the wagon. "Should we wake the little man?" he asked.

"Not now. I'll wake Caleb in a bit. He gets grumpy sometimes if he doesn't get his nap. So, this is it. It looks different without all the stuff that was here." Marissa said as she looked around. "There was a rock crushing machine over there," she pointed in the direction, "and over there was the cooking shack from what I remember, the bunkhouse was next to that. I think your shack was Jake's office and sleeping quarters." She walked over to an old log and sat down.

"Four years changes a lot." Tyrell responded as he opened the back gate of the wagon so that he could start unloading it.

"Are you going to start that now or are you going to show me around a bit first?" Marissa wanted to know.

"There ain't much to show that I know of yet. Heck, I don't even know for certain if there is an old outhouse around here."

"How about showing me the inside of that nasty old shack then?" she suggested.

"Certainly, follow me." Holding the door opened for her she stepped in. Walking over to the single window she looked out.

"I bet you'll get to see some beautiful sunrises from here." She walked the short distance to where the woodstove once was and looked up through the hole in the ceiling. "Yep you'll be able to see the stars." She smiled, "what are you going to do about the stove and pipe?"

"I reckon the stove itself will suffice, but I'll have to head over to the Hudu Creek Mercantile eventually, and pick up some new stovepipe. It is still in operation ain't it?"

Marissa nodded her head. "Yes it is. It's the only mercantile in the area unless you travel to Fort Mount or Salwood."

"Good, then I can pick up the stovepipe in the coming days. When and if, I ever build another shack I'll build a proper fireplace and hearth. For now, I reckon a piece of pipe is all I'll need."

Marissa nodded in agreement as they exited the shack and made their way over to the wagon. Gently she woke up Caleb while Tyrell slowly unloaded it. Finishing with that and with a spade in hand, he looked for a place to put a fire pit. Choosing a spot with a clear view of both east and west, he dug a shallow hole. Marissa and Caleb helped him gather the rocks that would go around it. "There, that ought to do." Tyrell smiled at their accomplishment as he added the last rock.

By now Marissa finished stacking some wood that she found scattered about and Caleb had a handful of small twigs which he handed to Tyrell for kindling. "Are you going to light the fire now mister?"

"Would you like me to Caleb?"

"That would be nice."

"All right then, so it will be." A few minutes later a relaxing fire gently warmed the evening air its flames dancing this way and that as a mountain breeze began to blow. They sat on blocks of wood that they took from the pile out back. Marissa handed out treats of biscuits and jam. A hot pot of coffee was starting to perk, the rich brew's aroma filled the evening air and mingled with the scent of cedar and pine.

The sound of the creek was audible in the background as it flowed by. A sunset on the western horizon added to the collage of everything else. Caleb was wrapped up in a blanket his eyes weary as he looked into the orange glow of the fire. He was so tired that he fell over fast asleep. Marissa and Tyrell both chuckled as they stood to pick him up to put him to bed on the bunk in the shack.

He must be pooped from all that hard work he helped with today," Tyrell remarked.

"Fresh air always does that to him." Marissa smiled as she put another blanket over him. "He won't stir until morning now. I guess that means it's only you and I at the fire. Or do you want to go to bed now too?" she questioned.

Tyrell shook his head. "I don't think I'm ready for sleep yet. There is at least two more cups of coffee in that pot outside and there is no point in wasting it. It's also a nice evening and I don't want to waste that either. Before I forget you'll have to put something against the bottom of this dang door to keep it from blowing opened," he mentioned as he grabbed his bedroll for when he did finally go to bed.

The two of them returned to the fire and he added another piece of wood. They sat close as they finished the last of the coffee and watched as the sunset faded to blackness. The fire cast shadows and warmed the evening air as they conversed about this, that, and sometimes nothing at all. When the fire was only a soft glow and there were more coals then flames they bid each other goodnight. Tyrell rolled out his bedroll next to the coals and Marissa headed inside and curled up next to Caleb. All-and-all it had been a good day.

As he laid there his hands behind his head, Tyrell looked to the sky, he had been back for five days and healthy for two. Calculating this he looked back to the first day he arrived. It was September 7$^{th}$ and from what he recalled it was a Monday, he was comatose for the first two-and-a-half days due to Marissa shooting him off his horse. He finally came to on the 10<sup>th</sup> and spent that night alone at the shack, which meant that it was now Friday, September 11<sup>th</sup>. *Not much longer and fall will be breathing down my neck, sure hope I'm ready for it,* he thought as he closed his eyes and waited for sleep.

It was the shriek of Marissa's scream's that made him jump up and grab his .45. Running the short distance to the shack, he flung open the door. Marissa was sitting up staring at the window and cradling Caleb. "What happened? What's going on?" Tyrell questioned as he darted inside.

"There was someone looking through the window. It scared the heck out of me!" she exclaimed.

"What?" Tyrell asked confused. "If there had been anyone lurking around out there Black Dog would have had a say." He lit the lantern and the shack lit up.

"I'm telling you, there was someone looking in on Caleb and me." She was certain of that.

Caleb was rubbing his eyes as though nothing happened and he yawned. "It was probably Teeka."

"Teeka? Who the heck is Teeka?" Tyrell wanted to know as he looked at Caleb and then Marissa with a look of befuddlement.

She was shaking her head and looking at Caleb. "Caleb, it wasn't Teeka, because we both know that Teeka is only your imaginary friend right?" she cooed.

"Teeka, is real Momma, I keep telling you that." Caleb rolled his eyes and slid off her lap. "Can I go back to sleep now?"

"Yes, yes you can." Marissa said as she rose and Caleb crawled back onto the bunk. Tucking him in, she walked over to the table and sat down. Tyrell was looking out the window assuring himself that no one was about. Satisfied, he joined Marissa.

"So who is this Teeka person?"

"She's supposed to be a friend of Caleb's, except no one has ever seen her or met her before. She's someone he made up to play with I assume. He has quite the imagination. I'm telling you though, there was someone peering through that window."

Tyrell half chuckled. "I reckon he gets his imagination from his ma. I don't know Marissa. Black Dog wouldn't allow anyone who wasn't supposed to be here, be here. If you know what I mean?" Lighting a cheroot he took a long pull on it.

"There is something that I guess I should have told you before...but I thought you would think that I was crazy. You'll probably think I'm crazy now too, but I'm going to tell you anyway."

Tyrell shrugged his shoulders. "I'm listening."

"A few years back when Jake and his crew were around they told Grandma and me that they had seen a young child all alone hanging around up here. It was odd because only Caleb and I were living in the area. I thought that they were making up stories for one reason or another, but they weren't. I saw the child myself once."

Tyrell sat there his mind blank as he listened to the tale. "How could a child be all alone around here and survive? I think they were making up stories to keep you on your toes. They were probably as bored as Caleb was when he made up his imaginary friend."

"Then how do you explain the fact that I saw the child once too?"

"Don't think there is anything to explain. I lived in these parts myself for a bit don't forget. I know how one's mind can play tricks."

"So, you think I'm crazy?"

"I didn't say that."

"You didn't have to I heard it in your words."

"No you didn't."

"Yes I did."

"No you didn't." They repeated it a few more times and then both began to laugh. It was funny in the sense that they were both simply teasing each other now. Tyrell even made a face and stuck his tongue out at her. As their laughter subsided they conversed like adults until he finished his cheroot. Then they returned to their respected beds. Tyrell walked around the shack checking on things, Black Dog at his side. He saw nothing out of the ordinary that would corroborate with Marissa's story of someone peeking through the window.

"I think she must have had a bit of a nightmare, Black Dog. I don't see a thing." He made his way back to his bedroll and for Marissa's sake, he tossed a piece of wood, on the dim coals and waited for a flame. Sleep took him quick after that and he woke in the morning quite refreshed.

Marissa and Caleb were still asleep and he added more wood to the fire. His pocket-watch read 6:30 a.m. The sun was slowly rising to greet the day anew and by the look of the sky he could tell that it was going to be clear and hot. Black Dog lulled nearby, the horses were socialising with one another, neighing, and farting as their tails swatted at black flies.

Pouring himself a coffee Tyrell thought about how to tackle the day. There was a lot to do. The roof needed fixing, the sluice box and rocker box both needed to be set up and it probably wouldn't hurt to scout the area. Taking a drink from the cup in his hand he heard the door of the shack open and watched as mother and son approached. "How did you sleep?" he asked as they made the distance.

"I had the best sleep ever mister." Caleb said as he sat down on a piece of wood. "You have a great place. I really, really like it here," he said as a matter-of-factly.

"You're welcome anytime Caleb you and your ma both." Tyrell rose and poured Marissa a cup of coffee then handed it to her. "What about you, did you sleep well after all the excitement of last night?" he asked as he sat down again.

"Other than the fact that someone was looking through the window, yeah, I did sleep good, better than I thought." Marissa took a drink from her coffee. "Caleb, if you run over to the wagon and grab the basket I'll make all of us some pancakes how does that sound?"

"Yummy." Caleb responded as he dashed over to the wagon. A few minutes later, he hollered back. "Ma, where is the basket? I can't see it. It's gone."

Marissa rose and walked over to the wagon herself. "Isn't that strange? I know it was here." She was a bit confused as she searched. "Hey Tyrell, you didn't move that basket I had did you?"

"No ma'am. I didn't touch it," he called back as he too rose and made his way over to them.

Marissa had a look of despair on her face. "Maybe whoever it was, that *'wasn't'* looking through the window last night took it," she commented as Tyrell approached.

"Maybe a dang racoon took it," he said, he knew how unlikely that was, but he was certain that there hadn't been anyone lurking around the night before.

"It would have to be pretty big racoon." Marissa said her hands on her hips.

"There has to be some kind of explanation, maybe it is in the shack. Caleb, why don't you take a look for me, please?"

Caleb shrugged his shoulders and jumped down from the wagon to go have a look. Tyrell was squatting on the ground trying to decipher if there were any footprints other than their own around the wagon, but saw nothing. He was shaking his head as he looked up and over to Marissa. "I don't know what to say." He shrugged, "I don't see any other prints here but our own."

"So the plot thickens?" Marissa commented.

"Let's not jump to conclusions, maybe Caleb found it."

Marissa stepped away from the back of the wagon and looked up the trail to the shack. "Nope, here he comes now and he doesn't have a basket."

Caleb ran up to them out of breath. "It isn't in there mister. I think Teeka took it." He said as he picked up a stick and tossed it towards the creek for something to do. "She get's hungry sometimes."

"Enough talk about Teeka," Marissa scolded.

"But Ma…" Caleb started before she cut him off.

"Never mind Caleb, go on, go play for a bit. Tyrell and I will look some more."

"Can I play down at the creek?"

"Yes you can. Be careful don't go far. Understand?"

"I won't Ma." Caleb responded as he darted away.

Tyrell whistled for Black Dog and tilted his head toward Caleb and the dog darted after him. "He'll keep Caleb safe. Now, we have an issue regarding a missing basket. I don't know what to say Marissa. I thought for sure it would have been in the shack."

"No, I left it right here." Marissa turned and gestured with her hand as to where she left it sitting.

"Unless it grew legs and ran away then I reckon something is awry. Could be something took it, maybe a bear if a racoon couldn't have."

"Or the visitor from last night... There was a bunch of stuff in it that I was going to leave with you, like sugar, flour, some sausage, that type of thing, but it is all gone now." She threw her hands in the air.

It was around that time that Caleb and Black Dog ran back from the creek. "We found it! We found the basket but it is empty. It was in the grass." Caleb pointed as he handed it to Marissa.

"Can you show me where it was?" Tyrell asked. His hope was that he'd find some kind of track, hopefully that of a bear so that he could prove to Marissa once and for all that there hadn't been anyone looking in the window the night before.

Caleb nodded. "Follow me mister," he led Tyrell to the spot. "It was right there," he said as he pointed. Tyrell crouched down and looked, but he didn't see any bear tracks or for that matter any tracks except Caleb's.

"That's sure strange. There aren't any tracks around." Tyrell squinted as he looked downstream and then to the forest on either side of the creek. "We ain't empty handed leastwise we got the basket. Come on Caleb let's go." The two of them walked back to the fire where Marissa was sitting.

"Did you find anything?" she asked as they approached.

"Nope, nothing at all, it's a weird little mystery. But you got the basket back at least."

"A lot of good an empty basket is. I'm a bit hungry and I'm sure Caleb is as well."

"I have plenty of jerky we can share and likely enough flour to whip up some biscuits. How would that be?"

Marissa took a drink from her coffee. "That sounds good to me," she responded.

They conversed back and forth as they ate their meagre, but hearty breakfast. As the morning sun warmed up, and with Tyrell riding alongside the wagon to keep them safe until they made the trail, Marissa and Caleb headed for home. "Take care Tyrell, and stop by when you can."

"Rest assured that I will. Maybe in a day or two, until then if you need me for one thing or another come on up and get me. I ain't going anywhere, I'll be here. The horse trail is the quickest route. It's only an hour's ride. You can't miss it. Just head west you'll see where the trail cuts into the wood," he hollered after them as the wagon creaked away and onto the trail.

"Will do!" Marissa hollered back as she and Caleb waved.

Tyrell smiled, turned his horse and headed back upstream. He noticed Black Dog was acting antsy. "What's the matter old boy?" He slowed to a stop. Black Dog was looking in the direction of the wagon trail, wagging his tail. "I get it, you, want to follow along with them eh? Probably not a bad idea if you did so. Go ahead, go on." Tyrell gestured. Black Dog looked once more in the direction of the wagon trail and then turned and sped off after them. "That a boy. Catch up and keep them safe." Tyrell watched as the dog cut through the forest in the direction of the trail. "C'mon Dutch, giddy-up, let's head back to the shack. We'll let Black Dog escort them back. No harm will come to them with him at their side. You and I on the other hand have a ton of work to get started. That hole in the roof being one of the things that needs doing."

A short time later, Black Dog startled Marissa as he darted out in front of the wagon. She let go of the reins in a sudden fit of fear and had the old Henry in her hands before she realised it was Tyrell's dog. "Hello there Black Dog. You scared the pants off me. You almost got a lead slug in your behind." She chuckled as she looked at Caleb. "Didn't he scare you?"

"Nope. I knew it was him. Hello Black Dog." Caleb said, "I was starting to miss you. Can I get down and walk with him Ma? I think he wants me to."

Marissa pulled on the horse's reins halting them to stop. "You sure can. Go on jump down."

"Thanks Ma." Caleb darted to the back and jumped to the ground. Black Dog pranced over to his side and licked at his face, causing Caleb to laugh. "See Ma, he missed me already too."

"He sure did. You guys walk close you hear." Marissa smiled as she watched Caleb and the dog frolic as they walked alongside the wagon. She felt better now that Black Dog was with them. She kept the wagon going at a snail's pace. It would slow them down some, but there was plenty of day left and there was no need to rush. It was actually quite relaxing and she enjoyed the sights and sounds as they traipsed onward. After a half a mile of walking, Caleb started to get tired and he jumped back onto the wagon and surprisingly so did the dog.

With both Caleb and the dog onboard now, Marissa snapped the reins and the horses began to shuffle along at a quicker pace. "Tell me Caleb, do you like Tyrell?"

"Yes I do Ma, I think he's funny. Especially the way he sometimes talks and stuff. Can he be my Pa?" Caleb asked innocently as he patted Black Dog and rubbed noses with him.

Marissa was lost for words for a few minutes, *if only he knew,* she thought. "I don't know Caleb. That is something we'll have to let Tyrell decide."

"What if I ask him to be?"

Marissa laughed softly. "No Caleb that is not how it works."

"Why not?" He asked in a sleepy voice as he now lay on the wagon floor next to Black Dog. Marissa thought for a minute on how to explain it to him, but before she could answer, he was fast asleep. For the remainder of the trip she was left alone to think. By the time they made the distance home, she still wasn't sure how to answer Caleb's question, and luckily, he didn't ask it again that day. Together, they unhitched the horses and corralled them. Then Caleb set about getting them some feed and tending to his chickens. The whole time Black Dog remained at his side. Marissa sighed as she sat in her chair out front with a cup of tea in her hand. She was glad to be home.

# Chapter 7

Back at the shack Tyrell was wrestling with the poles, he cut to repair the roof. He couldn't get them in place. They were too long, too short, or plain too big. He threw them to the ground and cussed as he climbed down the makeshift ladder. The ones that were too short and big he tossed over to the fire pit, the ones that were too long he sized up and cut again. Busy as he was he didn't notice that Dutch somehow managed to slip out of his tether and was half way back to Marissa's, and the mare of his own dreams.

Satisfied that the poles he cut would now fit correctly, Tyrell threw them back onto the roof and climbed back up. An hour later, they were all in place and ready for some clay and sod. Resting, he sat on the roof and looked out over the vast forest of evergreens and birch. Noticing that not too far away and hidden by some heavy drooping fir branches was a little building. He squinted to get a better look then smiled realising that what he was looking at was an old outhouse. "Thank God for that," he muttered to himself. Averting his gaze toward the creek and where Dutch, was supposed to be. His heart sunk when he didn't see him. "Damn it." He climbed off the roof and walked over to where he tethered him. Looking in the direction that Dutch's tracks travelled he knew that the horse headed toward Marissa's. He called the horse a few times and followed its tracks downstream to the horse trail. But, the horse never came.

*This day just keeps getting better and better,* he thought as he looked at his pocket watch. There was no point in going after the horse, in an hour it would be dark. Turning, he walked back to the shack, if Dutch didn't show up by morning he'd hike after him. For now, he was alone, no horse and no dog. *Could prove to be an interesting evening,* he thought as he made his way over to the fire pit. A few minutes later flames were dancing and a fresh pot of coffee brewed. Taking the time then, he walked the short distance to where the outhouse was and looked it over. It was in surprisingly good shape. Swinging open the door, a bunch of mad bees swarmed out. He ran in the opposite direction swatting at them with his hat as he made his way to safety. Only thing was they could fly faster than he could run and he was stung a dozen or so times. "God damn it!" he exclaimed. "The horse is gone, the dog is gone, and I damn near went in my trousers." He sat down and looked at all the stings that covered his arms. The ones on his face and neck hurt the most, but he'd live. There was no way he was going to let them have the last say, so he picked up a piece of smouldering wood from the fire and set off to rid the unfriendly critters.

Slowly this time he opened the outhouse door and stepped back. He waited to see if they were going to swarm him again, but they didn't. He peered in. His plan was simple and he threw the smouldering wood inside and closed the door. Again, he waited…and waited, finally the bees started flying out, hundreds of them. Most fell to the ground while others flew this way and that. He stomped on as many as he could. There was a legion of them, and if he listened close enough he would've probably heard them coughing, from the smoke.

Opening the door, he looked inside, and using a stick he knocked the bee nest down. If any remained in the hive they met their demise when he crushed it with the sole of his boot. *There, that ought to take care of that issue.* Safe now from their stingers he kicked the smouldering piece of wood out onto the forest floor. There was no way he could have picked it up without burning his hands. The entire piece was now burning from both ends. He unbuttoned his trousers, and peed on it. It hissed and smoked and finally went out as he finished. Then as though he'd been shot he grabbed at his manhood, bagging himself in the process. "OWWWCH, GODDAMN, GODDAMN!" he hollered as he danced around. The cause of his distress was evident when he looked down and saw that a bee, still attached to its stinger dangled from that part of his anatomy that no bee should dangle. He flicked it off. Although there were tears in his eyes from the pain he was in, he couldn't help himself and he started to laugh. Of all the stupid and crazy things that happened in his life, this one beat all. It was safe to say that the bees on that day had the last say. He sucked in a deep breath as he tucked it away and buttoned up his pants. Walking bull legged he headed back to the fire.

Sitting down with his legs spread wide he poured himself a coffee, lit a cheroot and shook his head as he contemplated the day's events. He was starting to get comfortable when he heard a rustle coming from behind where he sat. He wasn't able to spin around as quickly as he'd like due to his earlier misfortune of being stung in a certain area. But, he did have his gun drawn. Looking and ready to shoot, he saw and heard nothing. He continued to stare into the darkening evening, waiting, hoping to hear or see something but nothing jumped out or sounded.

Satisfied, he holstered his Colt and tried to get comfortable again. It took some doing, but he managed. A welcoming breeze picked up as he inhaled a lung full of cigar smoke, the breeze gently caressed the stings to his arms, neck, and face as he exhaled. But, down south there was no relief. He'd have to grin and bear it. Even as he sat there, he thought the incident to be quite humorous. How couldn't he? There was a lesson to be learned too. He chuckled to himself and shook his head at the ridiculousness of the life lesson. It was one, he knew, he would never forget.

Time slipped by and he downed another cup of coffee as he sat. He was content. The cool evening breeze felt good and the silence was nice, the fire warm. *What more could a man want,* he thought trying to make light of his current loneliness. It wasn't often that both his dog and horse were gone. He felt isolated without the horse and lonely without the dog. Removing his hat, he set it on his lap and ran his fingers through his hair. *I guess I should hit the sack,* he thought as he slowly stood and dumped out what was left of that night's coffee. He walked the short distance to the shack, opened the door, and hung up his hat. With the lantern lit now, he tossed his bed together. Then fluffed up the pillow that Marissa was kind enough to give him and removed his boots. Next, he hung up his holster and tucked his Derringer under the pillow. Satisfied, he lay down.

Staring at the ceiling with his hands behind his head, he waited for sleep. The recent amount of coffee that he drank however, was working overtime and all he could do was think. He thought about everything, including the things he was told years ago about Hudu Valley and Red Rock Canyon. The missing cattle and ghostly figures, witches, and goblins, the bones that The Wake Up Jake came across back in 1890 when they first started work on the Sloan claims.

He even thought about what old Bentley told him about all the men who went missing in the area. As well as the odd looking creatures that he saw in Fetor Valley, when he first came to Red Rock, six years earlier to claim his Grandfather's homestead. There was nothing that, he didn't think about as he lay there. His mind even raced with the possibility now of a wandering child. After all, something did run behind him that night as he sat by the fire. And, Marissa's basket did go missing. Things were certainly not on the up-and-up. The more he thought, the harder he found it to sleep. Perhaps it was the coffee. Perhaps it was anxiety and the fact that he was truly alone. Whatever it was he slept little that night. When he did sleep, he dreamt about all the things, he thought about.

Morning brought with it a sigh of relief to the bee stings, even the one down below. Tired as he was he wished for a few more hours of sleep, but instead stepped out into the cool dawn. Smoke continued to rise from the fire and he tossed a couple of sticks on it. While they began to take a flame, he relieved himself. He was thankful that his member didn't hurt when he did so, and that the bee sting didn't leave any lasting marks other than to his ego. It may have been as red as a tomato and a little oversized due to some continued swelling. That of course was to be expected. Shaking it off he tucked it back into his pants. He made his way back to the fire and warmed his hands. Today he'd walk down to Marissa's and gather his damn horse. The hike he guessed would take him two maybe three hours.

First, he'd slap some clay on the poles he used to patch the hole in the roof of his shack. There was some red clay along the creek bed. With that and sod he was confident the hole wouldn't leak. If all else failed he could always make some cedar shakes and use them instead. For now clay and sod would do. Pouring his first coffee of the day, he took a swig from the cup in his hand. It was bitter without much sugar and he sighed. *Going to need to make that trip to the Hudu Mercantile soon,* he thought. Spitting, he looked east to the rising sun. It was going to be a cooler day than last and it looked like some rain might come. He was hoping that wasn't going to be the case. He needed dry conditions if he was going to slap down clay.

Contemplating, he looked around. It was then he heard the sound of hooves, he rose quickly and cautiously waiting to see who might be approaching. He couldn't believe what came around the bend. It was Black Dog and he had Dutch's lead in his mouth. "Well I'll be. Black Dog you old scoundrel, I see you brought with you Dutch. Hello, Dutch," he said as he approached the dog and horse. "You outsmarted me but not the dog eh? That don't make me feel very good," he chuckled as he took the lead. "Sure glad things turned out as they did. Wasn't looking forward to the hike-especially since it looks like rain." He led Dutch closer to the fire pit and tethered him to a tree. It would give the horse shelter if it did decide to rain, and shade if the sun decided to take over the greying sky. "I reckon until I can build you a corral of sorts, this here will have to do. I don't need you running off again. No sir, I can keep my eye on you now." He slapped the horses behind as he headed back to the fire.

Black Dog huddled beneath the mountain ash near the shack and was content as he laid there panting. Tyrell walked over to him and patted the dog. "You're quite something else, you know that? I'm going to get you a piece of jerky, jus' cause." Tyrell entered the shack and gathered a couple pieces of the jerked meat. Black Dog's ears pricked up as he approached. He tossed one to the dog, "we're going to need some fresh meat soon. Our provisions are getting low and so is this jerked meat. In the next couple of days after we've settled a bit more, I reckon we should head over to the Hudu Mercantile," Tyrell chewed on the jerky in his mouth. "Pick up that stovepipe and few other necessities, maybe we'll invite Marissa and Caleb along. That'd be nice wouldn't it?"

He scratched Black Dog behind his ear and then made his way down to the creek, a spade and bucket in his hand to gather up some clay. He was surprised at all the pan fry trout, that darted this way and that, as he waded in knee deep to reach the red clay bank. Filling up the bucket, he headed back to the shack, and climbed the makeshift ladder to spread the first of the clay across the poles. The first bucket wasn't enough to smear all the poles and more was needed. By the time he retrieved the second bucket, the first bit was already beginning to heal and he smiled. *Yep, it's going to work fine,* he thought to himself, as he spread the second bucket of clay. Within four hours of adding the last bit of clay, it healed. Next, he added the sod. Finished and satisfied with the work he sat down on the roof and looked at his pocket watch, it was just past noon.

He accomplished a lot in the two full days he'd been up at the shack. And there was a lot more that needed doing, like a corral for the horse and he would have to get to work on the Sloan claims. It wasn't something he really needed to do with all the pouches of gold he had access to. He hid the pouches along a lonely trail when he left Red Rock back in 1890. All he needed to do was go gather them, but, what would he do with 160 pouches of gold? That was the question. He didn't even know the value. He recalled Grandma Heddy telling him way back when, that the gold he had with him, was as good as the gold coming from Australia. That the 20 pouches he brought with him were worth $15.00 an ounce. He recalled the pouches weighed near ten ounces each. What he didn't know is that the price now was $21.00 an ounce. It was enough hard cash to live comfortably for the rest of his life. For now, unless he was in dire need of some quick cash, the pouches would have to wait. Working the Sloan claims could be his cover up when he did gather the gold. He didn't want to deceive anyone, nor did he want anyone trying to deceive him. Keeping the pouches hidden for now was best.

It was then the thunder rolled across the sky followed by a crack of lightning so clear and crisp it sounded like a whip. Slugs of rain boiled down on him from the angry sky turning the fire into a puddle of ash. Grabbing the pot of coffee, he headed inside. It wasn't as warm as he would have liked and a nice fire would have certainly helped to dry out his clothes, for now however he would have to go without. He was still missing one of the key components to light a fire inside…a stovepipe.

Setting the pot of coffee on the table, he hung up his hat and removed his buckskin-shirt. He slipped out of his denim pants and slid into another pair. Sitting at the table he listened to the rain beat down hard and heavy. There wasn't much else he could do. The door flew open as a gust of wind whistled outside. Rising from the table, he closed the door and tossed his saddlebags against the bottom. "There that should keep it closed," he said as he made his way back to the table.

Making mental notes in his head on what he was going to need to make the shack a lot more comfortable and a lot less vulnerable to the coming fall and winter, he sat in thought. Not one who liked to sit around with nothing to do he pulled out his skinning knife from his boot, sat up, and carved, *TBS September 13 1896* into the table. He brought his cup to his lips and downed the last of his coffee. There was a half day ahead and if it kept raining and stayed cold, it wasn't going to be a pleasant one. He stood and walked over to the window, leaned on the counter and looked out. The clouds were dark and dismal but it did look like the sun was trying to burn them away. There was a chance that the day might not be a total loss.

Taking some time, he straightened out the shack and put a few things away. He had three cans of beans, coffee, a couple of potatoes, a can of peaches, flour, salt and a wee bit of sugar, a few thick sticks of jerky and two cheroots left. That was it; that was all. It didn't bother him much he'd lived on a lot less. He waved his hand through the air uncaring about food.

Removing his .45 Winchester rifle from the wall he set it on the table and began to clean and polish it. The rifle always looked best and shot better when it was shiny and clean, he removed his holster and did the same to his Colt .45s, and two shot derringer. His guns cleaned and oiled he rose once more from the table and peered out the window. It was looking more like an inside day after all

# Chapter 8

The rain finally began to taper off as evening approached. Finding some dry cedar and birch bark, he made a fire. The heat from the flames felt good and he huddled close to it. Dutch and Black Dog both managed to keep themselves dry. Tyrell took note of the old dog's limp as it made its way to him and the fire. He had picked the limp up a few months earlier and by the way, he limped now it wasn't improving. Tyrell scratched him behind the ear as the dog sat next to him. "You can feel that cold in your bones too, eh? Yeah me too, we're getting old Black Dog, we're getting old," he repeated as he continued scratching him behind his ear.

Black Dog panted and set his paw on Tyrell's lap. He chuckled as Black Dog wagged his tail. It was obvious what the dog wanted. Reaching over to the leather sack that he kept the jerky in, he looked inside. "We have four pieces left. We'll each have one now and before bed we'll finish the rest up. How does that sound?" he handed one of the bigger pieces to the old dog. Black Dog took it graciously and then traipsed out of sight into the undergrowth. Tyrell watched as he vanished into the darkening wood. The sun remained well hidden behind the clouds, as the late afternoon progressed making it darker than it should have been.

Reaching into his shirt pocket, he removed one of the two cheroots he had left. With a burning twig in his hand, he brought it up to the cigar dangling from his mouth and inhaled. In the distance only a quarter of a mile away a small pack of wolves were on a scattered hunt. They managed to track down an elk cow and her calf, only the calf suffered a fatality and now the wolves were on the move to take down its mother. They tracked it along the creek within shouting distance of Tyrell's shack.

Black Dog was well aware of the threat and he was now confronting the weary wolves. Growls and snarls were exchanged but Black Dog held his ground! Three of the wolves circled him while the other two remained in the shadows. Black Dog's instincts told him who the alpha male was and in a few seconds while the two younger males snapped at his haunches, he made his move. With fury, he pinned the alpha male to the ground holding its neck in his jaws.

The two younger wolves backed away with their tails between their legs. In a show of mercy, Black Dog released his grip. The killing party except for one vanished into the evening. The one that stayed behind remained hidden in the shadows. Black Dog's show of bravery and strength did not go unnoticed by her. She was smitten by him and it would be Black Dog that fathered her first litter. The dog stood motionless until he could sense that the pack of wolves were no longer a threat, ignoring the young wolf bitch in a show of dominance he turned and made his way back to Tyrell's side and the warming flames of the fire.

Tyrell heard the pitter-patter as he approached. "Evening Black Dog, looking for some heat eh? Make yourself comfortable old boy. I've decided that we ain't going to waste our time in getting supplies after all. We'll head to Hudu in the morning, how does that sound?" Tyrell spoke as though the dog would answer. Black Dog responded by licking his chops and rolling onto his side. Looking over to him, he smiled. "You know what Black Dog; I think I'm going to hit the sack. You're welcome to join me inside if you like. It ain't as big of a place as we might be use to but it's big enough. Going to join me or are you content in staying outdoors?"

Black Dog licked his chops and followed him inside. "I'm glad you decided to come in. It's likely to get a lot cooler this evening and it appears that the damn rain is once more on its way. We'll get a good night's sleep. Most of all we'll stay dry. Tomorrow, weather permitting we'll head down to Marissa and Caleb's to see if they want to come along with us to the Mercantile."

Black Dog found a piece of floor and curled up, sprawled out like a drunk the dog never twitched. He was comfortable there was no doubt about that. A crack of lightning outside cast a shadow at the little window, and Tyrell saw it from the corner of his eye. It startled him at first. He wasn't sure what it was that he thought he saw. Then as quickly as the lightning cracked it was gone, he stood and darted over to the window but the darkening forest never gave up any ghosts, or goblins. From experience, he knew that if there was a threat of any kind, Black Dog would make him aware. That wasn't the case though, the dog hadn't budged, and because of that he was confident, that what he thought he saw was nothing at all.

Kicking off his boots, he made his way over to his bunk and lay down with his hands behind his head and pistols at his side. His eyes were heavy and he was about to doze off when he heard the clip-clop of a horse approach. He raised an eyebrow and rose from the bunk. Black Dog by now was in front of the door as though he were ready to pounce on any foe coming through it.

Tyrell strapped on his holster and grabbed his rifle making sure it was loaded and ready, he approached the door. Cautiously opening it, he peered out but saw nothing. Black Dog never budged and laid there as calm as a pool of water. "What do you figure, didn't you hear that? Sounded like a horse approaching," he looked around once more, then shut the door. "I guess I was hearing things. If a horse and rider were hereabouts you'd be the first to let me know, ain't that right? I don't reckon there is a damn thing out there, that wasn't here in daylight, just my own imagination playing damn tricks on me?"

Sitting in the darkness, he listened to every sound the night made. Oddly, it was dead silent. No tree rustled and no wind whistled or blew. Black Dog was lying now on the floor next to him. Then as though stung by a hornet the dog rose and started to bark, as he made the short distance to the door his haunches raised and ready to attack or at least slow down any intruder.

A voice from outside could be heard. "Young Sloan! It is me Wilson." Tyrell tilted his head as he listened, the voice was certainly familiar, but he couldn't be sure that it was his old friend Wilson. Approaching the door, he tucked one of the Colts into his waistband, leaving his left hand free to open the door. Getting Black Dog to sit and stay, he slowly opened it to look out.

"What did you say your name was mister?" Tyrell could only make out a horse and figure sitting on it in the darkness.

"It's me, Wilson. Been a long time young Sloan but you can lower that pistol now."

"I'd rather not mister until you step closer so I can have a look at you."

"Fair enough, fair enough." The man repeated as he slid off his horse and approached. Sure enough it was old Wilson.

"I'll be damned! Old Wilson how the hell have you been?" Tyrell questioned as he tossed the .45 into his free hand and lowered it reaching out his right to shake old Wilson's.

Wilson came closer with his own hand outstretched, and the two of them shook hands for the first time in six years. "I knew right from the beginning that you weren't dead. I even tried to put a stop to the rumours myself. It did no good though. Most folks think you're dead."

"I don't mind a bit that some might think that. Come on in Wilson. I ain't got any coffee brewing but we can change that real quick."

"Nah, that's okay young Sloan." Wilson waved his hand through the air. "I'd much prefer to simply lay out my bedroll. I've been hard at it for a few days. This old body that I'm wearing is sore and tired," Wilson turned and retrieved his bedroll. "We can catch up in the morning."

Tyrell nodded and the two of them made their way into the little shack. "It ain't much bigger than a matchbox but you're welcome to lay out your bedroll on a piece of floor." Tyrell thought for a moment, "hell, you know what Wilson, you go ahead and take the bunk I'll lay down on the floor with the dog."

"That is mighty kind of you. Thank you very much." Wilson tossed his bedroll to the foot of the bunk.

"I figure an old folk such as yourself would be more comfortable on the bunk." Tyrell smirked.

"Old folk eh," Wilson was looking at him a smile across his face. "Indeed I am, yes sir. But I reckon I could still out ride a young whippersnapper like you." Wilson sat down on the bunk and looked around, "so, you're going to spend the winter in this little shack are ya? I reckon it'll suffice. My cabin up on Beaver Mountain ain't much bigger and I manage. I reckon you will too." Wilson bent over and pulled off his boots. "You best get your bedding, cause I'm about ready for some shut eye."

"Before I can do that you are going to need to get up so I can. Need a hand or would you prefer a walking stick?" Tyrell teased.

Wilson chuckled. "I can manage on my own. As for a stick you can certainly get me one so I can beat you with it." Wilson rose from the bunk grinning from ear to ear.

Chuckling at Wilson's remark Tyrell gathered his bedding. "There you go old boy, the bunk is yours."

"Don't be trying to make me sound as though I've gone soft. Years of hard-work and travelling puts more miles on a man than being a tenderfoot." Wilson winked at him as he laid himself out on the bunk.

"I wouldn't know Wilson, a tenderfoot I ain't."

Wilson pulled out his pipe from his woollen shirt pocket and filled the bowl with pipe-tobacco. "I see you got yourself a new horse? What happened to that no-good-for-nothing mountain horse, you once had?" Wilson used his thumbnail to strike a match, and brought the flickering flame to his pipe and inhaled deeply. "What was his name again...oh yeah, Pony. Dumbness name for a horse as big as he was, so what happened to him?" Wilson inhaled another lung full of pipe smoke.

"To make a long story short for now let's say he got old…" Tyrell responded as his mind drifted.

"That's fine. I know what it is like to lose a horse." For a moment an eerie silence filled the room. "The dog still has his legs he looks pretty good too for an ol' fellow." Wilson reached over and patted him. Bringing his pipe to his lips once more, he inhaled. "So, young Sloan whatever brought you back this way?"

"I reckoned I made a few mistakes and wanted to make them right. I've been kicking myself for the last six years over some of the things I've done. I'm going to make it all good though. That is my intent."

"Uh-huh. We all make mistakes. If you're here to better those mistakes than that is what you ought to do. No ifs or buts about it."

"That is what I reckon."

"Good. All right young Sloan; I think it is time to rest my tired eyes. We'll talk more in the morning." Wilson rolled over and faced the wall. In only a few short minutes, he was sound asleep. Tyrell sat on the floor his back to the wall and reminisced. It was hard for him to believe that six years had come and gone but they had. He had done a lot in those few years and some things he wished he hadn't but he had. Now it was time for redemption.

# Chapter 9

Wilson was kicking him in the ribs early next morning to get him motivated. "C'mon young Sloan rise and shine. Get up. Got the fire outside going and the coffee pot is on. Hurry up."

Tyrell rolled over and wiped his eyes, slowly rising he stretched and yawned. "Was going to head over to the Hudu Mercantile today to pick up some supplies and stovepipe. You got any plans Wilson? Care to join me?"

"I ain't got any plans. It is on my way I suppose." Wilson was scratching his whiskered chin as he contemplated. "I could probably use a few things myself. I guess I will join you. I'll head home from the Mercantile."

"You'd be more than welcome Wilson. I'd enjoy the company."

"Good, cause, I got a few more days before I need to head back to Beaver Mountain. It'll be a bit of a break I suppose. Come on now, the coffee is done brewing and it is always best when she's hot." Wilson exited the shack and Tyrell followed behind.

"How did you sleep on that crinkly ol' bunk?" Tyrell asked as he looked at his pocket watch.

"Like I've been sleeping on a bed of rocks, feels good, straightened my back out," Wilson chuckled. "It couldn't have been any worse than the floor."

"Wilson do you know what time it is? It ain't even five a.m. yet."

"Nope, near though."

"Near! Hell it ain't for another hour," Tyrell blurted as he sat down.

"There is nothing wrong with getting an early start on the day. Drink your coffee and quit being an ol' woman." Wilson smiled as he took a drink from the coffee in his hand. "The sun will be up soon and we can get. The Mercantile is a good day's ride and since we're heading that way, I thought we might take some time to check in on Marissa and Caleb. I ain't seen them in a few months."

"If you ain't seen them in a few months how did you know I was here?" Tyrell asked in confusion.

"Did you forget young Sloan? I'm a tracker, trapper and a prospector. I know these woods. I was out and about a few days ago and came across some tracks, a horse, and dog. There are no folks around here that travel with a dog, 'cept you. So I finished my business, and made my way to Marissa's. No one was there though, but I did find more tracks, which headed this way. Figured, you and Marissa needed some time alone so I kept my distance. It wasn't until yesterday evening that I headed this way." Wilson took a swig from his tin cup. The two sat in silence for a few minutes as they stared into the early morning flames of the fire.

"Is that old codger Fry still kicking?"

"Fry ain't been heard from in a few months. Some of us got together when he went missing, and we searched for him for three or four days but the old fellow wasn't found. Speculation is he moved on or plain died. The bears must've ate him if he died." Wilson shrugged his shoulders and sighed, "he's missed."

"Marissa told me he was still alive."

"That is because that is what Marissa knows. I haven't spoken to her since Fry went missing, it is one of the reasons I'm down this way. Thought maybe by chance I'd run across him. But, that ain't been the case so far. I continue to keep my eyes opened for him. Visited his claim a week ago, it don't look like anyone's been there in some time." Wilson grew silent as he reminisced.

"You'd never think a fellow like ol' Fry would go missing. I reckon he knows these woods and probably has a name for every bear and goat this side of old Heddy's mercantile. It is a damn shame Wilson." Tyrell took a drink from his coffee. The sun was starting to rise in the east and he looked in that direction. "Look at that Wilson, ain't that a miraculous sight the sun rising as it is."

"Tells me it is going to be a hot one today, it sure does look nice though. I'll agree with you there."

"Well, it'll be a good day to travel I suppose. I figure since we aim on stopping off at Marissa's, that I might ask if her, and Caleb would like to come along. They might need a few things. Tell me, Wilson, does the mercantile sell books?"

"Books?" Wilson asked with surprise. "What the hell do you want books for?"

"They ain't for me. Caleb gave me a few of his and told me I needed to do some reading, to practice the English language. He claims I talk funny half of the time." Tyrell chuckled.

"Yep, the mercantile sells books. I think in fact that is where Marissa buys them."

"I reckon I'll pick a few out for Caleb. What do you figure a young fellow like him likes to read?"

"Look at the books he gave you, that should give you an idea," Wilson stood from the fire. "Well should we get the horses saddled?"

Tyrell dumped what was left of his coffee into the flames. "Figure so, first though I'd like to be sure the fire is doused. Had enough problems with anxious flames the other day, don't need no more of that." Grabbing one of the horse buckets, he made his way down to the creek and filled it. Wilson stayed behind and saddled up the horses.

"Thanks for saddling up Dutch for me," Tyrell said as he made his way back and dumped the water over the small flames. "There that'll do it. I guess we're off then."

"As sure as the sun rises." Wilson replied as he swung onto his horse. Tyrell whistled for Black Dog but the dog didn't show.

"Damn, wonder where he's got to now. Ah, he'll follow once he sees we're gone." Tyrell mounted his horse and the two set off towards Marissa's and the Hudu mercantile. As they made their way, an odd and overwhelming sense that something was amiss came over Wilson.

"There is a strange feeling in these woods today," Wilson slowed his horse and looked around.

Tyrell pulled up beside him. "What's that you said?"

"It feels like we're being watched, probably just old age. Forget it young Sloan, let's make tracks."

Whatever, the feeling was that Wilson felt as they rode on kept him alert and cautious. He slowed down every now and again and looked around as though he were looking for something to jump out at them. He never spoke about what it was he was looking for, but Tyrell was no dummy. He knew that something was bothering the old codger. Realising this he cocked his rifle and set it across his lap. Suddenly Wilson's horse got spooked and it rose up on its hind legs.

"Damn horse!" Wilson shouted as he pulled on the reins and took control. "Did you see that? Something spooked my horse. I knew once we entered this wood that something wasn't right."

"What do you mean?" Tyrell asked with concern.

"I've been in these woods many times, today, was the first day I ever felt as though I was being watched by something I can't see. I hate when that happens." Wilson spat to the ground and removed his hat to wipe his brow. "Could be a hungry old mountain lion keep your wits as we carry on."

"Yeah, you bet," he responded with concern. "Thanks for the heads up." he wasn't about to let his guard down. There was another quarter of a mile to go before they would exit the woods. It seemed odd to Tyrell how Wilson was behaving, he never knew the man to be so damn quiet. He was as silent as the whispering breeze that gently blew. Finally, the horse trail exited the wood and their world opened up. "We're damn near there Wilson," Tyrell said as he caught up. "Kind of strange Black Dog didn't follow," he mentioned as he looked back.

"There are a lot more strange things going on than that. Not sure you noticed but we were followed for a distance." Wilson said as they continued on.

"What's that? What do you mean followed? I didn't see a damn thing and I reckon my eyes are better than yours." Tyrell half chuckled.

"Eye sight maybe, instinct not."

"Shit, you're getting old and squirrely. There was nothing in that wood but us and likely a few animals which are always there anyway."

"Let's hope you are right. Enough chatter let's get a move on. Giddy up!" Wilson heeled his horse in the flank and galloped away.

Tyrell stood back for a second and looked once more in the direction they had come, looking for both Black Dog and making sure there was nothing unfriendly following them. Satisfied, he too heeled his horse and sped off. He caught up with Wilson a short distance away. They could now smell smoke from Marissa's wood stove and every now and again the smell of fresh bread wafted in the gentle breeze. "Smell that Wilson?" Tyrell inhaled deeply.

"I sure do. Smells like home don't it?"

"Yep." In a few short minutes they were tying their horses to the horse pole. "Well, here we are Wilson," Tyrell said as they made their way to the door and knocked. He opened the door a bit. "Hello, anyone there?"

"Tyrell!" he heard a voice call out.

"Sure is. With an old friend in tow."

"Come on in. I'm in the kitchen. Who is the friend you have with you?" Marissa asked as she stepped into their view. "Wilson!" she hollered as she darted to them and gave him a big hug. "I haven't seen you since early summer. How have you been? Come in and sit down both of you."

"Why thank you ma'am." Wilson said as he removed his hat.

"What about me? What about my hug?" Tyrell smiled as he removed his hat and he and Wilson made their way to the table.

"Oh Tyrell, come here then and give me a hug."

Tyrell smiled and gave Marissa a big bear hug. "There, I feel a lot better now," he chuckled. "Where is the boy? I half expected him to answer the door."

"He is spending a few days at Len's house. He'll be back by mid week, I'm alone until then. I made fresh bread and I can get coffee going in a jiffy. You are going to visit for a bit aren't you?"

"We sure are. I smelled that bread a mile ago and wouldn't have a problem putting some down. Coffee sounds good too." Wilson replied.

"Good, get comfortable and I'll be right back." Marissa commented as she pranced off again to the kitchen. It had been a few days since Caleb left and the loneliness was overbearing. What a treat it was to have Tyrell and Wilson stop in on her. "Do you want strawberry or raspberry preservatives with your bread?" she asked from the kitchen doorway.

"Either or, makes no difference to me." Wilson said as he looked around.

"I'll bring both. You'll have to take your coffees black with sugar I ran out of cream yesterday when I made butter."

"That's fine we've been drinking it straight black. We're heading to the Hudu mercantile today. Would you like to come along?" Tyrell asked.

"That would be terrific. I thought I'd have to go there alone before Caleb gets back. Yes, I'll tag along. Maybe we should harness up the wagon. You still need stove pipe don't you?"

"I do. I reckon the wagon is a good idea. There are a few things I'd like to gather before the snow flies. I might as well get it all in one shot."

"It's settled then. After we have some bread and jam and a coffee, Tyrell and I will harness up the horses. Now where is that bread and coffee little lady?" Wilson asked as he winked at her.

"It is coming right up," Marissa returned to cutting bread and mixing coffee. "There, all done," she said as she brought a dinner tray with freshly baked bread, coffee and the preservatives. Setting it on the table she sat next to Tyrell and gestured for them to dig in. "Go ahead fellows, help yourselves. Tell me Wilson what brings you around?" she questioned as she took a sip from her coffee.

"Wasn't sure I wanted to bring this up but, seems ol' Fry has gone missing. That is one of the reasons I'm down this way. I had no intent on coming to Red Rock though. That is of course until I came across Tyrell's tracks heading this way. I figured I best make sure it was him and not some hoodlum." He took a bite from the jam covered bread he held in his hand.

"Missing? What do you mean missing?" Marissa questioned.

"It was a couple months ago when some of the old timers and me realised that Fry hadn't been around. At first we weren't too concerned though. Sometimes he's a bit slow in getting back to his claim on Beaver Mountain. But, for thirty odd years he ain't never not shown up before I head to my trap line on Grizzly Mountain. That's when I knew something wasn't right. He's always made it back by this time of year." Wilson smothered another piece of bread and filled his coffee mug. "We rounded up a crew of six men and we searched for near a week but there were no signs of him. His claims had been worked but they weren't active at that time. It seemed strange and it is still a mystery."

"That is terrible. Poor Fry, I hope he is found. It won't seem right without him travelling these parts."

"There are still a few possibilities aren't there?" Tyrell looked at Wilson. "Could be he might have travelled to

Salwood or Waldy. Don't know why he'd go there but if it hasn't been looked into it is a possibility ain't it?"

"A couple of us did go either way and there were no signs of him. Nope, we pretty much covered all directions and all possible outposts and towns that he might have gone to." Wilson inhaled deeply. "There is more. And now that I have you both together and there are no kiddie ears around, now is as good of a time as any to fill you both in on another concern in these parts, it has only come about recently," he looked deeply into each of their eyes. "There was a young Mountie that I bumped into a week or so ago up near Beaver Creek summit. We got to talking and he said a couple of farm hands not far from Fort Mount were found dead. Tore from limb to limb he claimed. Said it looked like they were butchered. When you hear stuff like that from a Mountie, you listen. I guess what I'm trying to get at is you both best be careful in these parts."

The small room grew quiet for a minute as Marissa and Tyrell took in what Wilson was jabbering about. Tyrell took a sip from his coffee. "Hoogley boogley, maybe it was that Ripper fellow who was once in London," Tyrell chuckled. "Fort Mount is a distance away I don't reckon we have anything to concern ourselves with. Could be they were tore apart by a bear. Butchered?" Tyrell shook his head, "I ain't going to go worrying myself about a tale like that."

"I don't know Tyrell, you have to admit, that there has been some strange things going on. Don't forget about the picnic basket." Marissa pointed out.

"That I am sure has a simple explanation, Marissa."

"A theory maybe but not an explanation, I would think." Marissa added.

"Tell me about this picnic basket and your explanation, young Sloan." Wilson put his hands behind his head as he waited to listen to the tale.

"Ah, it was nothing Wilson," Tyrell waved his hand through the air as though he were swatting at a fly. "When

Marissa and Caleb spent the night up at the shack a couple days ago. In the morning a basket she packed went missing. Caleb finally found it empty and down by the creek."

"That's not all. Tell him about the person I saw standing in the window," Marissa dared him.

"That too is explainable. I reckon it was the wind blowing the branches of the cedar outside. The moon was high that night and likely made a shadow which startled you," Tyrell chuckled.

Wilson was nodding his head. "Did you find any tracks near where the basket was found? Without track's things are hard to explain, young Sloan. Although, I do agree it was probably a cagey 'coon. I'd be hard pressed to make that an infinitive answer without some sign. Anyway, I just wanted the two of you to be on your toes. One friend missing is enough," Wilson leaned forward and finished what was left of his coffee. "I guess we best get them horses harnessed if you two plan on making it back this way today. I'll be heading to Salwood and from there back to my trap line near Grizzly Mountain. I was going to come back this way and give Tyrell a hand for a day or two but, I've decided to check one more place for Fry. A place that might have been overlooked, I'll be back this way again in late fall."

Tyrell and Wilson both rose from the table. "Sounds like another long ride ahead of you. Where is this other place?" Tyrell asked as the two of them made their way outside.

"He sometimes takes Crag Pass, might be he did this time too. Still, if he did and he ain't back yet it isn't a good sign." Wilson said in deep contemplation. "It'll be my last year up in that area. Going to sell off that trap line this spring, I'm getting to old to keep going as hard as I do. I have to admit though it has kept me young." Wilson chuckled.

"What the Hell are you going to do with yourself if you sell it?"

"I don't know. I'll keep my line up on Beaver Mountain; I reckon it has ten years of sustainability. After that I'll move to Salwood and retire for good."

"I can't imagine you retiring."

"Nor can I. C'mon let's get that wagon hooked up."

# Chapter 10

They travelled for an hour conversing back and forth with idle chit-chat. The sun was full and hot and it cast shadows along the trail they rode and on occasion these startled them, but that aside, it was a glorious day. "There is a creek up ahead, I reckon we might as well take a break there and let the horses drink."

"Sure thing, Wilson sounds good. I could use a bit of a rest myself. I ain't use to sitting on wood as I travel." Tyrell said as he twisted and turned in the wagon seat. "It is damn uncomfortable."

"That is why I choose packing mules or horses when I need to go a distance," Wilson chuckled. "Maybe you should look into that young Sloan."

"I intend to. Is old Everett still in these parts, he still selling mules?"

"He is, he does, but he ain't had any new blood in them mules in years. I reckon any one of them you might buy will be lacking a few scruples."

"A mule is a mule I reckon, most of them have an uncanny way of getting under my skin. The first two I picked up from him all those years ago constantly and consistently dared me to shoot them," Tyrell chuckled.

"After a day or two with the ones he has now you might shoot. There is the creek," Wilson pointed. The threesome pulled up to it. "That water looks good, going to have to have a slug of it and fill my canteen. There is no more water in these parts now until the mercantile." Wilson said as he dismounted.

Tyrell helped Marissa off the back of the wagon and grabbed his own canteen to fill. Filling their canteens and having a drink from the creek themselves, they led their horses to the edge and let them get their fill. Tyrell looked around. "This place ain't changed much. I stopped here with the mules and spent the night when I first came to these parts," he inhaled deeply. "That old fellow that lives down the trail some, what the hell was his name...?" he thought for a moment. "He was a good friend of Fry's. Damn I can't remember his name."

"You are thinking of Bill Waxley," Marissa responded.

"That's it, that's his name. He still around here too? I was thinking maybe old Fry is down that way."

"Bill has been dead four years now. His son runs the place. Fry ain't there; he and Bill's son ain't ever seen eye to eye. They're the worst of enemies."

"Where does Fry buy his feed? I thought Waxley was the only one in these parts."

"There is a fellow in Salwood. That is where Fry has been getting his winter feed. Marissa though still gets feed from Darrell, don't you?"

"Yes I do. I never knew Fry and Darrell never got along. Mind you, Darrell and I don't have much to say to one another. He isn't nearly as likeable as Bill was. That is for sure."

"Do you figure he's got any feed left? I reckon I'll be needing some? I don't care if he ain't the friendly sort." Tyrell questioned them both.

"He'll have some. Likely charge you an arm and a leg too." Wilson said as he knelt next to the creek again and splashed water on his face.

"Next year I'll get it from someone else. I reckon he's the only choice I have this time around."

"You'd be right; the fellow in Salwood has most of his stock already sold. If you want to buy from him next year, you best let me know now and I'll pass the message on."

"You go ahead and tell him Wilson. I'll get from Waxley this year," Tyrell splashed water onto his own face. "I reckon we've rested enough. The horses ain't drinking no more. Let's get a move on." Tyrell rose and made his way to the back of the wagon and helped Marissa board.

"Thank you," she said as she made her way to the front of the wagon. He hopped on behind her and moments later the three of them set off to finish their journey. "It is so beautiful through here," Marissa mentioned as they continued onward. Her gaze was upon all the foliage and wild flowers that grew on the trail. The dark forest looked haunting and peaceful all at once. Streaks of sunlight flickered through the pine trees that grew tall and proud along the trail as the wagon travelled onward. The echoing sound of the horse hooves, and the turning wheels of the wagon, took over the sounds of their voices as each of them embraced the serenity, and peace that was all around them.

"Beautiful don't always mean safe," Wilson pointed out. "Never let your guard down, and keep your eyes peeled. A few more hours and we'll be at Waxley's." Since earlier that day he felt as though something wasn't quite right. The woods to him were too quiet, too still. He slowed his horse and tilted his head to listen. *Either a storm is brewing or something has scared the animals off...* he thought as he traipsed ahead of the wagon.

"Where are you going Wilson?" Tyrell called after him.

"Going to mosey ahead for a bit young Sloan. Want to make sure the trail is clear."

"You don't suppose he's leaving us behind because it is so romantic through here do you?" Marissa asked with a smile.

"Hell, I don't know what that old boy is up to he's been acting strange since this morning," Tyrell said trying to lead away from Marissa's original question. She punched him in the arm. "Now what did you go and do that for?" he asked, as he looked at her confused.

"Don't you think this is romantic, the two of us travelling through this beautiful place?" she asked.

"I never quite looked at it like that...umm, I suppose now that you bring it up. I guess so. Sure. Yeah it does feel romantic in a sense."

"What do you mean in a sense?" she responded with a half scowl.

"I ain't much of a romantic. I don't know how to be romantic and I ain't no poet."

"Obviously," Marissa added as she rolled her eyes. Maybe in time there was hope for him, for now he was just Tyrell. "Haven't you ever picked flowers for a lady before? That could be a start you know?"

"I wouldn't know which type of flowers to pick. I ain't a gardener either." he chuckled.

Marissa shook her head. "I think deep down you are a bit of a romantic."

"Am not."

"Are too."

"If I am, it is a part of me that I ain't never saw."

"For now we'll say that you aren't a romantic," Marissa smiled at him and snuggled up to his shoulder. Tyrell smiled as he snapped the reins and got the horses moving a bit faster. It felt good having her snuggling him, maybe he was a romantic after all.

Wilson was well out of sight and ear shot, he was cresting a hill, and as he came to the top, he could see down near the bottom why the animals were so silent. A grizzly bear was feeding on a freshly killed moose. He slowed his horse down and stood stock-still. Slowly he untied the leather laces that kept his rifle firmly attached to his horse's saddle. The bear hadn't spotted him and he was thankful for that. Coming across a fresh grizzly bear kill with the animal feeding was a sticky situation. He cocked his rifle, he wasn't going to shoot, but being prepared and ready might save his life.

With his rifle loaded, he got his horse turned around and headed back the way he came. Galloping up to the wagon, he slowed his horse. "Whoa," he said, as he rose his hand.

"What's a matter Wilson?" Tyrell asked as he got his team to stop.

"About a quarter mile up the trail is a grizzly bear feasting on a moose. It ain't no small bear either. The damn thing killed the moose right smack in the middle of the trail. Not sure how to rectify this situation. Could fire a shot off at him I suppose but that might only draw his attention our way. Last thing we need is a pissed off grizzly come at us full bore. We could hold off here a bit and maybe it'll move on but he ain't never going to be far from his feast. Now is when I wish that dog of yours was near," Wilson spat to the ground.

"Yeah, me too, I'm surprised actually that he ain't near. I say we hold off here for a bit. It'll eat its fill and move on eventually."

"I say load your rifle and we'll head straight for him. The site of the horses and us might make him run off. Might piss him off too, it'd be a different story if he wasn't gnawing on a kill, then for sure the horses and us would scare him off." Wilson turned his horse so they were facing the same direction. "We'll carry on side by each. If the bear decides to charge we'll try to scare him off by shooting at him. If he keeps coming, we'll kill him. I hate to have to do that though, but that might be the only option."

With the three of them in agreement they continued onward. As they approached the area they were surprised that the bear had moved on. It wouldn't be too far away though. "Glad to see it took off, the damn thing is probably looking at us right now," Tyrell commented as they passed the kill.

"He is watching us you can bet on that," Wilson replied as they moved on. "When the two of you are making your way back this evening be careful in this area. A moose that big will keep the bear near until it is all ate up. Not to mention it'll attract a few more beasties. Just stay alert and keep your rifle near."

Tyrell nodded. "You bet. I reckon he'd have to be a big bear to have taken down that moose. I ain't never seen one quite that big in this area. Twelve hundred pounds or more I reckon."

"The bear is probably that heavy too, he's probably an offspring of Old Senile. Now that was a bear, ain't seen him though in years."

"Chances are he's likely dead by now. I remember the stories Fry told me about Old Senile. Any bear that can live through being shot dead twice is a bear I wouldn't want to come across."

Wilson chuckled. "Hell, there ain't no proof that Ol' Senile is dead. He just ain't been saw in a while. It don't mean he's dead young Sloan, no sir."

"He'd be near thirty years old if he was around. There aren't many bears that will live that long, if any."

"Nope, but then again there aren't many bears, that could take as many slugs as he did, and still get up and runaway to only be seen days later and shot dead again."

"True enough, true enough." Tyrell responded as they carried on.

Marissa throughout the conversation concentrated her efforts in staying alert. The trip up to that point was a treat, now though she was feeling a sense of fear. In all the time she lived in Red Rock and all the trips she made to the mercantile alone never once did she see a grizzly. It frightened her to think that she had only been lucky. She was grateful that this trip she was in the company of both of them. Still, she couldn't wrap her mind around the fact that she could have been alone. Suddenly the forest she thought that was so beautiful and peaceful seemed ominous and dark.

By 3:00 that day they arrived at the mercantile. Loading the wagon up with their surplus of dry goods, canned goods, lumber, screen, and stove pipe they bid Wilson good bye. He promised he'd be back in late fall or early winter. Marissa and Tyrell watched as he and his horse disappeared into the forest in the direction of Salwood. "He ain't changed all that much has he?" Tyrell questioned.

"He's too old and set in his ways to change. I wouldn't want him any other way," Marissa said. "Are you sure you have all that you need?"

"I reckon so. Anything else I might need I'll have to take from the land. We have a six-hour ride ahead of us and I don't want to spend any more time wrestling with what I have and what I need. Don't want to be travelling back to Red Rock in the darkness. Come on Marissa let's get." The two of them climbed into the wagon moving things out of their way so they could sit.

"It sure didn't look like we had that much stuff," Marissa commented as she moved a box of canned goods off the wagon seat.

"Between you and me we have enough goods to make it through winter that is all that matters. I'll have to make another trip down this way to arrange for feed from Waxley. There is lots of grass up near my shack, that will keep Dutch happy for a month or so, after that he'll be needing feed. Are you ready?"

"I am."

"Good, all right let's get going, giddy up," he said as he snapped the reins and the wagon slowly set off creaking this way and that as they went. Neither of them spoke much at first. They were content with their own thoughts. Finally Tyrell spoke. "We're getting close to Everett's but I ain't sure I want to stop."

"It is up to you. Do you need a mule right now?" Marissa asked. The truth was 'no'.

"Ah, not really, I reckon we'll continue on. I'd much rather make the distance to Red Rock before the stars are out. Stopping now will slow us down. We'll keep going." There was a look of relief in Marissa's eyes. She too didn't want to be travelling in the darkness not now, not after the earlier events of the day. The last thing they needed was to come across the same grizzly they managed to avoid as they made their way to the mercantile.

The sun was in front of them now as they travelled and it beamed down on them hot and hard. Tyrell turned the brim of his hat down to shade his eyes. Marissa on the other hand leaned back in the seat and closed her eyes. The sun felt good on her face and in only a few short minutes, she was gently sleeping. Tyrell chuckled when he looked over to her. "That is it Marissa, have a nap. I'll wake you if need be." He was quite content as they made their way westerly toward Red Rock. His mind drifted and he lost himself in deep thought.

There were things he wanted to tell her and things he didn't. One thing was for certain, he was falling in love with her again. He conjured up visions of them spending the rest of their lives together. It was a long shot, he knew. Nonetheless, it was a shot as long as he didn't screw it up again. She was the one of the reason he returned to Red Rock.

The way he left her years earlier haunted him every day that he was gone. This time he wouldn't leave. This time he was going to make things right. He had the means and desire but sometimes things didn't always pan out the way he expected, and he knew that. But if he didn't try to rectify the situation then he might as well have continued to drift. He could have easily returned to the gold he stashed and slipped away once more into the frontier. His mind was made up and for the first time in a long time, he felt good about the decision he made.

Paying little attention to the trail in front of him, and the rock that protruded out of the dirt the wagon lurched up and crashed down almost tossing Marissa out of the seat. The lumber bounced with a loud crash and one of the boards struck him in the head knocking his hat off and him to the ground. It was an embarrassing situation and he tried to cover his blunder by getting up quickly and dusting himself off. "You're awake now...? Good. I was getting a tad lonely."

Marissa sat there looking at him shaking her head. "Couldn't you have nudged me awake?"

"I reckon that is what I did," he replied as he picked up his hat and stood there like a child waiting to be scowled.

"Almost killed yourself too didn't you?" She was not at all impressed.

"No, no. Heck no. I...ah... umm well I suppose things could have been worse. I'm truly sorry I don't remember that rock being there when we came this way."

"That is because you went around it. Look at the wagon tracks Tyrell. They are on that side of the rock."

Tyrell looked down. "Yep, I see that now," he was blushing. "I guess I best fix the load," he rubbed the back of his head. "Ouch. I seem to have a good wallop on the back of my head, damn."

Marissa stepped off the wagon and went to his side. "Let me have a look." Tyrell tilted his head toward her so she could see.

"How bad is it?" he asked. She was almost laughing. The wallop he was talking about was the size of an egg. But it wasn't at all that bad. So she slapped the back of his head. "Hey what was that for?" Tyrell expressed as he ducked away from her assault.

"If you had paid attention to the wagon trail we wouldn't be stopped right now. That is what '*that*' is for." She shook her head and began gathering the few items that fell off the wagon.

"It isn't like I meant for it to happen. It was one of those things that man has no control over."

"Right," she looked at him with a smile. "If you were paying attention you would have control." Indeed that was fact and there was no use in arguing.

"I suppose. Now never mind all that. Let's get this wagon moving," he waved his hand through the air. "I ain't never been so damn embarrassed." Marissa held her tongue even though there was so much she could say. For now, she'd leave it alone. A few minutes later, they were once more on the move. From that point on, Marissa stayed awake. Next came the moose kill and Tyrell slowed the wagon down to a crawl. He handed the reins to Marissa and cocked his rifle.

"Looking good so far, it doesn't look like the grizzly has been back. That's always good. Keep her going little lady. Keep her going." He said referring to the wagon that now creaked by the dead moose. "Thank God that is over, clear sailing from here I reckon." He added as they passed the carcass and the wagon crept around the bend. "I feel better now that is over. You want me to take the reins?"

"I'd prefer it if you stayed alert with that rifle. We aren't out of the woods yet?"

"If your arms get tired, let me know and we'll swap." Tyrell looked along the brush-line relieved there was nothing unusual or out of the ordinary that caught his eye. Relaxing, he reached into one of the boxes pulling out a fresh package of cheroots. He opened the pack and offered one to Marissa. "Care for a cheroot?"

"I don't smoke Tyrell."

"Do you mind if I do? I feel as though I need one now after today's escapades."

"I don't mind. They're your lungs."

Tyrell nodded. "Thanks. I ain't puffed on one since yesterday." Striking a match he inhaled the pungent smoke. "Ah, that feels better. I reckon we're getting close to Red Rock. I can hardly wait to fix up that woodstove. The weather can change anytime after I get that pipe in."

"It'll be changing soon you can bet on that. Winter came early last year but it didn't last long. The cold did but not the snow. This winter it might be mild. That is what Len thinks anyway."

"I don't mind mild. I'll embrace a mild winter with my arms open. The last couple of winters I spent up north were torturous. And I mean that literally."

They grew silent for a few minutes listening to the birds as they squawked and chirped. They were both content in each other's company there was no denying that. It was like they had known each other for eternity. "I hear the creek we should take a rest there and let the horses drink."

"I agree, we will."

"Good. My backside is getting sore," he moved in the seat trying to get comfortable. "There that feels better. Still want to stop though, I'm a might thirsty."

As the creek came into view, Marissa slowed the wagon to a stop. They stepped off and made their way to a cold drink. Kneeling down they slurped a few cold mouthfuls and splashed water on their faces. "Ah, that feels good," Tyrell said as he filled his hat with water and placed it on his head. Squatting still, he removed his watch and looked at the time. "I reckon the sun will be settling when we get to Red Rock. Likely be dark by the time I get to the shack."

"If it turns out that it is too late for you to head back to your shack, you'd be welcome to spend the night with me." Marissa said in a coy manner.

Tyrell was surprised and the look on his face as he responded showed the shock. "I don't know Marissa, I appreciate your offer and all but..." he scratched his head, "I ain't sure, that'd be a good idea." He had good reason to reply like that, one out of respect for her and two he hadn't bathed in almost a week, he was at the least rancid.

"Why? Wants wrong with that?" she asked.

"Nothing I suppose, I, well I ain't comfortable doing that yet."

"Doing what?"

"Spending the night in your presence...I mean. I think I need to think about that."

"Think about it then, the offer remains," she was glad he answered as he did. He was probably right. *Perhaps another time would be better,* she thought. Even now as she looked at him, he was as handsome as he was when they first met. Caleb certainly had his eyes. She smiled and splashed some more water on her face. Rising from the creek, she led the horses over to drink themselves. "They are sure thirsty."

"It's been a long haul for them made even tougher now with all the supplies. They're good horses I'll give them that. You've done a good job with them."

"Thank you but, it was Len who trained them. I just feed and use them," she chuckled. "I guess they are done. We should get moving." Making themselves comfortable Marissa once more took the reins and off they went on their last leg of the trip. The two hour ride went without a hitch and finally they could see the cabin.

"There it is, *'home sweet home'*." Tyrell remarked.

"It sure looks beautiful against the sunset doesn't it?"

"As beautiful as the woman I'm sitting next to."

"Why thank you Tyrell. You are quite handsome yourself." Marissa smiled as she pulled the horses to a stop by the side of the cabin. "Now the fun of unloading everything starts." She said as Tyrell helped her off the wagon.

"It won't be so bad. A few minutes is all it'll take." Reaching into his pocket, he pulled out both his watch and his package of cheroots. "It's half past eight. We did pretty good I reckon," he drew a match and sparked his cheroot. "I'll finish the cigar and then we'll get cracking. I need to walk around a bit. That wagon ride has made my ass numb."

"Mine too; I think this winter I'll make a pillow for it. I don't remember it being so hard on the backside. But, it sure is. I usually sit on a folded blanket. I forgot it this time though."

"That would have made the ride more comfortable I reckon." By 8:45 that evening Tyrell, was on his way to his own shack and strapped to Dutch were his necessities and the length of stovepipe. The rest he'd retrieve from Marissa's in the days to come. Her horses were tired from the trip to carry on up to his shack. Besides, it gave him another excuse to visit her in the next couple of days when Caleb was back. The closer he got to his shack on Hudu Creek the darker it became. He could barely see the horse trail and travelled it under instinct most of the way. The sound of the creek brought a smile to his face. In only a few minutes, he'd finally be home.

# Chapter 11

After unloading his supplies and stowing them away, he lit a small fire. As the flames took on a life he whistled for Black Dog, he hadn't seen him all day and by now, he was getting worried. It wouldn't be the same sitting around the fire without him. He sat down and looked into the flames and drifted back to his earlier thought that day, regarding the fact the he needed a bath. Glancing toward the creek he had an idea, he could build a bath. He could dig a hole and divert a small stream into the hole. If his logic was correct it would fill up, the sun would heat it and he'd have a hole full of warm water. The ground he knew was mostly clay, a bit tough to dig in, but beneficial to the idea he was scheming.

Black Dog finally showed up to his relief. "There you are, you old scoundrel. Where the heck have you been? I've been to the mercantile and back again and ain't seen you all day." The dog walked over to him and set his paw in his lap as if to say sorry.

"No need in apologizing ol' boy. I'm glad you're here, I picked you up some fancy dog things, I think they're pig ears actually. Only thing is I left them behind at Marissa's. How about a cheroot?" he joked.

Black Dog licked his face and then curled up on the ground next to Tyrell's side. "Sure good to have you here with me." *Things are now as they should be,* he thought. Tossing another log on the fire, he reminisced about the day. It had been a good one. All the supplies he'd need to get him through winter, he now had. In a day or two once he mounted the stove pipe, he'd also have heat. It was sad though to learn about Fry, and the fact that he had not been seen in months. He shook his head as he thought back to when he first met Fry and the time the two of them were confronted by would-be robbers.

They made short work of the three and planted them in the ground along the trail heading to Heddy's.

A shiver ran up his back as Dutch's neighing and discontent snapped him back to the here and now. He stood up with a piece of flaming wood in his hand, and used it to for light made his way over to the anxious horse.

"Easy now, easy Dutch, what's a matter? What has spooked you?" he looked around, but saw nothing. "It's okay Dutch. There ain't nothing about, or that old dog would be snarling away." The horse finally settled after a few minutes, and once again, Tyrell found himself sitting at the fire.

Time slipped by.

It had been a long tiring day and he was feeling the exhaustion. With some effort, he rose from where he sat and dumped the coffee pot out into the slow burning flames.

"Want to come in, Black Dog? I'm heading inside." Black Dog yawned and whimpered, then followed him inside. Closing the door, he slid his saddle bags against the bottom. Removing his holster and tossing his hat on the table, he hung up his guns. "Going to sleep like a baby I reckon," he sat on his bunk for a moment not sure if he wanted one last cheroot. Instead, he took off his boots and swung into bed. "That feels good, damn feet been sweating all day. Good night Black Dog." Stretching out with his hands behind his head, he stared into the darkness and waited for sleep.

Black Dog woke him the next morning by licking his face and wanting to be let out. Tyrell tried to ignore him but it was useless. "All right, all right I'm up. You're worse than Wilson, you know that." Letting the dog out he kicked him in the behind in a friendly gesture, then made his way to the table and sat down. He gave his underarms a quick smell and almost gagged. "Whew that needs to be taken care of. Goddamn!" *Two things need to be done today, one I got to build a bath, two I got to take a bath,* he thought as he enjoyed the rancid smoke of his morning cheroot.

Looking out the dirty window, he did a quick weather check. Only a few clouds drifted in the sky. Pulling on his denim pants and a dirty shirt, he slipped into his boots.

Grabbing his hat and holster, he exited the shack. Coals still glowed from the fire the night before and he simply tossed on some dried wood and waited. He looked around for the best place to build his bath. Walking to where Marissa parked her wagon he kicked the ground with the toe of his boot. He was looking for the clay bed that he knew existed on either side of the creek, and smiled when he found it.

If he was going to build a bath, a clay bed would work best. It could hold water and the sides wouldn't cave in. He also wanted it to be big enough for at least two people and of course it had to be in continuous sun all day. The closer to the creek the better, and where he stood was the perfect spot. He carved an X in the ground with his boot heel and headed back to the simmering coals of his morning fire. Grabbing the coffee pot, he walked to the creek and filled it, and at the same time gave his face a quick wash.

The horse lulled under the tree where he was tethered and nibbled on grass. "How are you today, Dutch?" Tyrell questioned as he scratched the horse behind its ears. Of course, Dutch didn't have much to say. He never did. It was one of the reasons he missed Pony. At least Pony would fart or something. "I'll lead you to the creek in a bit for some water, Dutch. See you later."

Making his way over to his shack and gathering the shovel and pick that leaned against the outside wall he set out to build his bath. He used the pick to soften up the dirt. It wasn't as bad as he thought it would be. After an hour of picking, he started to dig out the square shape, making sure to keep the pile of dirt and clay to one side of the hole.

Inch by inch, foot by foot, the bath began to take shape. He stood in the center and stretched his arms out in all four directions, satisfied with the breadth. The depth was another thing he took into consideration it had to be at least waist deep. Another hour of digging and squaring of the sides he stopped. It was the right width and depth that he wanted. He crawled out of the hole and admired his work, while he rested for a few minutes. Next, he dug a small ditch to divert water into the hole from upstream of the creek. Once it filled he'd place a rock up at the creek where the fill stream was to staunch the flow, then he could decide where to divert it back into the creek, that part he knew was going to be the hardest. It was going to be a difficult task digging a trench through the trees and all their roots.

Sitting on the edge of the hole now, he watched as the stream filled it. He was quite pleased at his ingenuity and more so that it was actually working. He wiped his brow with the back of his hand, and sighed.

It took the better part of an hour for the hole to finally fill. He rolled a rock into the fill trench to stop the flow while he judged where the overflow trench should be. The water that filled the bath was dirty and murky. Once it settled though he knew it would be clean, and with an overfill trench the water would run out continuously once it got to a certain level keeping the pool of water decently clean.

The sun as he continued was hot and arid, his mouth was dry, and a few blisters were beginning to show on the palms of his hands. The overfill trench was the hardest one to dig out of the two. It finished now he splashed some cold water on his face and took a long swallow.

He soaked his bloody blistered hands to wash away the dirt and caked on blood. "Geez, that hurts a bit," he winced as he shook them dry. Making his way back to his bath he once more looked it over, *that is going to work nice, a little hard work and a bit of initiative is all it took. It is hard to believe what man can do once he sets his mind to it,* he thought. Walking now along the fill trench, he removed any debris that might staunch the flow, and then kicked the rock out of the way again to see if the overfill trench would work as he had envisioned.

With the overfill trench dug and ready he could let the water run continually or stop the flow anytime by putting the rock for the fill trench back in place. It was the simplest and most efficient way that he could have a supply of decently warm water. To make it even hotter all he needed to do was stop the flow and let the sun do the rest.

He waited again for it to fill and watched as it drained off constantly maintaining his depth preference. He didn't wait for it to clear or get warm. Removing his boots and clothes, he jumped in butt naked. The water wasn't too cold, surprisingly, and he dunked his head few times. It felt good to wash the week away and all the sweat that caked his body. This was a test bath. For the next one he'd make sure it was warm and that a bar of soap was handy. For now though, he was already starting to feel brand new. *Sure feels good to wash the stink off,* he thought as he dunked again. He held his breath under the cool water for as long as he could and shook his head back and forth.

Finally, he emerged and took in a big gulp of air. To his surprise, Black Dog had finally come home. Where he had been only he knew. "Hello there Black Dog. You've been gone all day." Tyrell pulled himself out of the water and dried himself with his shirt. "Where have you been?" he asked as he made his way naked into his shack to put on a cleaner set of clothes. Black Dog lulled next to the fire pit while he dressed.

Slipping on his buckskins he made his way over to where the dog lay, bringing with him a couple thick pieces of jerky. He handed a piece to the dog; Black Dog gently took it like he always did, then set it down in front of him and wagged his tail. "What, one ain't good enough?" Black Dog looked at him wagging his tail and perked his ears. "All right, here you can have this piece too." With that, the dog picked up both pieces and darted off.

"Hey, where are you going now?" Tyrell watched as the dog headed into the nearby forest, he simply shrugged his shoulders and shook his head, at least he knew Black Dog was okay, and that is all that really mattered. For a brief second he contemplated having a shave. "Ah, I'll shave and use soap tomorrow. Ain't much more I want to do today," he tossed a stick into the fire and watched, as the sun tucked itself away for another day. Lately it had been colder in the evenings and he noticed that now with his hair still being wet. *The season is changing, there is no doubt about that,* he reminisced as he added a few more pieces of wood to the flames that were beginning to dance in the bed of coals.

Rising from where he sat he made his way over to his horse and led him to the creek. "Sorry about being as late as I am in getting you to the creek. Got caught up in what I was doing." The horse didn't seem to care and stuck his muzzle into the cool running water.

It drank for a few minutes then Tyrell tethered him again and brought him a bucket of oats. He'd have to move the horse soon to a more appropriate place and to new grass. Dutch had been doing a pretty good job in gnawing down the bit he had now. "Done with them oats yet? Good boy, Dutch, that ought to keep you satisfied until the morning, eh. I'll get busy on a corral for you in the next couple of days.

The day after tomorrow, which I think is a Thursday we're going to head down to Marissa's, the boy should be back by then and we can visit for a bit. Still have a load or two of supplies to gather from her place. But, that ain't going to be for a couple of days, we have work here to do first. That dang stovepipe is what I'm going to work on tomorrow," Tyrell sighed. Turning on his heels, he made his way back to the crackling fire and sat down. A pleasant breeze picked up and the flames swayed this way and that. He stared into them as if mesmerized.

Yawning he looked around for Black Dog, it was almost dark and it seemed strange that the dog wasn't laying beside him, *hope he ain't out there chasing polecats,* he thought as he once more averted his eyes to the flickering flames. It was true the old dog was getting on in age, and one of Tyrell's concerns were that he wasn't as spry as he use to be. It wouldn't take much for a mountain lion, bear, or even a wolf to dispose of him.

The truth was, Black Dog, had been frolicking with the young maiden wolf that, had taken an interest in him. He brought her a piece of the jerked meat, like one brings his sweetheart a bunch of flowers. She was quite impressed with him and showed her appreciation by jumping this way and that, coaxing him to play. For three hours, the two of them didn't stop with their antics as they proved their cunning to one another. Now though three hours of play turned to a tranquil visit, nothing more just a visit.

It wouldn't be long though before the wolf would give in to him and Black Dog knew it. Licking the wolf's face, he headed for home. Surprisingly the timid wolf followed behind taking up a spot not far from the flickering flames and the odd man sitting there. "Look at you it is about time you came strolling back. Where and what have you been up to? I don't expect you to answer but I'm damn happy you've finally made it back. Now that you are here and the fire is petering out I'm going to bed."

# Chapter 12

The sound of crows squawking woke him bright and early the next day. Dressing, he made his way to the fire and set the coffee pot on the coals. Making his way up to the edge of the creek, he rolled the rock into place to stop the flow of water into his bath. The sun was rising and he could tell it was going to be another hot blistering day. The water would be warm when he was done for the day and he'd gather a soap bar and his straight razor and enjoy a nice warm bath. Looking around he thought he saw something stirring in a nearby bush.

Unarmed and ill-prepared in case of a confrontation by man or beast, he slowly turned then quickened his pace back to the shack and strapped on his holster. Feeling less vulnerable, he exited and sat down by the fire. Reaching into his shirt pocket, he pulled out his pack of cheroots. There was only one left in the pack and he tossed the empty package into the fire. With a twig, he caught a flame and brought it to the cheroot hanging out of his mouth.

The acrid smoke enveloped the early morning scents of coffee, and cedar, he inhaled deeply. The smoke felt good going into his lungs and he felt a sigh of relief as he exhaled. There was no doubt that it was a dirty habit and he was going to quit eventually. Until then he would enjoy every lung full.

With a cheroot dangling from his lip's he walked over to the creek. Squatting he looked around and reminisced. There was so much work to do and he knew there was very little time before the weather changed to colder days, and frozen nights. He would make it though he was certain of that. The stovepipe was his next project and then he'd move on to the corral. With those out of the way, he could concentrate on winterizing the shack so that he didn't freeze. *Yep, a whole bunch needs doing around here,* he thought as he rose and made his way back to the fire.

An hour later, while the sun warmed up the morning he began gathering the tools he needed to install the stovepipe. He gathered clay from the creek bed, which, he would use to seal the pipe in its place. First though, he needed to break away some of the clay and sod he used to patch the large hole where the old stovepipe used to be.

He was surprised at how well his quick fix worked. The clay was as hard as rock, and it took a couple hard swings from the hammer, to break away enough to be able to get to the short poles he used as the base to hold the clay.

With his axe, he chopped through the poles making the hole big enough to accept the new stovepipe. It was a tight fit at first and he struggled with it at the beginning. Finally, the stovepipe relented. He adjusted the height so that at least two feet of the pipe stuck out of the shack's roof and above the peak. He would make final adjustments once he was sure it was long enough to attach to the potbelly stove. Making his way inside he pulled the stove over to where the pipe extended through the ceiling.

The pipe of course was too short. It was an easy fix however, and all he did was give it a few good pulls until managing to get it fitted. As long as there was enough of it still extending through and above the roof he was set.

Once more, he climbed the makeshift ladder and looked at the pipe. A smile crossed his face as he climbed onto the roof. He was satisfied. *That is going to work fine, got lucky I suppose,* he thought as he began slapping clay over the hole and around the pipe sealing it from the elements of rain and snow.

An hour later, he was sitting on the roof enjoying the view of his surroundings. The sun was warm and a mild breeze tousled his hair. He felt good about the work he did and even better about the fact it didn't take him quite as long as he expected. Everything was coming together it was only a matter of getting it all done. He looked around from where he sat on the roof, looking for the best place to start building the corral for Dutch. Where he was tethered seemed like a good spot, he was close to the water and there were shade trees. Tyrell could see him from the fire pit as well as from the shack door; he decided that is where it would be.

Climbing off the roof, he parked himself next to the fire that glowed with coals. The coffee was still warmish so he poured a cup. Looking at his pocket watch, he noted the time to be almost noon and already he accomplished one task. Black Dog, he noticed was panting in the shade but something else caught his eye and that was the wolf which lay behind him a few yards away.

At first he wasn't sure it was there as a threat or if the wolf and Black Dog were friends. Cautiously he rose from where he sat and pulled out his pistol. "Black Dog come," the old dog slowly rose and traipsed over to him as though nothing was out of the ordinary. "You don't smell that damn wolf behind you or what?" Tyrell reached down and pet him. "Either you're sense of smell and sight, have gone for a crap or you're friends with that mangy wolf. Which is it?" Black Dog wagged his tail. "You're friends then? That's where you've been getting to. You're out there dancing with a wolf bitch. Hope you know what you're getting yourself into ol' boy. As much as I might protest I don't reckon there is much I can do about it."

The only thing he was sure of at that moment was the fact that in time there'd a bunch of whelps yelping and whining and generally making nuisances of themselves. *Oh well, so be it,* he thought as he took a long swig from his now less than warm coffee. "Yuk, that wasn't very pleasant at all." He poured out the rest. Grabbing the axe that was nearby he strolled through the tall weeds and over to the stand of cedar poles that he decided to use for Dutch's corral. It was while he was falling them that he a got a good look at Black Dog's new mate.

They darted not five feet from him in a gust of wind frolicking like two kids playing. Stopping what he was doing he watched them for a few minutes. They were in love there was no doubt about that. It was strange not to see any other wolves around. He watched them for a few minutes running and jumping through the woods and tall knapweed. It was obvious she was a rogue or misfit. It was going to be interesting to see what would come of it. Tyrell chuckled, *Hell, she ain't even going to be in heat until winter. I reckon though there ain't nothing wrong with a long courtship.*

He went back to his work knocking down another half dozen cedar poles. It wasn't quite dark when he made his way back. The sun had been hot all day and he knew his bath would undoubtedly be warm enough to clean up even at that hour. He fished through his gear and pulled out a bar of soap, his straight razor, a small mirror, and pair of long johns that he'd use to dry himself after his bath. It felt good to lather his body and shave the whiskers off his face. Done with his bath and shaving he climbed out and dried himself. Black Dog was lying near the fire pit and looking even closer now, he noticed that the wolf wasn't far off either.

"You and your friend done playing?" he asked as he approached with only the long underwear around his waist. It seemed as though the dog was bit embarrassed at what Tyrell was wearing and he covered his head with his front paws. "What's a matter ol' boy? Ain't never seen me dressed like this before have you? I'll slip into some clothes if that'll make you happy. I was going to do that anyway," he chuckled as he entered the shack and threw on his last pair of clean shorts, pants, and shirt. Grabbing a handful of jerky, he exited and walked over to the fire.

"I brought you and that friend of yours some jerked meat. Do you want it?" he asked as he handed the dog two thick pieces. Of course, Black Dog did he always wanted jerky. Taking the two pieces in his mouth, Tyrell watched as the dog pranced over to the wolf and set the pieces down. The two of them looked like a match made in heaven. He was surprised that the wolf felt comfortable enough to stay in view. It was surreal and almost haunting to look at her from such a short distance. Tyrell felt as though they were already friends.

Back at Marissa's, Caleb and Len were tethering up the horses. They just rode in from Len's house. "That was a fun couple of days. Wasn't it Caleb?"

"Sure was Uncle. I liked shooting that big rifle. It scared me though," Caleb smiled. "But I did pretty good didn't I?"

"You did. Maybe I will ask that sister of mine, if you can tag along with Sebastian and me when we go hunting later this fall. Would you like that Caleb?" Len asked as he gathered Caleb's over night gear.

"Ma won't let me. She say's I'm too young still. She'll get mad if she finds out I shot your big rifle. Don't tell her, okay Uncle."

Len chuckled and tilted his head. "If you don't want me to tell her, I won't. I wouldn't want her getting mad with me either. It'll be our secret for now."

"That would be better I think. Maybe next year I can go hunting. I'll almost be seven then." Turning he headed for the chicken coop. "I have to check on Captain Black and the hens."

"Are you sure you don't need any help?"

"I'm sure." Caleb opened the coop door and the chickens flocked toward him. Their squawks of excitement and surprise broke the silence of the darkening evening. "It's okay it is me, Caleb. Hello chickens," he said as he closed the door behind him. "I missed you. Did you give ma lots of eggs?" He looked over to Captain Black his rooster. "Captain Black, I missed you most of all. Guess what I shot Uncle Len's big rifle, but don't tell ma," he joked. "Did you miss me?"

The rooster stood up on its perch and flapped his wings. "So you did miss me? I'm glad ma kept you watered and fed." Caleb said as he looked into the water and feed trough.

"I'll see you all in the morning. Maybe I'll let you out into the yard, okay," he walked back to the door and turned. "Lay some eggs tonight. I want fresh eggs for breakfast. Good night chickens." Closing the coop door, he ran the distance back to the cabin and burst through the door. "Ma, ma, I'm back," he ran to her, and jumped up on a chair and kissed her.

"Hello young man," she said as she returned the kiss. "Len told me you had lots of fun?"

"I did. Sebastian and I caught some fish and ate them. They were really good, plus we built a fort. I'll show it to you the next time okay," Caleb sat down in his chair. "You will really, really like it a lot." His eyes were as big as saucers as he said that. Marissa knew when his eyes grew like that he was very proud of something.

"I bet I will. What did you build it from?"

"Some poles and stuff, we even had nails. Sebastian hit his finger when he was putting one in with an old hammer. It got all black and sore. He's okay now though, right Uncle Len?"

Len smiled and nodded. "I told him if he ever hit the wrong nail it was going to hurt."

Marissa chuckled. "Len, you are so mean sometimes. Poor Sebastian, I bet you teased him too?"

"Who? Me? Never," he smiled. "Anyway thanks for letting us have Caleb for the past couple of days. It is a real treat when he's around. He's turning into quite the little man." Len took a drink from the cup of tea he held in his hand. Marissa always made them a pot of tea, when he brought Caleb back, it was a way for the two of them to catch up before he would head back home.

The two of them would and could talk about anything. Their sibling relationship was as solid as any. He loved and adored his sister. She may have been naive in her time, but she had turned into quite the woman. If there was one thing he could wish for her, it would be happiness. Where she was now she seemed quite happy and for that Len was happy too. He would have never said 'no' to her if she ever asked him if she could move onto his land near Heddy's old mercantile. But, she would never ask and he knew that. Her happiness was where she was now. Len set his cup down on the table. "Caleb tells me that Tyrell is back and staying up on the Sloan claims. Is this true Marissa?" He was a bit forward with the question.

"Yes, yes he is. This land is his after all. I feel comfortable that he is near. Safe in a sense, it is good to have a friend that close."

Caleb was looking at her a bit confused on why the two of them seemed to be upset. "Wasn't I suppose to tell anyone Ma?" he asked.

"There is nothing wrong with Tyrell being here sweetie. You can let the whole world know. I only forgot to tell Uncle Len when he picked you up," she smiled at him. "Come on let's get you tucked into bed you look tired." Marissa rose from the table. "I'll be back in a minute, Len. Help yourself to more tea. Come on Sleepy Head and don't forget to give your Uncle a hug before you go to bed."

Caleb hugged Len's big shoulders. "Thanks for all the fun. I'll see you next time Uncle." Waving goodbye he followed Marissa to his bed. "Can I go back to uncle's again sometime?" he asked as he lay down in his bed. "He really wants me to."

"We'll see Caleb. There is lots I need for you to help me with here. But, we'll see. Good night sweetie, I'm so glad you are home." She leaned down and kissed him on the cheek. "Have a good night's sleep, okay."

"I will."

"All right, good night," Marissa exited the room. Len poured each of them a fresh cup of tea as Marissa made her way back to the table. "There, he's all tucked in and probably sleeping already." Marissa took a drink from her tea. "I guess you want to know why I forgot to tell you about Tyrell."

"Forgot?" Len questioned as he half smiled. "How about neglected?"

"That's fair," she replied. "I didn't tell you because it wasn't time. I don't know what his intentions are. I can't very well send him off his land."

"It isn't any of my business. I hope that you and he both know what you are doing." Len took another drink from the cup of tea in his hand. "I haven't got anything against him, other than the way he left you. I'm your brother, so at times that bothers me some," he took another drink from his cup of tea. "I hope he comes to his senses and realises what it is he has done to you and Caleb both. You could have all the money in the world Marissa, but that never buys a child's future. It helps them but, without a daddy around... well, let's say we know how that can end up. A boy growing up today needs a decent and disciplined man to point him in the right direction. I'm not sure Tyrell Sloan is either."

He was frank but Marissa knew it was an argument that she could not win, not yet at least. She knew without a doubt that in time she would stuff those words down Len's throat. Tyrell was a respectable man. He treated her right and cordial, was apologetic and sincere. Len couldn't know that though, he didn't known Tyrell like she did.

"I appreciate and respect your opinions Len, and like I said I don't know what his intentions are."

"I might have spoke out of order Marissa, and if I did I'll apologize before-hand." It broke the tension that the two of them were feeling. Len was always like that - to the point, and when he was wrong he didn't argue. "Anyway it's getting dark. I have a long ride ahead of me. I best get on my way," he rose from the table as did Marissa, and she gave him a hug.

"I love you brother," she said as she kissed his cheek. "Are you going to be all right heading back tonight? You could always sleep on the couch."

"Nope, no can do little sister. I have to be at least halfway home before I even consider sleeping. I'd like to make it all the way back if I could. Liz and Sebastian don't like being alone for too long. More importantly I got some pressing business to look after tomorrow."

"I see," Marissa replied as they walked to the door. "Len, before you go, I want you to know I appreciate everything we talked about and I'll be careful."

Len smiled. "Never be afraid to shoot first and ask questions later," he said teasingly as he made his way to his horse. "I'll be by again soon and remember if you need anything make your way to the farm. We're always there." He tilted his hat at her, turned his horse, and sped off into the evening. Marissa waved as he disappeared into the forest.

"See you next time Len." She quietly said as she turned and entered the cabin. Removing the kettle and cups they used from the table, she made her way into the kitchen and set them in the dish tub. Feeling the need for fresh air, she stepped out on to the back porch and leaned against the railing. It was a peaceful night and a warm September breeze gently blew.

Looking in the direction of Tyrell's shack, she smiled. She felt safe knowing he was near. *What are your intentions Tyrell,* she thought to herself. He never made anything clear, but then again she couldn't expect him to so suddenly after stepping back into her life. She thought back to those first couple of days and how she accidently found a wanted poster in his saddlebag. She wondered about that poster now. What did it mean? Was Tyrell a wanted man? Was he running from something? she shook her head. Tyrell wasn't the type to run. *I'll ask him about that one-day, unless he mentions it first,* she thought.

Glancing around one last time Marissa stepped back inside and closed the door. It was getting late and making her way to Caleb's room she checked on him, then kissed his cheek and made her way to her own bed.

Tyrell was contemplating the same thing and he rose from where he sat and poured his coffee out. "Are you coming in tonight Black Dog?" he asked the dog as he made his way to the shack. Black Dog wagged his tail, turned and darted into the evening shadows. "All right, see you in the morning." An hour later Tyrell was sprawled out on his bunk fast asleep.

# Chapter 13

The air was chilled when he woke the following morning. A light frost covered the ground. He made his way over to the fire and tossed a few pieces of kindling onto the glowing coals. Filling up his coffee pot, he stopped and checked on Dutch. "We'll be heading to Marissa's sometime, hope you are up for a short ride?" Tyrell scratched him behind the ears. "Turned out nippy overnight eh? You even have a bit of frost on your back," he looked to the east. "No worries Dutch, the sun will be on us soon." Slapping the horse's behind he made his way back to the smouldering pieces of kindling, which hadn't taken on a flame.

*I guess them sticks are a little to frosty,* he thought as he rooted around for a few drier pieces. Finding a suitable handful he tossed them onto the others then knelt down and gently blew into the coals. Finally, a fire danced to life. *There, now I'll get some coffee and vittles going,* he looked around to see if he could spot Black Dog and his playmate but it was too dark for him to see far. Tyrell sat down and waited for his coffee and salt pork.

He mixed up some flour, sugar, and salt so that the mixture was thick enough that he could put a dollop on the end of a thick stick and roast it, like a sausage over a fire. It was an old method that, he'd been taught in his younger days. It worked like a charm and when it was done all one would do is pull it off the end of the stick. It didn't take long and a few minutes later, he was eating salt pork and flame roasted bread, washing it all down with a fresh coffee.

Waiting for the sun to lighten up enough so he could see he looked to where, he remembered Black Dog and the wolf had been the night before. There was no sign of either of them. He made sure that he kept enough pieces of the salt pork so that he could feed them to the dog and wolf later when he finally found them, or Black Dog made his way back. Not the dog, nor the wolf showed by time that he decided he had waited long enough, especially if he wanted to make his way back to the shack before dark

A short distance away in the deepest part of the small creek the feral child known to Caleb as Teeka, was bathing. It was the sound of horse hooves that caught her attention, she tilted her head to listen. As the sound grew closer, she grabbed her old torn clothing and darted out of sight. Crouching behind an overgrown mountain ash, she watched with intent as the man and his horse appeared.

They slowed to a stop and looked in her direction. Tyrell wasn't sure why he pulled Dutch to a stop but, there was something that for a brief moment either caught his eye or seemed oddly out of place. He removed his hat and wiped his brow. "Does anything seem strange to you Dutch? I have an odd feeling right now that something is amiss."

He looked downstream to both sides of the creek, but whatever he might have seen or thought he saw, wasn't there now. "Maybe it's that damn dog and his playmate. I don't know. C'mon Dutch, giddy up," he heeled the horse and once more they set off.

Teeka knew exactly where the man was heading and knew he would be gone for the better part of the day. It was the perfect opportunity for her to scavenge things that, she could use from where the man stayed. Slipping into the old grey sweater and woollen pants she got from Caleb a long time ago she made her way cautiously to Tyrell's shack.

She hid in the undergrowth for a few minutes watching the shack to make sure there was no one about. Then she crept up to the door and slipped in. There were cans of food scattered about and she opened the one with the picture of fruit on it. Her sense of smell brought her to the sack of dried meat next and she helped herself to a dozen pieces. Not far from the sack of meat was a sack of potatoes, grabbing one she bit into it, even raw they were delicious. She filled her pockets with them and continued her search. Finding a box of bullets that looked to be the same size as the half a dozen she had back at her new hiding spot, she grabbed those as well.

An odd looking package with a picture of what looked like burning sticks caught her attention next. She broke open the pack and smelled them. About to bite into one she noticed one of them was in a tin cup on the table, making her way closer, she picked it up. Looking close she realised that one end was ash. This seemed strange, she studied it for a while, and then as if by instinct she put one end between her lips. For the first time ever she tasted the acrid flavour of the unlit cheroot.

"Uck, bad stuff," she said in broken English as she tossed the cheroot back into the cup. Removing her clothes, she tried some of Tyrell's on but they all were too big. Dressing she made her way back to the canned food and selected a few. Retrieving the empty can that she finished she exited the shack. Walking over to the pool of water next that was a short distance away. The water was so smooth and clear her reflection looked back at her. She ran her fingers through the water and was surprised at how warm it felt. "Good, for clean." There was plenty of time before the man and his horse came back. She once more slipped out of her torn clothing and slipped into the warm water. It felt wonderful and she splashed and laughed. Her sounds of glee echoed in the calm and silent wood.

It brought her back to the time when she was with her family, before the terrible attack that left her father, mother, and sister dead when she was ten. She remembered her mother warming an old washtub over the fire and bathing her and her sister. The water that she was in now felt as good as that. The memories of her family had been lost in time. There was very little she remembered of them.

For the past seven years, she lived in caves and old abandoned trappers cabins, and was lost to the world. Now at age seventeen the life she lived was all she knew. She spoke only minimal English due to forgetting the language. It wasn't until she befriended Caleb did she ever have a need to speak and by then she could only remember a few words. She and Caleb had been friends since he and Marissa made Red Rock Canyon their home. When the men with all their noisy machines left she made Tyrell's shack her winter home. With him being there, she was afraid of what might happen as the days and nights of winter set in. She could always count on Caleb to sneak her into his room when it was blistering cold. They had done that many times and Marissa was none the wiser.

Feeling clean and fresh now, she climbed out of the warm water and sat on the grass letting the warm sun dry her tanned skin. She ate another potato as she sat there, her mind drifting. It was a beautiful day and she smiled. Dressing now that the sun and warm breeze had dried her, she stood and walked into the forest and the big tree that was her shelter. The wind uprooted it years ago and the roots and hole from where it once stood made for a perfect shelter. She wove cedar boughs through the roots to protect herself from rain and frost.

On the ground were old woollen blankets she packed with her when she left her dead kin all those years ago. There were a few other things as well, like her father's axe and hunting knife, and a flint that she used on occasion to light a fire. In one corner of the shelter was her father's .45 Winchester which, was more for protection then to kill things. She found the gun to be big and noisy. She knew how to use it though, in fact had it not been for her father's occupation as a trick shooter. They would not have been on their way to the Pacific where he was due for an appearance.

They hadn't been rich, but they never went without. Her father's show name was 'One Shot Jack.' Known as William Jack Sloan, indeed it was true, Bill, as he liked to be called was Tyrell's half- brother. Neither of the two knew anything about the other's existence and it would only be by fate that Tyrell would soon learn.

Back in 1889, one year before Tyrell first made his way to Red Rock Canyon, William J. Sloan, his wife Amelia and their two daughters Rachel and Raylene Sloan were on a two week journey from the eastern prairies to the Pacific Coast where 'One Shot Jack' was expected to make an appearance. Under other circumstances, Bill, probably would have turned down the offer, but there was some family business, he wanted to look into that was on the way. They crossed into the western Kootenay's through the Canadian Rockies, from there they continued south-westerly in the direction of Red Rock Canyon.

There was a property that he knew of that belonged to the Sloan's, and that for the past three years it remained unoccupied. He being the only heir or so he thought, decided the property might be worth looking into. It would be a surprise for them all. He owed that to his young family. They had been traveling with him seven months out of the year as 'One Shot Jack' made a name for himself and a decent fortune.

He hadn't said a word to anyone about the land. For now, he wanted that to be a secret. What he knew is that it was 300 acres large, big enough to raise livestock and a family. He made a decision week's earlier before their fateful journey that the show he was scheduled to appear in would be his last. When it was over he'd settle down in Red Rock and take up ranching, that was his dream, and he knew it was their dream too.

He may have been a crack shot but he wasn't fast enough to kill the five men that attacked them, and that is where the dream ended. The only survivor 'Teeka' as she was known, her real name for now lost in time, learned how to shoot from her father so she was no slouch when it came to shooting.

Most of the time she used a spear to hunt small game and fish. Those were her staples and she usually ate them raw or dried the meat. She picked the wild berries, asparagus, and the wild onions that grew as well, just like Marissa. She even raided Marissa's meat and vegetable cellar when she needed to, but most times when she was terribly hungry, Caleb always managed to bring her food. She was grateful for that. There were many times she went without food when the fishing wasn't as good as it should've been. Or when she was unable to find something small enough to kill with her spear, the blue grouse and wild turkeys were easy to kill but sometimes they were hard to find.

For the past seven years, she managed and she would continue to manage, sometimes though it certainly got lonely. Was this her destiny? Is this how she was supposed to live? She often wondered about that. The memories of her past were just that, memories, and as it were she had very few. She often dreamt about how her family died at the hands of five vicious and callous men that bush-wacked them and raped both her mother and sister as they shot bullets into her father. It happened so quickly that he had no time to reach his rifle. For one reason or another, they left her alone as she huddled underneath their wagon, crying and waiting for the same fate. She covered her ears so she could block out her mother's screams as the men had their way with her and her daughter both.

Finally, what seemed like hours the men lit torches and tossed them into the wagon, then simply mounted their horses and vanished, into the misty grey morning. It was then she climbed out from beneath the wagon, the horror, and carnage that was all around her made her weep and quiver. A realisation came over her that she needed to protect herself.

Grabbing the axe and hunting knife along with the .45 Winchester and four boxes of bullets she made haste to get away and vanished deep into the woods. It was her only refuge and her only means of survival. It wasn't until she stopped running did she realise how lost she really was. Not knowing which way to go, she aimlessly wandered from that day on. It was a tough life, made even tougher due to her circumstances, and tender young age at, which, she was thrown into that life.

From that experience, she gained the ability to fend for herself. It was either that or succumb to the elements, the memories palpitated her mind unrelentingly as she reminisced. "Is over now, no think about it," she softly cried as she curled up wrapping the woollen blankets around her quivering body, while tears of anguish and sadness stung her eyes.

The panting and playful growls that sounded an hour later are what she heard next. Slowly crawling out from her hiding place, Teeka, cautiously looked around. Not far away she saw that the man's dog and a wolf were playing. She was already acquainted with the dog. It curled up with her a few times already when the weather was cold. The wolf though, was new. She smiled and laughed quietly as the two of them frolicked. Teeka was not intimidated by the wolf or its presence. She had been around them before. People scared her more than the animals she learned to live with.

Tyrell was making his way to the horse pole outside Marissa's cabin. He only managed to slide off Dutch before Caleb came running over from his chicken coop. "Hey, mister, my chickens laid seven eggs last night."

"Seven! That is quite a haul, how have you been Caleb?" Tyrell asked as he knelt next to the boy and looked at the eggs he had in his hat.

"Pretty good mister, pretty good, Uncle Len brought me home yesterday. Can you keep a secret mister?"

"That depends on what kind of secret I reckon, is it a good one or a bad one?"

"Ma, would think it was bad one," Caleb looked shyly away.

"I can keep a secret."

"Are you sure mister?"

"I am, go ahead tell me."

"I shot Uncle Len's big rifle and hit two cans that still had beans in them."

"Two cans! That's pretty good. What makes you think your ma wouldn't like to hear that?"

"Cause she told me I can't shoot her Henry until I'm older, said she didn't want me to hurt myself. Would ma's Henry hurt me mister?"

"That big old rifle sure would, it would even knock me on my butt," Tyrell chuckled. "I reckon your ma's gun would knock a bruise in both our arms," he stood up. "C'mon let's go see your ma."

"Sorry mister I can't I've got chores to finish up. But can you take these to her please?"

Tyrell reached for the hat. "Sure will Caleb. You don't need any help do you?"

"Not yet, maybe when I check on the cows." Caleb said as he slipped into chicken coop.

Tyrell smiled and shook his head. Tethering Dutch, he gently knocked on the door. "Hello, I'm here again," he waited as Marissa opened the door.

"Hello Tyrell, what a pleasant surprise. I see Caleb gave you the eggs?"

"Yes ma'am," he handed her the hat and eggs. "He seems quite chipper about getting seven."

"Lately they haven't been producing much or the dang fox keeps getting to them. How have you been?" she asked as she made her way to the kitchen.

"Quite good actually, I got my stovepipe in place and built a bath of sorts," he sat down at the table and tossed his hat on the floor.

"A bath?" Marissa questioned.

"Yes ma'am. It took a day but well worth the effort. I didn't have the supplies I would have needed to make a steam bath, so, I dug a hole," he smelled his armpits to make sure he was still decently fresh. "You didn't notice my stench ain't as bad?"

Marissa blushed as she replied. "I did, I also noticed your clean shaved face. And I do admit you are ruggedly handsome, man."

"Thank you, you look nice as well, but then again you always do."

Marissa chuckled softly noting his tone. "Would you like some fresh eggs and coffee?"

"I would, thank you very much Marissa."

"Caleb will be wanting some anyhow, might as well make enough for the three of us."

"I hope I ain't intruding," Tyrell replied.

"Don't be silly. Caleb loves it when you are here and so do I, if I were to be honest."

Tyrell sighed and inhaled softly. "I ain't too far away, just up and yonder. That is where I belong for now." He didn't want to get into what she was implying not yet, it wasn't the place or the time.

"I know, but you belong here too," she responded as she brought him a coffee.

"No Marissa, this is your place. Mine is up on Hudu Creek." He was desperately trying to get her to move on in a different direction with the conversation, he simply didn't want to talk about that yet.

"Whatever you think," she said as she finally got the hint. She needed to keep reminding herself that when the time was right and things were settled Tyrell would be a lot more comfortable and willing to talk. "Have you started sluicing yet?" Marissa added as she changed the subject.

"I haven't even looked for the placer tags. I think I can remember where they were. If things go as I expect them to I should be working them soon," Tyrell took a drink from the cup in his hand. "That is good coffee Marissa, thank you."

"Wait until you taste these eggs, with the supplies I picked up they'll be extra good."

"They smell good already," he paused for a moment as he inhaled. "Should I give Caleb a call?"

"Yes, you could. Thank you."

Tyrell rose from the table and opened the door. "Caleb!" He yelled out. "Your ma has breakfast ready, come and get it boy." He waited a few seconds and was about to call out again when Caleb finally came running from the barn.

"I'm here mister. I was checking on one of the cows she's due to calf in a few days."

"Calf? How the heck do you know about cows calving?" Tyrell asked with surprise.

"Geez mister I've grown up around cows and stuff." Caleb rolled his eyes as he made the distance to the door and Tyrell.

"I realise that but heck I ain't even sure I know about that stuff."

"Haven't you ever saw a cow calving?" Caleb asked as he removed his boots.

"I have so. They get big and fat and their teats grow." Tyrell replied with some humour.

Caleb started to laugh. "You're funny mister. You said teats."

"That's what they are called."

"Like I said mister, I know, I've grown up with cows." Caleb said as he and Tyrell made their way to the table and plates of eggs set out for them. "That looks yummy. Doesn't it mister?"

"Damn right it does," Tyrell was about to dig in when he felt the burning eyes of Marissa and Caleb, realising then that he swore. "I mean, ah, it sure does look good, thank you very much Marissa," he was nodding in shame.

"That is better, no swearing especially around the table." Marissa scolded.

"I know. I'm sorry I did." Tyrell cut his eggs with his fork and brought a mouthful to his lips. He looked over to Caleb who was looking at him with a faded smile and he winked at him. Caleb chuckled quietly and went about eating his own eggs. The sounds of plates being scraped and chewing mouths filled the house as the three of them ate in silence.

Being the gentleman that he was, Tyrell cleared off the table when they finished and offered to bring Marissa a coffee. "Yes, please. Thank you Tyrell."

"No thanks needed, it should be me thanking you for the eggs." Tyrell brought two cups of coffee with him as he returned and he set one down for Marissa. "It's hot and I hope sweet enough. I ain't sure how much sugar you use so I added as much as I do my own," he said as he sat down.

"That is fine. I don't like it to sweet."

"You don't mind if I smoke do you?"

"No go ahead, like I told you before they're your lungs." She smiled at him as she took a drink. "You made my coffee just right."

"Well, I reckon that is something we have in common, how our coffees are mixed," he smiled as he inhaled a lung full of the putrid smoke. By now, Caleb was slipping on his boots again and heading back outside. Tyrell gestured with his chin. "That boy must keep you on your toes."

"You don't know the half of it," Marissa chuckled. "He's a busy body there is no doubt about that."

"He seems to know as much as most ranchers do in cattle rearing." Tyrell smiled.

"Most of what he and I know, we've learned on our own and of course, we rely upon my upbringing on my father's cattle ranch. He has always been a very quick learner though," she took another drink of coffee.

"You ain't done anything wrong in raising him as you have. I expect that'd be how I'd want my son to be raised if I had one." Both Marissa and Tyrell knew that Caleb was his, but neither one admitted it to the other. For now, that is how it would remain. In time that would change, the makings were already in the works.

"I have done my best with him. He has a lot of his father's traits," Marissa was looking at Tyrell with sincerity as she said that.

Tyrell scratched the back of his neck with nervous anxiety. "I reckon I should gather the things I've come for, got to get back to the shack," he rose from the table and donned his hat. "Is it all right if I borrow your wagon for a day?"

"Of course, how else are you going to get that stuff up there? In fact it is early enough that we could help."

Tyrell didn't know if that's what he wanted or not, Caleb had already been on the trail for a couple of days if this was only his first day back. "No need for that. I reckon Caleb is tired from his trip yesterday. I can manage."

"Are you sure?"

"Of course I'm sure. I'll bring the wagon back the day after tomorrow if that is okay? Maybe then if you want to come up to the shack, we can ride up on horses. It only takes a little more than an hour that way. I wouldn't mind showing Caleb how to use a sluice box or shaker box. It is something he might be interested in. It also gives me some time to shape up the place. Making it more inviting."

"That sounds good, we'll still help you load it up." Marissa said as she now rose from the table and slipped on her boots. Tyrell opened the door for her and they made their way to the tarp where his supplies were stowed. Surprisingly no animals had ripped or torn anything apart.

"That is good to see," he replied as he removed the tarp. "Everything is intact." It didn't take long to load up the supplies onto the wagon, and it was light enough that Dutch could pull it alone. "There, that's it, all loaded and ready to make tracks," he said as he untied Dutch and hooked him up to the wagon. "Not sure this horse has ever pulled a wagon not even sure he's going to like it," Tyrell chuckled, as he stepped up and grabbed the reins. "Thank you again for the eggs this morning and the use of your wagon, Marissa. I'll have it back to you in a day or two," he said as he looked down at her and Caleb.

"About that, I was thinking that Caleb and I will ride our horses up instead. We'll take the wagon home then. You have a lot of work to do up there and you'll be able to get it done a lot sooner this way." Marissa said as she stepped back from the wagon, Caleb in her clutches.

"Sure, that would be appreciated. I should have asked you that in the first place. Just remember to take the horse trail, it cuts about three maybe four hours off the travel time. I guess I'll see you two in a day or so. Thanks again, Marissa and thank you Caleb for all your help in loading the wagon."

"Okay mister, we'll see you in a couple of days." Caleb said as he and Marissa waved. Tyrell nodded at them and winked, then headed for home. Dutch didn't seem at all temperamental about pulling the wagon. He obeyed every "whoa" or "giddy up" command that Tyrell gave. It was a peaceful journey back to his shack and he was quite impressed with Dutch's behaviour.

"You ain't such a lame horse after all, Dutch. Either you've pulled a wagon before or you just couldn't care. I dunno which, but I appreciate your cooperation. You'll be getting a good feeding of oats tonight, ol' boy. You sure will." Tyrell said as the wagon creaked along. With sound of water getting closer, he knew they would soon be at Hudu Creek and then it was only a short distance to the shack.

They had been at it for close to three hours, and once they made the distance to the creek, he decided they'd rest. He could use a stretch, the hard wagon seat was unbearable most of the time, and it hurt his back and numbed his ass. He hated that about that wagon.

The seat needed some kind of bounce or give. Since it didn't, it was like sitting on a rock and being jerked this way and that. Finally, Hudu Creek came into view. Slowing Dutch down to a stop at the edge of the creek so he could drink and rest a bit, Tyrell stepped out. Stretching his back, he looked the wagon over making sure all the parts and pieces that made it work were intact. Satisfied, he checked on the load that was stacked, everything was there. He jimmied a few boxes around and retied the heaviest pieces. From what he remembered of the creek trip when Marissa and Caleb came up with him the last time, it was full of bumps and humps, ruts and rocks, and Marissa was tossed around to- and- fro. The last thing he wanted was to lose something and have to back track to find it.

Walking over to Dutch and the creek Tyrell leaned on him. "We're almost home. We ain't got that much further to go." Tyrell smiled, he loved where he was. Tossing his half-smoked cheroot into the creek, he splashed water on his face, rose, and stepped back into the wagon and with reins in his hands he gave them a flick. "Giddy-up Dutch, let's get a move on." The horse didn't neigh a sound as he followed Tyrell's command and the wagon slowly crept to a rolling start. As it entered the creek the wagon lurched and sunk a few inches into the soft clay, but it didn't discourage the horse as much as it startled he who was commanding it. "Whoa, whoa, easy Dutch, easy does it." Tyrell said as his face went blank and he nervously sat up.

It only lasted a few seconds but was as unexpected as getting stung on the end of his manhood by a bee. Noting now that all was well and that Dutch managed to keep the wagon on course, Tyrell smiled. "Well done Dutch, I thought I was going into the drink for sure. That was close, would have likely caused me a bit of hurt too with the water being as low as it is."

Other than a few bumps and grinds, the rest of the way went well. Still, there was relief on both their faces as they finally made the distance back to the shack. Pulling up close he slowed Dutch to a halt. "Whoa, right here is good." He said as Dutch slowed and then stopped. "Good boy, Dutch. Good boy." Climbing out of the wagon, he removed the harness from Dutch and tethered him in his usual spot. He stroked the horse's forehead and scratched him behind the ear. "I am beginning to get a whole new respect for you." It was true, he was. Turning on his heel, he walked up to the wagon and began untying that which was tied, some of the knots were so tight from the travel he couldn't loosen them so he simply cut the rope. "There are more ways than one to untie a rope." He quietly joked to himself as he removed the boxes and gear. He stacked the few planks and boards against the shack, new rope, and old rope he hung from the side. Oats and a few salt blocks he piled nearby, tools he leaned against the shack, next he moved all his food stuff inside and piled it on the table, floor, and countertop. *There, done for the year,* he thought as he looked around, something felt odd.

He noted the pack of opened cheroots and picked them up. He couldn't make heads or tails out of why the pack was opened or why it was tossed on the floor. *That's a little different ain't it,* he thought as looked the pack over. All eight cheroots were intact none were missing. *Huh, racoons or a squirrel must've been looking for a treat,* he assumed as he set the pack on the table. With all the wooden crates and boxes scattered throughout the shack it shrunk in size. Tyrell stroked his chin, *once I get things put in their place and boxes out of the way, it won't look so small.* Leaving it for now, he stepped back outside and whistled for Black Dog, letting him know that he was back. What he wanted then was to sit down on something a bit more comfortable than the old wagon seat.

Making his way to the fire pit, he sat down in his usual spot and stirred the ashes. He decided if he saw a few coals he'd get a flame going, and cook something up. Everything he could want or need was only a few paces away and he deserved a man-cooked meal of beans, salt pork, and biscuits. To his surprise a few orange coals glittered and glowed, heck even if there weren't any coals he would have started a fire so he could have a feast. Breaking up a few pieces of wood, he tossed them onto the coals. Next, he put together some biscuit mix and cut a large piece of salt pork off the salted pork quarter that was hanging, and he tossed that into the one frying pan he owned. The beans he'd cook straight in the can because he'd always liked them that way best. It was indeed, a meal made in heaven. As the sky grew dark bringing with it a cold wind. Tyrell tidied up a bit and went to bed. It had been a long day.

# Chapter 14

Next morning he was once more woken by the sound of the pesky crows. It seemed as though he had just fallen asleep and wasn't too impressed with their constant cawing. "Damn crows, shut the hell up!" he yelled from his bunk. Covering his head with a pillow, he dozed a few minutes longer but the crows were unrelenting. "Ah, to hell with it, guess I'll get up and maybe go shoot some crow," he slowly rose and dressed, and made his way over to the fire. He tossed a cold biscuit to the dog as he sat in contemplation, listening to the cawing of the crows. They were a nuisance and he hadn't shot his pistols in a while.

He tried to figure out what tree they were in. Finally, he saw one and then another, a smile crossed his face as he rose. *I see you now you little devils,* he thought as he walked a bit closer. Pulling out one of his .45 Colt Rangers, he began shooting them from the branches. The pistol felt good in his hand and the sound of the echo was music to his ears. Anything was better than the cawing of all the crows.

The wood now grew quiet and he watched with a smile as crows fell from the tree like pinecones. "There you go you bastards. How's that for a wakeup call?" The surviving crows flocked to another tree a distance away. There were so many they blocked out the rising sun as they made their way to safety.

"And stay the hell away or I'll shoot the rest of you, you damn noisy scavengers." Loading his pistol, he slapped it into its holster and made his way back to his to his usual spot at the fire. "Showed them didn't I," he said to Black Dog. "I reckon there are six dead crows that the maggots can eat off of now. Damn, they've been a nuisance," he scratched the dog behind the ear.

"Oh yeah, you're looking for some jerky, ain't ya? Sorry about that I got caught up in the moment," he made his way into the shack and grabbed a few pieces. It seemed odd that they had gone through so much, but he took into account that he did eat a lot of it when he first picked it up. Walking back to the fire he handed the dog his usual piece but the dog wanted more, he could tell by the way he looked at him. "Right I forgot your lady friend would probably like a piece too." He handed the dog another piece and like every other time the dog darted into the undergrowth and out of sight.

Looking at his pocket watch, he wound it up. It would be another hour before he got up the gumption to carry on with his plan to start building Dutch's corral. He ate a few of the cold biscuits he made the night before, finished two more cups of coffee and then finally gathered the tools he would need for the day's task.

Working straight for three hours he managed to dig only six of the twenty holes that he estimated he would need, for the corral he had planned. It was tough digging and because of the tree which he was building the corral around, roots were an issue too. The palms of his hands stung as some of the blisters he got from digging his bath broke opened and began to bleed again.

It wouldn't be long before the callous' took over the tender bleeding blisters. He rested for a few short minutes, his back resting against the big tree. Dutch stood there looking bored and unenthusiastic at what he was doing. "It won't be today, it might be tomorrow or it might be the day after, but this here is where your corral is going to be. You'll have shade from the tree in the summer and when it rains it'll keep you dry. No more tethering. You'll be free to prance about."

Tyrell looked around at the size not realising that without the posts in place and because he was sitting down it looked small. "Well maybe not prance but you'll be able to move around. It'll work until next year. I'll build you a shelter with a roof over there, closest to the shack. I think that be the best place. That is the plan old boy. Maybe you'll feel better once we move you in." He wanted to get as much done in two days as he could, before Marissa and Caleb arrived to take back the wagon. Working hard and steady, and only breaking after every fifth hole, before the sun even set that evening he managed to have all twenty holes dug for the posts. Looking at his work, he realised that the corral, was in fact a decent size. Removing the bandanna from around his head, he mopped up the sweat from his face and neck. He was surprised that he managed to get it done in one day. Putting up the rails would be the easy part, he already had the nails and poles.

"What do you figure Dutch, how does she look?" he asked the horse as he approached with the shovel over his shoulder. "I figure you and I could use a drink." Untying, Dutch he led him to the creek. Of course, Dutch never neighed, whispered, or even broke wind. "You're so dang quiet Dutch, don't you ever fart? Quit being so damn uptight," Tyrell joked with him as they made the distance to the creek.

Soaking his hands, he washed away the dirt and blood from the ruptured blisters that mapped out his palms and winced as he did so. *That always stings a bit, good to keep them clean though,* he reminded himself as he splashed water on his face and took a drink himself. Rising, he waited for Dutch to have his fill of the cool mountain water. It was while he waited that again for the second time in as many days something caught the corner of his eye. He looked in the direction and squinted as he shaded his eyes from the sun, *I know I saw something that time, but where the hell did it go, and what in the hell was it,* he thought as he looked on. Then, as though it were a mirage he saw what he thought to be the head of somebody bobbing up and down in the thick under bush 100 or so yards away.

Unable to discern what it was exactly that he was seeing, he slowly untied the hammer laces of his holstered .45s, so he could have quick access to the pistols. Finally, he saw it again. This time there were two heads bobbing closely together, he shook his own head as he sighed in relief, it was

Black Dog and his mate traipsing towards him through the tall golden grass. He waited for them to get closer. "I see you and your friend have been out prancing." Black Dog ran up to him but the wolf stayed behind and disappeared in the tall grass. "How are you doing Black Dog?" Tyrell reached down and pat him. "You startled me coming out of those bushes, thought you were some renegade," he chuckled.

Unknown to him, Teeka had been watching him for the better part of the day, even laughing when she heard him talking to himself or his horse. She was quite amused at the man's antics. What brought her so close were the sounds of gunfire, which she soon learned came from the man's shack, the six dead crows she found were self-explanatory.

When she found them, she thought it was quite funny. She wanted to learn more about the man. Staying hidden, she watched him for the better part of the day, like she did many times before. All the trappers, prospectors, and cattle range riders she watched over the years in her mind were vicious and evil. In fact, she thought that about all men with good reason. This man though was different.

When Tyrell thought he saw something he certainly did, it was her as she made her way back into the shadows. Out of sight now and with the man not looking so intently in her direction Teeka too, sighed. "Close be careful next time," she muttered in one breath as she continued her gaze of him. "Safe now he not see." The sound of her own voice speaking words startled her. It was something she hadn't done in a long time.

Having watched the man for days and hearing him on occasion talk to himself and the animals only made her long for her own voice and words she knew. A smile crossed her face. "Is because of him, I can talk too," Teeka started to laugh quietly. She couldn't believe that she was forming words and sentences. It had been years since she spoke with such clarity. Words were forming in her mind that she forgot how to pronounce or read. The more she thought about speaking the easier she was finding it, it was like a switch turned on. It confused her at first and perhaps scared her a little, but it felt good. "Today happy day," she said with moxy as she turned and made her way back to her shelter, a crow in each hand.

Tyrell looked over to Dutch who, for the past 20 minutes slurped water. "All right old boy, you got to be finished by now." But the horse didn't budge or even lift its face out of the creek. "Seriously, really, you need that much water. You ain't a camel, Dutch. C'mon let's get you back," he led the horse back to the tree and tethered him. "I'll bring you some oats shortly." Making his way around the shack he looked at the stack of posts that the Wake Up Jake left behind when they vacated.

He counted out 20 of the best and began carrying them to their perspective holes. An hour later he was finished and sitting down on his bench around the fire. Midget flames snapped and crackled as he added a few pieces of dry wood. *Wasn't such a bad day after all, and I ain't heard a crow caw,* he chuckled as he thought about that.

An hour later he was debating if he wanted a bath or wash some clothes it was warm and early enough for either or. He decided clean clothes were more important. Gathering all his dirty laundry, and adding to that the clothes he was wearing, except of course his undershorts, which he kept on, he even had his holster strapped around his waist. From an outsider looking in he probably would have looked awful funny, but he didn't care.

Who the heck was going to see him way out there? Finally wringing out the last pair of wool socks and setting them on the pile of clean laundry he rinsed his hands off and splashed water on his face. Without his boots or socks on he walked up to where the rock was that stopped the flow of water and removed it. He would let it bleed into the bath all night and right back into the creek. In the morning he'd block it off again, and by tomorrow evening, it would be ready for him to bathe himself. For the rest of the evening he stayed close to the fire. He felt vulnerable wearing only his undershorts and holster but, his clothes hadn't completely dried yet.

A pair of pants, a shirt, and socks hung on a few skinny sticks that he pushed into the ground near the fire, in hopes that they'd be dry before he turned in for the evening. His choice of beverage that night was tea, he usually never drank the stuff but, it was different for a change. He sat listening to the crickets and the odd squirrel chattering in the distance as he slurped from the cup in his hand. It wasn't long before nature called and his gut rumbled. Slipping into his boots, he walked over to the outhouse to take care of business.

He should have paid closer attention to the clothes hanging near the fire before he made his way there. It was his wool socks, that caught the first spark and they began to smoulder. It was the gentle breeze that made his smouldering socks ignite, and burn through the stick that they hung from, causing a whole chain of events to take place. Next, his shirt went up in flames and a flailing shirtsleeve ignited his pants. Totally unaware of these events taking place Tyrell took his time sitting in the outhouse. Black Dog on the other hand was watching the spectacle from a distance and was somewhat confused at the entire thing. There was nothing, he could do so he laid down, and continued to watch as Tyrell's clothes charred and turned to ash.

By now, Tyrell was making his way back and it wasn't until he sat down again that he realise what happened. "You got to be kidding me..." he said as he stood up and walked over to where his clothes were. He didn't know whether to laugh or be mad. He had never seen anything like that happen before. Tossing the charred remains into the fire, he was glad that they weren't a good set. Sighing in derision, he made his way back to the bench and sat down heavily. *Was having a good day until that happened,* he chuckled. *I guess that is pretty funny, stupid too.* Black Dog now lay next to him. "Couldn't you have at least pissed on them?" he scratched the dog behind the ear. "I reckon you watched that eh, probably laughing your fool head off. I have to admit it does seem funny. I'm down now to three sets of pants and four shirts, plus my buckskins and a couple three pairs of socks." He grew silent for a moment as he pondered the situation. "That's all right I've managed on less before." Pouring another tea, he shook his head and stared into the flames laughing in his own mind at the dumb fool luck he had. *Could have been worse I suppose, might have been my winter long johns...*

Finishing his tea, he retreated to his shack and sat at the table. He hadn't used the woodstove yet and being without any dry clothes, he thought it to be a good opportunity to test it out. Gathering some kindling and a few pieces of firewood, he struck a match and set the kindling a fire. Adding one piece of firewood, he returned to the table. He was impressed that the old woodstove was working as well as it was. Not even a puff of smoke escaped. Nor did it take long for the shack to warm up. In fact, it got so hot he opened the window.

Bored now he began putting his supplies away and kicking the empty boxes out the door. It got darker than usual early on that night due to the changing season of course, and he lit his lantern so he could see while he stowed things. It took him an hour to get things in perspective and by then he was feeling tired, the shack sure looked good though. Removing his boots and holster, he curled up on his bunk and within minutes, he was sleeping.

# Chapter 15

His itching face and head woke him the next morning. He had forgotten to close the window the night before, and the mosquitoes and every other bloodsucking insect fed on him as he slept. He felt his face as he scratched it. There were lumps and bumps and he could barely see out of his left eye, it was practically swollen shut. *The critters sure feasted on me, should have closed the window. Damn,* he thought as he rose from his bunk. He walked over to the window to close it, and in the process, he stubbed his toe on the table due to his lack of vision. "Goddamn it!" he howled as he began hopping in pain.

He knew it was going to be one of those days. Sitting now, he looked at the toe he stubbed. It was turning purple. He shook his head as he limped to the window and closed it. *Stupid me, I bought screen for that window should have had it in place by now,* he thought. A more pressing task though was finishing Dutch's corral. The horse couldn't be trusted to roam freely he had a tendency to vanish.

Making his way to the clothes hanging on a rope near the shack entrance, he grabbed a set and dressed, then slipped into his boots. It hurt his toe a bit but he was able to wiggle it inside. Exiting into the early morning, he fetched water for coffee. He stirred the coals looking for any shimmer of life, but the heavy dew from the night before put the fire completely out. Using pieces from one of the wooden boxes he tossed out the night before, he struck a match and lit the tinder dry wood. It didn't take long for the flames to grow and for his coffee to start perking.

He followed the fill trench up to where the rock was and rolled it into place. By day's end he'd be able to have another bath, and hopefully the insect bites, that covered his face and head would quit being so damn itchy. For now, he would live with it. They weren't bad, if he didn't scratch them. Throwing another piece of wood onto the fire, he looked around in self contemplation. There was little doubt that fall was fast approaching. Poplar and birch tree leafs were falling from the clutches of the branches that birthed them. All the foliage that was once was full of life was now turning shades of red, purple, gold, and brown. Even the days were getting shorter. He sighed as he sat back down, Black Dog was nowhere in sight, it didn't surprise him much. Lately the dog had taken on a whole new outlook on life.

Finishing his coffee, he made his way over to Dutch's unfinished corral. The horse for the first time that he could remember greeted him as he approached with a couple of loud neighs. "Good morning, Dutch." Walking over to the horse, he patted him, "I reckon that is the first time you've said two neighs to me. That made my day."

Dutch bobbed his head up and down as he scratched him behind the ear. He was determined to get Dutch into the corral by day's end. Most of the rails were cut down already, enough to at least to get started. Turning he went to the first post and began filling the hole, and tamping it with a heavy pole. He finally rested, after the tenth post was in place he was half way done.

According to his watch, he had been hard at it for close to 2.5 hours. Although his hands were in agony from tamping and his palms bled, he felt good. Three hours later, he was admiring his work. Every post was planted into the ground and in a decently straight line. He was quite impressed with himself. "Turned out to be a better day than I thought it was going to be," he muttered to himself as he sat down in the shade. "There you have it Dutch, I'll get the rails up shortly. Once I figure out where to put the gate, you'll be able to move in. No more tethering." He was hoping for some kind of response, but Dutch really didn't have anything to say. "Speechless eh, that's all right no need to thank me."

By early evening, he was nailing up the last rail. He managed to go three rails high but really wanted to go four. *That'll do for now*, he thought as he made his way to where the gate was, and finished putting it in place. It was a bit of a struggle but finally there it was, Dutch's corral complete with gate. He was elated as he looked at it and he smiled, "hey, Dutch, got anything to say now," he made his way over to him and untied him from the tree setting him loose in the corral. "Go on, go have a walk about." Tyrell made his way over to the gate and exited.

Dutch neighed, and jumped, and began running to-and-fro, back and forth, up and down. Tyrell chuckled. "That a boy Dutch. Feels good to be able to move around a bit don't it?" For over 30 minutes that is all the horse did, and for 30 minutes he watched and encouraged him. It was obvious that Dutch approved of his new corral, there was no doubt about it. The horse made its way over to where Tyrell was leaning on the railings.

"Got that restlessness out of your system now?" he reached out and rubbed his knuckles up and down the horse's face. "I reckon I'll get you some oats. I think you deserve them." Stepping away he gathered a bucket of oats and set them down inside. "There you go Dutch, enjoy your oats. I'll be back and check on you later."

Walking over to the creek, he washed his blistered hands and splashed water on his face. "That's better," he said to himself as he made his way back to his shack and sat outside by the fire. It was too late for a bath he decided. All he wanted to do was rest his aching back. He went hard today and he was feeling the effects. Stirring the coals of the fire, he threw a couple of sticks in. If he wasn't going to do anything else, he wanted coffee.

Running his hand across his face, he noted that the insect bites weren't as pronounced as they were that morning. Even the swelling under his left eye seemed to be going down. He attributed this to the hot sun that baked his skin, and the sweat that boiled from his pores, as he built the corral. As the evening began to cool, he sat comfortably with a coffee in hand, and watched the low flames from the fire cast shadows.

He reminisced about why he was there. The most important reason of course were Marissa and Caleb. The other being the fact that there was a $5000.00 bounty offered for the shooter that ended lives of two dirt bags. Tyrell was that shooter. His name wasn't on the poster nor was there a very good picture. The man on the poster didn't look at all like Tyrell, thanks to Emma.

The only people that knew were the dirt bag and his friend, both pushing up daisies and of course Emma. He never did catch her last name but he would never forget her smile. Thinking back on how it all took place, Tyrell shook his head, it had been six years, and he still felt badly about the incident. It was around that time that Black Dog strolled home. Tyrell heard him panting as he grew close. "Hello there Black Dog. I was beginning to think that you forgot where home was," he turned and looked at him. "Looks like you've had a good romp, panting like crazy and covered in mud I see."

Black dog wagged his tail and whimpered as he lapped at Tyrell's face. "Almost seems as though you missed me?" he teased, as the dog licked his face. "All right, all right that's enough, have a lay down. C'mon Black Dog, sit." Sitting now Black Dog put his paw on his lap and wagged his tail. "I see. Jerky eh, all right, c'mon, let's get some."

They made their way to the shack and stepped inside. "Next month when Marissa does some butchering, I think we ought to buy a side of beef from her. You and I go through this stuff like cows in an oat field," he chuckled as he grabbed a few pieces of the jerked meat, and handed the dog two pieces. Black Dog turned and darted outside. "Just like I figured, gone," he watched Black Dog disappear into the evening.

Tyrell followed behind and sat at the fire. He brought with him a cheroot and he puffed on it. His life had come full circle. He made new friends and killed a few foes, broke a few hearts and had his broken. The only thing he was missing was a place where he could settle down once and for all. Even now as he sat there, he wasn't sure he'd stay. His heart and mind wanted him to but, his soul still wanted to wander. It was getting old just like himself, but even he had a lot of life left. The thing was, so did his soul.

Looking around, he nodded, this was where he, belonged. This was where he could fade into anonymity. It is what he wanted, he could learn to live with the turmoil and memories of his past, he knew in his heart, that Caleb was his redemption and Marissa his savior.

Although it was getting late, he felt less tired than he did the previous night. It was quite surprising actually considering the work he did. But, he was both excited and anxious at the visit he was expecting the next day. He didn't know what time Marissa and Caleb were going to show up, all he knew is that they were. Two days had come and gone since he gathered his supplies and borrowed her wagon and she was due to come and get it.

It gave him extra time to get ahead of the game, and he was certainly ahead. The corral was finished, his supplies were stowed away, and the shack itself felt good at night with the added comfort of an operational woodstove. If he brought the wagon back like they first discussed, he would have been behind by a day.

Next, he'd pitter-patter and slap mud in the gaps of the shack walls, but that wouldn't be until after their visit. He could fix the door in the morning before Marissa and Caleb arrived. He'd tack the screen in too. He wouldn't want Marissa or Caleb to be insect bait in case they spent the night, which he hoped they would. It was warm enough still that his bedroll would keep him warm enough outside by the fire. Sleeping arrangements wouldn't be a problem.

For one reason or another he looked toward the wagon and then back to the fire and then back and forth again. He stroked his chin and chuckled. While building the corral he didn't take into account where the wagon sat, and now it was blocked off by Dutch's corral. He stood up and scratched his head, he couldn't believe that he managed such fumble. There was no way it could go around without a lot more work than it was to knock off a set of rails. *Huh, that is something,* he thought as he gave in to the inevitable at sat back down. He couldn't see with both his eyes when he built it, and he used that excuse as a contributor on how he managed such a blunder.

Truth was, he simply 'was not' paying attention. *That is damn funny.* He shook his head, *ain't nothing like a good joke to end a man's day,* he tossed what was left of his cheroot into the fire. His last swallow of coffee filled his mouth with coffee grounds, and he spat. "Shit! The jokes keep coming, damn that was awful." He dumped what was left of the coffee into the fire and it hissed and filled his lungs with wood smoke. Coughing, he set the coffee pot down, turned, and made his way to his shack. That was enough for one night.

# Chapter 16

Early the next morning he removed the shack door. Using the lumber he picked up he tried fixing it so it would close tight. Winters could be brutal, the last thing he wanted was to be letting all the heat from the woodstove during a January snowstorm escape through the less than adequate door. Or for that matter the gaps in the logs of his shack. Those, for now were not an issue and would be a simple fix. The door however, was a different story and Tyrell was wrestling with the repair.

*Goddamn it! Should have built you from scratch,* he thought as he looked at the sliver beneath his nail, he kicked the inanimate door in a burst of defeat. "If it ain't one thing it is another!" he cussed. Lucky for him enough of the sliver was protruding, using his teeth he latched onto it, and in one quick tug and yank, the wooden splinter pulled out, from beneath his bleeding nail. Spitting it out, he shook his finger in pain and misery. Picking the door up, he knocked off all the new pieces and carried it over to a small tree where he leaned it up. Then walking a distance away as if to add insult to injury he drew his .45 and filled it with lead.

Splinters of wood flew this way and that, as slugs of lead tore through it, pummelling the ground behind, uprooting and tearing into small shrubs and leaving .45 slug craters in the dirt, and trees where the bullets finally rested. He was not impressed at how slow his draw was, but he did manage to get six shots off before it fell to the ground. Now it lay in a pile of rubble cut in half with pieces missing.

A short distance away and already watching him was Teeka, she was startled when the shots rang out. Up until that point of the day's events, she was quite amused with his antics. Again though, he seemed to have wasted bullets on something this time that he was obviously going to burn. It was strange behaviour as far as she was concerned. "First crows, now door," she said quietly to only hear her own voice. "Man wrong with him." She shook her head as she rose from behind the old log that she had taken refuge behind when Tyrell began shooting, and once more looked in his direction. He was standing with his arms crossed and looking in the direction of the shack and missing door.

Taking a couple of measurements with a stick and piece of rope he set about building a door from scratch that would fit snugly in the already semi framed opening. Not much of a builder of any sort, it took him an hour to do all the measurements and wood sawing. After piecing it together and nailing it solid, he stood it up and carried it over to the opening. It was a little shy of fitting perfectly but it was better than the previous door, and he nailed the hinges in place.

Opening and closing it a few times, he used his knife to shave some of the wood until it finally closed to his liking. "There, much better," he said as he retrieved a set of clean clothes from inside and made his way over to the bath. Slipping out of his three-day old dirty and sweat emanating shirt and pants he climbed into the warm water. It felt good and he dunked his head a few times. He scrubbed, and shaved and for a few minutes soaked. *Probably the best idea I've had,* he thought referring to the bath. Cleaned and refreshed he climbed out and patted himself dry with the dirty shirt. Then walked butt naked up to the fill trench and rolled the rock aside.

By the time he made his way back to his clean clothes water was already cycling through his bath and draining, he decided to let the water flow freely. Dressing, he walked over to Dutch's corral and checked on him. "How are you today?" he questioned the horse as he rested his foot on the bottom rail. "I guess you have clued in to the issue I have with this corral being here. Or should I say with that wagon being there," he gestured toward it. Dutch shook his head from side to side and neighed. "Are you shaking your head at me for being blind to the fact that wagon was there when I put this together? If you are, go ahead and laugh, I know I did. You know what that means don't you? Means I got to knock down this set of rails and that set of rails, just to get the damn wagon."

Dutch strolled over and bobbed his head. Tyrell reached over and pat him on the nose. "That's all right. It won't take but a few minutes and once we get her out you can have your space again. I'll get started in a few minutes. No rush today. Today is lay back day." He looked at the shack and clean new door, *almost looks like I knew what I was doing,* he thought.

As usual, Black Dog was out and about gallivanting with his playmate, and he sat alone around the fire puffing on a cheroot. He really wasn't alone though, because Teeka was near. She was not even a stone throw away as a matter-of-fact. She was slowly crawling through the grass towards the protection of the forest. She snuck close when she saw Tyrell going in the direction of the bath. She watched him with some apprehension and embarrassment as he scrubbed and cleaned himself.

Hiding once more in the undergrowth she looked back to where Tyrell sat. His back was toward her but she could see him, and if she listened from that distance, she could faintly make out his words when he spoke them. "I stay now here," she made herself comfortable and stayed out of sight. Black Dog and the wolf found her with her back against a tree, sitting there whittling a piece of wood. Teeka smiled as the dog approached and lay at her side. The wolf on the other hand kept a safe distance. Teeka reached out her arm for the wolf to smell her if it wanted to but it remained cautious and indifferent. Shrugging her shoulders, she went back to carving as both the dog and wolf napped.

It wasn't long before the man stood up and vanished over a knoll. Teeka rose then and climbed the tree she was sitting under. She could see him now and she watched as he began tearing down the corral. It was confusing to her, why would he do that? What was the purpose? She climbed a little higher and looked on, it was then she noticed why, and she laughed to herself. "I saw why now," she twirled her finger in a crazy gesture. The more she watched the man the safer she felt with him being so close. He was a nice man not like the bad ones she thought all men were like. A little aloof perhaps but otherwise civil, she didn't know who he was or why he was there. He was friends with Caleb and his mother that much she knew. She shrugged having seeing enough for the day. Climbing out of the tree, she glanced back one more time and then vanished into the forest.

Tyrell was hitching Dutch up to the wagon when Black Dog and the wolf appeared from nowhere. "Hey, Black Dog, are you here to laugh at my blunder too?" he joked as he finished hitching Dutch to the wagon.

"As soon as I get this wagon over and beyond the corral and get the rails back up, if you're still about I got leftovers for you. Plus I found those pig ear things I bought at the mercantile," he jumped up into the wagon and snapped the reins. Black Dog tilted his head and followed close behind as the wagon creaked beyond the corral. He heard the word 'leftovers' which meant an assortment of this and that's. He was excited and the wolf took that as key to get excited as well. In a burst of energy, she ran up to Black Dog and tackled him, and then ran in circles.

Black Dog responded the same way and the two of them as per usual vanished in the tall grass. Tyrell watched the spectacle and he chuckled. "If that ain't love, Dutch, I don't know what is," he said as he removed the harness from him and led him back to the tree. "Okay, this will be the last time you'll ever be tethered around here. I promise. It'll only be for a few minutes whilst I get the rails back up." Dutch didn't seem to mind and he snorted and neighed. "That's right, just a few minutes." Tyrell assured him as he hammered the rails back in place. A couple minutes later Dutch was once more dancing and prancing in his corral.

It wasn't long after that he heard the clip-clop of horse hooves. He stood up and walked into view. Sure enough, it was Marissa and Caleb. Tyrell smiled as he greeted them. "Hello there. How was the ride?" he asked as they pulled their horses to a halt.

"It was fun." Caleb was the first to say as he climbed off the horse like a pro.

"It wasn't so bad at all," Marissa added as Tyrell helped her off.

"Good to hear. It is a lot quicker, that route is."

"Wow, mister you sure have done a lot." Caleb said as he looked around. "What is this little creek for?" he asked as he pointed to the stream that bled back into the creek.

"That's the bath drain." Tyrell tried to explain as best he could.

"The what?" Marissa asked with a look of confusion on her face.

"C'mon, I'll show you. It is the easiest way to explain it." They followed him as he walked up to the bath pool. He pointed at the stream of water filling the pool. "That one is to fill it and that one," he started as he pointed to it next. "Lets the dirty stagnant water out when the water level gets to a certain height. Pretty neat eh?"

"That is pretty smart mister. Can I play in there?"

"You sure can if you want. But first I have to show you how to stop it from filling. Come on, another little walk."

"Lead the way." Marissa said as her and Caleb walked alongside him. "You've been busy that is for sure. Dutch seems quite happy."

"Hard to say what that horse feels but yeah, I'd say he's happy enough. He doesn't have to be tethered anymore and has a bit of freedom. Here we are," Tyrell said as he pointed to the rock. "We roll this into here and the water slows and finally stops. No more water streaming into the bath. The sun warms the water during the day and a warm pool of water awaits. Keeping clean this winter is going to be a different story though. I seemed to have forgotten to buy a wash tub."

"You didn't?" Marissa asked with a smirk. "Are you serious? How could you forget a wash tub?"

"I ain't sure how I managed that." The three of them began to chuckle as they walked back. "I thought there might be one around here somewhere. I just ain't looked yet. Could be there is. Jake and his team left a few odds and ends around, most of it will come in handy at one time or another."

"If you don't find one lying around here, I'm sure I have an extra one. You're welcome to it Tyrell."

"If need be sure, thank you very much."

"You're welcome. So tell me what else have you been up to?"

"Fixed the shack door, umm, the stovepipe is in but you already knew that. The stove works well too by the way. I used it the other night as a matter of fact. I'm slowly getting things up to par. What's new with you?" he asked as the three of them ambled on.

"Not much really. I haven't been as nearly productive as you. We do have butchering coming up in a few weeks and then I have to go through my books and calculate where I made money and where I didn't. It is a pretty blah time of year. I'm glad you are close, though."

Tyrell nodded. "Yeah, I feel that way too. I mean... I'm glad to be close to you and Caleb."

"I knew what you meant." Marissa smiled and took him by his arm. "Can I convince you to help with the butchering?"

"You don't need to convince me. If there is any man work or work in general that needs doing all you have to do Marissa is ask me. There ain't nothing two fair men like Caleb and me can't do. Ain't that right Caleb?" Tyrell questioned as he reached over and scuffled Caleb's hair.

"I'll work with you mister, I sure will."

"Good, I'm glad. I wouldn't want to work with any other man in these parts than you," Tyrell smiled. Finally, they were standing next to the shack and he demonstrated how well the door opened and closed. "It is better than the old one eh?" he gloated with a smile.

"I am truly impressed with all that you have done around here. Will I get a chance to use your bath Tyrell?" she teased when Caleb was out of earshot, "and would you join me?"

Tyrell's jaw dropped. There was nothing wrong with being straightforward but it shocked him just the same. He nervously scratched his face. "I reckon I certainly would if the moment arose," he grew flush as he said that.

Marissa chuckled at his innocent embarrassment. "No worries, Tyrell, I was a little embarrassed when I said that. I don't know where it came from, honestly," she flirted.

"I reckon we should have a coffee. What do you say?" he asked as he changed the subject.

"Yes, coffee sounds wonderful." Again, she took him by his arm as they ambled over to the fire.

Caleb was already seated and poking at the coals. "There is something really strange in those coals mister. It's all gooey."

Tyrell began to chuckle. "Those my friend use to be clothes, I was trying to dry them after I washed them. I wasn't paying much attention I suppose and a spark from the fire turned them into ash and that goo you're playing with." Both Caleb and Marissa were looking at him like, he was telling some kind of joke. "Really, that is what happened," he assured them.

Marissa shook her head and started to laugh. "I think you might need adult supervision, Tyrell."

Caleb sat there shaking his own head. "Yep, mister I think ma is right. You sure do some silly things."

"In my defence if you must know, I was in the outhouse when it all took place." The story seemed even funnier when he said that. This time all three of them began to laugh. "I guess it is pretty funny," Tyrell responded as he sat next to Caleb. "I was glad it weren't my long johns or wool pants. Then it might not have been so funny."

"Where is your dog, mister?" Caleb asked since he hadn't seen him yet.

"He's around, I guess I should tell ya's, that he has found a new friend, a rogue female wolf, least I think it is female. The way they play and frolic."

"A wolf?" Marissa questioned.

"Yep, I reckon it's a rogue, it has been playing with the dog for the past while."

"Wow, does that mean they'll have puppies?" Caleb asked with enthusiasm.

"Depending on how he treats her I suppose that might be the case."

"Aren't you afraid?" Marissa asked with concern.

Tyrell shook his head, "afraid of what exactly?"

"That a wolf is running around here and playing with your dog," she responded.

"Not really, it doesn't concern me one way or the other. The wolf hasn't showed me no aggression nor has it been bothering Dutch. I reckon Black Dog laid out some rules for her. I dunno I just know the dog comes and goes now more often than before. I can't get away with giving him only one piece of jerky, now he wants two and shares them with the wolf." Tyrell answered.

"If they have puppies, can I have one?"

"That I reckon will be up to your ma."

"Can I Ma, can I have one of Black Dogs puppies if they have some?"

"I don't know Caleb, a half wolf dog might be a problem for your chickens."

"I'll train him Ma, he won't touch Captain Black's hens. I'll make sure of that. So, can I Ma?"

"I'll see, Caleb. I'll have to think about it."

"All right," Caleb said as he stood and stirred the coals some more. "It would sure be nice to have a dog..." he mumbled.

Marissa and Tyrell looked at one another and smiled. "If your ma won't allow you to have one Caleb I'll keep one up here for you. How would that be?"

"I suppose, but I'd rather have him down at the farm with me, though."

"I know you would, but your ma might be right about the chickens."

"Black Dog doesn't hurt my chickens." Caleb replied.

"I know. Still that's just the way he is. His pups might be different."

"If you say so mister, I won't bug no more. Can I go swimming now?"

"Sure ya can, we can keep our eye on you from here. Ain't that right Marissa?"

"By all means Caleb, I just might join you later."

"Okay," he said as he darted over to Tyrell's bath pool.

"Quite the rambunctious fellow, ain't he?"

"He sure is, and the older he gets the more rambunctious he becomes." Marissa answered with a smile. The two of them conversed for a few minutes before Caleb started to yell.

"Hey Ma and mister, the dog is here!" he yelled from the bath pool. Lying down a short distance from Caleb as well was the wolf. Panting from all the running it and the dog did.

"Caleb, be careful! The wolf is close by." Marissa and Tyrell rose and walked over to him. "I hope that wolf isn't going to hurt him."

"I wouldn't worry about that Marissa. Black Dog is lying beside him. He wouldn't let anything happen to Caleb. Besides I'd drop it in its tracks if it decided to do something." Making the distance to Caleb, Black Dog ran to their sides and playfully hopped to-and-fro. "Easy there Black Dog, be nice, no jumping up on our guests," Tyrell scolded as the dog sat and wagged its tail. The wolf remained where it was and watched closely. It knew that if the people were Black Dog's friends then she didn't have to be afraid. It laid there like it was part of the family, without a care in the world. "Pretty docile I reckon."

"I have never been this close to a wolf. It is beautiful. I love her blue eyes. Is that strange for a wolf to have blue eyes?" she asked.

"I wouldn't know, ain't never been this close either, mostly because I never wanted to be. I reckon though, their eyes can be any colour, I dunno." Tyrell shrugged as the three of them looked on at the wolf not 20 feet away.

"It is pretty friendly I think mister." Caleb began to chuckle as the wolf rolled in the grass then stood and shook itself off and darted out of sight.

"I reckon we won't be seeing it again today. Maybe later but not while it is light out, it seems to like being around in the early morning and evening before dusk. The reason for that I speculate is because that is when Black Dog trots home and wants his beef jerky. That reminds me," he looked down at Black Dog who was looking up to him. "I forgot to give you the leftovers and pig ears. Sorry about that Black Dog, we'll get to it soon," Tyrell, said as he pet him.

"Are you all done now Caleb? We should get you out and dried off."

"All right, I was just starting to have fun." Caleb said with disappointment, but he knew with the wolf being around his ma was just looking out for him.

Tyrell reached down and helped Caleb out. "What did you think of that little man?" Tyrell asked referring to the bath.

"It was fun, even the water was warm. It is almost over my head too. But I know how to swim mister. Ma says I'm a good swimmer. Do you swim mister?" Caleb asked.

Tyrell never swam a day in his life, if he ever needed to, he might figure it out. He wasn't afraid of water by any means but if it was over his head, he avoided it. "Well," he scratched his head. "I ain't sure if I know how. So, nope, I don't swim."

"I've been swimming since I was three. I was scared at first too, mister, so don't worry. Maybe when you get older you'll know how."

"Older? I ain't very young now, Caleb."

"But you have a lot of growing up to do, least that's what ma says," he said innocently.

"Caleb!" Marissa scolded with embarrassment as a surprised look crossed her face.

"That's okay Marissa. I'd rather have a lot of growing up to do, then none at all. Once you stop growing up there ain't nothing else left and likely you're pushing up daisies, isn't that right Caleb?" Tyrell chuckled as he looked over to Marissa and winked. He knew she was probably right he did have some growing up to do.

"What do you mean pushing up daisies, mister?" Caleb wanted to know.

"Just a term some use when we go to heaven I suppose."

"Then I'm never growing up. I want to live for a thousand years, so I can grow up for a very long time." Caleb said as he now put it in high gear and darted back to the fire pit.

"I'm so sorry about that Tyrell I don't know where he heard that," she fibbed, she knew exactly where. It was Len though that said it and Marissa only agreed, so that she could change the subject. It really wasn't any of Len's business. Caleb must have over heard them.

"Ah, no worries, I already told ya, I have a lot of growing up to do." Smiling, he took her by the arm this time and the two of them walked back to where Caleb sat.

"Hey mister is that the old door?" he asked as he pointed toward the pile of debris. Caleb was certainly inquisitive. He never missed a thing.

"It is, as a matter of fact," Tyrell, answered.

"Why is it all busted up?"

Tyrell was feeling a little ashamed about the reason. "Was just practicing with my gun is all."

Caleb looked shocked. "Your gun did that!"

"Yep, it sure did."

"Wow. I haven't seen that before. You're a pretty good shot I think."

Tyrell chuckled. "I was pretty close to it when I shot at it."

"Boy, you shot it to pieces didn't you?" Caleb questioned with a little bit too much enthusiasm.

"Never mind Caleb, it ain't nothing for you to concern yourself with." Tyrell responded, trying to avert Caleb's interest. That last thing he wanted was for Caleb to want to shoot a gun more than he did already. Marissa, he knew wouldn't be impressed with that.

"When I get older will you teach me how to shoot?"

"Caleb!" Marissa started, "don't be asking Tyrell that, you aren't even close to being old enough to talk about guns, let alone shoot them."

Tyrell interjected. "Now settle down Marissa, the boy only asked a question. There ain't nothing wrong with a man wanting to learn how to shoot," he looked over to Caleb. "Caleb, when your ma decides you are old enough to shoot, I'd be more than happy to learn you how. You got to promise me that until then you listen to what she tells you. If she don't think you should be talking about guns and shooting then let it be. All right?" Tyrell nodded.

"As long as when I am old enough you'll teach me. Do you promise mister?"

Tyrell looked over to Marissa for her approval. She was looking back at him a little cross, but she gave him the facial expression that said, 'that would be fine'.

"I promise," Tyrell winked at him. Caleb stopped asking and talking about guns at that moment and turned his attention once more to the small flames of the fire.

"Damn. I forgot about Black Dog's leftovers. Caleb, do you want to tag along with me while I gather them."

"Sure."

"Good, c'mon then," Tyrell said as he rose. "We'll be right back Marissa." She watched as the two of them chatted and gathered the leftovers and pig ears. They were quite a pair the two of them. Their resemblance to one another was unmistakeable unless a person was blind. Caleb certainly was his father's son. A smile crossed her face and she wondered if her, and Tyrell, would ever make that clear to Caleb. He did deserve to know and Tyrell did deserve to be a part of his life. Marissa was beginning to doubt that their relationship, hers and Tyrell's, would amount to anything more than what it was now. Tyrell as far as she was concerned seemed to be avoiding that issue as much as possible, without reason.

There were reasons however. Tyrell felt guilty for the way he left. He felt guilty for the life of lies he lived afterwards, the men he killed and not just the ones Emma knew about there were others. As long as he battled the demons of his past, married life as far as he was concerned could jeopardise the lives of the ones he loved.

This may have only been an excuse but it did have a ring of truth to it. People were looking for him. None of which he knew would ever beat his draw, but the fear of ambush and surprise attacks was enough reason to be apprehensive. If the law ever discovered that it was, he who killed Heath Roy, and his dimwit friend Ollie, chances were he'd be hung or shot dead. That is why he wished that he faced the law after the shooting and given the chance to plead his case. Instead, he chose to run and he had been running ever since. Marissa knew nothing about that. If she did perhaps, she wouldn't feel so slighted, and would then have understood Tyrell's apprehension.

It took Tyrell and Caleb a few short minutes to round up the dog treats and to make it back to the fire. "Look Ma," Caleb said as he showed her the ears teasing her.

"Yuk, get those away from me," she joked back.

"They're only ears, Ma, they won't hurt you, or even hear you scream. That's what mister told me," he laughed. "Black Dog!" he yelled out, while Tyrell whistled. "Where do you think he is mister?"

"Give him a minute and maybe give him another shout."

"Black Dog, come on boy, we got leftovers for you." Caleb shouted out again. It only took another minute or so and there he was, wagging his tail and waiting for his feast.

"See, told ya he'd show, always does when food is involved." Tyrell set the bowl down and Caleb tossed him the ears. The dog didn't even pay attention to what was in the bowl, instead he snapped up both of the pig ears and headed into the forest.

"Where do you suppose he's going to now, mister? He didn't even eat the leftovers."

"I reckon he's delivering one of them ears to his friend. He'll be back for the leftovers." Tyrell sat down next to Marissa. "Can I pour you another coffee?" he asked.

"Thank you Tyrell, yes," she handed him her cup. "Do you still need winter feed for Dutch?" she asked as he handed her coffee back.

"I do, maybe next week I'll head to Waxley's, see if he has any."

"We probably have enough that we could share." Marissa mentioned.

"If it turns out that way I'll pay fair price. I don't want no handouts. Before that happens though I'd like to make sure Waxley ain't got any."

"What is the point in that? I know we have enough and you can buy it if you like."

"Well, if you reckon you have enough, I'll buy it as I need it. I only got one horse to feed."

"Sure we can do it that way if you like. I'll give you the first ten bales for helping us butcher."

Tyrell raised his hand. "I don't want any sort of payment from you Marissa for anything I might do for you."

"You are so stubborn. I'm only trying to help."

"I realise that and I appreciate the thought," Tyrell took a swig from his coffee. "I'd even like to start buying eggs from Caleb, how much do you want for a dozen eggs Caleb?"

Caleb's eyes grew big. "Really mister, you want to buy eggs from me?"

"They're the best eggs I ever tasted. Of course I do?"

"How about five cents a dozen, how does that sound mister?" Caleb was excited. No one bought eggs from him before.

"Five cents a dozen, I'd never turn down a deal like that." Tyrell reached out his hand and shook Caleb's.

"Wow, Ma did you hear that?"

"I sure did. You drive a hard bargain."

"How long does it take you to save up a dozen eggs?" Tyrell asked of Caleb.

"Two days, give or take," Caleb responded.

"What is the date today?" he questioned. He had an idea but wanted to be sure.

Marissa responded. "It is Sunday the 20$^{th}$."

"Okay, so we'll start our egg contract on Wednesday. You should be able to save a dozen eggs up by then eh?"

"Yes sir!"

"All right on Wednesdays and Fridays I'll come and get my eggs. How does that sound?"

"Every Wednesday and Friday sounds good to me mister. That's ten cents a week!"

"It might be more depending on how many I buy each time. Maybe on Wednesdays I'll buy a dozen and on Fridays I'll buy two dozen, or visa-versa, 'cause I'll have five days to wait for my next dozen. But, yeah it will always be ten cents a week at least," Tyrell was smiling as he said that. "Now, about the hay, how much do you want per bale?" he asked Marissa.

"I don't know." Marissa replied. "I only pay twenty two dollars per ton."

"I'll pay the same then, how'd that be? It works out to be by my calculations fifty cents a bale. That sound about right?"

Marissa nodded, "that is fair."

"All right then, I got my eggs and feed for the horse. I'm happy now. Even happier knowing I'm buying them from my two most favourite people," he took another slurp from his coffee and Marissa followed suit. "So, what do you folks want to do? It is early enough if you want to take a walk."

"I'd like to Tyrell but I think Caleb and I should head for home. It is a long ride with the wagon."

"I know," he said with disappointment. "You two are quite welcome to spend the evening."

"We can't, I'm sorry Tyrell. Some friends of mine, Mr. and Mrs. Vanrose from near where Len lives, are supposed to be coming by. They stop by every second Sunday and spend the night. Do you want to join us, you'd be welcome?"

"Thank you but, that's okay. I'll see you on Wednesday, ain't that right Caleb?"

"Yep, because you'll be coming for your eggs, isn't that right mister?" Caleb questioned to be sure.

"You bet," Tyrell responded. He was a bit saddened, and was really looking forward to the two of them, spending the night. Still, if they had other plans, then that was fine too, he had a lot of stuff to do to keep busy. They sat together for a few more minutes talking. Then they hitched up Marissa's horses to the wagon and said their goodbyes.

"We'll see you on Wednesday Tyrell." Marissa said as she and Caleb waved.

"You bet. Be careful on your way back."

"We will be. Bye for now."

Looking around for Black Dog, he whistled for him, Marissa and Caleb were out of sight by the time the dog showed up but he could still hear the wagon splashing through the water. "You go, follow them," Tyrell said as he gestured. The dog was more than happy to obey and he chased after the wagon with the wolf on his heels. "There, I feel a lot better now, there is nothing that is going to hurt them." He removed his hat and fiddled with the band as he walked over to Dutch's corral. "Well Dutch, we're alone once more. Sure gets quiet don't it?" he put his hat back on and petted the horse. "Kind of sad in a sense, that they couldn't have spent the night. But I guess I can't have things my way all the time, now can I?" he looked at his watch surprised that it was only 1:00 o'clock.

With at least six hours of daylight left, he decided to gather some mud and moss and went to work filling in the gaps of his shack. There was no point in putting it off. With nothing else to do now was as good of a time as any. It didn't take long nor was it strenuous. Three hours later the work was finished. Next, he rinsed the bucket and returned it to Dutch's corral with fresh water.

There was one last thing he wanted to do that evening and that was put the screen in the window. He cut the screen to fit and tacked it into place using thin pieces of wood. He looked around at the shack walls from the inside to see if he missed any gaps when he mudded it. The only light now was from the only widow, and he suddenly realised that with no light peeking through the gaps the inside of the shack was darker than he liked. He leaned against the counter, with his back to the window. Deciding to knock out a couple more windows, he could use canvas in place of glass, they'd be obscured, but some light would emit through. He looked around at the walls, contemplating as he looked for the best place to do that.

The one widow faced east so he decided the best place would of course be in the south and west wall, and possibly a smaller one in the door. He walked outside and around to the south wall and visualized where he wanted the window. Finally making his decision, he pulled out his knife and marked it with an X. He did the same with the west wall. Satisfied on where he would chop the windows out he turned and walked away. It would be a task for another day.

Although it looked like rain was coming the evening was warm, and he decided to take Dutch out for ride. They wouldn't go far, maybe upstream a mile or two, or head into the south forest. There were many, places, they could go. In fact, there were a lot of places he hadn't been, even if they stayed within a couple of miles of the shack. Saddling up Dutch, he led him out the gate, swung up on him, and headed south. "Never been this way yet, figured we'd go have a look-see." They traveled for a few minutes until coming to a ridge and he pulled Dutch to a halt.

"Ain't that spectacular, what a beautiful view," Tyrell mentioned as he looked on. There was a small valley below so thick he could only see the tops of the trees. There were however sporadic rock outcrops and a few clearings he could make out as well. *Wonder if that is Sloan land,* he thought as he gazed on. "All right Dutch let's get," he reined the horse along the ridge and followed it for a short distance. They stopped every now and again and looked around.

There was a lot of land there was no denying that. "Could have quite the cattle ranch up here, wouldn't that be something Dutch? We're going to have to make a day of this some time and do some exploring. What say you?" Dutch of course, never responded. A short while later, the creek came into view and they followed it. He noted game tracks, like deer, moose, and even the odd bear track. It would be a good place to hunt. The game trail was certainly well used.

They made it back to the shack as the sun began to set, and the clouds rolled in. "Looks like we might get some rain, good thing you got that tree to keep you dry." No sooner did he say that when the first rumble of thunder rolled across the sky. "Yep, I reckon it is going to rain. It won't be here for a while but, it is coming." Tyrell said as he looked up to the sky. With his arms loaded with firewood and coffee pot in hand, he entered the shack. Dropping the wood on the floor, he set the coffee pot on top of the stove. As the fire warmed the inside of the shack, outside thunder and lightning clapped. It only took minutes before the rain pelted down. *Sure hope Marissa and Caleb have made it home. I'd hate for them to get caught in this,* Tyrell thought as he looked out the window and slurped a coffee.

Looking at his watch, he calculated the time when they left. *I'd say they've been back home for close to an hour,* he thought as he turned and tucked his watch away. Setting his coffee down, he added another small piece of wood to the fire and removed the coffee pot. It grew dark in the shack as a black cloud precariously shut out the little bit of light emitting from the sky. Reaching over he lit the lamp on the table the soft glow lit up the one room shack. He looked down at the carving he carved on the first day that he arrived. Counting on his fingers, he counted how many days it had been.

"Yep, she was right, it is the 20$^{th}$." Tyrell said to himself as he remembered Marissa telling him so. He had been there for only seven days so far, and had accomplished a lot more than he expected. He sighed, he still needed to find the placer claim tags. It had been four years since the last time the claims had been worked, he wasn't sure he could remember exactly where they were.

The cattle ranch idea popped up in his mind again, it was something he knew he'd rather do, than bust his nuts trying to find more gold, hell he already had enough of that stashed away. Perhaps he and Marissa could become cattle barons. Aside from the few rocky and swamp laden areas, there was a lot that could be done with 300 acres.

What he needed he decided was a surveyor to come up and survey his land, all four corners of it. Where could he get someone like that he wasn't sure, but it was something to certainly look into. Out of curiosity, he looked through the pile of papers under the bunk, looking for the property description. There was a chance that the document might point out where the property stakes were. With longitudes and latitudes provided. He thumbed through a pile of documents but nothing jumped out at him. *Grandpa wouldn't have made it that easy,* he thought as he put the documents back.

# Chapter 17

It rained the entire night and the thunder is what woke him Monday morning. He tossed and turned most of the night until the rain slowed and the thunder became distant. Now it was at it again, and was so loud that it practically scared him out of bed. "Jesus Christ," he grumbled loudly as he sat up and shook his head. He looked out the window at the dark clouds, not a ray of sun was visible. He turned and sat down at the table, and then yawned.

Putting his hands behind his head, he put his feet up on the table and leaned back. Lighting a cheroot he inhaled a lung full of smoke and enjoyed the serenity for a few minutes, then standing, he donned his hat and buckskin jacket and strapped his holster to his waist. Exiting the shack, he whistled for Black Dog and called his name.

Black Dog however was nowhere to be seen. In fact, he spent the night huddled with Teeka. He kept her company and warm throughout the night, he only faintly heard his name. For a moment he tilted his head and listened, then went right back to sleep next to Teeka. His playmate, the wolf, was nearby as well but she wasn't nearly as willing to lie next to the girl child. She was still a bit strange to her. The wolf for now wanted to keep her distance. In time, she might befriend the child. Black Dog certainly had.

Tyrell looked around this way and that, hoping to at least glimpse the dog. Walking to Dutch's corral, he greeted the horse. "Morning Dutch, least wise you're about. Rained quite hard last night, didn't it? Looks like it is going to all day today too," he reached over and pet the horse. "You managed to keep dry I see, good. We'll get a shelter put up soon enough." He pointed in the direction of where he was going to build the shelter, "over there I think is the best spot, it looks level and I can see ya from the outside fire. Plus, once I get the window in on this side of the shack, I'll be able to keep my eye on you from there." Dutch neighed and shook his head. "What? You don't like that spot?" Tyrell chuckled.

The horse never responded. "I bet I got something you would like, how about some oats?" Tyrell asked as he continued to pat the horse and scratch him behind the ear. "I'll get some for ya, and bring them over to you under the tree, less you like porridge, 'cause that's what will happen in this rain. They'll get all soggy."

Tyrell turned and gathered the oats in a bucket and brought them to the horse. He climbed the rails and met him under the big tree. "Here you go, ol' Dutch. Enjoy," he set the bucket down and watched the horse eat for a few moments and then bid him good day and exited the corral. Again, he called for Black Dog, and again, the dog didn't show. *Well, guess I wait,* he thought as he made his way back inside.

It was while gathering water for coffee that the downpour came. He was soaked by the time he made it back to his shack. Lucky for him it was warm and cosy inside. Adding grounds to the pot, he set it on the stove. He slipped off his wet shirt and slipped on a dry one. Returning to the table, he sat. The rain outside pelted down unrelenting for the next few hours and he spent that time reading the documents, slurping coffee and puffing on a cheroot. He didn't just skim through the documents this time he paid as much attention to details and legalities as he could. There were no longitudes or latitudes for where the Sloan property stakes may or may not be. All he did find on one of the documented maps of the property was an area with four little marks.

He could tell that the area where he was now at the Sloan claims along with Marissa's place were both on the map. The four almost unnoticeable marks were north, east, south, and west of both places. It was hard for him to decipher the distances or even where each property stake was, if that is what the marks represented. It would take him a hundred years to find them. *Nope, ain't even going to try, I think I'll hire a surveyor, seems to be the only solution,* Tyrell thought as he stroked his face and looked at the document. Setting it aside, he peered out the window. Even though it was raining, he was hot. The stove certainly pumped out the heat.

Carefully removing one side of the screen, he opened the window and let some air in. He'd leave it open for the time being. The screen however he replaced and tacked it up. *Guess I didn't think that through,* he thought, *shouldn't have to remove the screen to open the window, that don't seem right.* He spent the next few minutes revamping the screen. "There that makes more sense now don't it?" He said to himself, he was content there was no doubt about it.

Adding another piece of wood to the stove, he exited the shack. It wasn't raining as hard, but it was raining. Again, he called and whistled for Black Dog, hoping that by now he was going to come. If he didn't he'd have to start to worry, and maybe even head off down the wagon trail to make sure Marissa and Caleb were home, he could take the horse trail but that would defeat the purpose, especially if the two of them were stranded or hurt. Usually, the dog would come and when, he did Tyrell knew all was well. Gathering his rifle, a few blankets, and handful of beef jerky, he knew if Caleb and Marissa were stranded somewhere along the wagon trail, they'd be hungry, cold and wet.

Satisfied that he had all that he would need he saddled up Dutch and headed downstream following the wagon trail. Even his rain jacket didn't keep him dry from the onslaught of rain pellets that bombarded him and Dutch as they continued. Not far from the shack he pulled Dutch to a halt and glanced downstream, the rain didn't help his vision, but coming his way was another man and horse.

"Hello," he called out as he pulled his rifle from the saddle scabbard and set it across his lap. He didn't know who would be out and about or who would want to be in this weather. Obviously though, someone was. Tyrell hoped it wasn't a hooligan or for that matter the law. He didn't want to come across either, although a hooligan was probably worse.

The man finally raised his arm. "Hello there," he said as he approached. "I haven't seen rain like this in a long while." The man commented in a friendly tone as he drew close and reached out his hand to shake Tyrell's. "I'm Darrel Waxley. We lost a few head of cattle last night in the storm."

"Waxley, eh, Bill Waxley's son, I reckon." Tyrell confirmed as he reached out his hand to shake the newcomers.

"That's me, yes sir. And you must be Tyrell Sloan?" The two shook hands.

"I am, and no I ain't seen any cattle out and about. Are ya sure they came this way?"

"As sure as the tracks that, haven't been washed away by the rain. I started tailing them last night. Once the rain hit though I lost them, I was lucky enough to pick up the trail this morning, they were headed this way."

"Uh huh, well, like I said, I ain't seen them. You're welcome though to scout around. My shack is upstream a ways. I'm on my way to check in on Marissa and Caleb. They left my place yesterday before the storm. I want to make sure they're safe."

"No worries there. I spoke with her late afternoon yesterday. She and Caleb were home then."

"Huh, is that right? Ya didn't happen to see a dog with them did ya?"

"Nope."

"Well, I guess if they're home than I ain't got any reason to be out in this rain. Care to join me at my shack for a coffee. It'll get you out of this rain for a few. Maybe I'll help you scout around for them cows you're missing."

"That'd be mighty kind of you."

Tyrell nodded. "Let's get," he turned Dutch and the two headed back the way they came.

"You knew my old man I suspect." Darrell said as they traipsed onward.

"I met him once. Years ago when I was passing through, I was on my way to the Hudu Mercantile and ol' Everett's place to buy a couple of mules. That's when I met Bill." The two of them traveled in silence until finally making it to Tyrell's shack. "You can tie your horse to the horse pole." Tyrell gestured with his chin. "I'll get Dutch put away and we'll go make some coffee."

"That sounds good to me." Darrell pulled his horse up to the shack and tethered him to the pole. He waited for Tyrell and then followed him inside.

"Welcome, to my shack in the woods." Tyrell said as he set the coffee pot on the stove and added wood. "Go ahead sit down."

"Thank you Tyrell." Darrell said as he pulled out one of chairs and sat opposite of the woodcarving in the table. Obviously, that was where his host sat. He took off his hat and tossed it to the floor as he looked around. "Was up here one other time when Jake and his crew were here. It hasn't changed much, other than all their equipment is gone."

"Nope, I ain't got no plans to change it either." Tyrell said as he sat down and offered Darrell a cheroot.

"No, thanks, I don't smoke."

"Yeah, wish I didn't either." Tyrell said as he sparked one up. "So, how many cows got away on you?"

"Two young heifers and a couple of steers, we managed to keep the rest."

"How many head you Waxley's running?"

"Close to three hundred head, only a hundred were set out on the range, we're rounding them all up now."

"Are they off to market?"

"Some, yep. The boys will drive them to Fort Sheppard. They'll be auctioned off there."

"Auction, eh? How does that work out for you folks?"

"Usually get ten or fifteen dollars a head. Depending on their health and size, are you considering running cattle up here?"

"I've thought about it. Maybe next spring, I ain't sure though."

"How many does Marissa have down there in the canyon?" Darrell questioned.

"Thirty or so I reckon. Not much more I don't expect."

"There is a lot of room up here to have cattle. I often wondered why she didn't hire a cow-hand and do just that." Darrell said, as he tasted his coffee.

Tyrell took a swallow himself. "I reckon Marissa couldn't be bothered, probably quite a handful raising Caleb. Plus from what I know, she grew up on a cattle ranch in Victoria. She probably has no desire to run cattle after growing up with it all of her life."

"Yeah, raising a boy around here can't have been easy. I have to admit she's done a good job with Caleb. I don't see them but once a year when she buys her feed. Every time Caleb seems to have grown. He's a good kid, going to be a hell of a man when he grows up. Can't say much about his old man though, I haven't met him, nor has Marissa, spoke of him, folks around here, leave it at that," Darrell finished his coffee. "Tyrell it was a pleasure meeting you and thanks for the coffee but, I got some cattle to round up." Darrell stood up and put on his hat.

"Just a minute Darrell," Tyrell finished his coffee too, "need any help?"

"That's up to you. You want to join me, that'd be fine."

"Sure," Tyrell stood and the two exited again into the rain. "Slowed down a bit least wise, might clear up after all." He made his way to Dutch's corral and saddled him up again. Two hours later finding the cattle downstream they rounded up the four of them. Darrell shook Tyrell's hand and thanked him for the help. Then he headed home. Tyrell watched as he vanished around a bend in the creek and out of sight. Turning

Dutch, he headed home himself. "That was an interesting visit, wasn't it Dutch? I know where to buy cattle now. I should have asked him if he knew any surveyors," Tyrell mentioned in hindsight.

By the time he made it back, the rain had turned to sporadic showers. The sun, that is what was left of it, forced its way out from behind the clouds. Tyrell inhaled deeply. There was nothing like the smell left behind after a rainstorm. Turning Dutch loose in the corral, and not seeing the dog, he yelled and whistled for him a couple of times. Finally, the dog and the wolf ambled towards him. He watched and waited until they were within earshot. "Spent the night outside in the storm eh?" Tyrell questioned as Black Dog approached. The wolf kept its distance lying down in full sight. "Had a stranger come by today, would have been nice to be forewarned," Tyrell chuckled as he pet the dog. "That's okay he weren't no renegade. It was Darrell Waxley from Hudu. I still wish the two of you would stick around, the horse don't say much, you on the other hand at least respond to conversation. Damn, horse anyway eh."

His saddlebags were close, and he reached over and pulled out the handful of jerky that he packed when he set off to see if Marissa and Caleb were safe. He knew now without a doubt that they were. Black Dog's presence proved that. "Here you go," Tyrell handed the dog a couple of pieces. He was expecting the dog, and wolf, to disappear like they always did once the jerky was handed out. This time though, they lay only a few paces away as they gnawed on the treat.

Tyrell watched with amusement and intrigue. It was odd in a sense, and he wondered why they chose to stay close. He looked around to see if it was because danger was near, but saw nothing out of the ordinary. The truth was, the dog and wolf simply wanted to lie where they were. The wolf was no longer afraid of Tyrell or for that matter Teeka, she had adopted them as part of her and Black Dog's pack, she had no reason be skittish.

Looking at his watch, Tyrell decided he sat long enough. Grabbing the axe, he walked over to the shack. As far as he was concerned, this was as good of time as any to chop out, the two windows. It didn't take long to get a hole chopped out for the first one that was big enough to put the saw blade through. Using a board as a straight edge, he pulled out his knife to trace out a square on the outside wall. Stepping back he eye-balled it to make sure it was square and a decent size. Satisfied he chopped another hole in the top corner of the square.

He estimated that each of the logs that made up the shack were near four to five inches in diameter. The window was drawn out four logs high and what, he reckoned to be the same distance in width. It was at minimum of 16 inches by 16 inches and a maximum of 20 inches by 20 inches. *Yep, that'll work,* he thought, as he slid the blade of the saw through the first hole in the wall and started sawing. He only needed to saw down each side of the square and after that he could use the sledgehammer or the axe head to knock out the loosened logs.

With some effort and a few curses later, he was ready to knock out the hole. He swung the axe head into the bottom log first, but it didn't budge. He tried a few more times, but the axe wasn't doing it. *Never send an axe to do a sledgehammer's job, I guess,* he half-chuckled as he caught his breath and wiped his brow. It certainly wasn't as simple as he expected. Rested, he picked up the sledgehammer and with as much power that he could exert he swung the hammer at the bottom log. Again, nothing happened except some of the old mud from the wall fell out and the shack shook minutely.

*Huh, what the hell,* he thought as he looked at the wall. He had cut through both sides. It didn't make any sense on why the cut pieces didn't simply smash out. He decided then to hit the log above. Stepping back, he prepared himself for another swing. This time his effort paid off, except he lost his grip on the sledgehammer and it went flying through the hole and crashed into the table breaking off one of the legs. He heard the commotion inside and poked his head through the opening. "Holy, that sure went flying," he said out loud, as he looked on. Using the axe, he tapped out the second and third cut log. Looking inside the shack from the outside, he looked down to the bottom log wondering why it didn't budge. It was obvious when he looked and he would have saved a lot of energy if he thought it through.

The reason the bottom log didn't give into the fight was simply due to an error in judgement. From the outside, it looked as though he had sawn through it, but he hadn't. Tyrell shook his head as he picked up the saw and headed inside to finish the cut. Once that was done, he only needed to wiggle and jiggle it a couple of times and it fell to the ground. He stuck his head out the window opening and looked around.

*Perfect,* he thought as he looked this way and that, he looked at the table knocked over in the middle of the room with its leg busted off. He picked it up and set it upright. He leaned on it to test its integrity. For now it would do. Making his way back to the new window opening he used the saw to square it off. Next, he grabbed the sledgehammer off the floor and exited to the south side of the shack where he went through the whole process again. It was easier the second time because of what he learnt from the first.

An hour later he was putting up the screen on the outside, and as the sun set, he fit the two windows with old wagon canvas. The screen would keep the bugs out and the canvas would let light it. If he wanted more light, all he would need to do was roll up the canvas. It was a big improvement. There were other improvements that, he could make as time went on, but for now, everything he did was good enough. It would get him through until spring.

# Chapter 18

He was refreshed and feeling good when he woke up Tuesday morning. From his bunk he looked out the east window glad to see the sun rising. Slipping into his denim pants, he pulled on a pair of socks and slid his feet into his boots. He picked up his shirt, gave it a quick smell to be sure it wasn't too dirty, satisfied he put it on. Strapping his holster around his waist, he exited the shack. It looked like it was going to be a glorious day. The fresh September morning air was pleasant and he inhaled deeply as he made his way to the creek for water.

Surprisingly, by the time the fire was lit outside and his morning coffee was brewing, both Black Dog and the wolf, were lying next to him. "You two must have explored all that you can. I haven't seen you as early as this in a while," he petted the dog. "Guess we have to come up with a name for you, eh, sweetheart?" Slowly he reached out his hand for her to smell him. "It's okay, I ain't going to hurt you any." The wolf however backed out of his reach and sat down again staring at him. "A little scared still I see. That's okay. I wasn't so sure if I wasn't scared when I reached out to you. I think I'm going to call you Shyaway, what do you think of that?" The wolf and Black Dog both looked at him curiously. It was a strange sound to them. "I guess that got your attention, do you like that?" he repeated the name. "I think Shyaway is a good name for you wolf. That's what I'm going to call you, Shyaway."

Sipping from his coffee, he stretched out his legs. Shyaway stayed where she was and Black Dog continued to lull next to him. "This is a cosy little circle we have going on here." Tyrell said to the wolf and dog. Black Dog sat up and pawed his lap. "Easy, ol' boy, yeah, yeah, I know. You want a treat. I did pick you up that bag of pig ears. We're going to slow down on the jerky for a while. It's got me all plugged up," he chuckled as he stood and retrieved the bag of dried

dog treats. Pulling two out of the bag, he handed one to Black
Dog, and then walked closer to Shyaway. "I know you want
this, so come and get it." He held the pig ear at arm's length.
Shyaway sniffed at the treat and crawled toward it. "That a
girl. Go ahead, it is for you." He reached a little closer toward
her and the wolf flinched a bit. It relaxed again but remained
cautious as it snapped the treat from Tyrell's hand. "Good
girl," he said as he crouched down and watched her.

Black Dog came over and jumped around, wanting Tyrell
to play with him and the two of them wrestled. Shyaway
watched with caution and confusion. She could tell however,
that Black Dog was playing, and eventually she too, tried to
join in by biting Tyrell's ass. Both a bit too hard and
unexpected, it was a start though, and Tyrell knew it. "Easy
there Shyaway. That didn't tickle one damn bit!" By now
Shyaway was a distance away looking at him as though she
herself was laughing. Tyrell stood up and rubbed his rear.
"Think that was funny, eh." Of course, he too thought the
same and he smiled as he shook his head. "Next time don't
bite so dang hard."

By now, the sun was high in the sky, so he entered his
shack wanting to know how much daylight and brighter it
was with the new windows punched out of the walls. He
rolled up the two canvas window covers on the south and
west walls. For the first time ever the shack came to life with
full sunlight. The new windows made all the difference in the
world. The shack seemed more pleasant. Rays from the sun
animated the dust that was floating around and the particles
danced as the light reflected off them. They were like streams
of glittering gold, moving this way and that on the air
currents. He smiled and nodded his satisfaction.

Walking over to the counter he opened a can of peaches
with his knife. Canned peaches were his favourite and he
took his time in eating them. He didn't know what he would
do for the rest of the day. Being it was Tuesday a bath was
likely a good idea. Tomorrow, he would go pick up his first

couple bales of hay and a dozen eggs from Marissa and Caleb. Walking to the creek, he rolled the trench rock in place. If he was going to have a bath, he wanted the water to be warm. It would take a few hours to warm up.

In the meantime, he decided to take Dutch for a ride. He wanted to follow the creek upstream and scout that area out above where they saw the game tracks. He packed his bedroll and loaded some food into his saddlebags, making sure his rifle was loaded and that he had extra shells for it and his pistols, he and Dutch set off, with Black Dog and Shyaway following close behind.

Two hours into his ride, he slowed Dutch to a halt. Looking into the undergrowth, he thought he saw the derelict remains of an old wagon or some other piece of machinery sticking out of the ground. Swinging off his horse, he walked the short distance and kicked some of the dirt and debris away. What he found was an old burnt out wagon.

Looking around, he started to find other things too. Linens, rusting cans, clothing, there were all kinds of stuff and it was scattered everywhere. He even found an old box of bullets. It was then he thought if perhaps he had come across Fry, and his heart sank for a second, finding women's clothing in a heap though changed his mind, he hadn't found Fry. *What the heck, have I found,* he thought, as Black Dog and Shyaway joined him. He looked around at all the debris deciding that it was nothing more than an old wagon and a pile of junk. It did seem odd, but as with all old places if one looked one could always find junk.

Unknown to him it was at that spot where Teeka's family had been slaughtered. The only people that knew were her and the killers. The rubble had been lying there for almost 7 years. Tyrell wasted no time in searching through the debris. He simply climbed back onto his horse and continued riding. They traveled further upstream. Black Dog and Shyaway took the lead, and Tyrell watched as the two of them darted over a crest and vanished out of sight.

A few minutes later, he came across an open plain. It wasn't that big and was surrounded with birch and pine. Even a few cedars stood out. "I think we'll rest here, Dutch," he slowed the horse to a halt and dismounted. His first thought was that it would be a great place for open ranged cattle. The creek was nearby and the mountain grass was knee-deep. It was turning golden now due to the changing season. There was no doubt in his mind that the grass would feed fifty or sixty head of cattle through the spring and summer months easily enough.

The more he thought about ranching. The more he thought that is what he wanted to do. He could leave the claims for now, and pick up a hundred head of cattle instead. He could easily get the thousand dollars or more that he'd need. It would only take a couple of days, to make his way to the gold hidden along the trail that led to the old Heddy's mercantile. That was another thing that; crossed his mind. Maybe he could buy Heddy's and get the mercantile back on track.

He ran his fingers through his hair as he crouched and looked around. *There are so many things I could do,* he thought. Deciding on one or the other was the biggest catch. Hell, he could do both, he knew there was enough gold. Obviously, the first thing was to make sure that he could find the place where the gold was hidden. It had been years since he'd been that way.

More than likely the trail would be over-grown. However, he did still have the map that Wilson made for him. The trees he marked back then would also help. He looked over to Dutch who was busy feasting on the tall grass. Tyrell took the opportunity then to have a bit of a rest himself. He thought about the gold and decided that he would retrieve it.

If he left Saturday, he should be able to make the round trip by Tuesday, he would be in need of it sooner or later anyway, and, there wasn't much point in putting it off. Once he got back and had the gold he'd do some more calculating, and maybe visit Waxley's boy and see what kind of deal he'd make for a hundred plus head of cattle. It would be a start. Rested now and with a clear vision on what he wanted to do, he climbed back into his saddle and he and Dutch headed back the way they came. It was mid-afternoon when they finally made their way back to the shack. "I'll get you some oats in a bit," he turned Dutch loose in the corral and walked away.

Making his way inside he grabbed his straight razor and bar of soap. With clean clothes in his hands, he walked over to the bath and stripped down. The water was lukewarm. Singing and humming he scrubbed and shaved. It felt good to be clean again and his face didn't itch now that his whiskers were scraped off. He jumped up and sat on the bank with his feet dangling in the water. Butt naked he looked around. Things had gone his way so far and the place was looking up. Dressing into cleaner clothes, he looked around for Black Dog and Shyaway. They should have been back by now, but he saw neither one. What surprised and even confused him was the whistle that came back.

The repeated whistle of course was an accident and Teeka herself was confused at the sound that she made. "Hmm make noise like he make." She tried again not thinking anyone could hear her, but Tyrell could. He tilted his head and listened. The first time he thought he might have heard an echo. He was convinced otherwise now. Echoes didn't sound like that.

Quickly he turned and walked back to the bath pool where he left his holster. Strapping it to his waist, he undid the two hammer laces that kept his pistols from falling out as he rode. Most of the time he always kept them tied, but, he was beginning to think, that maybe he shouldn't do that anymore. He didn't want to lose that half second it took to untie the two if he ever needed to draw. It could mean the difference between life and death. For now, he'd keep them untied, and his pistols ready to be drawn.

He was expecting someone to come traipsing out of the forest or ridding up the creek. Instead, only the sounds of the crickets and birds filled his ears. Uneasy as he was feeling about the whole thing, especially without Black Dog being near, he made his way to the shack and loaded his rifle. Ready now if anyone decided to take him by surprise. Tyrell scouted the area his eyes and ears trained for any unfamiliar sound or sight. As far as he was concerned there was certainly something amiss. Too many things were happening for him to continue to believe that nothing out of the ordinary was going on.

When he thought back to the picnic basket and the opened package of cheroots that he found but hadn't opened, to the amount of jerky that seemed to have gone missing, these and the feeling of being watched on occasion, much like right now, were happening to consistently to only be a coincidence. Perhaps Marissa and he too saw something or someone looking through the shack window. It did seem odd to him as he thought about that, the incident did happen on two different occasions.

Something was amiss. Someone or something other than himself was out there. If it were a man, then as far as he was concerned they were trespassing on Sloan land and if by accident or on purpose, he did come across someone other than Marissa and Caleb, living on the land, he'd see to it that they left. If it were a bear or other animal, he'd learn to live with the company. Sitting down on the bench, he leaned his rifle up. Using a stick, he stirred up the coals of the morning fire and added wood.

At least, four hours of sunlight remained of the day and he took the opportunity now while his coffee perked to bring Dutch his oats. The only sound he heard as he walked the distance to Dutch's corral, were the sounds of his own footsteps. "Hey, Dutch, I got you some oats, said I would, so here they are." Reaching over the top railing, he set the bucket down.

He waited a few minutes while the horse ambled over and stuck his head in the bucket. Tyrell watched as he fed, noticing that the horse's water bucket was empty he picked it up and filled it at the creek. Once more, he looked both upstream and downstream hoping to see the dog and wolf. If they were close, they were being ghosts, because he saw nothing. With bucket in hand, he returned to the corral. "Here you go Dutch, fresh water." He set it next to the bucket of oats. "You know what? I think I can come up with a water trough for you. That way you'll have plenty of water all day long."

Tyrell scratched the horse's face, as he contemplated. In fact, he could probably divert water from the creek to stream right through the corral. A small stream would constantly flow during the warm seasons. In winter, it would freeze solid and, he would be hauling water anyway. He continued to pet the horse. It gave him a moment to think. He decided to build a trough and line it with canvas that way it wouldn't leak much. Looking to the other side of the creek, he sucked on an eye tooth. In spring, he would extend the corral another sixty or seventy feet right across the creek, up and over the grassy knoll.

Dutch would have a little more room to move around and the creek would keep him quenched. Plus, there was a lot of grass that grew on that side. There was more shade too he was noticing. He continued looking in that direction visualizing it and the work involved. For now, he decided the trough was the quickest idea. Getting tired of sitting around he gathered the lumber, canvas, and tools he would need to build the trough and tossed them inside the corral.

Once that was done, he leaned on the top rail as he planned in his mind the square box he would build to hold water for the horse. Anyone else probably would not, have needed to think on it too long, but he was never much of a builder, he was learning though. Climbing over the rails with the blueprint etched in his mind he began building. It was around this time that Black Dog and Shyaway made their appearance, they lay outside the corral and watched. A short while later he noticed them. "Well, look who decided to come home. You guys should have been here earlier. We've been back for an hour or so. What took you?" Tyrell questioned as he continued with his work, relieved that both the dog and wolf were there.

The measuring and sawing were the hardest part of the whole deal. When that was out of the way, the rest was simple. He lined the trough with canvas, making sure there was enough to pull over the sides, these he tied tightly with rope so they couldn't pull inside and spill out the water. Standing back, he looked the trough over. By now, Dutch was near showing some kind of interest. "That'll be your water trough. I reckon it is deep enough that come winter it might not freeze solid. The next step is to see how well it works." He picked up the half-empty bucket of water he brought Dutch earlier and poured it in, but it barely covered the bottom of the trough.

It took ten trips back and forth to the creek and twenty buckets of water later before the trough was finally full. Leaning against the railings, he looked on and caught his breath. It took a lot more water than he expected. The sides of the trough were weeping a bit, but he knew that once the canvas was saturated it would stop. Satisfied it was going to work he climbed into the corral and removed all his tools and scraps of lumber. Then he made his way back to the fire pit. The dog and wolf followed him, lulling nearby as he added a piece of wood to bring the flames up. He ate a can of beans and a couple of day-old biscuits, tossing Black Dog and Shyaway the remaining four. He watched the two of them as they gnawed the hard biscuits.

"If you two haven't scared away the deer, moose, and elk from around here yet, chances are we might get lucky and bag us one in the coming weeks. Wild turkeys should be around soon too. Plus, we'll be buying a side of beef from

Marissa. There will be a lot of meat around here soon. Enjoy what I toss yous between now and then." He chuckled as he looked on and noted how disappointed the two of them seemed to have gotten such a meagre hand out. He looked solely at Black Dog and kicked a rock at him to get his attention. "Just teasing you ol' boy, I got pigs ears still. C'mon, if either one of you want one, you come to me this time." Walking the distance to the shack, he unhooked the bag of ears that was hanging on the wall in the shade. Selecting two, he hung it back up and tossed one to Black Dog who was already waiting patiently.

Crouching, Tyrell gestured to Shyaway to come and get hers. The wolf, reluctant at first only glared at the hand out in his hand. She knew what it was and desperately wanted it. After a few moments she stepped closer, but not close enough, Tyrell continued to coax and encourage her. It took the better part of fifteen minutes, before Shyaway took the last few steps forward and snaffled it from his hand. "See that wasn't so bad now was it?" he questioned as she pranced away and lay next to Black Dog.

# Chapter 19

Bright and early Wednesday morning, after a quick breakfast and cup of coffee he was ready to head to Marissa's. It was early morning and Teeka, by coincidence was out and about around the same time, watching him from a short distance as he saddled his horse and rode towards the horse trail, the dog and wolf trailing close behind. Again, she took the opportunity to invade his shack and rummage through his belongings. If it wasn't for the sack of potatoes and the canned goods, not to mention the jerky she had no reason to rummage at all. There was nothing the man had that interested her. She was somewhat surprised when she entered and the small shack was full of light. She danced joyfully around in the rays that shone through the two new windows. "He make better now I think." She said quietly as she searched for the bag of jerky and helped herself to a handful. Looking around she noticed a few documents sticking out of a box under the bunk. Curiosity welled up in her as she knelt next to the box and began going through it. None of it made any sense to her other than five letters that spelled out SLOAN.

She knew those letters. They were engraved in her father's rifle the .45 Winchester. She did her best to remember how it sounded and she said it a few times before it finally came clear, "Sloan," she said. "Sloan?" She repeated it a third and fourth time, then as fear and an overwhelming desire to cry came over her she stood up and with the paper in her hand ran out of the shack. She didn't stop running until she was in the forest. Sitting under a tree she began to cry uncontrollably, she looked at the paper and the name again. Wiping the tears from her eyes she used every bit of memory from the civilized world that she could conjure up, and did her very best to read the words that made up the document. It was of no use though no matter how hard she tried, she had simply forgotten how to read. "I keep," she said as she held the document. She knew that if she kept practising speech, she could, and would, learn how to read. Teeka stood up and put the document inside her shirt, it would stay safe until she finally made her way back to her shelter. For now, she wanted to soak in the man's bath. He would be gone for a bit longer, she knew. Cautiously she made her way back to the shack, and over to the bath pool.

She noticed that it wasn't as warm as before, but nonetheless she removed her clothes and slipped into it. Scrubbing herself clean and feeling refreshed she hopped up onto the bank and dangled her feet into the water, letting the sun warm and dry her. The mid-morning breeze blew gently across her bare skin, and in only a few short minutes, she was dry. Dressing, she slipped back into the forest and headed for her own home, the big uprooted tree.

Removing the document from inside her shirt, she added it to the other memorabilia she had managed to hang onto from the civilized world. The document and rifle however, were the only things with words on them and she was determined to learn what the words meant. It was strangely odd to her that the name SLOAN would be on anything other than embedded in her own mind. There was obviously a reason for it and she wanted to know.

At high-noon, Tyrell was on his way back to his shack. Strapped to either side of Dutch were two bales of hay and in his saddlebag were a dozen fresh farm eggs, he was going to fry a couple up as soon as he made it back. He could almost taste them as he thought about them. His visit with Marissa that day was a good one and it seemed as though they were coming to terms with where their relationship was heading. He even kissed her when he left. Now it was back to the shack and the comfortable loneliness that he chose to live with. In time, he knew the loneliness would be a part of the past.

It took longer than usual with the extra weight strapped to Dutch. They were in no rush, and they leisurely took their time. Finally, the sound of the creek could be heard and from there it was only a hop, skip, and jump. Tyrell reached into his pocket and pulled out a cheroot as they rested one last time. He dismounted and checked the eggs making sure none were broken. Noticing the bales of hay were snug and hadn't moved much he straightened them out anyway. Sucking on an eye tooth, he sighed. "We'll be home in only a few more minutes, Dutch."

Teeka, in her haste earlier that day, didn't close the shack door all the way and when Tyrell finally made the distance back, the first thing he did was pulled out his rifle and cocked it. He thought for sure that he closed the door that morning when he left. Why it was opened now made no sense to him. "Easy Dutch," he said softly. "We might have a visitor," he slowed Dutch to a halt and dismounted. Cautiously he made his way to the shack entrance and peered inside. Relieved when he saw no one was there. He shrugged his shoulders and un-cocked his rifle, then leaned it against the outside wall.

He walked back to Dutch. "I must not have closed the door, Dutch. I thought for sure that I did." Leading the horse to the corral, he set him loose. "There you go ol' boy, we're home." Closing the gate, he returned to the shack with his eggs. An odd feeling of something or somebody having being inside while he was gone came over him. He looked around for any signs that proved it either way, but nothing jumped out at him.

That is, until he noticed the disarray the box of documents were in. He knelt down and looked through them as far as he could tell everything was there. He scratched his chin as he looked around, *could be the wind stirred them up, if the door has been opened all day,* he thought to himself as he rose. That had to be the answer. Everything else seemed to be as it was when he left that morning. Satisfied, he exited the shack and started a fire. He wanted eggs and he was going to have some. Adding a piece of salt pork to the pan, he waited for it to render down before he added the eggs, three in total. Fifteen minutes later, he was eating eggs and salt pork. Every mouthful was a burst of goodness and he savoured every swallow. Looking over to the dog and wolf that were lying next to him, Tyrell smiled. "I guess I can't forget your pig ears. C'mon lets go get them," he rose and the wolf and dog followed.

"Here you go," he handed each of them one. Surprisingly, Shyaway didn't hesitate and took her treat from his hand without much coaxing at all. "Good girl Shyaway, good girl." The wolf only looked back for a second as it made its way over to Black Dog and joined him as they gnawed on the ears. Next he busted open a fresh bale of hay. "I reckon you'd like a leaf of this," he grabbed an armful of the hay and tossed it into the corral. "There, now all you animals have a treat and so do I. I have eggs." He said with enthusiasm a big smile across his face, "they're the best eggs I have eaten too."

On September 26, he headed north towards Grizzly Mountain. His destination was a chest of gold. He looked over the map that Wilson gave him years earlier. They were according to the map getting close to the top part of the canyon. From there they would need to head north-east for a couple miles. Eventually he knew things would start to look familiar. By mid-afternoon that day, he found one of the trees he had marked when he made his way to Red Rock Canyon, six years earlier.

Slowing Dutch to a halt, he dismounted to double-check. He nodded as he looked at it. They were indeed on the trail. He was somewhat surprised at how easy it had been so far, and that the trail wasn't as overgrown as he had expected. He swung onto Dutch's back and once more, they set off. Black Dog had no problem following the trail, he remembered it well, the scents, and the coolness of the dark wood, it was all familiar. Tyrell kept his eye on him knowing that if he followed closely chances were the dog would lead him to the small creek they needed to cross. Once they found that, it was all peaches and cream.

The trail would turn and head due north and as long as he kept the sun to his left, they would eventually be in the vicinity of where the chest of gold was hidden. Wilson's hand-drawn map and his memory of where he needed to go made the trip a lot easier. The map is what drew him to the first marked tree. From there the trail was easy to follow with Black Dog in the lead.

They rested when they came to the creek. He remembered when he passed it the last time that he marked a nearby tree. He looked for it now and sure enough it only took a few minutes and he found it. "Good," he said to himself as he looked around. They travelled for a couple more hours until the sun went down, and Tyrell decided it was time to set up an evening camp. In the morning, he would start looking for a plateau. Once he found that, he knew the chest of gold wasn't too far off.

He removed Dutch's saddle and tethered him to a tree. Black Dog and Shyaway continued to explore. As darkness came and Tyrell lit a fire the two of them finally appeared and lay down. "Good to see you two." He added another piece of wood to the fire. He had no pig ears for them, but he did have jerky. Reaching into his saddlebag, he retrieved three pieces. Handing one to each of them, he nibbled on a piece himself. They did well that day. He wasn't half-expecting to find this trail as quickly as they did, but he was sure glad they had. His coffee was ready now and he poured a cup of the steaming brew. It smelled good and felt warm in his hands as he held it near his lips and gently blew on it.

The evening air was chilly and he wrapped his bedroll across his shoulders as he sat and stared into the flames of the fire. It was a cold evening, up as high as he was, and he wished he had packed his long underwear. If it wasn't for the warmth of the fire, his teeth would be chattering. He wrapped the blanket tighter around his shoulders to keep the cold wind out. He shook his head, it was nearly the end of September, and anyone with a brain between their ears would've been bettered prepared to head into the high country. He was ill-equipped he realised.

Up until that point, he was quite pleased with how well things had gone. Now though as the evening settled in and it grew colder, things didn't look so warm and fuzzy. It was going to be a long night, and it wouldn't be the only one. He could count on one more night for sure. With any luck, they would be down lower in the canyon and it wouldn't be so brutally cold.

He added more wood to his fire to bring the flames up. Even Black Dog and Shyaway were feeling the bite as they huddled close together. Tyrell warmed his hands over the fire as he looked at them. "You two got the right idea, and if my flesh wouldn't burn I'd wrap myself around these flames. Damn! It got cold didn't it?"

Throughout the night, the weather was a mixture of tolerable to downright cold. By early morning, the only thing on his mind was to get moving, because, the sooner he made the distance to the plateau, the sooner they could turn around and head back to greener and warmer pastures.

He didn't even bother with coffee. Loading his gear, he saddled up his horse and set off travelling north. They were up high enough that the sun would beat down on them all day, as it coursed its way across the sky to another evening. They rested briefly every couple of miles and by that afternoon Tyrell could make out the plateau above them about three hundred yards away.

A smile crossed his face as he reined Dutch toward it. It was a steep climb and Dutch faltered a few times. "Easy there Dutch, take your time, I ain't in no hurry. The plateau isn't going anywhere." A few minutes later, they were on top of it and looking down. "Whew, we've made it ol' boy." Tyrell said as he slid off his horse. Dutch neighed in relief and shook his head. Taking Dutch by the reins the two of them traipsed the short distance to where he remembered the chest to be. It took another thirty minutes to find it.

Over the years, it became over grown with underbrush, and bramble, making it very hard to see. The biggest grin crossed his face. There it was. Slashing some of the bramble out of his way so that he could reach it he knelt next to it and opened it. Sure enough, all the fist sized pouches, remained as he had left them six years earlier.

# Chapter 20

It was mid-afternoon of September 28 when he finally made his way back. Two nights in near freezing weather left him with a bit of a cold. But the bigger picture was he was back at his shack with all the pouches of Sloan gold. Removing the saddle and saddlebags from Dutch, he turned the horse loose in the corral and tossed the bags over his shoulder as he made his way inside. He still felt the chill from the two nights out and he lit a fire in the stove and sat down at the table. It didn't take long for the shack to warm up and he lulled in the warmth as he contemplated.

Pulling one of the pouches of gold out from the saddlebags, he dumped the contents onto one of his tin plates. It brought back memories of a time that seemed long ago when, he first came to Red Rock, and spent almost a month doing nothing but sluicing and panning. He lost a ton of weight because he neglected himself, but that wasn't all he also neglected Pony and Black Dog. Why the dog ever forgave him he didn't know, he was just grateful that he had. He was struck with gold fever back then there was no denying it. The last thing he wanted was to live through that again.

It was probably due to that memory that he hadn't yet started working the claims. As he looked at the gold on that plate, he doubted he ever would. The more he thought about that time the more, he thought about cattle ranching instead. One thing was for certain, he was going to secure Marissa and Caleb's future, he wasn't sure how exactly, but it would be done. He dumped the gold back into the pouch and tossed it to the side. With plenty of daylight left and feeling the urge to get some fresh air, Tyrell exited the shack.

Both the dog and wolf were lulling in the shade. He walked over to them and knelt next to Black Dog. "Looks like you are as glad as I am to be back," he said as he looked over to Shyaway. "How about you girl, are you glad to be off

that damn mountain? Probably didn't bother you two at all
eh? Me, on the other hand didn't fare as well. I got a bit of
the sniffles and a scratchy throat," he started to cough and felt
a little queasy. "I might even have a bit of a fever, and am
certainly light-headed, but I'll get through."

Walking over to Dutch's corral, he tossed some hay to
him. He added a couple buckets of water to his trough noting
that it needed to be topped off, pouring the last bucket in, he
suddenly broke into a fit of coughing that lasted a few
breaths. Spitting to the ground and barely catching his breath,
another bout of coughing hit him hard, he grabbed his chest
as it rumbled, it made him wince in pain as he grasped a
breath.

"Goddamn! That was rough," holding his chest he took a
few slow deep breaths as he made his way back inside. There
was he knew enough water left in his canteen that he
wouldn't need to make a trip to the creek if he wanted to
make coffee. Removing his holster and boots, he stretched
out on the bunk and closed his eyes. He was hot, then cold,
dizzy then coughing. No matter how hard he tried to get
comfortable he couldn't find the peace.

Instead, he lay there with his eyes opened and his mind
racing most of the time. The few times he did manage to get
comfortable and was about to doze, he would breakout into
fits of coughing. Then his head would pound and the whole
thing would start over again. After five hours of battling for
sleep, he gave up, rose from the bunk, and sat at the table. As
far as he was concerned if he couldn't sleep, there was no
point in trying.

He noticed that as long as he was sitting up he didn't
cough as much, but his head pounded with voracity, he could
cope with that. It was the coughing, that, really beat him up.
Every time he did, his chest rumbled with agony as though
his lungs were slamming into each other in a ferocious battle
to cause him pain. Deciding to have a drink of water, he
stood up to get his canteen. The room spun this way and that,

everything, was garbled. Fumbling for the chair, he leaned on the backrest and waited for the room to stop spinning. It took a few minutes, but finally his equilibrium came back on-line and he stood upright. Taking a slow deep breath, he walked to his boots, and slipped them on and headed for some fresh air.

There was a beautiful sunset to the west, and he looked up at it for as long as he could, before he got too dizzy. There was something about the warm evening, and the painted sky that made him feel better. He walked to the creek and listened to the soothing sound of it for a few minutes, as it trickled by. He took his time walking back, it seemed the more he kept momentum the better he felt. Finally, by late evening he could lie down and get comfortable. It only took a few minutes before his eyes closed, and he fell into a deep slumber.

# Chapter 21

He battled the cold for the first day back. But when he woke the next day he was feeling better, glad that the coughing had settled and that he no longer felt as dizzy as he did the night before. He wasn't 100% better but he was well on his way. Dressing, he made his way outside. Coffee, eggs, and salt pork were on his mind. He battled a few coughing fits as he waited for his meal, but they were less aggressive and didn't last nearly as long. It was Wednesday and no matter how he felt he had every intension on making his way to Marissa and Caleb's that day.

He wasn't going to let how he was feeling interfere with that. Besides, he was now out of eggs. Drinking his morning coffee, he thought about the gold and where, he was going to hide it. Under the floorboards of his shack seemed like a plausible place. It would be easily accessible and he'd be able to keep his eye on it. If word got around that he was in possession of that much kitty, he'd be a sitting target for every hood-wink, from the Kootenay's to Alaska, and the last thing he needed was that kind of attention.

He finished his coffee and let his breakfast settle before he went back inside and pulled up a floorboard. He chose one of the boards where he piled the stove wood. With the task finished and the pouches of gold hidden, he stacked the wood back in place. *There, I reckon that'll do,* he thought, as he looked the board over making sure there was no visible sign that it may have been tampered with. Satisfied, he stood up, dusted himself off, and exited the shack.

According to his pocket watch it was 8:30 a.m., he wound it up as he made his way back to the fire. Black Dog and Shyaway were once again out gallivanting and were nowhere in sight. Tyrell decided he'd wait a bit to see if the two of them came back, before he headed to Marissa's. Looking toward the creek, he spotted two white tail deer, neither one of them big. They weren't worth the effort to shoot he decided. Instead, he watched as they drank at the creek then darted up the other side in one fluid motion and vanished before his eyes.

Filling his coffee cup one last time before saddling up Dutch, he reminisced as he thought about ranching. There were pluses and minuses. However, the alternative of working the Sloan claims and panning for gold wasn't nearly as attractive as cattle ranching or running a mercantile. With enough funds to do anything he wanted, made the decision harder to make. He felt compelled to work the Sloan claims, he felt compelled to help Marissa, and Caleb and he felt compelled to buy Heddy's Mercantile.

He remembered his last conversation with Gramma Heddy as they discussed the possibility of him buying the Mercantile, and Gramma retiring. Now she would never enjoy that part of her life. It saddened him, but so did the fact that Fry was missing. *Things and people change, friendships don't,* he thought as he sat there in deep contemplation. If he could ever convince Marissa to be business partners with him, he could finance all three. It seemed simple enough to him.

It was while he was saddling up Dutch that the wolf and dog showed up. "Good morning, how are you two feeling today?" he asked as he swung up onto Dutch's back. "Are you two going to tag along to Marissa's with us?" he turned Dutch and heeled his flank. "Giddy-up, Dutch, let's get." The horse obeyed and sauntered onward. "C'mon, Black Dog you too Shyaway. Let's go see Marissa and Caleb, c'mon," he repeated as the wolf and dog chased after them. Suddenly, without warning, Shyaway caught the scent of something and she darted up the creek bank with Black Dog close behind.

"Hey where are you two going to now?" Tyrell called after them as he watched them disappear. He never saw the two for the rest of the day. He arrived at Marissa's an hour later.

"Good morning Tyrell. How was your ride?" Marissa asked as he removed his hat.

"Same as always, a pleasure, how have you two been?" he smiled at them.

"I've been okay, mister. We have butchering to do next week. You're still going to help aren't you?" Caleb asked.

"Sure am, wouldn't miss it. Have you got my eggs?"

"They're in the outside cellar. I'll get them." Caleb slipped out the door.

"You don't look well Tyrell what is the matter?"

"I reckon it is a bit of a cold. It ain't nothing to worry about."

"I have some cold remedies. Would you like some?" she asked as they sat down.

"Nah, all's I need is some rest. I'll be okay, don't you worry," he said in a nasally voice as he sniffled.

"Are you sure?"

"I am," Tyrell nodded his head. "If you got tea or coffee, I'd be obliged," he hinted with a smile.

"Which one would you rather have? I can whip up either one."

"Whatever you prefer, it makes no never mind to me, as long as it is hot." He brought his hand to his mouth as he started to cough. "It's this damn," he began as he caught his breath. "It's this damn cough I could do without."

"I think it is some mint tea and honey that you need. That is a heavy cough, are you sure you are okay, I wouldn't want you way up there catching pneumonia or something as ailing. You really should take my advice and let me put together some cold remedies for you. It won't take long. You can drink your tea while I get them ready." Marissa was looking at him sternly. He could tell there was no way he could sway her otherwise.

"I guess I could use some, but, I don't want you and Caleb to short yourselves of any medicine. I'd make it through. I worry more about you and Caleb. Don't be giving away anything to me, that you don't have enough of."

"Tyrell, it is just herbs and teas. I have plenty. I plant and harvest them every year." Marissa said as she turned and made her way into the kitchen.

"You ain't giving me any of that stuff that makes me go loopy are you?"

"If you mean loopy as in sleep and rest, yes I am. I will tell you how much to use in your tea so that you don't get sick." Marissa said from the kitchen as she set the pot on the stove and added a piece of wood.

Tyrell was looking toward her confused. "What is the point in taking something that might make me sick? If I'm already sick? That makes no sense whatsoever."

"I don't mean sick as in nausea. I mean sick as though you are drunk. It won't kill you Tyrell."

"What won't kill me?" he wanted to know.

"The herbs I'm putting together for you so that you can have a tea at night until you are better. It will help with congestion, headache, cough, and sour stomach."

"The only tea I know of that does that is that damn tea the Ktunax use in their ceremonies. I was in one once you know. I didn't like seeing what I saw."

"Quit being a baby Tyrell this isn't like that. I wouldn't even know what they use for their ceremonies." Marissa answered as she continued getting the ingredients ready for him.

"I don't want to be back at my shack getting drunk either."

Marissa laughed at him. "If you follow the instructions I'll give you, I promise you won't get drunk either."

"What if I forget? I can't remember things like how much of this, how much of that."

"If it will make you feel better I can write them down. It sounds like to me that you're trying to avoid taking medicine."

"Am not. I just ain't sure I need it." The truth was he was trying to avoid it. He never liked taking medicine and was always able to fight most things off. The only time he'd ever used medicine were the few times bullets skinned his flesh. He could understand the purpose of medicine then, but for a simple cold or flu, who needed it?

"I'm still going to give you some. If you don't want to use it then don't, but I'd call you a fool."

"You wouldn't," Tyrell said with humour.

"Would too," she responded as she brought him his tea.

Tyrell pointed at it. "This ain't one of them get-better teas is it?"

"No. It is ordinary mint tea with honey." Marissa sat down with a bundled up cloth in her hand. "This is though," she said as she gestured to it. "All you have to do is add a pinch to boiling water and let it steep for a few minutes. You can add sweetener if you want, but I usually don't."

"What exactly is it? Looks like a bunch of wild flowers to me."

"That is exactly what it is."

"So I'm supposed to drink wildflowers?"

"Yes, Tyrell." She said as she rolled her eyes, "it is the Labrador tea that makes you sleepy and the mint that settles your stomach. The butter cup, raspberry leafs and dandelion heads help with a headache."

"Really?" he asked with doubt as he brought his cup of tea to his lips and took a drink.

"Just, try it. It can't hurt."

"All right. I wouldn't want to be called a fool," he smiled at her. "How much is a pinch?"

"The rule of thumb is as much as you can pick up with your thumb and finger." Marissa chortled as she took a drink from her own cup of tea. "If you decide to use sweetener, honey works the best."

"I guess I can remember that."

"So you don't need me to write it down," she teased.

"Nah, I'll remember." Chances were he'd never use the concoction, but he wasn't about to tell her that. "How are things going down here?" he asked with a serious tone.

"Not terribly bad, I suppose. At the beginning of the week two of our cows got sick and died. We dragged them up into the bush for the bears and coyotes."

"What happened?"

"They got sick on Saturday I think and by Sunday they were pretty much comatose. I found them dead Monday morning at feeding time. I can't be sure on what caused it, maybe they were bit by a sick rat or something. It is no problem though. Sometimes that happens. I've already spoken with Darrell Waxley he's going to sell me another four head at a discount. Who am I to argue?" she smiled as she sipped her tea again.

"I was thinking about ranching. I was looking for a partner too," he looked at her. "Would you been interested?"

"That would depend, Tyrell, what are you proposing?" she was curious.

"I don't know exactly. Ain't never ran a cattle ranch. You'd know better at what that might entail than I would. So, what does it entail?"

Marissa chuckled. "I know very little too Tyrell, I only raise a few head a year. Mostly they are for butchering and milking. I've only ever sold live cattle at an auction once. And that was while I was in Victoria after my father died. I'm pretty novice."

"I don't reckon it could be that hard for us to learn together. It would be something for Caleb when he gets older. Which reminds me, where the heck is he? Shouldn't he be back by now?"

"He's probably playing with the chickens, he'll be back. So, about this partnership are you seriously thinking about it?"

"I am, yes. I ain't got it in my bones anymore to be digging for gold. But, it would be a way to finance the operation. Plus, I have some money put away. I wouldn't mind parting with it a damn bit if I needed. I've been thinking about you and Caleb a lot these days and figured it was something the three of us could do together."

"You know Len asked me the same thing, but I told him no. He and Waxley would be our competition. Len runs almost a hundred head and Waxley over three hundred, I think. Do you think there is enough available pasture around here to run a hundred head or so?"

"That is a good question. I've done some scouting over the past little while. There is definitely enough land that, we could work to make into pasture. There is a real nice valley south-west of the shack. I ain't sure it is Sloan land but we could find out."

"Do you mean by surveying the land?"

"That is what I mean. There has to be a surveying company around these parts somewhere?"

"I'm sure there is, Len or Darrell would know. I don't think you'd be able to get one up here until the spring though."

"That don't mean we can't work out some details between us does it? I really want to do it Marissa and to be honest I want you and Caleb at my side. In fact, I won't even consider it unless that is so."

"Do you know what you are saying Tyrell? Maybe you're delusional from the cold you have," she chuckled."

"No ma'am, I ain't delusional from no cold, and I know what I'm conveying. I wouldn't have mentioned it if I was making idle talk. I am serious and want to do it." He brought his cup of tea to his lips and took a swallow, "I'd buy a hundred head today if you came in on it with me. I imagine though you want to think about it first. I'll finance the operation to start with, no cost to you whatsoever, only your partnership. That is all I want."

Marissa inhaled deeply. It was quite the offer and one that she was very interested in. Still, she did want some time to think it over. Her father's cattle ranch back in Victoria had been quite the undertaking and destroyed their family. It didn't mean that was what would happen with her and Tyrell. She turned her brother Len down because she knew that would have turned out badly. This though, a partnership with Tyrell and Caleb might work out. "You do know that a hundred head could cost upwards of two-thousand to three-thousand dollars don't you?"

"Maybe, but they could cost less too if we go to an auction. Waxley said there is one coming up. I ain't sure when though."

"When did you speak with Darrell?" Marissa asked with curiosity.

"Sorry, I forgot to mention that. The day after you and Caleb gathered the wagon from my place last week. A couple of his stock got away on him and followed the creek up near my shack. We shared a coffee and then I helped him round them up. He seems like a nice fellow."

"He does have a bit of his father in him and most times he is very cordial. There are times though he isn't so kind. He is a bit of a money grabber I think."

"We don't have to buy from him."

"No, you are right we don't if we decide to do this."

"I've already decided. I'm just waiting on you," Tyrell smiled. "But, I know it is a big decision so I'll leave it with you for a bit."

"Yes, please do. I really like the idea Tyrell, but cattle ranching can become quite an undertaking."

"Hell, we might even convince Wilson to join us. He wants to retire from prospecting and trapping soon. He knows a bit about cattle ranching and rearing."

"Let's not get too far ahead of ourselves." Marissa mentioned as she poured them each another tea.

"Yeah, you're right, no use blowing steam," he nodded as he accepted the fresh cup of tea from her. Deciding to change the conversation, he asked her about butchering. "What day next week are you planning on butchering? Is there anyone else helping?"

"Not this year. Len has his own butchering to do. It'll be only you, me, and Caleb. Unless Wilson happens to show up which, he has done before in the past. I don't know how he knows when to show up. He just does."

"That's Wilson for you. I had no expectations of seeing him the last time he was here. Like you said, he just showed up. He's a good man that is for sure."

"Yes he is. He reminds me of my father." Marissa smiled as she brought her cup to her lips.

"Your father must have been a great man."

"I suppose to an extent, but he too was a real money grabber, and very demanding. That is why Glen and Len left at such young ages and why they wanted nothing to do with the family operation after he died. Anyway, enough talk about that."

It was around that time Caleb finally came in. "Got your eggs mister. I picked through them to make sure you got the biggest ones."

"Thank you very much Caleb. I like those double yolks." Tyrell reached into his pocket, and pulled out a .10 cent piece and handed it to Caleb.

"Thank you very much mister! I'll go add this to my piggy bank right now," he said as he darted away.

"Well, I got my eggs and if you have a few extra bales of hay I could use them," Tyrell said as he stood from the table.

"Of course I do. Caleb," Marissa said loud enough for Caleb to hear her in his room. "I'm taking Tyrell out to the hay shed to get him some hay. Okay."

"Hang on Ma, I'll come with you." Caleb answered back as he added his dime to the piggy bank and ran back to meet them at the door. The three of them walked over to the hay shed conversing about this and that.

Finally, with the hay strapped to Dutch's back, Tyrell kissed Marissa on the cheek. "Thank you again ma'am for the hospitality and the hay."

Caleb started to laugh. "You kissed my ma. You kissed my ma," he teased.

"It was only a friendly gesture Caleb," Tyrell said as he reached out his hand and shook Caleb's. "Just like that was," he chuckled. "And thank you for the eggs," swinging up onto his saddle he tipped his hat, "I'll see you two next time, remind me again when are we butchering?" he asked as Dutch slowly ambled on.

"Early Wednesday morning?" Marissa replied, "that will give you a bit of time to get better. Caleb and I wouldn't want you working when you are sick."

"How come you're sick mister?" Caleb asked.

"A bit of a cold Caleb, I'll be okay. Your eggs will fix me up. I'll see you on Wednesday," he said as he and Dutch started off at a quicker pace. "That's when I'll gather my next eggs too, okay, Caleb."

"I'll have them for you mister, don't you worry. Get better, okay." Caleb called after him. Tyrell nodded and waved. "I think he likes you Ma, he kissed you." Caleb teased.

"I like him too I think," Marissa answered back as she watched him disappear into the horizon. "Come on Caleb let's go back inside and have some lunch."

"Are we having stew again? That is what I want." Caleb said as they went back inside.

"How about we have sandwiches and then have stew for supper?"

"Okay. Whatever you make Ma, I'll eat." Caleb sat down at the table in the chair that Tyrell always sat in. "Do you really like mister, Ma? I do, I think he is funny."

"Yes I do Caleb. I like Tyrell very much. He is a very nice man." Marissa said as she made them sandwiches.

"If you like him and he likes you how come you don't tell each other?" Caleb asked.

"Sometimes adults keep things away from each other I guess."

"Why?"

"There could be a lot of reasons."

"Like what?"

"Boy, aren't you full of questions," Marissa commented as she brought him his lunch. "For now, you don't have to concern yourself with what happens between Tyrell and me. We're really good friends, that is all, okay. Now eat your sandwich."

"All right Ma. Do I have to have a nap today?" Caleb asked as he began to eat.

"Do you want to have a nap?"

"I am a little tired, will you read to me?"

"Of course I will."

"Okay, after I eat, I'll have a nap."

"I might have one too." Marissa said as she ate her own lunch.


Meanwhile, Dutch and Tyrell were approaching the horse trail. "Guess what, Dutch? I had a talk with Marissa today about a partnership in a cattle ranch. I think she is interested." Tyrell mentioned out of the blue as though the horse cared. "Wouldn't that be something, her and I, and Caleb running a cattle ranch. Not sure what we'd name it but we'd have to name it something, maybe something like the Double R, meaning of course, Red Rock," Tyrell chuckled. "There are all kinds of names we could use I suppose."

He grew silent as he daydreamed and thought about all the possibilities. Time flew by as his mind drifted this way and that, and before he knew it, they were pulling up to Dutch's corral. Tyrell noticed right away Black Dog and Shyaway were laying a short distance away with a dead white tail buck lying near them.

He slid off Dutch's back and tethered him for a moment as he went to investigate. "Knocked down a little deer I see. I guess that'll keep the two of you happy for a time. It's going to bring the damn crows back too. Couldn't you have dragged it somewhere else?" He knelt next to them and petted Black Dog, he reached for Shyaway as well, but she was skittish and pranced a short distance away.

"You still ain't sure if you want to be friends or not, eh?" Tyrell shook his head as he stood up. "I hope you ain't going to mind me moving this carcass. We'll take it into the bush a ways. I can't leave it here. It'll attract unwanted visitors like bear, and those damn crows," he tied a rope around the deer's hind legs and started to drag it into the bush.

Shyaway decided that she didn't want him taking off with her kill, so she grabbed it in her mouth and started pulling it in the opposite direction like a tug of war. Tyrell turned around and looked at her. "Hey stop that. I ain't trying to steal the damn thing," he said as he continued trying to pull it into the bush while the wolf continued to pull it back. It was a battle between wit and brawn and quite humorous all at once.

Finally, after struggling with Shyaway pulling it one way, while he pulled it the other, he managed to get it far enough away from his shack, that it wouldn't pose a threat. "There, you two can feast on this for as long as you like. Keep in mind other animals are going to eventually smell it, so be careful." There wasn't anything, he could do about it, they had simply killed a deer, and no matter what they were going to eat it. That was all there was to it.

He untied the rope from the deer's hind legs and made his way back to Dutch who was not impressed with having to stand there with two bales of hay strapped to his back. "Awe, geez, I'm sorry Dutch. That damn wolf had me all disgruntled. I forgot all about this damn hay," he untied it and it fell to the ground. Removing the saddle, he set it on the top rail where he always put it. Taking Dutch by his halter, he led him into the corral and turned him loose. "I'll bring you some oats in a bit," Tyrell said as he closed the gate.

Picking up his saddlebags, he made his way into the shack and set them on the table. He took out the eggs and the cold remedy concoction of wildflowers, that, Marissa put together for him and set them both on the counter. Opening the cloth that held the concoction, he bent down and smelled it. It didn't smell bad, and he thought that perhaps he might use it. More worn out than sick he removed his boots and put his feet on the table as he leaned back with his hands behind his head. He felt good about the conversation he and Marissa had regarding a partnership.

Next thing he needed to do was to find out what an ounce of gold was going for. The last time he had anything to with gold it was selling for fifteen dollars an ounce, and that was six ago. For all he knew it was more, might even be less, he had no idea. Doing a quick calculation, although his math wasn't perfect he figured the total haul to be at least, twenty-thousand dollars give or take. It was enough money to make all his dreams come true, but it wasn't his dreams he cared about. What he wanted was to make Marissa and Caleb's dreams come true.

Although she never mentioned it in a round-about way, he knew Marissa did desire cattle ranching. He could tell, by the way she spoke about her father's ranch. As for Caleb, he was a natural with animals. There was no better way to draw that talent out of him than to let him grow up on a full-scale ranch. It was obvious to Tyrell that Caleb loved what he did with the chickens and cows they already had. He did a damn good job with them too, for a six-year old kid.

Another thing Tyrell thought about and would bring up to Marissa in time was schooling for Caleb, he'd be more than willing to hire for Marissa a schoolmarm/nanny. Only thing was, he wasn't sure if Marissa would be so willing. Caleb was already ahead of most kids his age, in reading and math, as far as he was concerned, and that was due to Marissa's involvement in teaching him, herself. She had being doing a hell-of- a good job so far. He decided not to step on her toes too much in that regard. If in time, he felt there was a need he would bring it up. Until then his lips were sealed.

Suddenly he heard what he thought to be the scream of someone in great distress! It pierced his mind like a nail in wood. Spinning around in the chair, he stood up and ran to the window. He noticed right away that both Shyaway and Black Dog were on full alert. Their ears were perked up and they were both staring towards where he disposed of the deer carcass. Again, the scream echoed, and the dog and wolf without hesitation charged in the direction. Tyrell quickly slipped into his boots and grabbed his rifle as he ran out the door following in their tracks.

It was too late though, both Shyaway and Black Dog were in a battle with a mountain lion. He immediately fired a couple of shots into the air in an effort to scare the cat away. He could tell the lion wasn't that big but it was certainly giving Black Dog and Shyaway a run for their money. Tyrell yelled at it and fired again, this time the lion made a beeline for the bush and vanished from sight.

"See. What did I tell you, that damn carcass is going cause me all kinds of grief," he said as he walked over toward the two of them. He was relieved that neither the wolf, nor the dog suffered anything more than a few scratches. "I reckon you each got lucky that time, next time that might not be the case. If that would have been a bear, you might be wishing you didn't kill the damn deer.

So, do me a favour refrain from killing things that you can't eat in one meal. Next time I'm going to burn the damn carcass, keep that in mind," he scolded as he looked at both of them. He knew Black Dog understood by the way he bowed his head as though ashamed for even killing the deer. Shyaway, on the other hand was wild and he knew that what he said probably landed on deaf ears. He was wrong though, because Shyaway was beginning to learn and Black Dog was her teacher.

Since he had his boots on and was outside anyway he gathered a bucket of oats for Dutch and brought them to him. "What do you figure, Dutch?" he asked as he set the bucket down and the horse sauntered over. Tyrell reached over the rails and scratched his forehead. "Quite the commotion with that damn pole cat eh? I don't reckon he'll be back, and I'm hoping Black Dog and Shyaway keep their kills to things they can eat in one meal. Like squirrels and such." He looked over to the wolf and dog that were lying down a short distance away. "Ain't that right you two?" he chuckled. "I think they have the idea now. Anyway I'll talk with you more in the morning," he turned and walked back to the shack. Another day of living tucked into his belt.

# Chapter 22

It wasn't even day light when the first crow he heard began cawing. He covered his head with his pillow to muffle out the sound. It worked for the first while, but, when he heard the cawing of what he thought to be a hundred of the pesky birds, he swung out of bed and dressed. "That has to be the worse wakeup call ever," making his way over to the window he opened it up and hollered obscenities loud enough to scare a few of them into flight. "Keep right on flying too you damn things," closing it now he turned and sat down at the table, realising then that he no longer felt sick, he reached for his boots and slipped them on, and flipped the page of his calendar. It was October 1, 1896.

Catching a bit of a chill he lit the stove and waited for the shack to warm. Looking out the window, he could see that there was frost on the ground. The better news was that the sun was rising in the east. In the background the few crows that remained tearing at the deer carcass continued to fuss and caw, it drove him crazy. He stormed out the door with his rifle in his hand and started dropping them where they stood. The sound of his rifle echoed and the few living crows that escaped his rapid fire flew off into the distance. *Maybe have some peace and quiet for a few minutes now,* he thought as he turned and went back inside.

An hour later, he was looking through the few timbers and planks that the Wake up Jake left behind. With those and the ones that he had, there was enough wood to get a good start, on a shelter for Dutch. It wouldn't be much of a shelter, but it would keep the horse warm, and dry and away from the wind, rain, and snow.

Making his way to the corral, he looked at the area where he was going to build. Dutch wandered over and stood at his side as he contemplated. He decided to use one of the corner posts of the corral and the one beside it, to get started. That way he could use the existing corral to build one side and the back. He estimated the size he would build and used his boot heel to mark the spot where he would need to put at least one more post. He scratched Dutch behind the ear. "I'll throw you a leaf of hay in a minute once I get all the wood and tools gathered, that'll I need."

A short while later he was all set up and ready to get to work. He must have picked the worst spot to dig a hole the ground was hard, rocky, and downright miserable to punch into. It took him the better part of two hours. By noon he was lining up the post with a piece of twine, making sure it was as straight as he could get it. He filled the hole and tamped the post in place once he was satisfied. The wind he knew blew from northwest and northeast, and those were the walls, he'd worry about for now and would build.

"You'll have protection once the walls are up and the roof is on ol' boy. I know it ain't quite a barn, but one day it will be. For now this shelter were building for you, and my shack, will have to get us through, we'll build appropriately come spring." Sitting on the top rail of the corral, he rested for a few moments and smoked. The sun was warm and if one listened closely, you could hear leafs from the trees fall to the ground, as gusts of a gentle fall breeze blew them from their branches.

It had been a cold evening for Teeka, and now, as the sun shone hot she was sitting on a big rock absorbing the heat from it and soothing in the rays. "Weather changing," she softly spoke as she pulled her knees up to her chest and rocked back and forth. She wondered if she should simply make her way down to Marissa and Caleb's, at least down there if it got too cold, she could always hide in the hay barn, or Caleb could sneak her inside his room. The man living in her winter shack had certainly made things difficult for her. With the weather changing, things were going to get a lot tougher. That much she knew.

By now, Tyrell was hammering nails and the sound echoed to Teeka's ears. She looked in the direction of the shack, then jumping off the rock made her way to her spying spot, and watched with interest, as Tyrell measured and sawed wood, as he continued building Dutch's shelter. It was the first time that she had been watching the man, since he arrived there, and began building things that, he didn't cuss, shoot, or throw things around as he went about his day.

He was actually impressed with himself as well. It was indeed the only thing he built since being there, that, he got right the first time. The roof was next and he took some time to plan it in his head before he started. He'd need six 12 foot poles that were a minimum of four inches in diameter to use as roof beams. Once those were in place he could decide how to build the rest. There were enough cedar slabs out back, which, he knew that he could use for the roof itself. And with a bit of sod and clay he could easily finish it to prevent it from leaking. Or, he could use what he had left of the old wagon canvas. However, there might be a time when he'd need that. He decided that a slab and mud roof would have to suffice.

All of a sudden, Teeka heard the galloping hooves of what she thought to be a hundred horsemen. It scared her, and she crouched down watching with intent as seven horses and their riders passed her by. She watched as the seven riders pulled their weapons and approached the man at the shack.

Tyrell had his pistols around his waist and he was ready for what might come, still it was a predicament that, he didn't want to be in. Who were these men and what did they want? It was the first rider that spoke.

"Look here boy's, we have ourselves a real live farmer." The seven men unknown to Tyrell were members of a cattle rustling outfit. They were in the area scouting out Darrell Waxley's herd and only by chance came across him and his shack.

"What makes you think I'm a farmer?" Tyrell asked as he continued to stare the riders down.

"You're either a farmer or a prospector and if you're a prospector you might have gold, you going to dispute you ain't neither of those?"

Tyrell spit to the ground. "Well sir, if you'd look around you might note I ain't got no cattle and there sure ain't no prospecting going on."

"You getting smart with me fella?"

"I don't see no point in that," Tyrell said as the men on their horses started to laugh.

"I reckon we're about to find out which it is you are. You going to pull them six shooters around your waist?"

Tyrell noted that Black Dog and Shyaway were hiding in the bush not far away ready to pounce. "I ain't sure. I reckon I'll leave that up to you," Tyrell said as he continued to stare the seven of them down.

"I'd say you're pretty cocky for a fella that stands alone in a horse corral." One of the riders said as the rest chuckled.

"I say we put a bullet in him or better yet one a piece."

"You might get a couple rounds in me no doubt about that, but I'll put rounds in each of you as well."

The seven horsemen began to laugh. "Shit we already have our gun's pulled mister. You think you'll be able to pull your pistols before we shoot. That is most unlikely ain't it fellas? If you want to live, you best drop that gun belt." Another rider taunted.

"I can assure you folks that I ain't dropping my gun's you better get that straight..." Tyrell began when the first shots rang out and two of the horseman fell to the ground. It wasn't Tyrell that shot them, Teeka had ran back to her shelter and gathered her rifle, when she realised the trouble Tyrell was in, and when she noted the first man getting ready to shoot, she shot first, and in quick succession fired again knocking a second man to the ground.

Tyrell, dodged bullets as the five remaining men began to shoot at him. Rolling to the ground, he came up with both pistols in his hands and fired back. Gun smoke and dust filled the air as the clapping of rifles and pistols echoed. The horses and their riders were taken by surprise, when Black Dog, and Shyaway darted out from the wood, startling them and making their horses rear up, knocking the riders to the ground.

Shots rang out from Tyrell's pistols as he put to rest two more of the unwanted visitors. The remaining three made a beeline for cover, and exchanged fire with him as he made for cover himself. Black Dog and Shyaway pounced on the three men, giving Tyrell that one second difference of being shot dead. He was about to fire at one of the men who managed to get away from the dog and wolf. But the sound of a rifle exploded in the distance, and the man grabbed his chest, as he began the dead man's fall to the ground. Tyrell looked around quickly trying to see where the shots were coming from, but he saw nothing.

Again, a shot rang out, this time from one of the remaining two men. It whistled passed Tyrell's ear, instinctively he pointed his pistol and fired back hitting the man in his throat. The man tried to return fire but instead he too gave in to death. The third man was in pain and screaming for mercy as Shyaway danced around him as though he were prey, and tore at his limbs. Tyrell called her off and made his way to the dying man.

He pressed the barrel of his .45 against the man's head hard and cold. "It don't feel so good being at the other end of a man's pistol for no reason at all now does it?" he pushed the barrel harder into the man's head. He could tell by the shape the man was in from being mauled by Shyaway that he didn't have a chance, and before the man could answer, he slipped into never-ending sleep.

Tyrell rose and looked around. Seven dead men lay on the ground and seven horses with saddles and gear were a short distance away. *What a mess this day has turned out to be,* he thought as he winced. He looked in the direction from where he knew the rifle shots came, but, again he saw no one. Black

Dog and Shyaway were at his side as he looked on, at the dead men, horses, and blood that soiled Sloan land.

Teeka herself had no idea on why she responded as she did, it seemed as though it was all reminiscent of when her family was attacked. She felt it was something she needed to do to help the man. It was a good thing too, because Tyrell knew right from the get-go, that there was no way he would have come out on top with seven guns pointed at him. But, he wasn't about to let the men get away with killing him without killing as many as he could.

He looked down at Black Dog. "You and Shyaway go, go see if Marissa is okay. She could be in trouble with men like these roaming around. Stay put if things ain't right I'll know if I don't see you back here in a couple of hours. Go, go now Black Dog," Tyrell gestured as Black Dog and Shyaway disappeared in the forest. He knew the dog understood every word he said, and that he would indeed be back if things were okay. He didn't know how Black Dog understood his plights half the time, but he did, and that was all that mattered.

Gathering up the seven horses Tyrell tethered them. He didn't know what he was going to do with them but he'd have to do something. It bothered him that the day turned out as it did. Scouring through the dead men's belongings he kept that of which would be useful and buried the rest with the bodies and their saddles.

It took him until late afternoon to dispose of them. Next, he looked the horses over for any visible branding, and satisfied, that there wasn't any, he turned them loose and shooed them off. They'd either make their way back to where they came from, or they'd end up being someone else's property. He didn't care either way.

Black Dog and Shyaway were back now, and so he knew that Marissa and Caleb were fine. With the dog and wolf at his side, he made his way in the direction of where he heard the rifle shots come from. It only took a few minutes to find a spent cartridge casing. He looked in the direction of his shack and the corral. It would have been a tough shot to kill three men from where he stood now. It was a shot that he wasn't even sure he could make himself.

He looked around for more signs but found nothing. *This is where the shots came from there's no doubt about it. Why wasn't I shot,* he thought. Looking at the cartridge casing, he was surprised that it was from a .45. He tried to remember if he knew anyone that owned a .45. Marissa and Wilson both used old Henry rifles, so it wasn't either one of them.

Tyrell shook his head. *I don't know who you are,* he thought as he looked around. *But, I owe you one.* He wanted to continue with his search to discover who it was that fired the rifle but it was starting to get dark. It seemed like a better idea to head back to his shack. In the morning, he'd saddle up Dutch and start looking again. With luck, he might be able to pick up a trail or something. He whistled for Black Dog and Shyaway who seemed to have gone off gallivanting.

The truth was they were with Teeka and sitting with her as she huddled in her shelter shivering from the cold and anxiety from killing the three men. It was Shyaway that finally laid her head on Teeka's lap. It was as if she felt Teeka's discontent. Black Dog sensed the correlation between both their body languages and he tilted his head as he licked Teeka's face, sniffed Shyaway, and exited Teeka's shelter. For now, he would leave the two of them alone.

He wanted to be certain that there was no more danger. Alone, he walked the perimeter of the shack, and Teeka's shelter, then finally made his way back to Tyrell, who was sitting by the flames of the fire and sipping on day-old coffee leftovers. It was bitter but Tyrell wasn't in much of a mood to care. Shivers rolled up and down his spine, as he thought about how close he was to dying that day. *What are the chances,* he thought, *that something like that might or might not happen again.* He shrugged his shoulders knowing that, there was nothing, he would have done differently. It simply came with the territory. You lived or you died and he wasn't ready for the latter.

Inhaling a lung full of smoke, he looked out across the horizon. If folks came looking for the seven men he knew where they could find them. He flicked the last of his cheroot into the fire and stood up. Filling Dutch's bucket with oats he walked over to the corral. He was still overwhelmed with what took place and his head was in a fog.

"Here you go, Dutch," he said as he set the bucket down. Leaning against the corral, he looked around and sighed. "I guess we'll finish with your shelter in the morning, Dutch. Damn shame what took place here today," he spit to the ground and wiped his brow. The best thing for him to do was to forget about it. The men got what was coming to them. What bothered him more than protecting his property and killing four men was that someone else had helped, which made him think that they were already following the men for whatever reason. But why then would that person or those people involved disappear? That made no sense. He was however determined to find out, who, what, and why.

"What do you figure, Black Dog?" he looked over to him. "Hey where is Shyaway?" he questioned as he looked for her. It was by luck that she showed up panting beside Black Dog. "You must've been hiding in the shadows, eh girl? Well, c'mon I got pig ears for you." Tyrell said as he turned and bid Dutch good night.

"See you in the morning ol' boy." He walked toward the shack and bag of pig ears hanging from the nail. Opening the bag, he tossed one to both the dog and wolf. "Going to join me by the fire for a bit?" he asked as he hung the bag back up and walked over to the fire. Tossing a couple of pieces of wood onto the flames, he sat down and stretched out his legs. Using the light from the fire to view his pocket watch, he noted the time to be 7:30 and already it was near dark. *Only a week ago it was light at this time,* he thought as he put the watch back in his pocket. *Days are getting shorter and nights are growing colder, soon enough, I'll be indoors by this time. Seems odd,* he thought as he stared into the flames.

An hour later, he made his way inside and lit the stove. It took a few minutes for it to warm up. He sat at the table and lit his last cheroot of the day. Pulling out the shell casing he found from his pocket, he studied it. Tomorrow he would again search for the shooter whom earlier that day killed three of the seven men, whom intrusively with ill intent intruded his world. Taking a long pull on the cheroot that dangled from his lips, he exhaled. *I reckon whoever shot those three men, is a damn fine shot. I need to find out who it was and why they did it.* He butted out his cheroot and made his way over to his bunk. Slipping off his boots and out of his clothes, he pulled his long johns on and sprawled out.

# Chapter 23

He didn't stir the entire night and when he woke on Friday, he was feeling good. The sun was shining brightly and the sky was as blue as a Jay. He looked out the window and smiled, *today will be a good day,* he thought, as he leaned against the counter. Still in his long johns, he stoked the fire and ate a can of peaches. Then adding a few more pieces of wood to the small flame he put the frying pan on the stove top and waited for it to get hot enough, to cook hotcakes and salt pork.

It didn't take long and soon he was finishing his breakfast, with a fresh cup of coffee, and a morning cheroot. He was set. He was full, warm, and ready to face the day.

Things went according to plan and by mid-afternoon the roof to Dutch's shelter was finished. Sitting, he smoked as he gazed around. There was still clay and sod to add but he wasn't in a hurry. For someone who rarely built anything successfully he was doing okay. A smile crossed his face as he looked around with satisfaction. "With thee hands, I have created thee."

Chuckling he inhaled a lung full of smoke. Now that he was caught up with the things that he needed to do, he climbed off the roof and led Dutch out the gate and to his saddle. "Are you ready for a little ride ol' boy? We need to go have a look-see, down there at the south-east corner. I have a sneaking hunch that we're going to find something. I don't know what, but, there is something for us to find. I'd bet on that," he said as he swung onto the saddle and gave Dutch the command to go.

A few minutes later, they were traipsing through the wood. The forest was so thick with obstacles that it was next to impossible to find any type of track whatsoever. Tyrell knew with the forest as thick as it was, that a man could live for a hundred years there, and never give it away. It made him wonder that's for sure.

He looked back the way they came surprised that he couldn't even see their tracks. In fact, he was blind to notice anything out of the ordinary except for a few broken branches. To find even those he had to be looking close. Slowing the horse to a stop, he looked around and decided the best way to carry on would be on foot. There was no point in risking Dutch getting all tangled up.

Dismounting, he realised that some of the undergrowth was as tall, if not taller than, himself. On Dutch's back things looked bad and from where he stood now things looked even worse. It was a jungle. It was quite possible he himself would have got lost if he wasn't aware of his surroundings.

He led Dutch forward avoiding as much of the overgrown, this, that, and the other thing as he possibly could. There was a clearing up ahead that he could faintly make out and he turned in that direction. "Got some sunlight up ahead, Dutch, I reckon we'll rest once we get there. Ploughing through all this bramble and overgrowth ain't no easy task, eh?"

Although the area he was heading for was close, it took another fifteen minutes to break through the forest, and into the clearing. It was magnificent and surrounded by tall cedar and jack pine that reached to the heavens. The clearing itself he guessed to be 100 foot by 100 foot easily. It was clear of bramble and undergrowth. It looked as though someone previously had actually cleared the land at the particular spot decades earlier.

Perhaps it was a garden, or burial ground. Whatever it may or may not have been, it was spectacular. The thick forest that obscured the clearing made the place impossible to see, unless you were right on top of it, or you knew where it was, or happened to get lucky like he did. *What are the chances of someone else finding this place?* He thought, as he led Dutch to the edge of the clearing, and tethered him to a tree. Unless he travelled to the spot four or five more times himself, he knew that even he, would have trouble finding it again. Walking to the center of the clearing he took a simple bearing from where he stood using the time of day, and the placement of the early fall sun. It wasn't an accurate bearing, but, it did put a mental picture in his head, on where the place was located. Once rested enough, they broke through the bramble again, he laid a few rock markers on the trail, so he could find his way back.

An hour later, after struggling and leading Dutch through the overgrown forest, he could hear the creek a short distance away, and he headed in the direction. Finally, the bramble thinned out and he could ride the horse. Once the creek came into view, he followed it upstream to another patch of overgrown forest. Then cut directly northerly in the direction of his shack. It was another part of the forest, he hadn't explored very well.

The ground due to being so close to the creek was damper than the other forest and a lot cooler. The cedar trees stood tall and were massive. Sporadic stands of poplar and birch were scattered here and there. It grew warmer and drier as he travelled closer to his shack, again, nothing stood out to suggest that there was anybody in the area, other than himself.

Contrary to that thought however, a short distance away, Teeka heard the horse and was on full alert. She wasn't sure who it was yet and she armed herself with her father's rifle, as she scurried away and hid. Her jaw dropped when she saw that it was the man and his horse, and that they were within spitting distance of her shelter. Surprisingly they ambled right by and continued toward his shack. Teeka waited impatiently until the sound of the horse grew silent, then, she stood from where she was hiding, and followed them. It only took a short time before the horse and man came into view. She tucked behind a tree and waited until she thought it was safe to continue.

It was then Black Dog, and Shyaway, met up with Tyrell and he slowed Dutch to a stop. "Well now, look who we have here. How are the two of you doing? Ain't seen either of you all day," he said as he dismounted and petted the two of them. "I guess we're close to the shack eh?" he couldn't tell if he was or wasn't, but, running into the two of them reaffirmed that he likely was. Suddenly, the dog and wolf darted in the direction of Teeka. Tyrell watched as they pranced away, "well, it was nice talking to you, too," he teased as he swung back into his saddle. It was then he caught the glimpse of Teeka. She startled him at first, and he pulled his pistol and pointed it at her, to only see that she was pointing her rifle back at him. If it hadn't been for the dog and wolf, Tyrell would never have seen her.

The two of them stared down each other's gun's not saying a word to one another as their eyes locked. Instantly everything he was told, about Caleb's, imaginary friend and the feral child folks claimed to have seen in the area, filled his head. He could tell she was scared but she held the barrel of her rifle steady as she glared at him. Tyrell spoke one word as he put his pistol back in its holster.

"Teeka?" he questioned as he looked on. "I'm Tyrell. I'm not going to hurt you," he spoke softly as he slowly dismounted. He had no idea then that he was looking into the eyes of his niece, "you are friends with Caleb?" he questioned as he stepped closer.

The look on the girl's face was that of terror. He heard the audible click, as she levered a bullet into the chamber. Tyrell raised his hands. "I am friends of Caleb, too. I see you are also friends with my dog and that mangy wolf," he said hoping to set the girls mind at ease that he, wasn't going to hurt her. His heart was pounding and his mouth dry as he took another step forward. All the girl had to do was pull the trigger and that would be the end of him. He reached out his hand and repeated her name. Teeka slid further around the tree but the barrel of her rifle remained pointing at his chest. He wasn't sure if he should get back on Dutch, and slowly ride away, or if he should stay put, and try to reason with the young girl.

Black Dog was in a predicament himself. He was loyal to Tyrell but Teeka was also a friend. He felt uneasy about the entire situation, and wasn't sure what it was he should do. Finally, Teeka lowered her rifle and peeked around the tree. The man was still standing there unarmed. She stepped away from the trunk of the tree, and was now in full view of him.

She was dressed in old clothes that were ragged and torn. Her face was dirty with sweat and her hair wasn't very well kept. In fact, it was hard for him to tell what color her hair was exactly. What did stand out, were her amber coloured eyes. Beneath it all, Tyrell, knew he was looking at a very attractive young-lady. She wasn't a child at all. They stood motionless for a few moments. Finally, Teeka pointed to him. "Sloan?"

Tyrell was surprised at her response and his eyes grew big, *how could she possibly know that,* he thought before he answered. "Yes, I'm Tyrell Sloan. Your name is Teeka, right?"

The girl looked at him and nodded.

"Are you hungry? I have food back at my shack," he pointed in that direction.

Teeka was looking at him oddly almost laughing because of the funny movements he made with his hands. She repeated the word 'hungry' as best she could. "Hunry," she said confused.

"Gree, gree. Hun-gree," he repeated putting emphasis on the ending of the word.

"Hungry," she said. There was a look of accomplishment in her eyes and her entire face lit up. She repeated the word a few more times. "Yes, hungry."

"Would you like to come with me to my shack?" he gestured again with his hand as he pointed towards it. "I have food."

Teeka tilted her head and looked at him. "Friends," she pointed to Tyrell and back at herself as if trying to confirm that he wasn't going to hurt her.

Tyrell nodded. "Yes, we are friends. In fact I believe I owe you my life. It was you that shot those men yesterday wasn't it?" he questioned as he imitated shooting a rifle. Teeka knew by that gesture alone what he was talking about and she desperately tried to find the words to reply.

She pointed at herself, "yes, I shoot men." She pointed to Tyrell's holster. "Pull away gun shoot." She now pointed at Tyrell as she tried to say his name, "Trell, they man men pull gun and shooting Trell."

Tyrell was looking at her as she said that and was grinning from ear to ear. "I understood every word you said, yes I did," he said as he looked at her with sincerity.

"Trell hear words. I talk," she said shyly knowing how silly it actually sounded but she was getting it. It wasn't because she couldn't talk, it was because she had forgotten how, never having much of a need. It wouldn't take long though, before she would remember words, and how to form sentences.

"I reckon so. I imagine the words I speak sound dang awful funny to you too. We just need to listen is all."

"I watch yes you many times as you build with wood. You not man to bang nails."

"What do you mean?" Tyrell asked with a slant of humour. "I know how to use a hammer."

Teeka softly chuckled and shook her head. "Nope."

"Nope what?"

"You shoot door and crows with gun." Teeka responded as she smirked.

"You witnessed that did you?" Tyrell felt a bit embarrassed. She was right it was an awful waste of bullets. "Well, it was a bad day and I needed to blow off some steam I guess."

"Trell make nice water?"

"You watched me build that to did ya? I think it is the best thing I built so far." The two of them chuckled. It was odd and refreshing all at once. Here they were two perfect strangers quite unexpectedly running into each other, and now conversing as best they could, as though they had been friends for years. "How did you know that I was a Sloan?" Tyrell asked as he point to himself.

"I hear Caleb, ma, say Sloan." Teeka fibbed embarrassed to tell him the real reason that she snooped through his stuff. Nor did she want to let him know how odd it seemed to her that her family was also Sloan. She couldn't understand the correlation between the two names, because that part of her life was lost to her. Every Sloan she knew was dead.

"You heard Marissa say my name?"

Teeka nodded. "She say name to brother."

"I guess that makes sense. You heard Marissa and her brother speak of me?"

"Yes. I know for since you be here," she pointed to the ground referring to the entire area. "Is man Sloan. Now Trell."

Tyrell smiled. "You can call me Trell as long as you like but my name is Tie-rell."

Teeka looked at him. "Not Trell, but Tie-rell."

"Yeah, that's it, Tyrell."

"Teeka name umm. Thinks yes."

"Teeka?" Tyrell questioned as though he was unsure that was what she was trying to say.

"Yes," she was smiling from ear to ear. "I know there is name from before this place. I not know it now."

"Teeka?" Tyrell repeated still unsure what she was trying to get at.

"Yes, we friends."

"I thought we already established that," Tyrell said as he smiled at her. "The longer we stay put here the hungrier I'm getting. Come back with me I'll cook us some food."

"I go with Tyrell," she stepped forward and Tyrell helped her into the saddle and then swung on himself. He didn't know what he was going to do with her, what he did know is that he couldn't turn her away, not now, not ever. Obviously, something went terribly wrong in her life. There was no other explanation on why a young girl, who he guessed to be in her late teens, was doing way out in the middle of nowhere. Not only that, she was one, if not the only reason why he was alive at all. If she didn't help kill the men that were jostling him the day before, he knew he would likely be pushing up daisies. It astounded him, how she was able to make the shots, but, she had and he was breathing today because of it. He owed her something there was no doubt about it.

Neither one spoke a word as the shack came in view. Slowing Dutch to a stop, Tyrell helped Teeka down, and removed the saddle from the horse's back and turned him lose in the corral. "Here we are," he said as he gestured her toward the shack. "Trell's humble shack in the woods," he teased as he led her inside. "Go ahead grab a seat. I'll get cooking. Do you like beans?" he asked as he lit the stove. "We can eat beans and salt pork. How does that sound?"

"You cook. I clean in water."

"Indeed, you are quite welcome to use my bath," he knew what she was talking about.

"Is okay I do," she was looking at him as she nodded hoping for his approval.

"Well, I don't see any problem with that. Feel free. I'll get some food cooking," he grabbed the bar of soap and handed it to her. "You can use this too if you like," he felt idiotic as he said that, "I mean, umm, I ain't saying you're dirty." He felt really awkward now, "it's just soap and you can use it if you like."

Teeka took it from him and smiled. "It makes bubbles and clean dirt."

"Yeah, that is exactly what it does."

"I use," she said as she made her way outside and over to the bath. She took her clothes off, and sat on the bank, as she dangled her toes, testing the water. Satisfied that it wasn't too cold, she stepped in and began scrubbing using the soap. The slippery softly scented bar, felt good on her dirty skin, she hadn't used soap in years, and it made her body feel silky and fragrant. Over the years, she had kept herself clean by simply washing in the cold creek, and it didn't always clean her. But it got rid of most the dirt. What she was standing in now was better than any creek. Deciding that she was as clean as she could get, she climbed out and slipped her clothes back on, and made her way back inside.

"Here," Tyrell said as he set a plate of beans and salt pork in front of her as she sat down. "I hope you like it."

"I say yes to your thanks." She responded as she began eating. It was clear that she was grateful for the meal.

"You are quite welcome," he said as he turned and filled his own plate. Sitting across from her now, he too dug in. There were questions each wanted to ask the other, but for now, they were content in sitting in silence as they ate. The only sound was the din of forks scraping across the tin plates, as the two of them finished. "Would you like more?"

"No for now. I must go back."

"Back where?"

"To where my sleep is," she replied as she stood from the table.

"It looks like it will be a cold evening you may sleep here."

"No, is better I go back."

"I can't stop you Teeka but I do want you to know I am here if you need anything."

"Cold get I come back."

"Yes, yes, please do. If for any reason you want to come back."

"I in morning will see how I feel. Come back then, yes."

"I will be waiting for you," he replied as he walked her to the door. "You are welcome here anytime Teeka. I am always around. Even if I'm not, help yourself to whatever you need." He gestured with his hand that his door would always be opened. She thanked him again and pranced off. Tyrell looked over to Black Dog and Shyaway gesturing that they follow her and keep her warm for the night. Black Dog didn't need asking twice. He watched as the dog and wolf vanished into the forest and out of sight. *I wonder how long that girl has been in these woods,* he thought as he made his way inside. Marissa was going to be surprised the next time he saw her, and told her that Teeka was real. He looked through the little amount of clothes he owned trying to find something, that might fit her better than what she was wearing now. He found a pair of pants as well as a shirt, and some socks without holes. He looked the clothes over, *they might be a bit big but they'll keep her warmer than the rags she's wearing now,* he thought as he set the clothes on the table.

It was almost dark by the time Teeka made her way back to her shelter. She was pleased that the dog and wolf followed her, and were now lying beside her on the cedar boughs, she used for her floor. She wrapped herself up in the woollen blankets, as her mind drifted to the confrontation and introduction, of herself and the man at the shack. "Tyrell be nice man. I safe with him," she snuggled up to Black Dog and Shyaway then closed her eyes and fell asleep.

# Chapter 24

That Saturday he woke early and dressed excited in the sense that he would see Teeka again that day. Tossing wood into the stove, he went outside to relieve himself. The sound of a flock of Geese overhead, confirmed that indeed colder weather was fast approaching. He walked over to the stack of lumber and looked at it, *likely got enough wood here to build another bunk and put up a wall,* he thought as he knelt down and began counting the pieces.

He decided that was exactly what he was going to do. He would build her a bunk, and a small room. Standing he made his way back inside. Looking over to the west corner, he decided that was where he'd build the room. It wouldn't be anything fancy, but Teeka would have a warm place to sleep, and as much privacy, that he could accommodate her with.

All he needed to do was build two walls. One he would build off the west wall of the cabin, and another from the north side. He guessed it would be ten by ten foot long not very big, but not very small either. The entire shack he assumed was twenty by twenty foot, maybe bigger, maybe smaller. Either way the small room could easily fit.

Gathering the tools and lumber he would need, he built the bunk first using his own bunk as the blueprint. It took him less than an hour. He tested it by lying on it himself making sure it could hold weight. Satisfied, he measured where the walls would go. Using a piece of charcoal from the outside fire, he marked Xs on the floor where the corner supports, would be. For the walls he could use, either cedar slabs, or the 1x6x10 foot boards, that were left of the stack he bought.

He scratched his head as he visualized the walls, confirming with himself that he knew what he was doing. Outside he gathered two 10-foot cedar slabs that were close to the same size. Next, he picked out a couple of poles from the pile he had, and with the flat side of the slab facing him. He laid one of the poles on the ground. Bringing the rounded side of the cedar slab up against the butt of it as tightly as he could, he nailed it in place.

He did the same to the other end of the slab, then added the top slab in the same manner, so that when he stood it up inside his shack the slabs flat side was to the floor and ceiling, making it easier to nail in place. He looked over the partially framed wall and crossed his arms. The wall frame looked taller than what the shack's ceiling was. He had no choice, but, to tear it apart. Finally, with the frame apart he moved everything inside and started fresh. It took him another three hours to frame-in the room.

Pulling his watched from his pocket, he noted the time to be close to 12:00 p.m. He exited the shack to have a quick break and cool off. Making his way over to the creek, he slurped up a cool drink, and dunked his head. The water was a lot colder than he was used to, and it took his breath away. Back inside, he once more gave himself approval, of the work he was doing.

It was then he heard the pitter-patter of Black Dog, and he went outside to meet him. Tyrell reached down and pet him. In the distance, he saw Shyaway and Teeka making their way towards him and he called out. "I thought I might have seen you sooner. I'm sure glad you are here now," he said as she approached closer.

"I slept well. Dog and wolf keep me warm. I watch for a time, what is Tyrell now done."

"Hurry up and I'll show you," Tyrell replied as he gestured for her to follow him. "I took some time today to build an extra room. I want it to be yours," he pointed at the incomplete walls. "I know it ain't finished yet, but it won't take much longer."

"For me! You build?" she asked with both excitement and apprehension as her mouth fell opened.

"Yes, for Teeka. It is going to get cold soon and I reckon I owe you at least shelter and food. You can accept or not, just know it'll always be here. What do you say?"

She tried to speak but the words were all mixed up, "owe Tyrell, owe nothing to me."

"Yes I do, Teeka, I owe you because you saved my life. Let me help you. I ain't got no intentions on hurting you. Stay here until we can find different or better accommodations. You no longer have to hide in these woods alone. There are people that can help you, me being one of them."

Teeka was speechless as she made her way over to the table and sat down. She looked around and back to Tyrell, then back to the room being built. "I for seven snows have been alone way out here. Colder than this times..." she trailed off as she reminisced, "I like room," she looked to the floor, as though trying to decide. It was when she started nodding, 'yes' I bring back here stuff."

"So you will stay?" Tyrell wanted to confirm.

"Caleb, ma, think what?"

"I reckon she will be happy to have you as a friend. There ain't no other women type around here. I think the two of you will get along fine."

"Okay, I stay with," she said with a smile as tears pricked the back of her eyes. "I'm thankful," she said without a stutter or misused word.

"I'm grateful that you have accepted. Do you need help gathering your things?"

"No, very little, I go now. Tyrell finish room," Teeka said as she rose from the table.

Tyrell chuckled. "I will. You come back as quickly as you can. You hear."

"Bring stuff fast. I see you soon," she said, as she slipped out the door heading in the direction of the uprooted tree that had been her home since he had arrived.

Tyrell watched as she disappeared into the woods and out of sight. By the time, she returned later that day with her meagre belongings Tyrell had finished her room. "There is the room," he said as he pointed at the finished product. For not being much of builder, his work had paid off. The room looked good and the walls were solid, the only thing missing was the doorway. It was the look on Teeka's face, that brought it to his attention. "What is a matter? You don't like it?" he questioned.

Teeka was shaking her head and smiling, "How I sleep in there?"

"What do you mean? You use the bunk." Tyrell responded as he looked over to the room realising then what she meant. His face grew red with embarrassment and he shook his head. "Hmm I see. No door," he looked at her and bowed his head. "I guess I should have thought that through...," he said as the two of them began to laugh.

"I said yesterday to Tyrell, not one for hammering nails."

"It ain't the hammering of nails that I don't know how to do it's the building of things that sometimes I don't pay attention too. I'm getting better though," he rolled his eyes as he sat down across from her. "Since there ain't no doorway yet, any thought on where you might want one?" he asked as he pulled out a cheroot and lit it.

"In wall so I can get to inside."

"I realise it'll be in a wall. Which wall would you like the doorway to be in? That is the question," he smiled as he inhaled a lung full of smoke.

Teeka rose from the table and walked over to the west wall, "here is place to put door," she looked back to Tyrell who was nodding.

"Yeah, that is the best place. In fact that is where I thought I put it."

"Tyrell put there now, be okay," she shrugged as she made her way back to the table and sat again. She wrinkled her nose as she looked at him, "smoke stink, from that." She said pointing at the cheroot dangling from his lips.

"I know, Marissa, says the same thing. I only have a couple packages left then I'll quit," he said as he butted the cheroot out on his boot heel. "I'll cut that door out now," he stood and went back at it. It took a few minutes but finally there it was in all its splendour a second room inside the shack, "how does that look?"

Teeka stood at his side and smiled. "Now I can inside put stuff." She gathered her belongings and set them on her bunk. She looked around inside the small room and she smiled at him. "Thank you."

"No need in thanking me. You'll be warm and safe that is all that matters," Tyrell said as he walked back to the table. "Are you hungry? I can make us some food."

Teeka came out of her room. "Tyrell sit. I make food."

"Sure, I don't know what you like to make but I do have canned goods and stuff," he pointed toward the counter. "Do you see anything you like?"

Teeka walked over to the counter and looked at the canned goods. She pointed to peaches, "I think I like these."

"Indeed. I love peaches. That is what those are."

"Peaches, yes," she said as she looked at the word on the can and studied it. Next, she grabbed another can and Tyrell told her what that was too. She went through the entire list of canned goods that he had, and he told her what every can was. She put four cans on the table and pointed at the words as he helped her pronounce them. "Sardines," she said and Tyrell nodded. "Corn, peaches, beans. Yes, I say right?"

"Yep, that's what those cans are. I got plenty of each too. These," he said as he picked up the can of sardines. "Are probably something you wouldn't like. In fact I don't like them much myself, but, Black Dog does. I got them for him mostly."

She looked at him confused, "Sardines, yuk?"

"No, but they ain't anything one could eat a lot of," he opened the can and showed her what was in it. Putting one in his mouth he chewed, and offered her the tin, so she could try one.

Teeka wrinkled her nose and shook her head. "Little fish in creek better."

"You certainly wouldn't be wrong about that." Tyrell finished the can of sardines, "yep, wouldn't want to eat many of those," he said. Teeka opened the can of peaches and the two of them shared those. "These. I could eat a lot of. Peaches and beef jerky are my two favourite foods." Tyrell commented.

Teeka was looking at him, "what is jerky?"

He reached over to the leather sack that held the beef jerky and handed her a piece. "That is beef jerky. It is meat."

Teeka smelled it and smiled. "I eat this before. I dry fish same as this."

"I've eaten dried fish before too, and you're right, they are kind of the same. Least wise made the same way, almost, I reckon. Both dried fish and meat are good. Before I forget, I found some old clothes of mine, that I ain't worn in a while," he pointed to them at the foot of his bed. "There is a pair of pants, a shirt, and some socks. They're yours if you want them," he said as he finished his jerky and stood up, "I best get my mess cleaned up before it gets dark. We don't need to be stumbling over tools and wood." Rising from the table, he gathered the tools scattered across the floor and put them away. Returning inside Teeka had on the clothes he provided. They were a little big but were better than the rags she had been wearing.

"These are warm clothes." Teeka said as she looked at him, "fit not very well, but warm. Thank you, Tyrell."

"You're quite welcome. I'm glad you like them. They'll do for now I reckon," he gathered the scraps of wood and piled the shorter ones next to the stove. The others he tossed in a pile near the fire pit outside. "There. All cleaned up now."

The two of them sat in awkward silence for a few minutes not knowing what to talk about next. There were many things they could have spoken about, but, some of those things weren't important yet. Instead, they talked about Black Dog, and Shyaway and his horse Dutch. Their conversation carried on until the sky was dark and they had to light the lantern to see.

"I don't know if now is the time to ask but, how long have you been on your own out here. You said before seven snows." Tyrell mentioned.

Teeka looked at him confusingly, "Tyrell what?" she asked not knowing exactly what he was asking.

"Umm, how many snows have you been out here again?"

"Oh yes, I understand," she grew silent for a few moments and started counting on her fingers, "seven times the snow comes, and the grass grow."

Tyrell was aghast, "you've been out here on your own for seven years?"

"Seven snows, yes." She lowered her head as she reminisced, "it was me very young. I think." Once again, she looked at her fingers and counted. "I was this old," she said as she held up both her hands.

"You were ten years old?" Tyrell was confused. There, were other questions, he wanted to ask. Like why had she lived in the woods so long, what brought her there in the first place, had she simply gotten lost? Did she have family near? These questions and many others were questions that needed answers. If she was simply lost, maybe he could help her find her family. If there was another reason she was alone, then it might be his prerogative to mention it to the law, so that they could help her. Without the answers though, he didn't know which way to turn, so he simply asked her. "What happened? Why are you alone out here?" When he asked those two questions he could tell by the look on her face that she wasn't very comfortable talking about it.

"I cry to sleep at night, when I think, of those things. I tell you. Family killed by men."

"Your family was killed by men?" Tyrell wanted to confirm.

"Men yes. Is why I shoot those men yesterday that try to kill Tyrell."

"I am sorry to hear about that. You have no family left?"

Teeka only lowered her head and shook it. "No. Tyrell is Sloan. My family was Sloan."

"What? Your family was named Sloan too?" he asked with shock.

Teeka rose from the table and gathered her rifle which, Tyrell hadn't looked at yet. At first he wasn't sure if she was going to shoot him or not, and he raised his hands. "Whoa, I didn't want to get you mad," he was a bit nervous. "I hope your intent ain't to shoot me."

"I show you name, not shoot," she handed him her rifle and pointed at the engraved words on it which read, 'SLOAN' on one side and W.J. Sloan on the other. "This was my papa's rifle. He does show for people."

Tyrell looked at the engraving. "I, I umm didn't know there were any Sloans in these parts except me. Can you remember anything else, like the place where you came from? And what was your father's name?" he was now enthralled at learning all he could about her family. Chances were they were related one way or the other.

"I have no memory of papa name, nor my ma. I had sister too. I remember this. We live on flat land. No trees like here."

"So your family is from the prairies?"

"Maybe is that place what it is called?"

"You said flat land and no trees. There is only one place like that and is called the prairies. Mostly farmers and ranchers, did your family live on a farm?"

"Farm," she repeated unsure what he meant.

"Yes, like Caleb's. Did your family have a place like that?"

"Chicken and moos. No we move around lots."

"What do you mean move around?"

"Papa, shoot for people to watch." She was trying to explain to him, what it was her father did for a living, but she could tell it wasn't making much sense, to Tyrell. She tried another approach. "Papa, people pay to see him shoot."

"People paid to watch him shoot?" Tyrell questioned again, as he looked at the .45 Winchester. "I think I'm beginning to understand. He was a showman with a rifle, a trick shooter?"

Teeka was nodding her head excitedly. "Yes he did shoot tricks. People pay to see. We travel for shows," she grew silent again as she thought about her family. She was trying to grasp something else that would help explain to Tyrell, where her family came from, who they were, and where they were going when they were attacked. But there was nothing there in her mind that she could so easily grasp.

She had forgotten, and made choices not to remember, thinking she would never have the need. There was one thing that she could remember, and it was a memory she would rather not have, but it was what, her dreams were made of at night when she tried to sleep, "I show Tyrell place where... ma, pa, and sister die. I know this place where is at."

Tyrell looked at her, "you know where your family was killed?" he asked with a heavy sigh.

"Yes. I show. Come," she began to stand up.

"Wait, it is too dark now Teeka. You can show me tomorrow. Is it far?"

"Not far." She said as she sat back down somewhat withdrawn. She had lived with the past for too long. Now, being friends with Tyrell, and answering his questions she was beginning to feel the weight of her past lifting. "We take horse. Not long to get there."

"Yes we will take Dutch," Tyrell, answered. He grew silent as he contemplated what he learned about Teeka so far. One, she was a Sloan. Two, her father was a trick shooter who travelled. He had seen a few shooting shows in his time, and he wondered if he had ever seen her father's show. He couldn't recall ever hearing the name 'Sloan' at any of the events he did see. Of course, he wouldn't have because

Teeka's father used the name 'One Shot Jack' when he performed. There was so much more to Teeka's story that he wanted to know. For now however, it was getting late and his bunk was calling his name.

"It is getting late, I think I will turn in," he said as he rose from the table. "I'm going to check on the horse and Black Dog first."

"I come with, I see dog and wolf too first." Teeka said as she rose from the table. Tyrell opened the door for her and the two of them stepped out into a cool evening.

"It is a cold one tonight," Tyrell said as he looked to the sky. It was a clear evening and a millions stars dotted the sky. "Yep, going to have to light the inside stove tonight. It is going to get colder before morn."

"Yes, cold. I thank Tyrell for room. Not so warm under tree."

Tyrell chuckled, he was glad he found her, and even happier that she decided to take his offer of food, and lodging and that she could have them for as long as she wanted. After all, she was a Sloan. What side of the family she came from, he wasn't sure all that mattered is that they shared, the same last name. He'd learn more about her and her family soon enough. The two of them walked side-by-side as they made their way over to Dutch's corral. "Evening Dutch, how are you?" Tyrell questioned as he reached over the top rail and pet him.

Teeka climbed up on the rails and reached across to Dutch as well. "Dutch good horse," she said as she ran her fingers along the horse's forehead.

"Do you like horses? I have a sneaking hunch there are seven horses running around here somewhere. Maybe we'll find one. Would you like your own horse?"

"Not bad man horse, no."

"Why? The men that rode them were bad, not their horses."

"Hmm, maybe right, I think about horse from bad man. We see maybe, I think about it."

Tyrell chuckled, "well, we ever see one of them and you decide you want it. I reckon the corral would hold another. Dutch might like the company."

They stood out in the cold evening for a few minutes more, and continued with their idle chit-chat. "Is time to sleep now, Tyrell, we get wood for inside fire."

"You bet," he followed her and the two of them grabbed an arm full of wood from the pile outside. "We got enough wood here to last a couple of nights." Tyrell said as they entered the shack and tossed the wood on the floor. A few minutes later, he blew out the lantern and the two of them retreated to their bunks. "Good night Teeka," he said as he curled up.

"Yes, morning soon. Good night." The crackling fire lulled them both to sleep.

# Chapter 25

Sunday, October 4, Tyrell was frying up salt pork and eggs, when Teeka came out of her room. "Good morning Teeka. How did you sleep last night?" he asked as he tossed some eggs and salt pork onto a plate and handed them to her.

"I slept well, I was warm," she looked at her plate of food, "You must eat too. We need to go to place. I show where family was."

"Yes, I will eat. Have you ever had coffee?" he asked as he set the pot on the table.

"Coffee?" she questioned not sure what it was.

"Yeah, coffee," he poured her a cup. "It is hot, be careful. I add sugar to mine. Would you like some sugar too?" he simply added some sugar to her cup, and then gently blew on his own, gesturing her to do the same. Then he took a sip. She followed suit and copied his every move. "What did you think of that?" he asked as he started in on his eggs. "Did you like that?"

Teeka still had the cup in her hand and she took another drink. "I like. Is good and warm, sweet too, thank you," she said as she took another sip.

Tyrell smiled. "I'm glad you like it. How about your eggs, how are they?"

"Everything good," she said as she set her cup down and continued eating her eggs and pork. The two of them sat in silence as they finished their breakfast. "Tyrell is better cook than builder, but, he learns. Like me, I learn more words every day. You make hot dark water taste good too," she was smiling as she said that. "No hot water, coffee I say to mean."

Tyrell began to chuckle. "I knew what you meant. I understand most of what you say. Some things though, don't make any sense whatsoever. But you'll learn our tongue again soon enough. I reckon anyone who hasn't lived amongst other folks for as long as you have, would suffer the same at speaking English. Caleb tells me I don't speak it proper either. So, we'll work on both our English speaking, even if we have to take lessons from Caleb himself," he smiled at her as he took a swig from his coffee. "All the books that boy reads, he can teach us both I reckon."

"Caleb, he has read to me before. I listened and tried to read. But it is hard. I remember something's for words. We talk and I remember more every time. Is good."

"Just like I said before, it'll all come back to you. You only need a bit of time and that is all we have out here."

Teeka nodded her head, "we go now to family place?"

"Sure, we'll saddle up Dutch and be off," he said as the two of them stood from the table and exited the shack. A few minutes later, Dutch was saddled, Black Dog and Shyaway were present, and his rifle was slipped into the scabbard. "There, I reckon we're good to get," he looked at Teeka and helped her onto Dutch's back. "Which, way?" he asked as he swung up himself.

"Up creek that way." she pointed.

"All right, c'mon Dutch, giddy-up," he said as they set off with Black Dog and Shyaway close behind. "I went for a ride a few days ago up along this creek. I came across an old wagon. Might that be where we're heading?"

"Wagon all broken. Up creek, also fire burned."

"Yep, that was what I saw. Didn't see nothing else though."

"Maybe is where I take you now. Could be, I show you, maybe then we know if it is where you went."

"That seems logical. Could be a totally different area I suppose." They journeyed on for a couple of hours and the closer they got to the area the quieter Teeka grew. Tyrell knew then that they were getting close, to the same wagon wreck he discovered a couple of days earlier.

"There is, see right there." Teeka pointed as tears welled up in her eyes.

"This is the same wagon wreck I found. Are you sure you want to get closer?" he slowed Dutch to a halt a few yards away.

"I will stay, you go alone."

"Sure. You stay here with Dutch," Tyrell jumped off the horse's back. He didn't know what he was looking for but there had to be evidence somewhere amongst all the debris. He scoured the wreck looking for something that would identify Teeka and her family. It was Shyaway, that discovered the first human remains.

Over the years, they obviously had been scattered by wild animals. If it hadn't been for the wolf, he would never have found them. Not far from the first horrid discovery was another partial skeleton, and another. The last one he found was that of a child.

His heart raced, and he felt sick to his stomach, he had found three skeletal remains, among or near the old burned up wagon. He felt anger and sadness all at once. A Christian burial was the first thing that came to his mind. The second thing of course was revenge. Whoever killed Teeka's family deserved nothing less than death themselves, and he felt compelled to be the one to see to it.

Teeka remained near Dutch as she looked on. She could tell that Tyrell had found something. She wanted to go forward and look for herself, but, something held her back. Instead, she called out to him, "have you find something," she hollered to him.

Tyrell could only look at her and nod. "What did find?" she asked.

"Your family," he replied not knowing how else to say it.

"I must see," she walked towards him.

"No Teeka, you do not want to see this," he said to her. It didn't stop her though. Standing next to him, she looked at the discovery herself, and began sobbing as the memory of that horrible day, years earlier palpitated her mind like never before. For seven years, she stayed away from that place, and for seven years she had been haunted, by that fateful day. Tyrell consoled her as best as he could.

"We will bury them properly. That is all we can do for them," he said as he held her head against his shoulder as she continued to sob. "There was nothing you could have done…nothing at all. You were young. You must remember that," Tyrell continued to console her. "We will bury them with the dignity they deserve Teeka. They are kin and they will be buried on Sloan land."

He looked up to the sky as tears pricked his eyes, *if I ever find the men that did this, I won't be sending them to you Lord. Hell waits for them and my bullets will send them there,* he vowed.

It was a heavyhearted moment, the good that could come from it however, was that perhaps Teeka could have the closure she needed. And of course her family would now be buried. Holding her now at arm's length, he looked into her tear-flooded eyes. "You too Teeka are a Sloan," he paused for a minute. "I'm your family now. C'mon, let's get the tools we'll need to bury them Christian like," he said as he tried to snap her out of her reverie. Finally, she responded.

"Yes, bury them," she said as she turned her head and walked back towards Dutch. "Tyrell hurry, come. We bury ma, pa here, in pretty place. Need shovel though at shack."

Tyrell looked at her and nodded, "right behind you Teeka. Right behind you," he said as he crouched one last time. Removing his hat, he looked at the remains. *I ain't sure which Sloan you may have been, but, I reckon there ain't many which would have known about this place. Makes me think you must be blood, and so I'll see to it that Teeka is taken care of,* he promised. He wanted to know more about the Sloans he was looking at. For now, though he knew very little except that he was looking at their skeletal remains. He needed to learn more. And, he would. Rising, he bowed his head one last time as he put his hat back on, then turning he made his way to Dutch. "We'll get what we need and come back. We'll put them to rest today Teeka," Tyrell said as he heeled Dutch and the three of them set off towards the shack, to gather the tools they would need.

It was while they recovered the bodies that he found some documentation in a small wooden box. The box itself was broke and battered, but, the documents inside did survive to a degree, they were wet and dirt-covered, and he placed them in his saddlebag. Once they dried out, they might shed light on who these Sloans were. Those were the only documents he found that dreadful day, as he pulled the last skeleton from the vegetation, and debris that, had hidden it for all these years. With the remains laid out, he and Teeka fell silent as they looked on.

Teeka never spoke the entire time, as they wrapped up the remains in the old woollen blankets, that she kept when she escaped the bloody slaughter. She shed tears only when the last shovel of dirt was tossed on the last grave. "They," she began to sob. "They will rest in peace now. They ghosts to heaven. Yes?"

"Yes, they will rest in peace now. And heaven does wait." Tyrell was looking at the wooden crosses as he said that. "I think they would have wanted to be buried here."

"Is nice, with trickle sound from creek, ma, pa, and sister, sleep now in peace," Teeka said as she knelt next to the graves.

Tyrell looked to the west and smiled a solemnly, "they'll be under sunsets forever."

"Place is easy to find, walk up creek to visit, you visit too?"

"We, I, the two of us will visit you can count on that Teeka."

"Maybe small circle around with fence, too?"

"If that is what you want."

She looked toward Tyrell. "Yes," she paused, "Tyrell, I feel happy, the sadness leaves me this day. I miss family though, how can I feel happy?"

"I reckon you could be both. Happy that your kin have been buried, and sad that they have been, only normal feelings I think," he replied as he gathered the pick and shovel. He looked on toward Teeka who remained at the gravesides of her family and watched her. Wanting to leave her alone for a few more minutes, he sat near the creek on a big rock, and smoked a cheroot. His mind was fogged as he sat there, and he was beginning to feel overwhelmed with the whole scenario, he inhaled deep lung full of cigar smoke and exhaled.

Teeka called out to him. "Tyrell, I and you can go to shack now. I prayed for them, I feel better, my heart is happy too."

Tyrell stood and walked over to her, "we can plant flowers or something here in the spring, but we can come back before the snow flies and put up a fence. Short like the one, Marissa did for Grandpa Sloan. How does that sound?"

"Yes, before white cold comes. We go now Tyrell."

"After you ma'am," he gestured with his hand for her to take the lead, he wanted to have a say at the graves as well. He knelt down and removed his hat. "Like I said earlier, I'll take care of Teeka, and when I learn more about you, I'll let you know what I've learnt. I ain't sure if you are cousins, aunts or uncles, or what. I do know you are Sloans and I'm going to do my best in finding out which Sloan's you are. Rest assured Teeka will be okay," he stood now, "until next time, Rest in Peace, Sloans." Turning, he made his, way to his horse, "how are you felling Teeka?" he asked as he stood beside her.

"I feel different, happy."

"Relieved perhaps?"

"I think yes, relieved. I will miss them differently now, I know I can visit them and not be scared." Tyrell listened as she said that, then, he helped her onto the saddle, he nodded his response and then swung up himself.

"C'mon, Dutch, let's get," reining the horse in the direction of home, they headed back. The two of them rode in silence, as Dutch ambled on. Tyrell could feel, and see the relief that now surrounded Teeka. Something he knew, that she never felt in many years. She would no longer, have to hide in the fear that had consumed her, since the deaths of her family. Tyrell was now, the closest thing to family that she had.

Two hours later, they were finally home, and were sitting on the bench at the fire pit, watching the dancing flames of their fire perform for them, in the gentle breeze that blew. Black Dog and Shyaway lay on the ground next to them, panting from the day's travels. "Teeka," Tyrell began as he looked to her. "This place here," he gestured toward the shack and surrounding land that went on forever. "You can call this home. You belong here as much as I. You are a Sloan and I'm a Sloan so you could say we are kin."

"Kin," she was a little bit confused at what that meant. "Like friends? Better though I think. Family, yes?"

"That is right, family."

"New family...." she trailed off as she looked into the flames of the fire. She was thinking back to something her father once said, about his own father and that his name was, John Henry Sloan Jr. It only began to make sense to her then.

"Yep, new family, you and I," Tyrell said as he added another piece of wood.

"I call you Uncle."

"Uncle, what do you mean?" he knew she was remembering something by the look on her face.

"Pa say onetime, Henry Sloan, his pa. Was he your pa too?" she questioned. She remembered enough about how family names worked. If Tyrell's father was also Henry Sloan then there would be no mistake that indeed he was her Uncle.

"That was his name, yes. The young John Henry though, not the one that lived down where Caleb and Marissa now live."

"Yes, that is same Henry."

"Are you sure about that?" Tyrell asked confusingly. His old man never spoke of another son but, then again his old man was full of secrets. "If that is true then your Pa was my half brother."

"I know that yes, Henry Sloan was my pa's, Pa. Sis and I never met him, only pa speak of him few times, maybe three. But I remember him saying that, now." She paused for a few moments as her mind became clear, "you are my uncle," she was certain, now.

Tyrell sat there in awe, "I guess I'm your uncle then, ain't that something," there was nothing more, he could say, he didn't know either way. There was no reason for Teeka to lie, and she certainly proved that her last name was Sloan. Tyrell scratched his head, then reached into his pocket and pulled out a cheroot. "Is there anything else you can remember Teeka? I'm as curious as a pole-cat now," he replied as he inhaled a lung full of smoke.

The papers he found that day were tucked away in his saddlebags and wouldn't be dry enough to open for a few more days. He hoped that there would be more information on who Teeka and her family were, but, until then he couldn't doubt a word of which she spoke.

"There are bits and pieces of family fluttering my mind." She said as clear as day without so much as a stutter or misplaced word. It even surprised her, "I am starting to understand, what we speak. English."

"I noticed that over the past couple of days. You have really come along way with speaking."

"It is because you talk to me." She smiled, "you also talk to yourself, and sometimes I hear."

"Yes," he began to chuckle, "yes I do. I talk to myself and the damn animals, crazy eh?"

The two of them fell silent, their attention now drawn toward the warm flames of the fire. "I am glad we found each other Teeka. We have the Dog and wolf to thank for that. If it weren't for the two of them, I'd have passed you by. I knew though, that someone was around these parts. I knew for sure when you fired upon those men that were here. I was I must say, quite surprised when we met though. I wasn't expecting on finding a young lady, or, for that matter another Sloan. There is a lot we're going learn about each other as time passes I'm sure."

# Chapter 26

It was cold when the two of them woke the next morning. The frost on the ground outside proved how cold the evening had been. "I should have kept the woodstove stoked. It sure got cold over night didn't it?" Tyrell questioned Teeka, as she sat down at the table while he lit the fire.

"I slept well, and didn't notice. Ground out widow is cold, frost out there."

"I noticed that, it'll warm up in here in no time, now that I got the fire going," he stood up and gathered the coffee pot. "I'll get us some fresh water so we can have a coffee. On cold days like this, hot coffee puts the skip back in my step." Tyrell chuckled as he exited the shack and made his way over to the creek. Even the creeks edges had froze overnight. The thin layer of ice cracked away, as he scooped up water with the pot. It was cold enough out that he could see his own breath. Black Dog and Shyaway he noticed were nowhere in sight. He shook his head as he looked around, "hope the two of you leastwise kept warm overnight," he said to himself as he entered the now warm shack.

Black Dog and Shyaway had in fact stayed quite warm that night. Even now in the early morning, they were warm. They turned Teeka's old shelter into their very own den. It was theirs now. They had rooted around and made it more to their liking. Black Dog even marked it as his territory. It was the perfect den as far as the two of them were concerned. It was both warm and dry what more did they need?

Tyrell made his way over to the woodstove and set the coffee pot down. "Even the brim of the creek had ice on it this morning. We might have an early winter this year."

"Winter is pretty sometimes, but is cold."

"Pretty, maybe, but I still don't care much for it," Tyrell said as he looked toward the coffee pot. "That seems to be taking it's time to finish isn't it?"

"Only put there now. You need to be patience."

"I think you mean patient," Tyrell corrected her as he smiled.

"Yes, Patient, I mean," Teeka wrinkled her nose at him and smiled back, "I listen and learn."

"You might learn forming sentences, but I ain't much of an English teacher. I don't speak it as properly as I should. Caleb and Marissa are the ones to learn that from," Tyrell chuckled, "which reminds me in the next couple of days I have to head down to their place, they got some butchering to do. I reckon you might as well come along too. We can set Marissa's mind at ease by introducing you. She's been on Caleb's back ever since I got here. She doesn't believe that you are real. I reckon when she learns that you are a living body, she is going to be quite surprised."

"I come, yes, I like to see Caleb again. Be better now, won't have to hide from Marissa anymore. They butcher cows?" Teeka asked.

"Yep, I ain't sure how many though. I told them I'd help. Plus, I have to pick up my eggs from Caleb and a few more bales of hay from Marissa."

"You not get hay from man in valley?"

"Waxley? Nope, I've made arrangements with Marissa to buy my hay from her. I only got one horse don't need much hay."

He had no idea that one of the seven horses, that he shooed away a couple of days earlier, was only a quarter of a mile away, and making its way back to his shack. It was a young Appaloosa mare that had somehow managed to lose the six other horses it was running with.

"What are we going to do today, Tyrell?"

"What do you want to do?" Tyrell responded as he looked over again to the coffee pot which by now was perking. "Right now, I reckon I'm going to have a coffee. Would you like one?" he stood up and made his way to the pot, and brought it back to the table.

"Yes, thank you."

Tyrell poured each of them a cup, "maybe today we could go for a hike and hunt for some meat. I'm getting a little tired of salt pork," he said as he took a swallow from his coffee. "A nice buck or bull Elk would suffice. I ain't had any venison in a long while. What do you say?"

"We walk together with guns, look for hunt animal? I like to do that. Yes. We can hunt. I not shoot big animal before."

"Really, today might be your opportunity to do just that. I found a game trail up the creek a bit. Looks like it is being used, we'll start there and follow it some. How does that sound?"

"You bring horse, Dutch?"

"We could use the horse, or, we could simply walk and talk."

"We walk and talk, I like that," Teeka said as she brought her coffee to her lips and took a drink, "when is time to go? Soon?"

"Let's enjoy our morning coffee first. Are you hungry? I can make us some hot cakes or biscuits?"

"We should stay hungry, for meat tonight. We share fruit can?" Teeka rose from the table and grabbed a can of peaches, "we eat this and old biscuits from day ago, no waste good stuff, like always you do."

"Sure. I wouldn't complain about that. I don't usually eat breakfast unless I'm making it for others. Coffee, biscuits, and maybe a piece of jerky, is all that I need in the morning. Of course when Marissa makes breakfast I eat."

"If I make breakfast, you eat then too."

"I would. There ain't no man including myself that can cook like a woman in the kitchen. Nor is there a woman that can cook on an open fire like a man," he chuckled.

"I cook only on fire, be careful what you say."

He was smirking when he looked at her, "sounds like a challenge, you think you can out cook me on a fire eh?" Tyrell questioned with humour as he scratched his chin.

"No think, I know," she said with humorous conviction.

"Well we'll have to see about that. If we manage to get us a deer or elk today we'll have a cook off."

"You don't sound, as though we will get a hunt animal. We must think yes we will, then, it happens."

"What the heck was that you said?" he knew perfectly well what she meant, but he noticed as of late that the more they talked the better she spoke.

"I say, you have to think good things. Then good things happen."

"Okay, then tonight when we come home with some meat we'll have a cook off."

"Yes. I prove to cook well on a fire."

"You got yourself a deal," Tyrell smiled at her and winked. It was quite pleasant for him to be able to talk to her. It was even more pleasant when she talked to him. It surprised him how quickly she was coming around, with her speech, and how well her speaking had improved, in the three days they had known each other. She was no dummy. It might take a few more weeks, before she finally spoke with the clarity, one would expect of a seventeen year old, but there was *no doubt* in his mind, that eventually she would. To him it didn't matter. He already understood most of what she said anyhow.

Teeka on the other hand wanted to speak with coherency. To make that transition Tyrell realised that he would have to improve the way he talked around her. He was no teacher though, that much was clear. He could only help her so much. He reached over for the coffee pot and topped off his cup. "Would you like more?"

"One last cup and then we hunt. I am excited to hunt with you and gun. So I can cook meat at fire." Teeka was smiling as she held her cup up for him to fill.

"Sounds good, we'll finish these and be off." Tyrell responded as he poured her more coffee.

"You have enough bullets?" Teeka teased. "I only need one."

Tyrell smiled, it was likely true she already proved how good of a shot she was. "One eh, sounds like another challenge. Who gets to shoot first?" he teased back.

"From before, I remember girls go first."

He quite enjoyed her sense of humour and wit and began to chuckle. "Yep, it is that way still. All right, you get the first shot." A few minutes later, they gathered their rifles and exited into the cool morning. They only walked a few paces along the creek, when they heard the distant sound of something running. Stopping abruptly the two of them listened. "Sounds like a horse," Tyrell said as he looked in the direction. Immediately Teeka's instincts were to hide but Tyrell stopped her. "Hold on a second Teeka, you don't have to run and hide every time you hear a horse. It could be friends. Besides we're armed."

Teeka slowly and cautiously made her way back to Tyrell's side. "You are right. I don't need to hide anymore, this is Sloan land," she said with clarity and pride.

"That's right we belong here," Tyrell looked at her and smiled. "It is only one horse anyway. One person can't be much of a threat." The sound of the horse got closer as the two of turned and walked back the way they came. They were surprised when they made the distance back that, standing outside of Dutch's corral was a horse. Tyrell recognized it as one that was ridden by one of the men he was forced to killed days earlier. It was the nicest one of the bunch, an Appaloosa mare. "Looks like Dutch, has himself a new friend and we got ourselves another horse," he said as he and Teeka stopped and looked on. "Ain't no use in spooking it. I reckon it'll be here when we get back. We'll give it some time to get use to Dutch. C'mon, let's finish our hunt. I'm expecting venison tonight."

"A bad man's horse, it is pretty though. I like."

"Once we get her corralled it might as well be your horse. I don't need one."

"A horse for me?"

"Sure, why not?" Tyrell asked as he looked at her.

"I not have my own horse ever. I think about bad man's horse, not sure I want a bad man's horse."

"Like I said before, the horses from bad men, ain't bad horses, only their riders were." Tyrell mentioned as they ventured on. They walked in silence and listened to the creek as it flowed by. The sun was warm by the time they made the distance to the game trail. The two of them stopped and knelt down next to the trail and read the recent tracks. "Looks like deer have been here," he pointed at one of the tracks. "That one there I reckon is a buck, nice sized track too." He rose and looked into the forest where the trail led. "We should follow the trail. I don't reckon them deer are much further ahead."

"No, they are close," Teeka said, in fact she already had visual contact. It was funny to her that the great man hunter couldn't see the animal. "I still have first shot, yes?" She asked with a smile.

"Of course, but you ain't going to get a shot, off if we don't find an animal to shoot."

"I already find."

"What?" Tyrell asked looking around he couldn't see a damn thing. "What do you mean?"

Teeka brought her finger to her lips. "Shhhh, Tyrell not so noisy. Look," she said quietly as she pointed toward a little knoll a hundred yards away on the other side of the creek. Tyrell still couldn't see anything and he squinted. Finally, the buck lifted its head and looked in their direction. A smile crossed his face when he saw how big it was. He was about to comment when the shot rang out, and the buck toppled to the ground. He quickly looked at Teeka, who was standing beside him with a smile across her face. "See one bullet," she began to chuckle.

"That was a hell of a shot, well done. Good eyesight too. I didn't see it until it lifted its head."

"You go alone to clean. I can't like doing that. I wait."

"What? What do you mean I have to clean that animal alone?" Tyrell questioned with confusion.

"I shoot. You clean," Teeka responded as a matter-of- fact.

"Well...that don't seem fair at all," Tyrell said as he turned and waded across the creek. "Damn female, anyway," he muttered quietly to himself, as he shook his head and smiled. Making the distance over to the buck, he drew his knife across its throat and waited for it to bleed out. Teeka's shot pierced both lungs. It was an instant kill. When he noticed that he smiled, *she can sure shoot,* he thought as he now went about drawing and quartering the buck. He guessed it weighed a hundred and fifty pounds, empty of guts. It was certainly big enough to provide meat for a few months. It didn't take too long to get it butchered, and with a half each strapped to their shoulders, they began their walk home.

It was early afternoon when they finally arrived. Removing the weight of the meat from their shoulders, the two of them sat down to a well-deserved rest. "We'll hang the meat in a bit. Whew," Tyrell inhaled deeply as he wiped his brow. "That was quite the walk with that animal strapped to our backs wasn't it?" he sighed as he stretched out his legs.

"It was a heavy walk. Glad not far too."

"You mean, 'not too far'." Tyrell said as he winked at her and smiled.

"Yes. Not too far. It could have been though, lucky we see hunt animal fast."

"Yes, it could have been a lot further of a walk, if we hadn't spotted it as quickly as we did. I wasn't even sure we were going to see anything today."

"Animals all around, you only have to watch to see. I win first challenge, one shot only," she began to chuckle. "Next time, you can have first shot."

Tyrell looked at her, he couldn't argue. Instead, he waved his hand through the air in a playful gesture. "Yeah, you win."

It was a short time later while they were hanging the meat and had cut a few big thick pieces off the carcass when Black Dog and Shyaway made an appearance. At first they were startled at the new horse that was nearby, and chased after it until Tyrell whistled and called them back. "You two ain't got to worry about that mare that's Dutch's friend and soon enough it'll be a fixture here," he looked over to the mare that was now standing in the creek a short distance away. Averting his eyes back to the dog and wolf, Tyrell smiled. "I haven't seen either one of you since yesterday. I reckon you've both been out gallivanting and chasing game eh?" he scratched the dog behind its ear.

Rising, he walked over to the fire pit, the dog, and wolf close behind. Of course, they made their way over to Teeka and sat next to her. "We're about to light a fire and cook some venison. If the two of you stick around for a bit you'll get your chance to enjoy some yourselves," Tyrell said to the dog and wolf as, he struck a match and lit the fire. "There. That'll get going good soon enough," he added another piece of wood and then another. Sitting down he lit up a cheroot and inhaled deeply. "Should we cook up some beans to go with the meat?" he asked as he exhaled.

"No, we cook round things, umm... called botato. Right on orange hot rock in fire."

Tyrell inhaled another lung full of smoke and smiled. "You mean potato, and those orange hot rocks, are called coals."

"I say botato, what do you mean?"

"You said BOTATO," he chuckled. "They are called POTATO. It is what you said but with a 'P'."

Teeka was looking at him confused. "P? I don't need to pee."

Tyrell started to laugh at her innocent mistake, "no no, not pee. The letter 'P', here, I'll show you," he picked up a stick and drew the letter 'P' and the letter 'B' into the ground. "There, see that," he pointed to the letter 'P'. "That is the letter 'P' and this one here is the letter 'B'. They sound the same but they ain't. So, when you say Potato that is with this letter," he pointed toward the letter 'P' again. "What you said was Botato and that is with this letter," he pointed to the 'B'.

"Ahh, yes, potato," Teeka repeated with a smile. "I see now, yes."

"Good. I'm glad you understand. It is easy to make a mistake like that."

"That evening as they ate their meal, Tyrell admitted that, the meat Teeka cooked was degrees better than his. He didn't get it. They used the same cut of meat, the same fire and the same type of stick, yet Teeka's was better than, his. He chewed and swallowed the last piece and smiling he looked over to her. "I ain't sure what you did different than me but, I'll admit the venison you roasted was tastier than the hunk of meat I cooked. That is challenge two that you have won."

"I win again," she smiled.

"We all get lucky once in a while," he teased. "I think maybe you should take over the cooking when it needs doing," he continued jokingly.

"You show me how to cook hot cakes. I will cook them for you, too."

"I wouldn't complain one bit. I ain't had a woman cooking for me, for as long as I can remember, except of course Marissa and a few others that cooked when I visited. But you don't have to feel as though you have too."

"I know, still I want to cook for you." Teeka looked into the flames of the fire, "woman of family always cook, where from I come."

"That ain't always true. Woman nowadays do a lot of other things too. Take Marissa for example, she raises cattle and provides for Caleb. There ain't no-one helping her either. Never feel as though your obligation because you are a woman, is to cook and clean, because that ain't the way it is. Men like me, and there are a lot of us out there, do all that on our own, you know, cooking, and cleaning when we feel it necessary."

"When, man alone, he has to. Same as when woman alone, together man and woman work animals, but woman always cook." Teeka said with conviction.

Tyrell began to chuckle, "all right you can take over the cooking, but let me do it once in a while too."

"Okay, but you can make coffee all the time."

"Sure. I'll make the coffee you'll cook. We'll share the other chores that need doing. I'll take care of the outside stuff." Tyrell said as he poured himself a coffee and lit another cheroot.

"Outside stuff," she wasn't exactly sure what he meant.

"Yeah, like feeding the animals, chopping wood, and fixing things. Like leaky roofs," he inhaled a lung full of smoke. "You know stuff like that."

"Feeding animals and wood chopping, yes, but maybe I too should help with nail hammering." She teased, "I see from over there," she pointed to where she always hid when she use to watch him. "From there I see how you build." Teeka shook her head and smiled, "I help next time with hammering nails."

"Hell! You've already out-shot me, out-cooked me and now you want to out-build me too," he said with humour as he shook his head and chuckled. Teeka saw the humour in his statement and began to laugh.

"You make day's fun, with thing sometimes you said."

"You mean, 'things I sometime say', make you laugh. That's good. Without laughter, I reckon life would be pretty boring, wouldn't you agree?"

"I like to always be happy. It feels good to, laugh. I have not laughed much, but, at what I see animals do in time once in awhile. When you come here, I laugh every day. Thank you, Tyrell."

Seven years of fear, running, and hiding and having no one to talk too had turned her heart stone cold. Now though in Tyrell's presence she was waking up from that misery. She had not felt the happiness, love, or kinship she felt then since the time of her families murder. It was no wonder it overwhelmed her and she secretly wiped away the small tear that trickled down her cheek.

"I reckon it was God's doing that made us cross paths. There ain't no reason to keep thanking me Teeka. There is more at work here than what you and I could figure out." Tyrell paused as he took a drink from his coffee. "I look at it this way. You've been out and about on this land longer than I. And I bet you didn't even know it was Sloan land, yet, you lived here all that time alone most of it except on those occasions you visited with Caleb. Now don't that seem a bit odd to you, that this is Sloan land and by God if you ain't a Sloan.

That, young lady is God's work... ain't mine." Tyrell winked at her and smiled. "Even though I ain't as sure as I'd like to be for my own benefit which Sloan you and your folks are, a Sloan is a Sloan as far as I'm concerned. If I never discover nothing else about you and your family, your name alone gives you as much right as me to be on this land, and all the riches it has too," he fell silent for a moment, as he inhaled a lung full of smoke from the cheroot in his hand. Looking at her again, he continued. "There ain't many of us Sloans around anymore."

"I only know my, ma, pa, and sis. And name sometime spoke, Henry Sloan. Is all Sloan's I hear of, now I know you too. God's work maybe is true." Teeka looked into the flames of the fire again. It was while looking into those flames, that a switch in her mind turned on, as the memory of her real name flashed behind her eyelids, RAYLENE. Jumping up from where she was seated, she screamed with both excitement, and confusion, as the vision flashed again and again. It was so abrupt that it scared the crap out of Tyrell.

"My name, my name, my real name is Raylene Sloan!" she said out loud as she began to shake and quiver at the realisation. More memories and names flooded her mind. Sisters name Rachel, pa's name, William Jack Sloan, ma's name Amelia. I...I..." she started to faint. Luckily, Tyrell was quick on his feet and caught her before she fell into the fire.

"Whoa, that was close. Teeka, Teeka," he repeated as he lay her down on the ground. He slapped her face lightly to snap her back into the here and now, "Teeka!" he said a little louder, finally Teeka took a deep breath and opened her eyes.

"What, what happened?" she asked as Tyrell helped her up.

"You fainted after scaring the crap out of me and screaming a bunch of names."

"Yes, I remember now more. My name is..." Tyrell cut her off there.

"Hang on a second Teeka, take a moment to catch your breath. We have nothing but time," he wanted to be sure that she was okay before carrying on. He had already heard the names and they were etched in his brain now because of the way they were thrown at him. It was as if Teeka had been in some kind of a trance. It frazzled him a bit, but he could understand what a shock it must have been, after all these years to remember all at once.

Calm enough to speak now, Teeka looked over to Tyrell. "My name is Raylene Sloan, my sister was Rachel... she was very young when those men killed her, 5 or 8 years old I think. Why did those men not kill me, Tyrell?"

"I haven't the answers Teeka...or should I call you Raylene?" Tyrell asked with sincerity.

She was looking away from him in deep contemplation. She was trying to decide what name she did prefer. Raylene was her name, but, she had grown used to Teeka. "I think I like, Teeka Raylene Sloan," the smile on her face at that moment was brighter than any star in the sky. "I still go by Teeka though. We know names of my family now."

"Yes we do. I am glad you remembered. How does it make you feel are you okay? It is quite the thing to remember all at once."

"I feel like the day we bury them, relief, happiness and some sorrow. It is not good though to remember what happened to them."

Tyrell inhaled deeply and sighed, he couldn't imagine what she had gone through back then. Or for that matter what she had endured since. The thing was, not he, nor her, could ever change the past. "We go through many obstacles in life, we endure them, and we learn from them. We also live through many tragedies, sorrows, and disappointments. These things though give back to us courage and the knowledge of kindness," he stopped there as he waited for her response.

"Where though does happiness come from after bad things happen?"

"Happiness is all around us, every day. I get joy from waking up every morning and watching the sunrise, and at night watching it set. Plus, I get joy and happiness when I'm in the company of those I care about. Like you, and Marissa, Caleb and the horse, the dog and that gnarly wolf too, not to mention friends, I make or meet on my way through life. I ain't saying there is no time to feel sorrow or mourn about what has happened, what is going to happen, and so on. But there has to be a time when we accept those things. We have to learn how take them for what they are, and move on. I'll never forget my friends or family that have died, or been killed. I do know they'd want for me to be happy and to keep them close to my heart, which I do and will."

"I see. I do understand what you say. I like happy feeling better than afraid or sad and by self. It is better to keep happy memories."

"I guess that is what I'm trying to say, yep," he knew then she got the gist of it. They sat in silence and listened to the fire as it warmed them while the evening grew cool. There was a north-westerly breeze, that blew, and it forced a few sparks from the fire to take flight and dance in the darkening sky. They looked like fireflies as they twirled this way and that, then, disappeared into the black void of evening. Black Dog and Shyaway now rose from where they lay at Tyrell and Teeka's feet, and like the sparks from their fire, they too, faded into night. Tyrell watched as they slipped into the darkness. "I reckon them two have found themselves a den," he said as he turned back to the fire.

"Yes, I think they now use my old shelter, they came to that place on cold nights," Teeka said as she continued looking into the fire.

"I bet you are right. I didn't even think about that. Well, least we know they're happy. See, happiness, Teeka." Tyrell said as he rose from the bench and smiled. "Like I said it is all around us," he poured the remainder of what was left in the coffee pot, over the flames to dampen them. "I reckon it is time to head indoors and get the ol' stove lit and settle in for the evening."

"We had a good happy day today, Tyrell. Tomorrow will be good too." Teeka said as she followed him to the shack.

"It was a good day Teeka. In fact, one of the better days I've had in a while. We went hunting we learned a few things about each other when we conversed around the fire. Even the dog and his companion came for a visit, and tomorrow we'll have ourselves another horse. That Appaloosa mare now has Sloan written all over it. And last but not least we ate some darn tasty venison," Tyrell chuckled as he opened the door for her. Whether Teeka wanted the horse or not, Tyrell, didn't see any reason, not to put her in the corral with Dutch. Eventually Teeka would learn that the mare wasn't bad like the man who once rode her. Besides there wasn't anything wrong with having an extra horse, except the fact that he would need double the hay. It didn't matter though he knew a good horse when he saw one, and that Appaloosa was a damn fine horse in his mind's eye. Closing the door behind them, he made his way over to the wood stove and lit it. It had been a long day but a day worth living.

# Chapter 27

Ten miles away and setting up their evening camp were two Mounted Police Constables. They were on the trail of a gang of men that reportedly had been rustling cattle. There were seven men in all and each one of them had a noose waiting for him. Not only were they stealing cattle and pillaging homesteaders, but they were also suspects of a few ghastly murders that took place. If it could be proven, they were the perpetrators, then for the murders alone, they would hang. If it could be proven that they were the rustlers only, they'd still hang.

"I think we are getting close to them Mitch. The only thing is there are a few homesteaders out this way. I sure hope they haven't met up with these men."

"Not sure if by now it would make much of a difference. They've been three days ahead of us the entire time. If any homesteaders around here have met these men chances are the damage is already done." Mitch the young Constable spit to the ground. He was 23 years old and a young go-getter full of piss and vinegar most of the time. But he knew how to track and he knew how to shoot. As for the law he knew enough about the legalities of this, that, and the other thing that they had made him a Constable at age 18. If the truth be known, he had no use for outlaws and would just as well shoot them then waste taxpayer's money. "And if that is the case why waste the Judge's time? Why not just shoot them when we find them?"

"Because, that isn't Justice, you know that Mitch."

"Justice? It is just a bureaucracy that is all that is, Timber." Mitch responded as he added another stick to their fire. Timber McCann was a senior Mounted Police Constable, pushing 50, he had followed in his father and grandfather's footsteps and was known as one of the best Constables on the Mounted Police force. He was a big man with greying hair and a heart of gold. He was joyful and pleasant most of the time. When it came to the law, he upheld it with dignity and respect. There were two sides to every story as far as he was concerned and he believed in innocent until proven otherwise.

Mitch knew that, still, sometimes Timber got on his nerves and not always did he like the way Timber apprehended prisoners. He was always so gentle and soft spoken. Mitch, on the other hand was the total opposite. He was aggressive, quick to draw his gun and not a bit afraid to go one-on-one with any man. One could say his methods and Timber's soft-spoken word is what made the two of them a dynamic force for the Mounted Police. They had worked side-by-side since Mitch first put on his Mounted Police badge and red uniform.

They had apprehended and brought to Justice more than twenty hoodwinks in the five years they worked together. Out of those, Mitch probably shot and killed a half a dozen and beat up as many. He was always within the law though and so he was allowed to continue to wear the badge and uniform. Timber often wondered if Mitch deserved the honour.

"Bureaucracy or not, we're meant to be peace keepers and law enforcers. That is what the oath you took five years ago and that uniform and badge that you wear represent. Keep that in mind while we get closer to those men. Understand?"

"There is no need to remind me about that. I know. I also know that those men, may very well be, the same damn men that have ravished innocent women, and even a child for Christ sake. I don't know about you but that doesn't make me feel very good."

"You said it yourself Mitch, *'may very well be'*, they may *'very well not be'* too. Keep that in mind."

Mitch tossed another block of wood on the fire and rolled out his bedding. "We'll see," he responded as he covered himself up and closed his eyes. The comment didn't go over so well with Timber and he voiced his opinion.

"There will be none of that 'we'll see' crap on my watch either Mitch. We follow the law when we round these men up. We arrest them and we bring them in with dignity. It is up to the Judge and people of the Law Courts to decide their fate."

"You are such an ass sometimes Timber. You and I both know that at the least these men are cattle rustlers. That alone takes away from honest men and women that raise the damn things. That is their lifeline. Why should those men be given a lifeline? They are nothing more than menaces to the poverty stricken, law abiding and honest working class. An ounce of lead goes a long way in putting things right and doing it quickly too. It could take weeks if not months before black hoods and nooses are slipped over their heads. That to me sounds like a lot of unnecessary living for the likes of them."

"Damn good thing you aren't a Judge you know that Mitch?"

"Yeah, well someday, I just might be. Good night Timber." Mitch pulled his bedroll over his head and once more closed his eyes.

Timber sat by the fire and thought about what the young whippersnapper said. The kid was right but, the law was the law and those that broke it no matter how foul the crime, still had the right to prove their innocence. It is not that Timber shied away from his gun, in fact, he had killed a few men as well in his time of wearing the badge and uniform, and each time he pulled the trigger he didn't feel any better about it. He rose now and laid out his own bedroll. Tomorrow they would be that much closer to bringing the fugitives to Justice. With that thought, he too closed his eyes and slept.

# Chapter 28

Teeka woke before Tyrell the next morning and put a fresh pot of coffee on the stove. The scent of the fresh brew wafted towards him and woke him from his slumber. He looked over to the table where Teeka was sitting. "That sure smells good Teeka. I haven't woken to the smell of fresh coffee in a long time. Usually it's me that gets it cooking, so I'm already awake." He chuckled at his morning joke as he swung out of bed and dressed. "It was a bit warmer last night wasn't it? I was sure cosy anyway. I slept like a lamb, how about you?" he questioned as he sat down.

"Not very happy, today Tyrell curse come."

Tyrell swallowed deeply, he knew exactly what she meant. He just never expected her to say so. He scratched his head in nervousness. "Umm, do you need something, ahh... We have toilet tissue," he said with embarrassment as he looked around for some. "I know there is some around here somewhere." He stood from the table a bit embarrassed and franticly began looking for something Teeka could use to keep her from menstruating all over the place.

Teeka, feeling as she did found humour in his extreme desire to help her and she chuckled. "I have already protected below. Tyrell, sit and have coffee. Worry not."

"Umm, well, ahh, maybe I should go check on the horse," he said as he scratched his chin. "I have to tell you Teeka, I feel kind of odd, knowing...well, you know, knowing that you are having that issue or curse that you call it."

"Is normal part of life, Tyrell sit and have coffee." She said with urgency as though taking control. Tyrell didn't want to argue, not then.

"Yeah, that's what I'll do. Thank you Teeka for making it," he said as he sat down. He poured each of them a cup. Bringing the fresh coffee to his lips he gently blew on it then took a drink. He didn't know how he should behave. He was nervous and didn't want to say the wrong thing. He knew how women could get when they were menstruating. So he decided not to say anything. The last thing he wanted was Teeka, getting mad at him, for saying something that he shouldn't. He looked across the table, he could tell, she was not very happy. "The coffee is really good Teeka, better than what I make anyway," he said as he took another drink.

Around this time, Mitch and Timber were beginning to stir. The fire had kept them warm most of the night and now it barely flickered. Mitch added a piece of wood to bring the flames up and he held his hands over the flames to warm them. "Not a very warm morning is it Timber?"

Timber was rubbing his hands together to knock the chill from his fingers too. "The evening was warmer that is for sure. How's that coffee coming?"

"It'll be ready soon enough. Hope this weather change isn't going to stick around. It wasn't this cold a few days ago. It might be that we're in for a chilly winter." Mitch poured them each a coffee now that it was done, and he handed one to Timber. "Getting tired of black coffee too, next time let me pack the supplies."

"Black coffee isn't going to hurt you any Mitch, man up would you. Quit being a sissy." Timber joked.

"Sissy? Hell I'm no sissy Timber I just happen to like cream and sugar with my coffee."

"Yeah, so do most women."

"Keep it up you old prick," Mitch replied as he took another drink from the cup in his hand. Setting his cup down he unfolded the map that they had and with the light from the fire looked to see where they were. "It looks like we're getting close to a canyon of sorts another ten miles or so."

"That would be Red Rock Canyon. Most of it if not all of it is owned by the Sloan family. Not sure, any of them are around though. We had a case up there six or seven years ago. A mining outfit was working dirt and came across a few skeletal remains. They turned out to be the remains of the

Farron family I believe it was. They had been reported missing years earlier, but, no one ever found them or learned what might have happened to them, until that outfit discovered their bones, and final resting place." Timber pointed out.

"When I think about it, I seem to remember a few years after slipping into this blood red uniform reading that report. Strange that it was never solved or no answers were proven. Considering I read that one of the skulls had an old axe wound. Doesn't that spell foul play?"

"Could also spell accidental, you have to learn to quit being so damn quick to judge, Mitch."

"Sure, it could have been an accident. I wouldn't argue that, but, once the bodies were put to rest, no one did anymore investigating to prove it either way, did they? No sir. It turned as cold as the ground that case did. Now is that Justice, Timber, or just plain laziness?"

"There wasn't much else anyone could do Mitch. The remains were a few decades old already and no witnesses ever came forward or hollered 'foul'. There are likely hundreds of cases that have had the same outcome where they have turned cold, that is."

"I've always wondered about that, 'cold cases'. What is exactly meant by that? I'll tell you. It means someone has tossed those cases into a drawer and forgot about them. That is the problem I have with what we call Her Majesty's Justice."

"I can't argue with you Mitch. I tend to agree a lot of cases end up as a file number with no conviction or witness reports whatsoever. I think lack of manpower is part to blame."

"Manpower? I don't think so. How many rookies are put on the Royal Mounted Police force a year? Ten at least, why not have them going through those cases? Manpower has nothing to do with it in my opinion, Timber. Nope, it is how the damn force is run," Mitch took a swig from his coffee and looked to the rising sun. "I guess we should be thinking about setting off soon. We don't need those men getting any further ahead. Hell, Her Majesty's Justice awaits them."

Timber stood up. "You make some good valid points Mitch, still we don't need you going all rogue. Keep in mind what that badge and uniform represent."

"Like I said to you the last time you said that. I don't need no reminding of what they represent." Mitch poured out what was left of his coffee and what was left in the pot over the fire. "I'm ready to ride, how about you, you old bastard?"

"As ready as you, let's get." The two of them rounded up their bedrolls, saddled their horses, and set off in a north-westerly direction heading straight for Red Rock Canyon. They picked up the trail they were following a few minutes later and it cut deep into the forest. Following it, they came across an evening camp that the men may have used. "It looks like they spent an evening here." Timber said as he slipped off his horse to have a look.

Mitch remained in his saddle and looked around himself. "Nope, this isn't one of their camps unless of course they're running with a dozen or so bovines."

"I noticed that. Could be the cattle were here afterwards."

"You are always such a damn sceptic, you know that Timber," Mitch shook his head.

"Being sceptical until proven otherwise is all part of this job," Timber replied.

Something caught Mitch's eye and he swung off his horse. "Yep, goddamn you are right," he said as he knelt down. "The cows were here after the men. Looks like a half a dozen plus one horse headed west here," he pointed in the direction as Timber made his way over to him. Mitch stood and slapped him across the shoulders. "For an old fellow I'm sure glad you still have your wits," Mitch chuckled. "Otherwise I might have left this place and tried to pick up their trail somewhere else."

"All right, so we know they aren't heading to Red Rock anymore. Looks like they're heading more in the direction of

Waldie, they make it that far and they'll be on a riverboat and well on their way up north or down south for that matter. We wouldn't have a hope in hell of catching them before they cause more havoc and death. Damn. I wish my bloody horse could fly," Timber replied as he and Mitch swung back onto their saddles, and continued following the old trail made by the seven horsemen.

As Mitch and Timber drew closer to his shack Tyrell, was outside trying to round up the Appaloosa mare that had been hanging around. Teeka, on the other hand remained indoors to deal with her curse. She watched from the window as Tyrell tried and tried again to catch the horse, she even laughed a few times at it and Tyrell's antics. The horse wasn't keen on falling for his schemes and tricks and it kept a good distance from him.

Even when he had a bucket of oats in his hands did it come within an arm's reach. Finally, he decided to set the oats down and walked back the way he came to watch her. She meandered up to the oats and knocked over the bucket to feed on the grain. Tyrell watched with gumption as the horse portrayed some of the old traits Pony use to have. This made him want that horse even more, and he smiled. *I get you in that corral missy, and you'll be a Sloan horse in no time at all,* he thought as he looked on. For now, he would leave the horse alone.

He decided that since the sun was starting to beat down hot and heavy, it would be a good day to let the bath pool warm up. God knowing he needed a bath, and by now so did Teeka. He'd let her bath first and if the sun remained warm he'd bath later. If not there was always tomorrow. He kicked the rock into place to stop the water flow, and then made his way back to the outside fire pit and bench, where he sat in the silence of the morning. Black Dog and Shyaway appeared a short time later panting, and waiting for a handout of some kind. Tyrell looked at them and chuckled, he knew what they wanted. Standing, he made his way over to the fresh deer Teeka killed and sliced off two thick pieces. "Here you go, a couple chunks of this ought to keep you happy for a bit, I reckon," he tossed the two pieces to them. They snapped up the handout and headed into the shade to feast. Over the past few days, things had been hectic. Men had died, kinships found, and kin had been buried. Now, as he sat there it all bounced around in his head almost overwhelming him. He sighed and inhaled deeply.

Since he first made his way to Red Rock back in 1890 his life had never been the same. And when he returned this time just when he thought things were going to be normal again, he discovered that Marissa was a mother. Next, he learned Fry was missing, and Grandma Heddy had passed away. Then of course, the death of the seven men, he, and Teeka shot, and the discovery of her and the fact that she was a Sloan, and that he might have had a brother. It was almost too much to handle all at once. *Hard to understand how life works sometimes*, he thought as he sat there and contemplated.

By now, Teeka made her way outside and sat next to him. "Tyrell looks very troubled. What is wrong?"

"Ah nothing really, I was just thinking about what has all taken place since I came back to Red Rock."

"Do you wish you had not come back?" Teeka asked with concern. "We not know of each other then."

Tyrell looked at her, "I only wish I never left the first time. You and I would have crossed paths sooner I'm sure of that. I would have been here for you and for Marissa and Caleb. But I ran off like a fool and I wish now that I never had." He couldn't count how many times he wished, or thought that on his two hands, but it was all true. If he never left in the first place in all likelihood, he and Marissa would have raised Caleb together. They would be years ahead of themselves in their relationship, and God willing they would have been wed. He would have discovered Teeka years earlier, and would have been there for her as her only living kin, saving her all the pain and turmoil of growing up in fear, hunger, and homelessness for all those years. He felt partly to blame for how horrible Teeka's life had been so far.

Teeka was looking at him sullenly almost as though she was reading him. "It is not your fault for how I came to be here, it is the fault of the men who ambushed my family."

"I appreciate that Teeka but, in a sense had I been here you may have then only spent a year, maybe two without kin. Don't you see your life would have been different perhaps, and that saddens me, that one small difference could have made a greater difference to all involved."

"It will be different now. You said once, 'it is what it is', that we learn things from sorrow. Is what you said."

"I did say that didn't I? I guess when I think about how things have come about you are right. It could have been different and who is to say it would have been any better. A good example is when those men came here," he began as he pulled out a cheroot and lit it. "If you weren't around then, I wouldn't be around now."

"Yes, like that things happen for reasons. Like you say," Teeka was smiling now realising that she had snapped Tyrell out of his depressed state.

"For a young wild woman," Tyrell teased. "You're damn smart, you know that Teeka?"

"I am young wild woman you are crazy man." They began to laugh out-loud. "I call you from now on, crazy man." Teeka teased back between breaths as they continued into peals of laughter.

"Young Wild woman and Crazy man, that is us Teeka, that is us indeed." Tyrell said as he caught his own breath. "I haven't laughed like that for a long while. It sure feels good doesn't it?"

"I laugh like that watching Crazy man build." Teeka chuckled as she rose. "I go back inside now and lie down. Stomach knots make me feel bad."

Tyrell understood what she meant and nodded at her. "Yeah, you go ahead Teeka and lie down. I'll stay near." He was glad she had come out for the little bit she had, it was always nice talking to her not to mention the little bit of fun they always had teasing each other. Tyrell remained seated for a few more minutes, then he made his way over to the wooden box, he set in the sun behind the shack so Teeka didn't find it. He didn't know what it contained, and thought it best to read through it before, letting her know about his discovery.

Perhaps it was a little bit selfish on his part, but it was more his concern for her, and what the documents might or might not read, that he didn't want to mention the box to her. He assumed that by now the documents had dried enough to at least read a few. If they weren't he'd leave them in the sun a bit longer, and maybe spread them out on rocks, so they would absorb the hot rays from the early fall sun. Opening the box, he looked at the contents and slowly removed the folded papers. The top ten were dry enough that he could peel them away from the buddle. But, the years of weather made the papers impossible to read. Mould grew deep in the wooden box itself, and the papers had disintegrated. They were nothing more than faded memories of a family's history. Whatever was on them not he, nor Teeka, would ever know.

He closed the box and carried it back to the fire pit. There was no point in keeping anything so useless, so he lit a fire and when the flames were high, he tossed the entire wooden box and all its contents into the dancing flames. He felt good about the fact that he didn't know any secrets, or for that matter, learned something he didn't want to learn.

Tyrell stared deep into the flames and watched as the box and all it held turned to ash. All hope he ever had in discovering who Teeka and her family were other than Sloans, now dissolved into nothingness. She would have the life she deserved and nothing less. She was a Sloan and for the first time since meeting her, he accepted her as his niece, and until the day, he died his niece she would always be. It was as if by some divine intervention or hand that they discovered each other. He would have liked it to have been under different circumstances, and not because of death, but like he always said. 'It was what it was'.

He stood from the fire and walked over to his bath, the sun had been beating on it for almost three hours. Dipping his hand in he felt the temperature, it wasn't quite as warm as he had wanted it to be by now but it was getting there.

Turning he walked over to Dutch's corral to check on his water and feed. The Appaloosa mare hid in the bush not far away, and watched as he approached. "Afternoon Dutch, how are you doing today?" Tyrell questioned as he put one foot on the bottom rail and reached out to pet him. "I reckon you got your eye on that mare, eh? I don't blame you. I do too. She's a pretty thing ain't she? Only wish she'd quit being so damn skittish. I'd like to put her in there with you.

The two of you could keep each other company and maybe I could convince Teeka, to ride her. I reckon that girl is going to need her own horse sooner or later. It might as well be that mare, eh?" he looked toward the bush where the mare was hiding, and he took a few steps in her direction. He spoke soothingly as he approached her. "Hello there girl, I ain't got no intent on hurting you, just want to be your friend. And Dutch, well, he'd like for that too. What do you say?" Tyrell began as he reached out his hand to show her that he wasn't a threat. It didn't help and the mare turned quickly kicking up dirt and farting, as it crashed through the forest and across the creek. It stood stock-still on the other side and glared back at Tyrell, not only was she glaring at him, but as he turned and walked back to Dutch's corral, so was he.

"All I was trying to do Dutch, was make friends with her. Shit, don't give me that look. She ain't gone far, she'll be back. No worries." Tyrell assured the horse. Dutch though, turned and ambled back to the big tree in the middle of the corral as if giving him the cold shoulder. "Awe, c'mon Dutch. I'll leave her alone for now." He looked into Dutch's water trough making sure it was full, then tossed a few leafs of hay into the pen. "I'll leave some out for her too, Dutch. She'll be back."

It was the abrupt sound of a galloping horse, that, made him stop and look back, to see the Appaloosa mare in a full gallop heading straight for the corral, and in one graceful jump cleared the corral fence. "Whoa! Now that was something! Holy mother of God, I ain't never saw that happen before!" He was dumbfounded as he watched both the mare, and Dutch begin playing and kicking up dirt. Snorting and horse farts echoed, as the two of them danced around. Tyrell stood there in awe and watched in disbelief. A smile of both shock and hilarity at the whole thing crossed his face.

All the commotion outside woke Teeka from her slumber and she came out to see what was going on. "You have caught the horse I see," she made her way to where he was standing.

"I didn't catch her, she jumped right in, as gracefully as a deer over deadfall," Tyrell responded.

"What?" Teeka questioned, as she looked onward.

"She just jumped in. The craziest thing I ever saw." Tyrell said as he looked at Teeka and shook his head. "I couldn't believe it."

"You mean, horse, jump inside, no gate?"

"That is exactly what I mean. I tried catching her but she darted off and across the creek. The next thing I know she's running at a full gallop straight for the corral, and in a blink of an eye cleared the fence and jumped inside."

Teeka was looking at him as though he had completely lost his mind. "I think you make joke Crazy man." she rolled her eyes at him.

"As God above being my witness that is what that horse did. Honestly. That is exactly what happened."

"The horse then, must be a jumper, I think then."

"Damn right, good jumper at that. I reckon that is as good as any name to call her too, Jumper. What do you think Teeka, should we name that mare Jumper?" Tyrell questioned as the two of the walked over to the corral and watched the two horses jostling each other in horseplay.

"Jumper is good name for it. Jumper, she is pretty horse, maybe I ride sometime."

"Certainly, there is nothing wrong with her she isn't bad. She does have a bit of attitude I think. She'll be a good horse for you Teeka." Tyrell said as they continued to watch the two of them play. "I almost forgot I have the bath warming up it should be ready soon if you want to take a bath."

"I will yes, have a bath. I use Tyrell's soap too?"

"Of course you can that is what it is for," Tyrell looked back at the two horses. "Ain't they something? Look at how they're playing. Old Dutch hasn't had so much fun in a long time."

"He seems happy to have friend. I go now and have soap bath," Teeka said as she turned and walked away.

"You go ahead, Teeka, I'm going to stay here for a bit and watch the horses." Tyrell leaned on the top rail and watched as Jumper and Dutch continued to court each other. Finally, both horses approached him and snorted as he reached out to pet each of them. "See, told you I wasn't going to hurt you none. We're going to call you Jumper, do you like that name?" Tyrell questioned as though the horse would answer. To his surprise it did. It bobbed its head up and down and side to side, then, pranced away farting and snorting as it went. Dutch followed suit and once more, the two of them began to play.

Tyrell pulled out his package of cheroots and put one between his lips, he had never felt so content, as he did now. He inhaled a deep lung full of smoke as he looked over to the bath, where Teeka was drying off, and slipping her clothes back on. Tyrell watched as she made her way over to him. "Was it warm enough for you?"

"Not so warm as before, but I am clean and feel better."

"Good. I'm glad you are feeling better," Tyrell responded as Teeka sat down beside him.

"I think it is tomorrow we see Caleb?"

"Yes, tomorrow we'll be heading to Marissa and Caleb's. How does that make you feel?"

"I like to meet Marissa in person, very happy to see Caleb, long time since I sit with him."

"I figure you and Marissa, will get along fine. Like, I told you before, you are the only other girl around here. She's probably going to love the company."

"I want it to be like that. I think it will be nice."

"I have no doubt about that, none whatsoever," Tyrell said with sincerity. "It will also put her mind at ease and prove to her that Caleb, wasn't making you up. I think that bothered her, thinking that he had an imaginary friend, named Teeka." Tyrell chuckled.

"Caleb and me have been friends for a long time. Since he could walk I think. I always ran away when Marissa come to check on him. I watch him grow through window and when he outside with Marissa. Later he talks and we play games and stuff. Very nice he is. Sometimes, he, make me think of baby sister, when I miss them. Is it okay that I sometimes think of them?" Teeka wanted to know.

"Of course that is okay. I often think about my old man and he's been gone for a very long-time."

"You not think of your ma?"

"I never knew my mother. Only my old man," Tyrell looked into the flames. "I would have liked to have known my mother but never did get the chance."

"She move away?" Teeka asked with curiosity and concern.

"Nope, she went up to the starry sky when I was birthed." It was hard for him to talk about it, and most times he never.

But with Teeka's innocent questions he felt they deserved all the right answers.

"What? She go to starry sky when you were a baby?"

"Yep."

Teeka now looked into the flames herself she felt sorry and saddened for Tyrell. "That is very sad, Tyrell."

"Don't let it sadden you. I grew up fine. Besides, it is what it is, ain't that right?" he smiled and winked at her as she turned and looked back at him.

"Yes like you said. Only a little sad though Tyrell?" Teeka questioned.

"Yeah, only a little bit." The two of them averted their eyes to the fire and grew silent. Deep down, he was more than a little saddened. He thought back to all the women who draped their arms around his old man, none of them were mother figures. Can-Can dancers and brothel inhabitants that is all they were. He did give his old man credit though, for raising him on his own. There weren't many words, he could say about him. He spent the majority of his younger days being looked after by so-called relatives, while his old man was out on the range, herding cattle, chasing women or gambling.

There was no denying the fact however that he was a good poker player. He often earned his year wage playing the game. Those were the best times when his old man would win big, and wouldn't have to be gone everyday earning a wage, and leaving him alone with people he didn't know. During those times, Tyrell and he would often travel to distant towns, and his old man would spoil him with sweets and toys. Sometimes they would go on long distant hunts, 'shooting expeditions' his old man liked to call them. It was during these expeditions that he was taught how to shoot.

The best memories though, were the ones when his old man finally gave up all his pleasures, and began working from home as a leather-smith. He made saddles and clothing, jackets and hats, knife sheaths, the list went on. He had a reputation, as was one of the best leather artisans in the whole of the Northern Provinces. Even after all that, and finally settling down and raising Tyrell through his teenage years, he still owned the reputation as a gambler, hot head, and a mean SOB. There weren't many folks that liked him as a person, but, they came from far and wide to buy his work. The years of gambling, drinking, fighting, and riding the range however, caught up with him, and he died, when Tyrell was relatively still a young man.

In a sense Tyrell followed in his footsteps, the only difference between the two was that he never enjoyed that lifestyle as much. He always wanted to do more with his life, than only being a gambler, gunslinger or range rider. His forte was always enterprise, so when the opportunity to take over his Grandpa's land came about, he jumped at it. It was hard for him to believe in fact that he had left it once, and the six years he'd been away, he hadn't accomplished a damn thing, except made some enemies, and stirred up demons. He shook his head as the thoughts permeated his mind. "Well I guess I'll take my turn in the bath. Probably could use a shave too."

He went inside and gathered his shaving soap, razor, and a change of clothes. He happened to find another set of clothes that he hadn't worn in months, but, they were fresh and clean and from what he remembered didn't fit him anymore. *These might fit the girl,* he thought as he unrolled them and looked them over. *Can't imagine I had a waist that small once,* he looked down to his stomach, indeed he had put on weight, or had just got plain fat. "I best try to trim that down I reckon," he said to himself referring to his stomach, as he exited the shack and told Teeka about the clothes.

"Thank you, I fit into them later okay?"

"Sure, makes no never mind to me," he responded as he walked over to the bath and undressed. The water was certainly not as warm as even he would have liked, for now though, that is all they had to keep clean. It was undoubtedly warmer than their alternative which was the flowing creek. A few minutes later, he was drying himself off and dressing. He walked up to the creek and kicked the rock out of the way, so that the bath, could clean itself out over the next couple of days until they needed bathes again. He stood for a few minutes to make sure the water flowing down the trench didn't get backed up. There wasn't as much flow as there use to be. The glaciers, and mountain lakes that fed the creek, were obviously freezing up for a long winter's nap. Looking to the north at the dark blue mountains in the horizon, he noted that there was snow on a few of the higher peaks.

By the time he made it back to the shack, Teeka was dressed in the fresh clothes he put out for her. She was very pleased with how they fit. "I like these. Better fit than others. What say Tyrell?"

Tyrell looked at her and indeed, they fit her better. She didn't look like a lost girl now wearing baggy clothes. She looked like a prim and proper teenage girl, appropriately dressed for the terrain and lifestyle they lived. "I reckon they fit you nicely. A little baggy around the waist I see, but that is what belts are for, and I have a few of those," he walked over to his bunk, and dug through a couple of wooden boxes until he found the one he was looking for. It was one that, his old man made. Tyrell had never worn it, preferring to look at it as art. "Slap this through the loops," he handed it to her.

Teeka took it from him and gawked at the intricate designs, and turquoise beads, that were inlaid throughout the belts design. "You sure you want me to have?"

"Of course I do. I ain't never worn it. Thought I could at least give you something new. You know who made that?"

"No, whoever done the making is very well at doing it. Who made it Tyrell?" Teeka asked as she continued adoring the belt.

"My old man made that," Tyrell said with pride and honour. He may never have always got along with his old man, but, he always respected him.

"I hold close forever, because it made by Grandpa. I never know him. It is very special Tyrell," she bent over and kissed his cheek. "Thank you, Uncle. You give to me a family again. That is why tears of happiness come from eyes."

Sometimes the smallest gifts one could give, were the best gifts. "No use in getting all teary eyed. C'mon slap that belt through the loops. Let see how it looks."

She cinched it up and locked in the buckle. It was certainly a work of art, and it looked beautiful, around her waist.

"That is a nice belt Teeka, it looks very nice on you." Tyrell said as he nodded his approval.

"It feels very nice to wear. Pants no need string now to tie up. Thank you very much again Tyrell. Is okay if I put pa's knife on belt?" she asked as though she had to.

"By all means, there ain't nothing wrong with wearing a knife in these parts, as far as I'm concerned."

Teeka made her way into her bedroom and gathered her father's knife, then looped the belt through the knife's sheath. She looked down at how it looked but wasn't satisfied, so she removed it. For now, she decided she wouldn't wear the knife. The belt was too pretty for that.

"I keep belt like is now, no knife," she said as she sat down across from Tyrell. "I like the way belt looks without big knife, maybe later. What does Tyrell want to do now? It will grow dark soon. Maybe coffee?" she asked.

"Sure, we could have some coffee. I wouldn't mind that one bit. I'll get the water," he rose from the table and grabbed the coffee pot. Exiting into the now cool evening he looked to the sunset, it was as peaceful as his day had been. He inhaled deeply the mountain air as he knelt down and scooped up water for their coffee. Today would be the day he would always remember, as the day of revelation. From that day on without a doubt, he was Teeka's uncle.

# Chapter 29

Wednesday, October 7 was butchering day. That morning
Caleb and Marissa rose bright and early and began preparing
for the day. After a hardy breakfast, they rounded up the four
steers they were butchering that day and corralled them.
"Think mister is going to come Ma?" Caleb asked as he
closed the gate.

"He said he would."

"I guess I should gather his eggs then. I think he wanted
two dozen. I hope I have that many." Caleb said as he darted
off to the chicken coop. Marissa went inside and started
planning the food she would serve throughout the day. She
planned on sandwiches for lunch and a pot roast for dinner.
She would bake bread and a couple of pies, and a simple
vanilla cake with cream icing to serve with their dinner.
Marissa looked over her ingredients making sure she had
everything she needed. Satisfied, she sat down to a fresh cup
of tea and cinnamon.

She was excited about the day and even more excited that
Tyrell was coming to help. It had been a week since his last
visit and she was in desperate need to have some adult
companionship. The more she thought about him, the more
she wished that he was with her all the time and not miles
away living in some shack. But, that was his decision, and for
now she knew she had to accept it.

There was always the slim chance that maybe today would
be their day, and they would fall into a lovemaking embrace.
Marissa chuckled, as she thought about how unlikely that
was. He had been back in her life for more than a month, and
still, the two of them hadn't bed down together. Tyrell hadn't
even put a move on her. It confused her somewhat, and she
often wondered since his return, if he was even attracted to
her. Then again, she also knew he was trying his best to
prove his love to her, by taking things slowly and gracefully.
He felt ashamed for the way he left, and guilt for not being

there for both her and Caleb. These things she knew he needed to come to terms with, if a life together, could ever be expected. How long it would take him she didn't know. As for herself, she was ready to spend her life with him now. *Perhaps,* she thought, *I should blatantly tell him that I'm ready.* Marissa took a sip from her tea as she contemplated the idea. Instead, she decided she would give him until spring to ask the question and if by then, he didn't she'd make history and propose to him.

She sat in silence for a few minutes. Suddenly Caleb began hollering at the top of his lungs from outside. "Ma! Ma! It is Teeka! Ma, hurry up Tyrell and Teeka are coming!" Marissa jumped up from her chair not sure what Caleb was hollering about and exited the cabin. Caleb pointed. "Look Ma! Tyrell and Teeka," he said as he ran over to Teeka as she slid off Dutch's back, and jumped into her arms, "Teeka! Teeka!" he yelled with excitement as the two of them hugged.

Marissa's jaw dropped and her eyes grew two sizes as she looked on in both shock and intrigue. "Good morning Marissa," Tyrell said as he swung off Dutch, as though nothing out of the ordinary was taking place. He walked over to her and gave her a hug and kiss on the cheek. Marissa stood there dumbfounded a look of *oh my God* on her face. "That's right, Caleb wasn't kidding when he said he knew Teeka," Tyrell chuckled. "In fact she's been here for as long as you and Caleb have been."

"I, what... I, I don't understand. Teeka," she said as she looked at the young girl and smiled. "I am so very pleased to meet you." Marissa was at a loss for words and didn't know how to react. It was all so shocking, so unbelievable.

"I am happy to meet Marissa too," Teeka said with effort making sure she said everything correctly.

"Teeka, you spoke very clear." Caleb looked over to Marissa, "sometimes Teeka gets words mixed up, right Teeka?"

"I'm learning from Uncle Tyrell."

"Uncle?" Marissa questioned confusingly.

"Yep," Tyrell began, "you got coffee brewing? I'll tell you all about it. I'm sure Teeka and Caleb have some catching up to do, ain't that right Caleb?"

"Yes, come with me Teeka, we'll go to my room and read." Caleb said as he took her by the hand. She smiled and waved at Marissa and Tyrell as her and Caleb passed them by.

"Quite a surprise eh?" Tyrell questioned.

"I, I, I'm totally lost for words... How can this be...I, oh boy, I need a tea. Come on Tyrell, I'll get coffee brewing, unless you don't mind some tea."

"Either or works for me," Tyrell said as he took her by the arm and opened the door for her. "You are in for quite a tale," he said as they sat down at the table.

"I bet I am." Marissa poured them each a cup of tea. "There. Okay, I'm all ears Tyrell." Tyrell took a drink from the cup of tea she poured him, and then lighting a cheroot, oddly enough the last one he had, he began his tale. Marissa listened with intent and eagerness, as Tyrell told her about the seven men, and how he found Teeka, to only learn later she was a Sloan, and had lived on the land ever since her, family had been slain, and that her father was his half brother and so on. He didn't miss an iota of the tale and by the time he finished, Marissa knew as much as he.

"So, there you have it. Teeka is my niece and lo and behold, I had a half-brother. Strange isn't it?" Tyrell asked as he finished the tale.

"It is so hard to fathom that poor girl living all alone all these years. Obviously, she is the child that people have claimed seeing in these parts including me. For her to be your niece, that, Tyrell is the working of someone with great powers, like the Lord above."

"I wouldn't argue against that. If I could confide in you I wasn't sure at first if I wanted her to be kin or not. It kind of gave me a scare. I mean I don't know anything about raising a girl. As the days went by though and what she could remember of her family and the things she said I knew she was my kin," Tyrell nodded. "It was quite a shock to learn."

"Maybe it is time we address another issue?" Marissa began, "I know I haven't told you this before but I am sure you have already guessed. Caleb is your son. You knew that didn't you?"

For a moment Tyrell was silent, 'yes' he did know that but to hear her say it confirmed his assumption. His eyes welled up with tears, and he looked at her. "I did know that, Marissa, but, I figured it wasn't my place to say. I'm sure glad you did though," he fell silent as he looked into the cup of cold tea in front of him. "Does Caleb know?"

"I think he has his suspicions. He's no ordinary little boy Tyrell. I think he knows a lot more than what we think he knows."

Tyrell was glad things were out in the open now, and he figured the next thing he ought to do, was ask her to marry him. He wasn't sure how to go about asking though, and in fact, he didn't even have a ring at that time to offer her if she accepted. What he did know, is that he truly and deeply loved, Marissa and now, he could love Caleb like a son, not that he didn't already, because he certainly did. Now though, things were different. Marissa had admitted that Caleb was his son. That changed things somehow. He looked across the table to her and in one breath simply asked her to wed him. Marissa almost fell off her chair and in fact did spill her tea all over the table.

"WHHHAT! Do you don't know how long I have waited for that question," she stood up from the table, and ran into his arms almost knocking him and the chair he was sitting on over backwards, onto the floor. "Of course I will marry you." She said as she kissed him and wrapped her arms around him. Finally, after all this time her wish had been granted. She kept her arms wrapped tightly around his neck, as he tried to speak.

"I love you to death Marissa. I always have," he said as he held her tightly. For a few moments time stood still, as they wept with happiness in each other's arms. "Quite the thing we started here I reckon." Tyrell said as he looked at her. "I ain't sure now that I should have asked yet. I ain't got a ring for you...," he teased.

"Ring or no ring Tyrell your fate has been sealed." She chuckled as she got up from his lap and made her way back to her chair. "I'm speechless Tyrell, I really am. I didn't think you were ever going to ask me to wed you. I have longed and wished for this day ever since our first time when Caleb was conceived. You did break my heart back then, when I returned from Victoria and found that you were gone. I cried myself to sleep for the first year. Then when it was said that you were dead I cried longer and harder every time I thought about you. It was hard for me to look at Caleb and not see his father." Marissa fell silent as Tyrell digested what she said.

"I made some bad judgement calls, and made a few too many wrong decisions there is no doubt about that. I never once forgot about you though Marissa. I often wondered how I could feel so lonely without you when we had only known each other for a few days. As I traveled through those years though, I began to realise why I felt that way, it was because I was truly and madly, in love with you. You swallowed my heart full the first day our eyes met. And now I ain't ever going to lose you again."

"That was beautiful Tyrell it really was. And you have always said you weren't a poet. I never want to lose you again either."

He reached across the table and took her hands into his. "So, when do you want to make it official, Mrs. Sloan?" Tyrell smiled and squeezed her hands. "Remember though I ain't got no ring just yet. You can bet I'll get one though, with the biggest shiniest diamond I can find."

Marissa smiled at him. "I honestly don't need anything prissy. It isn't to prove wealth, but to prove the love we have for each other. Besides, I'm a cattlewoman for God sakes Tyrell. My hands are always digging in dirt or throwing hay to the cows. I don't need anything extraordinary. A simple gold band is good enough for me. As for when, I want to make it official? I say to heck with the butchering today. Release the steers, gather the children and load up the wagon! We're going to the Preacher in Salwood."

Tyrell's mouth dropped he wasn't expecting to wed that soon. "Umm. Ah, well galdarnit Marissa, I, I wasn't expecting it to be today."

"You did ask me when, didn't you," she said as she looked at him.

"I did, yes indeed. I, well ain't never done anything like this before. Ain't you women supposed to wait until spring or something. Ain't that when most folks get married?"

"Spring has come and gone Tyrell, and I don't want to wait until it comes again. Are you getting cold feet already?" she teased.

"Hell no. I want you to be Mrs. Sloan as sure as I want ..." he was cut off there when someone began knocking on the door. They both looked at each other and in unison said, "Wilson."

Tyrell rose from his chair and opened the door. Sure enough standing there with a grin from ear-to-ear was Wilson. "I hope I didn't get my dates mixed up. Today is the day we're butchering ain't it?"

"Wilson! You old codger it is sure nice seeing you again." Tyrell said as he gestured him inside.

"Hello young Sloan." He tilted his hat to Marissa, "how is the little woman?" he asked as he kissed her cheek.

"I couldn't be better. It is nice of you to come by. I was hoping you'd be here."

"I said I'd be here, so, here I am," Wilson sat down at the table. "Where is Caleb? I brought him a couple of leghorn hens."

"You did what?" Marissa asked with a smile.

"Bought him a couple of leghorn hens, I had a pig for him too 'cept the damn thing didn't like following my horse. It served up nice on the spit though."

"What, you ate the damn pig?" Tyrell asked as he shook his head and chuckled.

"Like I said young Sloan it weren't too cooperative in following my horse. The leghorns were in a sack, still are too. So where is Caleb? Caleb! Hey boy! I got ya a couple hens for your chicken coop," Wilson hollered out. Caleb came running out of his room, trailed by Teeka. Wilson's eyes grew big. "Who is the young lady?"

"This is Teeka, sir." Caleb said.

"Teeka? You mean she's that friend of yours that everyone thought was imaginary?"

"Yes sir." Caleb replied.

Wilson looked her up and down and then looked at Tyrell and Marissa then back to Teeka. "What the heck has gone on since I was here last?" he asked as he once more looked back to Tyrell and Marissa. They were looking at him with smiles on their faces.

"I'll get coffee started." Marissa said, knowing that Wilson would want to hear the entire tale.

"I'd love some coffee, make it good and strong. I detect a long winded story of sorts." He paused for a minute as he looked at Caleb. "Best get them leghorn hens in the coop. They've been bouncing around on my horses back for a day or so. No worries though they're still alive. Go now get them in the coop Caleb."

"I'll do it right away mister, and thank you for bringing them to me. Come on Teeka, you haven't seen Captain Black in a while. I think he misses you," he said as he and Teeka exited into the early dawn.

"So what has been going on young Sloan?" Wilson asked as Tyrell sat down.

"Maybe we ought to wait for the coffee." Tyrell joked.

"That suits me. It is early still, we'll have plenty of time to butcher," he looked toward Marissa, who was in the small kitchen getting the coffee ready, "looks like, you have only four head to butcher this year, how come?" Wilson asked.

"Only three customers this season, I think it is because of Waxley. He offered a better deal I guess. I don't know."

"That son of a bitch is under cutting ya eh? His old man would never have done that."

"Not sure if it is under cutting or if it is the market. I think this will be the last year I do any private butchering. Next year I'll drive them to the market, and auction them off. That seems to be the way things are going these days," Marissa said as she made her way back to the table and sat down.

"You're going to need a lot more, than the thirty or so head you're running now, if you want to make money at it that way."

"I know but I'm not worried about it yet, it is just a thought. So, how have you been Wilson?" Marissa asked.

"Surviving I suppose. I found Fry. He's alive and well. I travelled through Craig Pass. Over to Waldie, and the old Mercantile, and back over Grizzly Mountain, to his one claim, I knew he had worked. I tell you, I was some shocked when I saw him there. Most of us thought he was dead. But, nothing is going to kill that old fellow, 'cept himself."

"That is good news. He's okay then?" Tyrell questioned with relief.

"Yes that is good news," Marissa added. "I have missed him coming around. I hope he is well."

"As good as he was ten years ago I reckon. Got lucky this year, made two years wage from one of his claims. Said now, that he's going to likely sell them off, and retire." Wilson started to laugh, "I can't imagine that old bastard ever retiring."

"No kidding, he's about as likely to retire as you are, Wilson." Tyrell responded as he chuckled.

"Nope, I'm done this year young Sloan. I'm selling off my trap-lines and the few measly claims I have staked. I'm too damn old to keep up with it all."

"You are only as old as you let your mind think, Wilson." Marissa said as she smiled at him.

"Well, whether that is the case or not I'm tired of the wet and cold. I've actually been contemplating raising hogs."

"Hogs?" Tyrell questioned with surprise.

"Yep, there is a good stable market for hogs." Wilson said as he pulled out his knife and started cleaning his fingernails, "how is that coffee coming Marissa?"

"I'll check it." She said as she stood up and walked into the kitchen, "it is ready now, do you guys want cream and sugar?"

"Either way suits me fine, I'm contemplating a story being told which I hope to hear soon. So, black as night and strong as a bull works too." Wilson replied.

Marissa poured each of them a cup and set them on a tray with the coffee pot.

"Here you go." She said as she set the tray of coffee down. "Sugar and cream is there too," she sat back down and waited for the men to get their coffee.

"Thank you, Marissa." Tyrell said as he took a drink from his cup.

"Yes indeed thank you kindly. Now, about this tale I'm waiting to hear?" Wilson took a swig from his coffee, "I'm ready to hear it," he said as he nodded at them both. So for the second time that day Tyrell told the tale.

"I knew something was awry when we travelled from your shack to here the last time." Wilson said as he poured another coffee, "do you remember what you said to me young Sloan?" Wilson harassed.

"I reckon it would've been along the lines that you were crazy or senile, or both." Tyrell started to chuckle.

"Yep, I reckon that be the gist of it. Ain't so, crazy or senile now though am I?" Wilson smiled.

"I wouldn't say that Wilson. I reckon you are as crazy and senile as ever, maybe even a bit more so."

"You keep right on reckoning young Sloan," Wilson took a drink from his coffee. "I sense something else going on here. What are you two holding back?" he asked as he looked at them, he wasn't stupid, he could see it in their eyes, that something else hadn't been mentioned. Marissa's face lit up as a smile crossed her face. It was so vibrant that Wilson didn't need to be told. "You got to be kidding! It's about damn time! I reckon. Congratulations! When are the festivities?"

"We ain't decided yet. Now, before you get all huffy Wilson, this took place around the same time you knocked on the door." Tyrell mentioned as he looked at Marissa and smiled.

"I'm here now! Leave the butchering and kids to me. Jump in that wagon and get over to the Preacher's in Salwood! C'mon!" Wilson said as he stood up and practically forced the two of them out the door. "I don't know why Marissa has waited as long as she has for you young Sloan. But damn it, she ain't waiting no more. Not while I'm here, no sir. Now get the horses hooked up to that wagon and get. I don't want to see either of you until Marissa is Mrs. Tyrell Sloan!"

Everything was happening so fast neither Marissa nor Tyrell could get a word in edgewise. Marissa didn't seem to mind though. She was smirking the whole time.

"Jesus, Wilson you old goat settle down. I ain't even got a change of clothes or my money satchel." Tyrell complained.

Wilson reached into his saddlebag and pulled out a handful of dollar bills. "Here's some money and you don't need no change of clothes. Salwood is less than a day's ride and it ain't even sunrise yet. No more arguing young Sloan or I'll kick you in the seat of your pants."

Teeka and Caleb were standing outside the chicken coop confused looks on both of their faces. "What, happening?" Teeka asked as she looked at Caleb.

Caleb shrugged his shoulders. "I don't know. I've never seen mister Wilson act like that."

Wilson, noticing the children standing there, smiled and winked at them. "Your ma and Tyrell are getting married Caleb!"

Caleb's mouth dropped open and he ran toward Wilson, Teeka trailing close behind. "What?" he asked full of excitement, as he got close. If what he heard is what he thought he heard, he was at that moment the happiest kid on earth. "Did you say ma and Tyrell are getting married, holy crap! Oops, I didn't mean that swear word, mister."

"Don't worry about it, Caleb," Wilson commented. He had a grin across his face as big as a horseshoe. "Yep, your ma and Tyrell decided this morning they was getting married. You, me and Teeka are staying here behind we got butchering to do."

Caleb began jumping up and down. "I'm so happy. I'm so happy. I'm going to be able to call Tyrell, Pa. I knew he was going to be my Pa, because I wished for it. I sure did," he said as he stood with Wilson, and Teeka, and watched as Tyrell clumsily harnessed up the wagon. "Do you think I should help him? I don't think he's having much luck." Caleb mentioned to Wilson.

"Nope, I reckon we'll stand here and watch," Wilson replied as he softly chuckled. Marissa was already sitting in the wagon. She looked beautiful as she sat there, a smile across her face. An aurora of light it seemed, had encompassed her, she was radiant. Tyrell, on the other hand, wasn't so pleasant. Not yet at least. He was a little grumpy, because of how he was coerced, by Wilson. Still, as he finished harnessing up the horses, he found himself smiling.

"There, I reckon we're good to go." Tyrell said as he looked back to Wilson, Caleb, and Teeka.

Wilson was standing there with his arms crossed. "There ain't no use staring, young Sloan, get those horses moving." Wilson said as he nodded.

Tyrell shook his head and smiled. "All right, let's get. Giddy-up," he said as he snapped the reins. The three of them watched as the wagon disappeared into the horizon.

"Which one of you two knows how to make coffee?" Wilson asked. They answered in unison that they both knew how. "Good, I reckon I need another cup. C'mon you two, let's get this day started. Caleb, you can round up the butchering knives, and if the young lady will make us another pot of coffee, I reckon in no time at all the butchering will be done." They followed Wilson back inside and went about the tasks he had given them. "What do you think of your uncle getting married, Teeka?" Wilson asked to start a conversation.

"He talks often about Marissa and Caleb. I'm very happy." Teeka said from the kitchen as she prepared another pot of coffee.

"It has been a long time coming that is for sure. By the way Teeka, excuse my manners, but, I don't think we've been formally introduced. I'm Wesley Wilson. I know who you are, now you know me," Wilson began to chuckle. "Your uncle has been a friend of mine for a long time. I regret to say though sometimes, he needs a push to get motivated."

Teeka made her way back to the table and sat down across from Wilson. She was very amused by the big burly man who wore an old hat with a band of animal teeth around it. "I hear Tyrell mention you before ago also. It is very nice to meet you old Wilson." Teeka smiled, "I have some trouble sometimes to talk. Tyrell tell you about that?"

"He did indeed, but I understand everything you've said. Hell, the English language can be spoken so many different ways half the time it don't matter none, if you make a mistake." Wilson replied as he ran his fingers through his salt and pepper beard, "I know folks that don't even speak, they just grunt," Wilson said jokingly, "so, never worry around me if you make a mistake with words, I probably wouldn't notice anyhow."

Teeka began to chuckle. "Old Wilson, you, like Tyrell say are crazy," she teased.

"It is the young whippersnappers like your uncle that make us old timers crazy," Wilson joked. "Now if that coffee is ready young lady, I'm ready for some," he looked around for Caleb who was foraging in the pantry. "Hey Caleb you got them knives yet?"

"I'm getting them, yes sir."

"All right, don't cut yourself. Be careful."

"I will. Ma always puts them in this wooden box," Caleb said as he set it down on the table and opened it. "Yes sir, here they are," he pushed the box over to Wilson who looked inside.

"Yep, that's them. All right, so we got the knives what else we need Caleb?"

"Ma uses her old Henry to put them down. Should I get it for you?"

"Nope, I'll use my own rifle." By now, the coffee was finished perking and Teeka brought the pot to him.

"Coffee is done now old Wilson." She said as she put it down on the table. "I try some, very strong. You like that way?"

"Sure do. Strong coffee is the best coffee," he said as he poured himself a cup. He blew on it and took a drink, "yep, that is strong. Thank you very much Teeka for making it. I'd have been like a big bull moose in that tiny kitchen, if I tried making it myself."

"Old Wilson you are welcome." The three of them conversed while Wilson finished his coffee. When the sun rose fully, they headed outside to the corral, and the work began. By late afternoon only one steer was standing. The other three were butchered, cut into halves and waiting to be hung in the cellar.

"I think it is time to have a rest. Caleb, Teeka, c'mon have sit down." Wilson said as he made his way over to a block of wood and sat. "We're doing well. One more to go and that'll be it. You two can work alongside me anytime, you're damn hard workers both of you," Wilson inhaled deeply. It had been hard on him, but nothing in life as far as he was concerned was ever easy. "Black Dog is going to have some good scraps tonight, I reckon. Which reminds me," he looked around. "I ain't seen him yet today. He's still alive ain't he?" Wilson asked the two.

"Lately the dog and wolf are together lots," Teeka said. "They'll be around when they see no Tyrell or me at shack. They'll come here."

"What, dog and wolf?" Wilson asked with interest.

"That's right mister Wilson. Black Dog has found a girlfriend for the winter," Caleb said.

"If it is a wolf it won't be for the winter. Nope, wolves make friends like that for life." Wilson replied with a snicker.

By this time, Tyrell and Marissa were getting close to Salwood. "I can't believe that damn Wilson, you know that?" Tyrell said as he half chuckled, "forcing us to the Preacher's like this. Damn him anyway."

"I don't know. I am glad he did," Marissa teased. "I really didn't want to wait until spring."

"I would have liked a little bit of courting first."

"You already courted me Tyrell," Marissa reminded him, as she smiled and kissed his cheek. "Wilson is a good and trustworthy friend, and he will always have my respect, and admiration."

"I suppose you are right," Tyrell said, as they grew silent. If Wilson hadn't forced him that day to get the marrying done, he knew full-well that he would have dragged out the commitment for months. *Yep, guess I should be thanking the old codger after all,* Tyrell thought as the wagon rolled on. For as long as he had known Wilson, it was Wilson, who was always the first to get things done. Whether it was helping him build a fence or a roof, it didn't matter to Wilson, when he was around he was always there to help, with whatever needed doing. Obviously, he thought their marriage needed doing that day. Tyrell shook his head and smiled. He was blessed to have such a friend like Wilson.

At 6:00 o'clock that evening, as the church bells of Salwood chimed in, Tyrell, slipped a simple golden band on his wife's finger, and he and Marissa were married. They booked an overnight hotel room, and celebrated their union like, all married couples do. It was the best night, of both their lives and one that neither of them, would ever forget. "Hard to believe this day started off to be an ordinary day isn't it?" Tyrell question as Marissa lay her head on his chest.

"Yes. But it was beautiful day wasn't it?"

"Indeed it has been. Did you think this morning when you woke up that you'd be Mrs. Tyrell Sloan by the time you went to bed?" Tyrell asked as he smiled and played with her hair.

"No. But I am more than honoured that I am."

"Me too Marissa, me too," Tyrell inhaled deeply and closed his eyes to relish the moment. He felt some guilt as he lay there thinking about Marissa's family. Weddings he knew were an important event for a bride and her family. The way he and Marissa wed certainly wasn't the norm. Marriages like that only happened in gambling towns. It didn't seem to matter though certainly not to Marissa, and since he had no family except for her and Caleb, it made no difference to him. As long as Marissa was content with how they got married, then it didn't matter, what anyone else thought. Legally and in the eyes of the Lord, they were husband and wife. It was what it was.

Back in Red Rock, Wilson and the kids were hanging the last side of beef in the cellar. They had worked hard the entire day, and finally, the job was done. Wilson sighed in relief as he sat down on a log. "How the two of you feeling?" he questioned. "Tired I bet?"

"We did good didn't we mister?" Caleb asked as he sat next to him.

"You both out-did yourselves. I'd say you worked as hard as me most of the time," Wilson chuckled. He was about to say something else when he heard the voices of two men. Tilting his head, he listened with caution. "You kids hear that?" he asked as he stood and cocked his rifle, knowing that at best he only had one bullet in the chamber. That didn't matter though he'd beat the other to death with the butt of the rifle, if they were there to cause harm.

"What did you hear, mister?" Caleb asked.

"Shhh, boy, listen. I think there is someone approaching."

"I hear now too," Teeka said. "I think two men and two horses."

Wilson looked at both Caleb and Teeka and brought his finger to his lips to silence them. "Keep still," he said as softly as butterfly. He wanted to be ready if there was trouble brewing. He kept his eyes averted along the dark edge of the forest. Seeing movement, he moved to a better position to make certain he knew which direction they were coming from.

He singled to the kids to huddle down and to be quiet. Finally, he saw the red tunics and sighed. "It's okay kids, it looks like it is the Mounted Police. I ain't sure what they'd be wanting around here but I best have a talk with them." Wilson stepped out of the shadows and waved at them as he spoke. "Hello there," he said as he approached. "Not often we see Mounted Police up in these parts."

"Good evening sir." Timber said as he slowed his horse down to a stop. He reached out his hand to introduce himself. "I am Sergeant Timber McCann and this here is Constable Mitch Hannigan. We represent the Mounted Police."

Wilson reached out his hand to shake Timber's. "Name is Wesley Wilson. It is an honour to meet you Constables. What brings the Mounted Police to Red Rock?" he questioned as he stepped back.

"Perhaps you can send your kids off indoors. There isn't no need, in frightening them," Mitch said as he looked toward Caleb and Teeka, his eyes locked with hers and he nodded at her. From what he could see of her she was a beautiful image, and from what she saw of the young Constable made her heart skip a beat. "Nice family you have mister," he added as he smiled at Teeka and tilted his hat in a cordial gesture.

Wilson looked over to Caleb and Teeka. "You two go on and get cleaned up. The Constables would like to have words with me."

"Yes sir," Caleb said. "Come on Teeka let's get washed up we're done for the day." Caleb urged but Teeka stood there staring at Mitch, her heart beating a mile a minute. She had never felt like that before. Finally, she smiled at him and waved, then followed Caleb back to the cabin.

"They're out of earshot now." Wilson said as he looked up to Timber who was still sitting in his saddle. Mitch on the other hand had swung off his horse and was picking at his teeth with a long piece of grass.

"Do you know who lives up there along the creek?" Timber asked as he pointed in the direction of Tyrell's shack.

"I sure do. Tyrell Sloan lives there. He owns all this land for as far as your eye can see, why you asking?"

"We've been following a group of men that are suspects in a cattle rustling ring. They might even be responsible for some other crimes that I'd rather not get into," Timber said as he inhaled and sighed. "Mitch and I were able to follow their trail to your friend's homestead up on the creek. After that, the trail runs cold. Have you spoken with your friend lately?"

"I have. Just this morning as a matter of fact, I sent him and Marissa McDowell which lives in the cabin over yonder off to get married." Wilson chuckled, "that ain't a word of a lie, neither."

"Really?" Mitch questioned. "That seems kind of odd, doesn't it? How do you send a man and woman off to get married?"

"You'd have to know the two of them to understand I suppose." Wilson answered.

"Well I don't know the two, how about you explain it to me?" Mitch asked.

Timber butted in though. "Now come on Mitch. It isn't any of our business on how or why. Goddamn it boy you got to learn to be a little more diplomatic." Timber looked to Wilson and shook his head, "I'm sorry for the young whippersnapper's attitude, Mr. Wilson."

"Don't give it a second thought Sergeant," Wilson replied as he waved his hand through the air. "I can tell you I ain't seen anyone in these parts since getting here this morning. I don't recall Tyrell mentioning seeing anyone either." Wilson lied, he knew what had happened to the men Tyrell had told him that morning. But, it wasn't his place to say and so he wouldn't.

"Tyrell and his Misses ought to be back some time tomorrow night. Maybe it be best, if you came back then, he'd know better than I, if he's seen anything out of the ordinary. I'm sure he wouldn't mind the two of you camping out on his land somewhere." Wilson paused, "there ain't anything I can offer you regarding the men you two are looking for," he finished.

"We aren't going to be able to sit idle. The longer we stay in one spot the further away they may get ahead of us. Nope, it's still early enough that we can continue toward Waldie. Could be they may have gotten on a riverboat. We'll be back this way though in a few days time, whether we come across them or not, we can set your minds at ease. We'll talk with Mr. Sloan then. For your own safety keep the women and children safe, and keep any rifles you have at the ready. These men aren't the friendly sort. Thank you for your time Mr. Wilson," Timber nodded his appreciation. "Come on

Mitch saddle up," he said as he turned his steed and headed north.

Mitch lazily climbed into his saddle. "Right behind you Timber," he said as he looked over to Wilson, "like Timber said, keep the women and children safe, until you hear back from us. The men we're tracking all have nooses waiting for them. That ought to give you an idea on what kind of men they are. Until next time Mr. Wilson, good evening." He turned his horse and followed Timber.

Wilson watched until he couldn't see them anymore then he turned and made his own way back to the cabin.

"What is man on blonde color horse? What does old Wilson mean, Mounted Police?" Teeka questioned Caleb as they waited inside.

"He's a Constable for the Mounted Police. They track down bad guys, and bring them to jail. Sometimes they even hang them. I sure hope Wilson isn't a bad guy," Caleb said with some concern.

"I don't think old Wilson is a bad man."

"You are probably right Teeka. I was just saying." Caleb shrugged his shoulders as he sat down.

"Caleb, when I seen man on blonde horse, I feel funny. What is that?"

"I don't know. Maybe you are in love," Caleb teased.

"Like the Princess in the book we read, maybe, I see."

The cabin door opened and Wilson stepped in.

"What did the Mounted Police want mister Wilson?" Caleb asked as Wilson made his way to the table and sat down.

"They're out checking on the homesteaders in the area. Making sure everyone is okay. That's all. They'll be coming back this way in a day or two. You'll get another chance to see them then. They want to have a word with your pa," Wilson said as he looked at Caleb. "Now ain't that strange to hear, 'your pa'." Wilson chuckled, "I reckon by now he is too. I guess that means also that the two of you are cousins."

"Cousins?" Caleb said, with excitement. "Like me and Sebastian?"

"I reckon so, yep," Wilson answered.

"Holy! I got a new cousin and a pa all in one day!" Caleb said as he ran up to Teeka and hugged her, "we're cousins now Teeka, we're family."

"I'm very happy too at this. You get a new pa, and I get bigger family, Marissa now aunt and you are my cousin. Plus, I meet old Wilson." Teeka said as she smiled and sat down.

The evening proceeded as they ate biscuits and talked about this, that, and sometimes about nothing at all. It was quite a treat for Wilson. He had no grand kids, no nieces, or nephews, or for that matter any kids of his own. Being able to sit and talk with Caleb, and Teeka, without adult interference was a welcoming change. He told them stories about hunting, trapping, prospecting, ghosts, and even goblins. The kids sat and listened with amusement, interest, and sometimes with their eyes as big as saucers.

"You have known Tyrell for a long time haven't you mister, Wilson?" Caleb asked.

"I sure have. I even knew his grandfather which lived right here in this cabin, long before Tyrell came here. Heck, I even knew the old dog which fathered Black Dog. Yes indeed. Tyrell and I go way back. I've known your mother longer though, by a year or two. Met her, when she worked at Heddy's mercantile, yep, I've been around for a long time kids." Wilson chuckled as he winked at them, "anyway, I reckon that is enough talk for tonight. I'm a might tired," he yawned and stretched. "We did a good day's work today kids and now it's time to lay our heads down and get ready for whatever tomorrow might bring." Wilson rose from the table, as did Teeka and Caleb.

"Yes. I am tired too mister," he looked over to Teeka. "I'm sure ma won't mind if you sleep in her bed Teeka. Mister Wilson always takes the floor by the wood-stove." Caleb said as he now yawned himself and rubbed his eyes.

"Good night mister Wilson. Good night to you, too, Teeka." Caleb said as he made his way into his room and curled up on his bed.

"I go to Marissa's bed to now. I say good night like Caleb did to you. See you tomorrow old Wilson." Teeka said as she ducked into Marissa's room, and snuggled into the bed. In only minutes, the cabin grew silent, as its three occupants fell into an exhausted state of sleep.

In the days that followed and as Tyrell, Marissa, Caleb, and Teeka, settled into their new roles in life. Tyrell and Marissa convinced Wilson, to move into Tyrell's shack on Hudu Creek and to take a paid position, as the lead cowhand for what they at the time envisioned, as 'The Double R' cattle ranch. It wasn't yet a reality, but, their plans were concise and so Wilson agreed. With Wilson's help, they shifted all of Tyrell and Teeka's belongings however meagre from the shack to Marissa's cabin, and at the same time added on another room. Timber and Mitch true to their word regarding their return showed up during this time. With more questions than they had answers. It was their hope that Tyrell was the man who could answer some if not all of them. In only a few sentences from Tyrell, the two Mounted Police were satisfied.

It took two days to excavate, identify, and transport the bodies and to round up six of the seven horses, they had been riding when Tyrell shot and killed the men. Teeka, and Mitch, struck up a relationship and became fast friends. No one knew how serious it was, until Mitch, one day turned in his badge and red tunic, and moved in with Wilson as Wilson's right hand man. And a new era in the Sloan family legacy began. The gold that Tyrell hid under the floorboards of his old shack all 160 pouches remained where he hid them. The gold claims, Sloan 1, 2, and 3, as far as Tyrell was concerned would never be worked, unless Fry himself worked them.